ACCLAIM FOR
JOANNE BISCHOF

The Gold in These Hills

"*The Gold in These Hills* by Joanne Bischof is a captivating story of hope and love. I sat down to read just a couple chapters and found myself completely caught up in the story until I was reading the very last page, and wishing there were more. I believe readers will be instantly caught up and drawn into the story. Joanne is a masterful storyteller giving the reader a great deal to think about and consider as they pour over her books."

—TRACIE PETERSON, AWARD-WINNING, BESTSELLING
AUTHOR OF OVER ONE HUNDRED NOVELS, INCLUDING THE
LADIES OF THE LAKE AND WILLAMETTE BRIDES SERIES

"Joanne Bischof is a master storyteller, weaving the past and present into a rich story bursting with hope and heart. *The Gold in These Hills* reminds us that just about anything can be restored with a little faith and a whole lot of love. Bischof never disappoints!"

—LIZ JOHNSON, BESTSELLING AUTHOR OF *THE RED DOOR INN*

"Anchored by Joanne Bischof's exceptional prose, *The Gold in These Hills* is a gripping tale of hardship and healing woven brilliantly within the well-researched world of gold mining. And presented with characters which possessed not only depth but grace, this stirring dual timeline would not let me go. Not to be missed!"

—ABIGAIL WILSON, AUTHOR OF *THE VANISHING AT LOXBY MANOR*

"Echoing with the ache and joy that come with the search for truth, home, and healing, *The Gold in These Hills* is courageous and captivating in its authenticity. Joanne Bischof, in her signature style luminous with heart and depth, explores Johnny and Juniper's unique stories as they cross time to intertwine in a restorative journey not to be forgotten . . . and through this

mystery-laced tale of gold, Bischof offers us a treasure even more priceless: that of hope."

—AMANDA DYKES, AUTHOR OF *YOURS IS THE NIGHT*,
SET THE STARS ALIGHT, AND THE 2020 CHRISTY AWARD
BOOK OF THE YEAR, *WHOSE WAVES THESE ARE*

"*The Gold in These Hills* mines the gritty depths of marriage while leaving the reader resplendent with hope. Joanne Bischof is quickly becoming one of my favorite authors."

—JOLINA PETERSHEIM, BESTSELLING AUTHOR
OF *HOW THE LIGHT GETS IN*

"With all the warmth, lyrical storytelling, and rich historical detail I've come to anticipate with every book by Joanne Bischof, *The Gold in These Hills* swept me away into two beautiful storylines filled with characters who captured my heart. I absolutely loved the way the historical and modern stories wove together with both heartbreak and joy to create such a compelling read. With emotional depth and gentle romance, Joanne Bichof's latest is a testament to not only her writing voice, but the beauty of redemption and new beginnings."

—MELISSA TAGG, CHRISTY AWARD-WINNING
AUTHOR OF *NOW AND THEN AND ALWAYS*

"*The Gold in These Hills* by Joanne Bischof is a beautiful unfolding of two stories where the greatest treasure isn't found in gold but lies in the beauty of forgiveness. In Bischof's usual style, she digs to the heart of the characters and refines them through trial into becoming better versions of themselves, so they shine with greater hope in the end. The faith thread in the historical story line, in particular, showcased how grief and heartache can be transformed by humility and forgiveness."

—PEPPER BASHAM, AUTHOR OF *HOPE BETWEEN
THE PAGES* AND *MITCHELL'S CROSSROADS*

Daughters of Northern Shores

"Initially, we have insight into the characters' thoughts and feelings, revealing how actions become haunting memories that cannot be shut out by drink or drugs. Over time, these memories demand a response, and it is a tribute to the Norgaard family that they choose a difficult, redemptive path to satisfy their inner turmoil . . . *Daughters of Northern Shores* is a very nice read with some historical references evoking Norwegian immigrant life."

—HISTORICAL NOVELS SOCIETY

"*Daughters of Northern Shores* fulfills every promise made in *Sons of Blackbird Mountain*. The entire cast of characters grows, fitting and shaping into their new roles. Romance thrives within a marriage. The sea heals the soul. We get new life and new love, but the old wounds still run deep. Somehow, Bischof manages to make the familiar fresh and new, creating a read that is equally exciting and familiar. And, she continues to be the best at writing strong, real, flawed men. They carry the story on broad shoulders, tucking the reader in safe and sound."

—ALLISON PITTMAN, AUTHOR OF *THE SEAMSTRESS*

"Bischof's effortless prose and emotionally driven scenes captivate the reader from beginning to end. Characters so real you begin to believe they are. The Norgaard brothers and their families will steal your heart. Beautifully eloquent, this grace-filled tale is one not to be missed."

—CATHERINE WEST, AUTHOR OF *WHERE HOPE BEGINS*

"Laced with lyrical prose, *Daughters of Northern Shores* is a story of redemption that gripped me from its first moments. I savored every gorgeous detail, and the characters continue to live with me even now. Bischof is a master at enfolding readers in her story world and bringing them along on a journey of the heart."

—LINDSAY HARREL, BESTSELLING AUTHOR OF *THE SECRETS OF PAPER AND INK* AND *THE JOY OF FALLING*

Sons of Blackbird Mountain

"*Sons of Blackbird Mountain* is a quiet gem of a historical romance. Refreshingly real and honest in its depiction of flawed but lovable individuals, it introduces characters readers will want to meet again."

—CBA MARKETPLACE

"Christy and Carol Award-winning author Bischof (*The Lady and the Lionheart*) creates endearing characters and a heartwarming story line in this unforgettable novel about the power of family, love, and the true meaning of home. Fans of Kristy Cambron, Julie Klassen, and Susan Meissner will love this one."

—*LIBRARY JOURNAL*

"Bischof (*The Lady and the Lionheart*) transports readers to late 19th-century Appalachian Virginia in this moving historical romance . . . With fine historical details and stark prose that fits the story, Bischof skillfully weaves a tale of love and redemption in rough Appalachia."

—*PUBLISHERS WEEKLY*

THE
GOLD
IN
THESE
HILLS

ALSO BY JOANNE BISCHOF

Daughters of Northern Shores

Sons of Blackbird Mountain

The Lady and the Lionheart

My Hope Is Found

Though My Heart Is Torn

Be Still My Soul

To Get to You

This Quiet Sky

THE
GOLD
IN
THESE
HILLS

a novel

JOANNE BISCHOF

THOMAS NELSON
Since 1798

The Gold in These Hills

Published in Nashville, Tennessee, by Thomas Nelson. Thomas Nelson is a registered trademark of HarperCollins Christian Publishing, Inc.

Thomas Nelson titles may be purchased in bulk for educational, business, fundraising, or sales promotional use. For information, please email SpecialMarkets@ThomasNelson.com.

Unless otherwise indicated, scripture quotations marked KJV are taken from the King James Version. Public domain.

Scripture quotations marked NKJV are taken from the New King James Version®. Copyright © 1982 by Thomas Nelson. Used by permission. All rights reserved.

Publisher's Note: This novel is a work of fiction. Names, characters, places, and incidents are either products of the author's imagination or used fictitiously. All characters are fictional, and any similarity to people living or dead is purely coincidental.

Library of Congress Cataloging-in-Publication Data

Names: Bischof, Joanne, author.
Title: The gold in these hills : a novel / Joanne Bischof.
Description: Nashville, Tennessee : Thomas Nelson, [2021] | Summary: "Two second-chance love stories, hope across the centuries, and the legacy that binds them together"-- Provided by publisher.
Identifiers: LCCN 2021011129 (print) | LCCN 2021011130 (ebook) | ISBN 9780785241355 (paperback) | ISBN 9780785241362 (epub) | ISBN 9780785241379 (downloadable audio)
Subjects: GSAFD: Love stories.
Classification: LCC PS3602.I75 G65 2021 (print) | LCC PS3602.I75 (ebook) | DDC 813/.6--dc23
LC record available at https://lccn.loc.gov/2021011129
LC ebook record available at https://lccn.loc.gov/2021011130

Printed in the United States of America

21 22 23 24 25 LSC 10 9 8 7 6 5 4 3 2 1

For Aunt Laura

Look, I go forward, but He is not there,
And backward, but I cannot perceive Him;
When He works on the left hand, I cannot behold
*   Him;*
When He turns to the right hand, I cannot see Him.
But He knows the way that I take;
When He has tested me, I shall come forth as gold.

JOB 23:8–10 NKJV

HISTORICAL NOTE

While most of the characters in the coming pages are fictitious, the mysterious rise and fall of the gold mine town of Kenworthy, California, was a true historic event. Many of the buildings mentioned within the story once stood. While the town has now vanished and tales of the lackluster mine faded into legend, I've had the honor of exploring the territory myself—searching for clues to the past. I've also had the pleasure of exploring some of the historic Cahuilla landmarks around my mountain homeland. Since different regions have different dialects, for those curious about the pronunciation of the tribal name *Cahuilla*, it is spoken [kuh-wee-uh] and rhymes with Spanish words such as *tortilla*.

At the back of the novel, I've shared an inside look at these local explorations, including some of the history-hunting adventures that reached into every scene of this story. It is my hope that each page you hold will paint a picture of this land that I hold dear and, most of all, of the people who have shaped it—then and now.

PART 1

CHAPTER 1

JUNIPER

SEPTEMBER 1902

I t's paramount that my daughter and I survive the coming winter, yet ghost towns are not for the living. Still, this desolate place with its remaining miners and abandoned buildings is home. If only I could count my husband among their dwindling numbers. But no soul has seen him since the gold mine was boarded up months ago.

Now over a dozen shirts flap on the laundry line—all belonging to the men who bring me their washing each week. The hems and tatters are more recognizable than their names, but I know each man's voice and who scrubs his neck or not. They pay coins for the service, and while it's tedious work on top of managing this farm alone, I'll do what's needed to keep food in front of my little girl.

Tilting my face to the sky, I breathe in deeply. There's a sound this land makes when it rises with the sun. The hens raise Cain from their coop, and the louder they get, the more likely my daughter and I will have eggs for breakfast. At the ruckus they're stirring up, it's going to be a good day. At least a good start to it. There's nothing worse than pulling a chair up beside three-and-a-half-year-old Bethany only to have so little to spoon onto her plate. Last night there was only rabbit stew enough left for one, and that was after I'd watered it down.

I went to bed on an empty stomach so that my daughter wouldn't have to.

Probably why I'm listening to the chickens just now, weighing the odds.

The morning is crisp today but not frosty. Five thousand feet above sea level, this mountain is only a few days' ride from the Mexico border. It's hotter than blazes from June to September. This summer was especially dry, so autumn is tiptoeing in gently. As I work, the linens stretch like soldiers in a line, and they represent souls. Lives. Pasts. Futures. Plucking free the next set of wooden pins sends another miner's shirt tumbling into the basket.

When the stamp mill was in operation, the whole town of Kenworthy was astir. Noise rang from one end of town to the other from the clackety steam engine and its massive, churning belt and the steel stamps that the engine powered up and down. Daily the heavy feet pounded atop ore carved from the mine, pulverizing the chunks of rock—proving their worthlessness year after year. Up and down the stamps crushed as miners unloaded carts of ore. The hungry beast ground anything it was fed, including our futures, and families were just as hungry for a sign of gold. Some sign of hope.

Now the mine is quiet, and hope is as dusty as everything else. All we hear is come nightfall when all the abandoned dogs that have turned wild howl at the moon. That is Kenworthy now.

"Pardon me, ma'am. I don't wish to startle you."

I turn. A man stands only a dozen paces away. My heart threatens to still at the sight of broad shoulders lit by the morning glow. Hope dies as quickly. It is not John—my husband.

This man grips a hat in his hands. He's pale. Not sickly so, just nervous. At least he's not holding a bucket as the others did, feigning the need for milk when they've come instead for a wife. I steel my features so apprehension won't show. "Washing's turned out on Fridays," I say even though he isn't one of the regulars.

"Apologies, ma'am. I didn't come for wash work." He surveys the open landscape as though to steel his nerves. To his credit, his eyes don't graze my form as other men's have done.

Another shirt comes down. I fold it swiftly. Chores need doing, yet as eager as I am for the breakfast eggs, I'm more enticed to have this conversation away from the confines of the barn.

The stranger steps closer. In the haze of dawn I can just see that his features—while plainly laid out—are clean. He's freshly shaved. Built strong, if not lean, from hard work. His hands know the grit of wood and earth, and that is just what any woman in this land longs to see.

"I'm afraid my answer must be no." I state it loud enough to be heard. Clear enough that he'll believe.

He halts. Lowers the wilted hat to his side. "I haven't asked anything yet, ma'am."

Warmth tinges the back of my neck. Before it spreads into true embarrassment, he continues.

"I don't have much to offer, Mrs. Cohen. If you seek passage away from here for you and your child, I have it at the ready. There's a group of us leaving for Arizona at week's end."

"There is no parson in town, sir." No means of marrying. I fold a threadbare coat.

"No, but there will be one along the drive. I mean that honorably, Mrs. Cohen."

There are so few people left here in Kenworthy that I can't help but wonder—will this be the last batch of settlers to escape a darkening fate? Is this the end, then? The final bridge to freedom before winter has us cornered? This miner knows as well as I do that women will be as scarce in the next stretch of gold country as they are here. I am one of few, and while I still wear a ring, he must believe as others do that my husband is no more.

Mr. Cohen's widow. When did that become my name? John has been gone so long that the locals have written him off for dead. Have I? The distant answer keeps me awake night after night.

"I've got a good sturdy wagon, ma'am. Healthy team of mares. Our group leaves in three days for a claim on a homestead north of Phoenix. There's talk of gold—"

I want no more talk of gold. No more promises from strangers. "A kind gesture, sir, to extend such a living to my daughter and me." The words nearly tremble on my lips. Is it wise to surrender this opportunity? It will be the last. This man is young and strong. Close in age to my twenty-seven. He seems to have a good head on his shoulders. How glad I'd be to wash laundry for just one miner again. I could step away with him and forget all about John Cohen. Be scrubbed clean of this abandonment.

I married a stranger once. It could be done again.

Reaching out, I snatch a bandana that's bending over itself in the grass, tossed and folded by the breeze. The way this man watches me with gentlemanly interest suggests he's mulled on this offer for some time in his bachelor's shanty. A pursuit that, while unwelcome, is no less romantic. However, there is no room in my heart for romance. Not even in the light of a rising sun. Nor with another miner placing hope on myths. Now there is only room for practicality and, if I'm honest with myself, devotion to another.

How will I forget the warmth of John's skin or the light in his eyes? The way his voice used to lower to my ear? Or all the ways he kept us safe and well? It might be a lost love that I hold to, but it is a love that I could not begin to describe to this stranger. "I must decline, sir. I am not free for marriage."

"But—"

Having hoisted up the heavy basket, I'm already starting for the house. My hair, in its long braid, bumps against my back as I regard him again. "Good day to you, Mr. . . ." I regret not knowing his name after all he just offered. His very life. "Mr. . . . ?" Raising a hand, it shields the sun.

A scar on his cheekbone deepens as his eyes squint. Does he sense a seedling of chance? Wiser would it have been not to inquire, but I don't wish to be callous to these men who have no other women to pursue. There are dozens of miners and millers for every maid.

At the sound of his name, I wish him well on his travels.

I start away, hoping he won't follow. This one seems kind. Though most of the others were as well. Men tend to be kind when asking for a woman's hand.

I deposit the basket on the porch, and he's striding across the meadow. It's likely not shame that slumps his shoulders but loneliness. A lump of regret fills my throat. I am sorry that it must be this way. I am sorry to injure this man who is perhaps more isolated than even I. It's likely he's never married or known a woman's affection. Only the most brazen of miners frequented the saloon with its female occupants. The structure no longer stands. The torn-down lumber built the wagons that carried the painted women away.

By the time the sun crests the nearest trees, there's only the wind on the grass. I clear my throat to fight the sadness. Tonight I will pen his name inside my Bible where three other names now reside. Each man—each offer—is one that I remember. Although they are all gone from Kenworthy, as this man soon will be, I recall them in my prayers. It is there on my knees that I offer up a petition to the Lord for their safety and guidance.

Drawing in a deep breath, I listen to the land. Being the sixth child to a poor family was hardly restful, but now, with those days past, it's a sweet comfort to recall the ocean breezes of San Francisco where I was raised. Even memories are something to be thankful for, aren't they? As for the here and now, there's plenty to be glad about.

I aim for the barn, and in passing its many windows, my reflection peers back. This frail shadow of a woman wears my flannel dress with rounded buttons up the front. Her waist is also my own because it looks like a broomstick despite the skirt pleats. My hips are narrow, making John's old pistol holstered there even more noticeable.

In the barn, I milk the cow with practiced hands, garnering a sparse return. She'll need to be bred again soon, which will require a careful trade.

Back outside, I balance the pail of milk and a basket of eggs. The trek across the yard brings me past the young oak tree that grows wild between the house and the barn. The sapling is the same height as me and as old as Bethany. It is our tree. I like to imagine that one day it will watch over us.

For now, it is thin and fragile, bending against coming winds. Rather like myself. Whenever I look upon this young tree, I remember to dig my roots in deep and strong, drawing up the water of life so that I can remain unwavering in my faith and this existence here. It is far from easy, and so I look upon the tree nearly every day. Watch the way it bends with grace in the wind.

The house is warm when I push past the door. Upstairs, little Bethany is likely nestled under the covers like a cat's nose in a mound of yarn.

At the stove, my empty stomach cramps as I crack eggs into a bowl. Feeling faint, I whisk in the fresh milk and a pinch of sugar. The custard warms and thickens. The last of this week's bread is hid away, so I slice the final crust into two wedges and press them into the mixture to soak up the rich nourishment. Into the oven the pot goes to finish baking.

The clattering of breakfast and the fresh crackle of the fire must have woken Bethany. She comes down in her nightgown, tiny hand sliding along the railing that her father shaped a few years back. This house is the grandest in Kenworthy and was built by John himself upon the founding of the town. The mine owner who once lived here vacated the premises last year, and John purchased the house from a third party for only eight dollars. The first-floor windows alone cost that much. With other buildings abandoned, including the post office and two-story hotel, those of us still here make the most of what's been left behind.

I grab the railing to scoop Bethany up in a morning hug. John's handiwork on the railing is like silk. I would say the same for the head of hair on the daughter he gave me.

"Breakfast is just about ready. How about you set the table?" I say.

Her small slippered feet pad around the kitchen, the sound warming my heart as she fetches two bowls from the low cupboard, one at a time in her tiny hands as I have taught her. She used to want to lay a third setting for her father, but no longer does. If she misses him, it shows only at bedtime when she beseeches the Lord through closed eyes to keep her papa safe.

We always say "Amen" together.

It's after those prayers that I always return to my room alone again. The window across from my bed overlooks the most beautiful ranges of timberland I've ever seen. The forest hems in this high valley. It's as though God built up this mountain from dust then decided to press His thumb against the top, leaving behind the wonder of a valley that dwells up here with the clouds, shaped and shadowed by the mountain peaks that rise higher still.

On the desk surface beneath the window rests a pile of new paper. Plenty of chances to continue writing to John. He'll want to know how his daughter is faring. He'll want word from me, his wife. Surely he will.

I tell myself this every day despite the fact that he hasn't written in months and there's nowhere to send my own correspondence.

Perhaps he's chasing gold again now. Perhaps he has found a new love and that is why he never returned. Still, I hold on to hope, beginning every letter with *Dearest John*. It's human nature that if you believe something long enough and deep enough, it's hard to quit. Did he wake up hungry too? A practical wife might wonder if he's still alive, but his silence isn't due to death.

It never was.

Bethany is chatty between spoonfuls of the thin custard, and while her vocabulary is still hard to understand at times, her voice has grown clearer over the last months. The chair—too big for her—becomes just right as she shifts onto her knees to better reach her bowl. We talk of our plans for the day, and while it will look much like all the days before, we try to conjure up something to stir in newness and possibility. We agree upon a picnic behind the house for her dolls. Acorn caps and leaves shall be the fare. She plans a concoction of sun-warmed pine bark for the pretend tea. Oh, how her voice fills the day with possibility. It's there in the thoughtful tilt to her head that I see her father. I hope she knows it, but reminding her of him might dampen the moment.

I was twenty-two when I found his advertisement in the newspaper in San Francisco. I'd only stumbled across the month-old periodical while wadding it up to light the stove. There I had knelt, the spinster daughter of a lower-class laborer, holding the petition of an unmarried miner in Southern California. A John Cohen willing to pay a woman's passage to the wild south. With seven of us already living in a cramped apartment that almost never caught the sun, and with several of my siblings already married, including the spouses that boarded with us, I secretly longed for a taste of adventure. For freedom. I wrote to John not only for this but for the warmth in his newsprinted lines. Words describing not himself but the land he called home, which was as telling of his spirt as anything else could have been. I thought of fate then, and decided to believe that if he was yet awaiting his bride, then I would be the one he was meant to find.

It was less than a month later that I came here to this boomtown.

Despite finding myself beholden to a stranger, I saw that John had kind eyes and an even kinder patience. Our exchanges were quiet, and in those first few hours of knowing him, I sensed that I was safe. A man of few words, he'd bunked down on the floor beside the fire in the one-room shanty he called home back then. He rose the following day for the backbreaking work alongside other miners. That evening, I fixed us oats with honey, and he placed wildflowers inside a jar for me. The earth drew him in for days on end as he picked for gold, returning home dusty and spent. Some evenings I found him asleep outside the cabin where he'd been trying to take off his boots. As the weeks melded into months, I gladly awoke on quiet mornings with the taste of his kiss on my lips.

As the mine proved empty of any gold—whispers of it having once been *salted* rising among the townsfolk who'd risked all on a hope and a promise—he began to take on extra shifts, passing his every waking moment within the mine. It became a lonely time, his quest for gold. I saw it as an obsession. He claimed it was an even deeper need.

The longest he'd stayed by my side was just before Bethany's birth. I'd never been so grateful for anything as I was for the life growing inside me. Not because I was going to be a mother, nor him a father, but because I wasn't alone. On the night our tiny daughter made her entrance into this world, it had been his hands, confident and steady, to help ease her body from my own and lay her in my arms.

He'd smiled at me with those gentle eyes, and I had known then and there that I loved him. Now, these years later, the town is all but empty of life, and I no longer hear the sound of his voice.

So have passed nearly six months of his absence. Now, on the cusp of watching the trees turn from green to amber again, my soul bends with the ache for assurance. Bethany and I have a home, and for that I am thankful, but the rooms and surrounding land lean empty without his presence. I feel ashamed to love him. I feel more ashamed to hate him. And so it is upon the closing of each day that I settle at the upstairs desk beneath the window and write the two words that somehow keep me from coming apart at the seams. The two words that are the very reason I say no to each and every man who offers us a new life.

Dearest John.

CHAPTER 2

JOHNNY

I squint up at the four-paned window of the cabin where a squirrel perches on the windowsill, gnawing on a pine cone. The overgrown rodent chucks the tattered remains of his supper onto the hood of my '06 Ford just as I turn to the Realtor. "I'll take it."

"Mr. Sutherland. May I call you John?"

"It's just Johnny." I pull a flannel shirt from the truck bed and tug it on over a work-stained T-shirt. The rogue squirrel drops another chunk of pine cone, but I'm not worried about the truck. The frame is already bent from rolling over on the highway some months back. It's still plenty drivable after the accident and sturdy enough that my kids are safe whenever I buckle them in.

The Realtor's polished loafers crunch on autumn leaves as he steps around the vehicle. The stats on this property light the screen of the tablet in his hand. I'm surprised there's internet all the way out here. Telephone wires stretch across the far skyline, but they seem

13

dismal when compared to the wide-open range where pine trees are kings and hawks soar for miles without seeing so much as a gas station. It's so remote and distant that simply standing here feels like another world.

"Johnny." The Realtor angles his screen so I can see it. "I have three other locations to show you today. I think you're going to want to keep looking."

This home has all the right specs, though. Two stories, off the beaten track, and it looks about as put through the wringer as I am. Plus, the yard has direct access to some of the best hiking and bouldering around. I smooth my hands together, as calloused from construction as from gripping granite handholds. "I like this one." It would give me a place to stay that wasn't the back half of my buddy's garage, and if I can fix it up enough to flip it in the next year, I'll end up with enough income to secure a good lawyer. Or if the next custody round goes well . . .

It's impossible not to grip the back of my neck and close my eyes. It's impossible not to try to imagine the sounds of their voices here. If a judge grants me shared custody of the kids, I could instead hold on to this place and have somewhere to bring them. That makes it hard to swallow. Only time will tell, but I need to do all I can for every day of the unknown. "Tell me more about the inspection." It was done after the last prospective buyers were interested in the place a few months earlier. The property passed, but I don't know details.

"Well," the Realtor says with a pause. "It came through surprisingly well for a structure of this age." He leads me around the eastern wall. "The house is believed to have been built just prior to the turn of the last century."

Over a hundred years ago.

"In the 1930s the exterior was papered over and shingled. That was all removed in the late seventies when the original log siding was exposed once more and resealed."

I run a hand along the wood. It's rough and grayed with age, but it's solid.

No longer consulting his tablet, the Realtor continues. "This was done so the city could use the cabin for historical reenactments."

"I remember those." My parents used to take my younger sister and me when we were kids. Employees of the estate would dress up in olden-day costumes, and we kids gobbled down two-dollar hot dogs and cups of lemonade then tried to pan for gold. My mom used to pack me an extra T-shirt because of how wet I'd get. My sister some-how always managed to stay dry.

"The reenactments are what generated funding for the upkeep and conservation of the property," the Realtor's saying. "As you know, a bathroom has been installed on the ground floor. It's nothing to write home about but it *is* functional."

"No plumbing upstairs, though?"

"None." The Realtor bends to inspect a piece of wood stick-ing out of the dirt. A broken sign announcing the hours of the old gift shop. He pitches the piece of wood toward a pile of rubbish that needs to be hauled away. "And there's also no central heating. There's a wood-burning stove, but it will have to be replaced eventually. Electrical is up to date, though it only services two of the three rooms for lighting. The only outlet is on the ground floor."

I nod and can just hear the words *buyer's remorse* ringing between my ears. I try to ignore it. I can handle electrical and don't mind a rough-around-the-edges bathroom. That can all be renovated. It's not just my contractor's license that says so, or fifteen years of restoring homes. It's a sense that just about anything can be restored if you go about it the right way.

"Recently, a nearby conference center contacted the owners with an offer on this property. Their plan was to put a horse-riding camp here." He thumbs toward a nearby meadow that could have housed new pens and stables. "But the conference center lost the grant needed to afford the purchase. That's when the family put it on the market to the general public. The Cohens admire this place but are both in their eighties with no children. They just can't maintain it any longer. They hope to see it land in the right hands. Someone who will appreciate its value and history."

I ponder that as we walk toward a two-story barn that rises amid pines standing opposite the house. It's the kind of barn you'd see on a country calendar. The structure is run-down in places, but it's clear why the online listing described this property as "charming." After crossing through tall weeds, I peer through one of the many barn windows at a mess of old equipment. There's a loft above. Judging by the load of crates weighing it, the rafters are sturdy, but the above flooring is warped and needs to come down. I thump my concrete-splattered work boot against the stone foundation. It seems solid. I step away, feeling like a kid on Christmas and terrified by it. I'm not supposed to feel this burst of anticipation.

"And that?" I point to a smaller building.

"That's the old well house. It's out of commission these days. This place was hooked up to the water district in the late nineties."

"Okay."

Slowly rolling back the cuffs of my flannel sleeves, I linger in the middle of the yard. The Realtor has already shown me inside the house. The rooms are small and poky, and the stairwell tight enough that I have no idea how to get a mattress up it. Stepping back to the open door of my truck, I lift the file that lists the other houses the Realtor plans to show me today, stopping at the flyer for this very cabin. The pristine picture depicts something out of the 1800s, and the real-life view is even more impressive. Maybe the history is a draw for some people, but I have other reasons. Reasons a lot closer to home . . . if I could just have a home to put them in.

"Up until how recent were the historical reenactments?" I ask.

"As a museum, this place closed about three years ago. There just wasn't the funding anymore. Most of the museum features were auctioned off, but a few items are stored in the barn."

I eye the price again. "You're sure this is all the family's asking?"

"Yes, but the price comes with a cost. This place needs a huge deal of work."

When a pen slips from his folder, landing in the leaves, I retrieve it for him and hand it back. "I've got the tools."

"The driveway needs serious grading to repair it, and the road to the highway isn't accessed by snowplows in winter. You'll be on your own for maintaining your road."

I've done enough construction work in my thirty-two years to know that his concerns are valid. But there's room in the budget to replace what needs fixing, and I've got a snowplow blade for the front of my truck. And since my wife dumped me exactly six months ago for her district manager, Austin, taking the house and the kids in the aftermath, I've been enough in the thick of life to not mind some good, clean snowfall. I can handle the road. The hallway. Outdated electrical. Just get me up here into these woods, give me some quiet, and maybe I can find the two things I need to regain.

The kids. And my soul.

I would add my wife to the list, but she's insisting I sign divorce papers. Still, it isn't over until it's over, so I tuck the girl I promised forever to onto the list for good measure.

Stepping across the yard, I survey the massive oak tree that shades the back end of the lot on the eastern side. It somehow shapes a perfect triangle with the two structures. Near to the barn, but far from the road, the huge tree is so sturdy it had to have been planted about the time this home was built. It would be the perfect spot for a swing. I can just see seven-year-old Micaela sitting there on the leaf-mulched ground, having a tea party, while Cameron sits in one of those red baby swings as I push him back and forth.

Despite the fact that we live in the same town, I haven't held my kids in over seventy-two hours. To say that I am eager to buy the first place with the perfect swing tree in the yard is something I don't know how to explain to the Realtor. I try not to notice the width of the porch and how it would be just right for two chairs and a little table in between. Maybe even a deck of cards. My wife and I used to stay up late into the night playing cards on the floor of our first apartment. Two college newlyweds in love. That seems like a long time ago now.

The Realtor continues to list reasons why I shouldn't buy this place.

Nodding, I turn the wedding band around on my finger. My hands are so scuffed and hardened from work that after half a rotation the band wedges snug. Like truck tires that can go no farther into the thick of it.

"I can't legally stop you from signing on the dotted line," he says. "I can advise against it, *heavily*, and will continue to do so. And I'm sorry about your divorce—"

"I'm not divorced."

"I see. But maybe you're finding yourself in a position of uncertainty. Impulse buys happen for a lot of reasons . . ."

I take the flyer from him and fold it square before pocketing it. As I do, he scrutinizes the scar splicing up my forearm, which is the proud guardian of a metal plate and half a dozen screws. Turns out my truck isn't the only thing that survived that night on the highway. "This isn't an impulse buy." Having watched the market for months now, I've already seen a few places, but nothing has been right. That changed last week upon discovering the new *For Sale* sign staked out by the highway after I'd hiked back to climb with a buddy from town. I had forgotten all about this place. As teens, some of my friends and I had come out to see if it was haunted, and one of them had picked up a rock and thrown it through a window. Smacked straight through yesteryear. Reckless of us, and the window's since been repaired, but

I still feel a degree of responsibility to help the rest along. There's something about this place and me. We belong together.

I glance to the stairs that once creaked beneath a bunch of boys looking for adventure. Stairs that are just asking to be climbed again. This time for real. Not because of a legend or juvenile curiosity, but because this place was meant to be a home. Whoever built it wouldn't have done such a solid job otherwise. This cabin shouldn't still be standing over a century later, but it is.

Speaking of impossibilities, *I* shouldn't be standing here, staring down a pending divorce with a woman who recently informed a ridiculously good lawyer that she'd married the wrong guy a decade ago. I shouldn't have a pacifier in the cupholder of my truck while the car seat sits empty, and I shouldn't have a CD of Disney songs in the player while my daughter is at swim lessons with Austin Steals-My-Wife-Jerk-Face, but I do. Maybe other dads would ease up on those things in light of a wife battling for full custody, but I'm not giving up on my family. I can't. And since I can't yet bring myself to sign divorce papers, I'm more than eager to sign something else. Something that offers hope instead of brokenness.

Even if I only buy the house to flip it, this place would keep my hands busy and give the kids a much-needed adventure along the way.

The Realtor releases a slow sigh before speaking. "Let me show you other properties. Give you a chance to see what the market holds, and give it all some time to really sink in. We'll crunch some numbers, and I'll show you some comp houses and the school specs. No decision needs to be made today."

I nod. That's fair. After we climb back into my truck, I free the emergency brake and crank the wheel to turn around in the tree-lined drive. As dust billows up behind the back tires, I try not to think about how a hundred years ago it would have been a wagon and horses ambling along this same curving lane. Maybe a man with a family. The image fills me with an ache.

We head back down to the main highway while the Realtor describes where we're driving to next: a move-in-ready ranch house near the lake. Within the span of a few hours, we make as many stops and both fulfill our promises. I see the rest of the homes on his list, and he ends our day by leading me into his office that stands between the Presbyterian church and the bakery in the middle of this town where I grew up and where my kids will too.

Despite the impressive properties I just saw, I need to claim the house from the previous century. The one where I broke the window. If she'll still have me. For so long she's sat empty and alone that it may take some coaxing to win her back. Houses are delicate that way. But there's something in me that can't stand to watch something else be alone.

As for that night with the pebble and my buddies . . . the past is history. Yet when the Realtor sits across from me at his desk, drafting up my offer for the perfect swing tree and the woodland porch with room for two, it seems the rest of the story is about to begin.

CHAPTER 3

JUNIPER

SEPTEMBER 1902

Git!" A greasy-haired miner kicks from where he's seated on his wagon, frightening the dog who is trying to clamber up into the moving box bed.

I help Bethany move aside on the road to make space for the commotion. Up ahead and just out of sight is the main street of Kenworthy, but this man isn't heading there. He's veering with other wagons into the valley that will soon lead them off the mountain and to new possibilities. The man who offered me marriage is somewhere among them.

Having hung back, the dog sprints forward again. Its fur is matted with mud as it tries to clamber into the jostling bed of the wagon once more. The man swings another kick, and the dog cowers to the dusty road. The creature, a female, slowly stands on shaking legs, but the man doesn't so much as look back.

I shift my hold on two bundles of clean laundry and, with

21

Bethany close, we stay clear of the lineup of wagons bound for the flatlands. When the last one passes by, Bethany skips ahead. Dust billows around her. I call for her not to go far. She's lithe as a fox on the uneven terrain. A courageous adventurer who has never feared forging ahead. I see myself in her in these moments and hope she knows that she instills courage in me by simply being her brave, beautiful self.

The dog is watching us now—her eyes too big for her face. Kneeling, I set aside the laundry bag and pat my hands together, coaxing her closer, but she scampers off. Toward town, fortunately, which allows me to watch her as we venture that way too.

Overhead, the sky is bright and clear, and the distant hills are soft in the daylight. With every glimpse of this view, I am in awe of such beauty. Of how a valley could dwell so high up in the sky, five thousand feet above sea level. It is no wonder John spoke of this place in his advertisement for a bride. The sheer notion of it had been so different from the view through the windows of my family's apartment. Of brick buildings stitched together with too many laundry lines, casting shadows above as carts clattered by, trollies clanged, and factory whistles sounded the end of each day.

Here, the sky is so wide open you can't take it all in with a mere glimpse. It takes a team of horses an entire day to climb this mountain over dangerous switchbacks and steep ravines. Such a trying journey to reach a mysterious stretch of land that welcomes the soul with a hush.

Up ahead, the fledgling town of Kenworthy is never hard to spot. Two clapboard buildings garner attention first—the squat post office and the two-story Hotel Corona. The wood that built them is nearly new despite the fact that they stand abandoned. It's not possible to spot the mine from here, and I'm glad. We gave all we had to the mine, and it offered nothing in return.

Those who built this town built it on the dream of gold that never existed. The glimmer discovered some years before sank no deeper into the ore than the craggy surface. Instead, the mine had been salted—gold loaded into a shotgun only to be fired off inside the mine to coat the walls with false promises. Who would deceive the founders so? How does a man hold his hands steady and conscience clear as he pulls the trigger? However he managed, the salting was a falsehood that caused a town to rise from the arid land only for hearts to break in its shadows. Tens of thousands of dollars were poured into its founding, and now the final wagon train leaves behind its dust.

This place that was built on hope has now died upon regrets.

Bethany slows for me, and there's a lonesomeness in the way she and I walk side by side down the center of the road. In the fact that I wear a pistol holstered at my hip. The town's one sheriff rode out months ago, and while most of the troublemakers followed soon after, I mean never to be caught unaware. The harsh truth about a ghost town is that you're not supposed to still live here.

The few who remain? We are the forgotten.

The last in a town that will soon fade to nothing.

Bethany and I make two, as does Edie, the shop owner's daughter, and her invalid father, Reverend Manchester, who isn't long for this world. Beyond that are several lingering miners as well as a schoolteacher I've never met. Bethany is one of only a few young ones now, so it's hard to imagine how the woman will remain. If she does, it would be nice to have another friend.

Winter whispers that it's on the way as I follow Bethany toward the mercantile. The dirt road running down the middle of Kenworthy holds only two men now. Only two.

One is Oliver Conrad. He's kneeling in the center of the road, sharing a morsel of food with the abandoned dog. It's a comforting sight. As I watch, he smiles some to me, but it's the kind of smile you share with someone when trapped in the same bad dream. An understanding as sad as it is kindred. We don't speak often since Mr. Conrad bears a difficult stutter, but he has always been kind. The sight of him—his dingy shirt and roughened hat—reminds me of John.

Thought of John drives a constant sharpness deeper into my gut. There is a pain to love. In the risk to willingly give your heart to another. It's a pain that gives cause for one to kneel at night and press on with faith in the unseen. I know because my knees are worn and weary.

The second man is one of the Cahuilla cowhands who works at the nearby ranches. I have heard him called Señor Tiago and have seen him with horses of every color and size, so I sense he is more than a cattle herder there. Most of the Cahuilla cowboys keep to the opposite end of the valley, but this one ventures into Kenworthy often. I couldn't begin to count the number of times he has stepped from the mercantile with a new tin of tobacco in hand. He is perhaps only a few years older than me.

His skin is as brown as aged leather, and his eyes glint dark like onyx from beneath his tattered hat. His shirt, a grungy white, drapes open at a smooth chest. He simply watches me pass by from the porch of the empty Hotel Corona, where he's settled in the shadows—easy and quiet. I've never heard him speak, and even if he were to voice something, it wouldn't be a language I know. Only some of the ranch hands speak English, and it's perhaps by their whispers that those of us in town have learned that this man is an *hijo de shaman*—shaman's son.

Oliver Conrad and Señor Tiago regard one another in passing. The native man spits a stream of tobacco juice, and Mr. Conrad tips up his chin. I do not think they like one another. But I have not ventured into town to worry about these menfolk. It is my dearest friend I have come to see. Bethany has already disappeared inside the mercantile where my friend's sure to be found.

At the open door, I hear Edie before I see her.

"Lands, June, get in here and fix this for me." Edie struggles to untangle two different sizes of rope that she's pulled from a box. She mutters a stream of curse words, and when Bethany starts to repeat one, I scold them both.

Edie ceases her monologue and winks at me. "If you let her go to school, she'd learn to speak proper, you know?"

"She's still too young for school. And if she spends less time around you, she'll learn to speak proper." Ah, how this woman is good for my soul. Especially with her laugh that fills this mercantile more than all its provisions. It brims with the sound of her girlish spirit that's as wild as it is strong.

Edie is not yet twenty, and with no mother was raised to hold her own among the roughest of men. "Coffee's hot, June."

The air smells of it, mixed with molasses, which means she's been baking.

"Pour yourself a cup and sit just here." She waggles the box of rope as though that will make rescuing her from this task more tempting.

I chuckle and, having the patience she lacks, set aside the bundles of clean laundry to do as she asks, ensuring the labels are pinned visibly in place on each smaller bundle of clothes. Men know to come here and collect it just as soon as Friday rolls around, and they drop off sacks of what needs scrubbing. I'm curious, now, to know which bundles will remain in a few days' time. How many men pulled out today, forgetting I had their laundry in hand?

Edie calls to me to come help *now*. Her long-legged stride is more apparent in the rawhide britches she wears. How is it this woman has the patience to decipher telegrams when they come through the wire and yet can't wait two seconds for anything else? Bethany tries to match her step for step as they walk the outside length of the polished counter. My daughter's chin is jutted upward, just like her tall companion.

Edie fetches a box of paper dolls from her back bedroom, and Bethany settles down beside the counter with the bounty. They're friends, those two, and while most mothers wouldn't warm to the idea of their daughter in the company of a woman who smokes a pipe and could curse a pirate to repentance, Edith Manchester is as genuine as she is loyal. She's a swig of cold water on a hot day. Just what the souls in this town need, and why her mercantile continues to be the lifeblood of Kenworthy.

Delicate leather fringe swishes down the length of each pant leg as she returns with a steaming cup for me and a plate of gingerbread for us both. Under her arm is an envelope with my mother's handwriting. The mail must have come in yesterday. She thrusts the plate toward me. "You must try this. It rose and did all the things it was supposed to!"

She offers me the letter as well, and I gladly tuck it into my apron pocket. Something to read by candlelight. News from home is always welcome. Just as welcome is the square of gingerbread she lowers into my hand. I don't take a bite until I see Bethany sink her teeth into her own square. My heart whispers a prayer of gratitude for the extra nourishment today. We eat enough to get by, my daughter and I, but barely, and as I savor my own bite, it's impossible not to be thankful for Edie's kindness.

Edie settles across from me. Her blouse is that of a woman, fresh from a catalog. It's tucked into the leather waistband where her pistol is twice as imposing as my own. An oversized coat drapes her narrow frame despite us being indoors. Her auburn hair hangs free, and there has never been a ring on her finger. Men have sought her, but each discovered that you don't tame a woman like Edie. Rumors abounded once that she nearly ran away with a fella, but either the hearsay wasn't true or she changed her mind. She's as vivid as she is headstrong, and God bless the man who will someday love her in all these ways.

Edie returns briefly to one of the back bedrooms, where her invalid father is abed. Doubtless the truest reason she stayed behind.

Reverend Manchester silently occupies a chair by the window during the daytime, and come nightfall, it takes all of Edie's strength to move him to his bed, where he is just as still. Having suffered a spell last year back, he requires her help with a spoon to even eat. I can just glimpse her adjusting his blanket before slipping back out.

Edie cares for him faithfully in this forsaken land, and it makes her only more admirable.

When I'm seated near the fire, the box of tangled rope pulled into my lap, Edie returns and leans near enough to whisper, "Your beau was just in here."

I gawk at her. "For shame. Mr. Conrad is not my beau."

She smirks and takes a square of gingerbread. She must have been using saddle soap earlier because when she waves a hand haphazardly, it stirs up the faint scent of lanolin and beeswax. "I was speaking of the other one. The one who left with the others." She arches an eyebrow as though puzzled by my choice to stay. But of anyone, I know this woman understands loyalty. "So . . . did he ask you?"

"Ask me what?" The rope begins to unravel beneath a patience that Edie, for all her qualities, lacks.

She drags a stool across from me beside the fire. "He was in here three weeks in a row asking after you."

"He was not." My face flames with embarrassment.

"Was too. Asked me all the time about you."

"Well, you'd do well to keep your mouth closed." If she only knew that I would give up a thousand hellos from a thousand men for the chance to see John once more. But she doesn't know this because I've kept the longing pinned deep inside. Like a hidden pocket that I let no one see into. Perhaps it is pride—the burning need for me to be strong. Not fragile or weak. Perhaps it is because I scarcely acknowledge that place myself. Only when I am alone, and can cry freely, do I concede how much my heart still beats for a man who is lost to me.

"I just told him you were the best cook in fifty miles." After tasting her gingerbread, she scrunches her nose. "Maybe a hundred. And that you aren't afraid of just about anything."

Actually, I'm afraid of a good many things. "Edith Manchester. You encouraged him."

"Did not. Just was honest, 's all." When she reaches for a rope to help, I bat her hand away. She'll only make it worse again. "So what did you say?"

"I told him no. I'm not going anywhere, and I'm certainly not marrying him." With no proof of John's whereabouts, it would be against the law for me to remarry. But what I also don't mention is that while the letter from my mother will doubtless hold another bid for Bethany and me to come and live with them, I'm not ready to leave. Maybe this mountain has made me stubborn like itself, or maybe it's something much softer. Perhaps it has more to do with the reason I saved the flowers John used to gather for me. Some linger dried on the windowsill by the bed. Memories that are planted like seeds. Seeds that haven't yet blossomed into hope, but the possibility is enough for me to not yet surrender.

"Maybe *you* should have married him," I counter. "You could find a town that's big enough to hold your personality."

She grins, flashing straight white teeth. "Can't leave Pa. And I sure can't take him along. No . . ." She shakes her head and breaks her piece of gingerbread in half. "This here is the spot for me." Still perched on the stool, she leans back to peer out the window. "It's strange to see the streets this empty."

The way she sits, her coat having fallen open, I notice her midsection is bowed out some. Not as lean as usual. She straightens again. Adjusts the coat, folding it carefully over her middle as she jabbers away some more about the latest news—that five men were arrested near Yuma after being accused of salting several gold mines across the West. Perhaps even the one here. "I think they're gonna talk more on it at the meeting," she adds.

I should pay closer attention to such a critical detail, but I'm distracted by what I just saw. "Edie."

She grabs for the box again, and I let her have it only to lean forward and brush one side of her coat away.

Her eyes shoot wide as she yanks it snug. "What'd'ya do that for?"

"Edie." This time the name comes out solemn. Despairing.

She rises, crosses to the counter, and plops down the box of rope. From a glass jar there, she pulls out a taffy for Bethany, who's content as ever with the paper dolls.

I follow the young woman. All the way to the storeroom where she sets to work arranging cans of beans. Wanting to startle her no further, I simply stand there. Waiting. Finally, she grips the nearest shelf and hangs her head.

"How far are you?" I whisper.

She shakes her head. "I'm not certain." She falls quiet then finally adds, "Shy of three months, I think."

I gulp. Edie's with child. And she's not married. It's hard to forget the sight of the abandoned dog on the road. The way it was shoved away from the wagon. A mother with no husband to speak of will be treated little better.

"Is the— Is the father still here?" Regret burns within me to have to ask. The pain deepens at the sorrow on her own face. Her chin is trembling. "Oh, Edie." I pull her into a hug.

She weeps silently against my shoulder. It's a cry that's harnessed so as not to alert Bethany or the sleeping reverend. A soundless sob that fractures me to my core.

I brush the hair from her damp cheeks and hold her face so she'll look at me. "Please tell me who the father is. Maybe it's not too late." Though if she's almost three months along, it could have been nearly anyone.

She shakes her head. "There's nothing to be done."

"Is he a miner?"

"No."

That eliminates half the men who were in town.

Her eyes flash with urgency as I grow pensive. "It sure as shootin' wasn't John," she adds. "That may be crass of me to say, but I can't, for one minute, think of you fearing such."

Warmth heats my limbs as the stun from those words collides into me. It's quickly tempered with relief for what she's generously offering. Slowly, I manage to nod, believing her with all my heart. Believing John with the same.

It's a relief, still, when she speaks on. "You don't know his name." She swipes at her eyes. "So don't ask for it."

"If that's what you wish." My heart is trying to slow in my chest. "Edie, you can't do this on your own."

She tips up her chin. "I'm just fine. Listen, June. This little bit ain't goin' nowhere for a while yet, and it ain't gonna get much bigger today. So let's just let it alone for now." She wipes her eyes with her sleeve then pulls the coat snug across her middle again.

"Of course." I touch her arm, giving a squeeze of assurance. "I'll go check on Bethany."

I step away, passing in front of the window where, less than an hour ago, the last wagon train pulled away. The offer of marriage from yesterday comes to mind, and it's more than a relief that I said no. Not only does my heart beat for one man and one man alone, but I could never leave Kenworthy now. Not with Edie and her father stranded here alone. There is no midwife, no doctor. Edie has only her father, whose unfocused eyes stare out the window from where he huddles in his chair. Abandonment is not a fate I will resign them to. This empty place is our home . . . or what will break us. Either way, we are here until spring.

CHAPTER 4

JOHNNY

Dust churns beneath rubber as I make an easy right onto the property drive. At a rut in the dirt road, the two-by-fours in the bed of my truck rattle on top of the tailgate. Rye, my overgrown Labrador, stumbles on the bench seat beside me. I scruff the top of his yellow head, and he lies down, whining. The climbing gear piled on the floorboard rattles—a pile of orange quickdraws and some loose carabiners clanging with every jerk of the truck.

"Almost there, buddy."

This is the first time I've brought him out to the cabin, and he sniffs the air, trying to make sense of the place. The sale on the Cohen house is a short escrow, so I should close next week. For now, the family gave consent for me to get the inside stair railing up to code. I would have gladly bought the materials, but they insisted on footing the lumber bill and paying for my labor. I couldn't argue with the first, but I'm not sending them any other invoices. They've been generous enough. We've never met, but they seem like the kind of folks you'd want to have over for Sunday supper.

The Cohens are in their eighties, and since they've already lost this house to time and finances, it's the least I can do. Extra handy that the week is wide open. Emily took the kids to a beach house until Monday, and while I'm eager to make up the time with them, the next few days will be perfect for getting the cabin up to par. The historical society has been maintaining it the last few decades, but a house this old? These four walls and I are about to spend a lot of time together.

The truck jerks again, splashing drops of hot coffee through the plastic lid on my to-go cup. I grab the drink from the holder and steady it. My crew and I just wrapped up a kitchen remodel in town, and we intentionally scheduled our next job for a week out, giving us all some needed vacation time. The guys didn't mind, and I don't either. At some point, I'll hire them to come out here to help me with some work in the barn, but I can tackle most everything else on my own. And with clear blue skies overhead and wind stirring acres upon acres of grazing land, the solitude is welcome.

I heave in a deep breath and rest my elbow on the rolled-down window. How is it that being out here makes troubles seem farther away? Vast, open sky has a way of doing that. Of reminding us of how small and quick life is when compared to the whole of time.

Still ambling down the dirt road, I just spot the roofline of the barn when my phone rings. *Please don't be the lawyer.* We have a phone conference scheduled for this afternoon, but I'm not ready yet. I fish the phone from the center console. It's lit up with my sister's name.

Thank God. "Hey."

"So, Mom told me about the house you bought." Her voice holds its trademark cheerfulness.

"That was fast."

"And? That's all you're gonna say?"

"What do you want to know?"

"Details!"

Rye rests his oversized head on my leg as I ease the truck to a stop. The vehicle settles, and I rest my elbow back on the windowsill. Dust churns, slowly. The house is just as I remember it from when last I was here, but something about this moment feels even more real.

"Alright," I say. "It needs some dry-rotted fascia board replaced above the eaves. Got half a flat of it in the bed of my truck along with pressure-treated two-by-fours for the upstairs gabling and some quarter-inch round to trim out an old hopper window."

"Oh, stop," she laughs. "I want the *details*, not the blueprints."

I grin. We both know our mom told her everything already, so I wait.

"It sounds like an amazing property." She sighs, and it's wistful—part envy and part worry. "It also sounds totally crazy. But I don't blame you for needing a change of scenery."

It's nice that she understands.

"Is it really part of an old ghost town?"

"Last part standing, they say."

"Wow. Johnny. That's incredible. Do you remember what the town was called?"

Surrounded by the property now, it's hard to imagine that there was ever a town around here with buildings and people. Now it's just pastureland across the whole valley to where the mountain peaks rise up. Not a single wagon track or even the memory of one. Hikers and a few mountain climbers pass through, as I have, but that's it. Even the road out here is just a glorified footpath. "I can't remember what the name was, but it's in the file. I'll look it up today and let you know."

"I want every detail." There's energy in her voice that's worth more than the supplies in the back. "Do you need some help? I've got a couple of free days coming up. I would love to check out the place and lend you a hand."

"That'd be great, Kate. Come anytime."

It would be good to see her, and my sister is one of those women who can decorate an empty room and angle couches in the right direction. Since my wife doesn't yet know where the kids will be staying when they're with me, having a woman's touch beforehand won't hurt.

After we set a plan, I drop the cell on the seat and sigh just as Rye does. "Well, boy." I thump his thick back. "Here we go."

Climbing out, I hold the door so he can jump down, then I grab a manila envelope from the glove compartment. Rye keeps pace at my side all the way to the porch. There, he lunges up and sniffs at a pile of pine needles in the corner. I turn the manila envelope over, and a set of keys slides into my palm. The deadbolt loosens with a click. Rye backs up, paws clacking on weathered porch boards. When the door creaks open, he sits.

I find the nearest wall switch, and the room floods with light. It's a strange kind of homecoming. Just walking in. Flipping a switch. *Bam.* Here's your new life.

The bottom level of the cabin is empty. The ceiling is low, depicting its era and a time when people were shorter, but it's just spacious enough that I don't have to duck. Against the wall stands a wood-burning stove that's not an antique and still looks plenty usable. The papered walls are bare, with only a few tiny nail holes where frames or mirrors once hung. On the wall beside the stairs, the same kind of nail holes rise at a steep diagonal with the slant of the steps. As I climb, I smooth my hand to the papered walls. The roughness of my palm catches on a paper edge that has curled away from the wall with time.

My other hand grips the smooth, spindled railing. The dark maple is so well seasoned that it'd be a shame to wreck it. Crouching,

I examine the evenly spaced balusters. Maybe the railing can be salvaged somehow. Whipping out a tape measure, I double-check the handrail height and once again confirm that it's only thirty-two inches. Modern codes dictate that railings must be thirty-four inches, and while this building is so old I don't think anyone would throw a stink about it, I'd like to have everything as safe as possible for the kids. I can't imagine swinging a sledgehammer and smashing through this creation, though. There's got to be a way to modernize the railing to code while preserving the beauty of this craftsmanship. Whoever designed the railing from hand tools alone cared about the ones who would touch this—the eyes that would notice it each and every day.

Needing to double-check the home inspection report, I fetch my bag from the truck and grab the house file from it. Thumbing through the documents, I spot the historical write-up as well. The miniscule text is faded and warped as though photocopied from an old book.

Good time to let Kate know before it vanishes from mind again. I shoot off a quick text.

Town was called Kenworthy. House was built 1890s-ish.

I turn my attention to the rest of the inspection report, barely reading ten words before the phone dings.

So cool! I'll swing by the library and see what they have in the local history section.
Just look it up on the internet.
Libraries are better.

Chuckling, I return the papers to the file. It's starting to make sense why she likes to poke through library shelves. The history really is interesting. I've only ever been drawn to this place for its hiking paths and boulders. I tend to notice textures more than words.

Like this house and the surrounding landscape. Those are the tales I best understand, and this one is beginning to take shape, begging for attention. If only I could glance over my shoulder and tell this craftsman, "Well done." The next best option is to give the design full respect while breathing new life into it.

Since there's no point waiting for the lawyer to call, I get right to work, starting at the bottom of the handrail. With a wadded-up cloth and rubber mallet, I manage to tap loose two balusters without anything splintering. Rye dozes by the door, and I can hear squirrels scamper across the roofline. I rest the individual balusters beside the stairwell and slowly work upward. There's a satisfaction in knowing that my kids will climb these stairs, holding on to the rail as they drag blankets, or play beneath them as a makeshift fort.

But first, I have to tell their mother that I've bought a hundred-year-old farmhouse. The finances are no biggie since Emily has already laid claim to her side of the assets. I'm using funds from my last two reno jobs—income that I earned after she filed for separation. As much as I hope to still win her back, I also have to keep placing one foot in front of the other. To keep living. I've learned the hard way that days of depression in the back end of your buddy's garage is no way to really live.

I've already crunched some numbers to see what it might cost to flip this property. If everything goes as planned, this place could be back on the market for spring. In the meantime? It's a cool place to live. Even if a number of factors still depend on Emily. During our last sit-down, her lawyer suggested we do things peaceably in his office. If we can agree on matters, we could avoid court. I don't blame her for liking that idea, but everyone was missing what I wanted.

To stay married.

It's not that I'm delusional. I get the point that she isn't in love with me anymore, but while she isn't exactly my favorite person on the planet these days, I also know that marriage is hard work. I'm not going to go down without doing everything I can to keep this family whole. There's another problem, though, which is out of my control. The state of California allows for her divorce petition to finalize by default whether I consent or not. Meaning that even if I don't want to play the game, I get picked for the losing team regardless. The only one who can stop this is her.

Rye lifts his head the same moment my phone rings. It's gonna be the lawyer.

I answer, and a thumping heart is instantly in my throat.

"This is Johnny." He gives his stiff greeting as I tap the speakerphone then set the cell on the step above me. Absently, I push the sandpaper forward and back in slow strokes. The lawyer seems to take this as my greeting.

"Well, I'm sure you don't need me to beat around the bush," he begins. "I'm calling to inform you that Emily is requesting that all the documents be signed by you and returned to the office here by the end of the month. In exchange for your timely cooperation, she has agreed to your request of a fifty-fifty custody share of the children."

It's a strange sensation—what happens to my heart then. Mixed with a rush of joy over a guarantee of more time with my kids is the pain that my bride is this eager to end our marriage.

I set the sandpaper on the nearest step. I hadn't even realized I was still holding it. "I'm sorry. Can you say that again?"

He does, and I'm certain that the parts of me that are dying will never come back to life again. The only thing that keeps me upright is thought of the children. Of the time I get with them by agreeing. "What about my accident?"

"The caseworker signed off on it. Confirmed that you posed no danger to the children and that since no drugs or alcohol were involved, and since it was the first incident on your driving record, not to mention reoccurring incidents with that stretch of highway for other motorists, there was no valid reason to take it further."

Relief slams my chest so that I have to sit down. Ever since the day I rolled my truck, Emily has threatened to use the incident in court as petition that I'm reckless and irresponsible, so as to gain full custody.

Closing my eyes, I rub fingertips against my forehead. The lawyer explains the rest of the details. All I have to do is sign the documents, and this mess will close up shop. Emily would be free of me, and I would get my kids equal share.

"And if I don't agree to sign?" The guy who says this is the same version of me that once raced Emily down the football field one night when we were in high school. It's the sound of her laughter under the stars and our bare feet on the grass that summon the words out. The longing not to end my life with her.

"Then the divorce will go through by default, and you'll have zero say in the outcome of how your assets are divided up. Including child custody."

"No say at all?"

"No, Mr. Sutherland. I heavily suggest you engage in this process. While my top priority is to my client, I believe it's in her best interest for this to be settled mutually."

With the sandpaper nearby, I take it up again. Fold it in half. "How much is this phone call going to cost?"

"I charge four hundred dollars per hour. She's requested you pay fifty percent of legal costs as part of the negotiation."

"Then here's a sixty-dollar question. What are the odds of stopping this moving train?"

"I'm sorry?"

"How often do you see a couple reconcile? This late in the process, that is?" With the phone still on speaker, I stare at the sawdust twirling in the air. The way it's coated my hands. Hands that are scuffed and calloused from years of climbing sharp granite and gritty limestone.

"Not very often, Mr. Sutherland."

"But it's happened before?"

"A time or two."

"If I stall, will it cost me the kids?"

"It may. The proposed arrangement is just that. Consider it an offer from your wife. It won't be on the table for long. You could counter, but it's risky. If this goes to court, things will get messier and take significantly longer. Not to mention it will cost much more than my base fees. In addition, the accident on record may work against you in front of a judge. If that happens, you'll have significantly less time with your children."

If a judge opens up that accident report, they'd know that my arm was broken in three places and repaired on the operating table. They'd also know that I busted my nose and broke two ribs when I slammed against the driver's door during impact. The judge would also know, if he or she asked me, that I was driving too fast because I was so dadblasted sad. That I hit ice because I couldn't see straight for the tears. But what they wouldn't know or care about was that I'd gunned my truck down the highway that day because I'd just seen my wife on the arm of another man as they exited a vacation rental cottage early one morning. A little cabin tucked away from it all. Their bags were sitting beside his car.

But I have to swallow that pain, so instead, I think of Cameron and Micaela and how badly I want to kneel down and catch their running hugs. The kind of hugs they give me the moment their mom unfastens them from their car seats. I need those kids like oxygen. And since the caseworker confirmed that I pose no threat to them, I have to take what I can for them right now. I have to take what I can, and it's killing me to do so at the loss of my wife whom I have loved since knowing her.

I want to hear the kids' voices again. Their sweet, young laughter. I want to wake up with popcorn on the bed and them sound asleep after a movie night. I want to buy extra milk so that we can make oatmeal with raisins just like Cam likes it and stir chocolate syrup into our glasses for Micaela. But then there's the memory of the woman I loved under the stars and the way she caught my hand as we ran all one hundred yards. The sight of her smile, even in the moonlight. "Can Emily give me a few more days to decide?"

"Yes. I'll let her know we spoke and that I'll be in touch with you again next week."

"Thank you."

"And, Mr. Sutherland?"

"Yes?"

"It was her idea to retract her intent to fight for full custody. I believe we can both agree that such a decision is generous considering her initial stance."

Unsure how to answer, I turn the wedding band around my finger, frustrated that her compassion makes it harder to truly stop loving her. Even when that kindness is for the purpose of setting herself free.

CHAPTER 5

JUNIPER

OCTOBER 1902

Dirt crumbles against the garden fork as I plunge it into the
earth. Lifting breaks ground enough for potatoes to tumble
loose. My hair, which is gathered back with a tattered cloth, tumbles
over my shoulder, and while it is clean, it hasn't been combed today.
The shirt tucked into my striped skirt was once John's. Rolled back
to the elbows, it's too large for me, but who is here to care? The sight
we must make as Bethany gathers potatoes into a bucket with soiled
hands and I dig at the earth for more. To think we used to dress up
in our Sunday best for the horse races and festivities Kenworthy once
exhibited.

Now, the day holds only the reality that our crop is weak from
this dry climate and my poor farming skills. We move down a few
inches and manage to unearth what little there is. As the autumn sun
hits the potatoes' soiled skins, I can't help but think of new life and
how instead of burying something into the ground as we do in spring,

41

we are drawing it out. The notion makes it impossible not to think of Edie and the life that has begun inside her. In truth, I thought of her and the coming baby the moment I opened my eyes this morning.

Did she shed tears in the night over it?

Who fathered this child? The mystery will unveil itself with time if Edie chooses to confide in me. I pray she will. Not for my own knowledge but so that she will know she is safe. Edie has sufficient provisions, and I do not fear for her life, only her heart. For men? It matters not. What price do they have to pay? But for us women, we are the caretakers of all that they leave behind.

I swipe a gritty forearm over my eyes to push back stray strands of hair while Bethany reaches for a potato with dirt-creased hands. The same small hands that helped drizzle water from the buckets I hauled from the pump all summer long. Now her breath fogs in the cold, and a knit cap covers her spry little braids. She is dearer than life itself, and a glimmer of hope rises that Edie will feel this dearness and not despair.

Lord, show us Your mercy.

"Let's finish one more row, then we'll go in and fix some supper," I call.

Bethany has paused to draw shapes in the dirt with a stick. She's not yet four but does the work of an older child and has more than earned the break. Leaving her to play, I finish the row, and by the time the basket is filled, she shows me her earthen drawings. I admire each wobbly creation.

"They're *so* fine." I ruffle the scrap of calico tying her braids. "I think this will call for soup tonight," I say, and together we snap off dark-green leaves from the narrow chard patch. In her pasture pen, the cow is grazing contentedly.

Edie has everything she needs at the mercantile but doesn't garden, so I'll bring some chard to her along with good, fresh milk. It's a simple offering, but the purpose of it helps push back the shadows of what our reality actually is. Come what may, I must hold on to gratitude. Gratitude tosses starlight into the darkest of nights. Sparse plates become plentiful, and fears lose their crushing hold. It is in our hearts where we are rich, and I have spent too many bleak hours in despair to not fight forward toward hope.

Standing here, I glimpse the two-man saw abandoned in the distance. It leans against the felled tree that John hauled into the yard in early March. He'd borrowed a horse and skidding chains that frosty day and was as gentle with that animal as he was with everything he encountered. Even as I think of it, I run my dirt-stained hands together, recalling the way he would lace his fingers through mine and kiss the back of my hand. He did this often—no rhyme or reason to it except to silently say that I was his and he was mine.

My gaze drops to the rusted saw once more before I turn away from the memories. Befitting its name, the saw is too cumbersome to manage alone. I haven't the strength, and now the abandoned tree trunk waits, as I do.

The thought dies when the sound that all mining families fear shudders the silence. A coarse rumble echoes down from the distant hills where the mine is tucked from sight of where we stand. A faint plume of dust begins to rise. Who would be in its depths? *Something* or *someone* has caused the commotion. Fearing the latter, I clutch Bethany's hand and urge her to follow.

As we hurry through dry chaparral, crisp grass clings to the hems of our dresses and pokes into our stockings. Bethany's steps are so short that I swing her into my arms and rush faster. I still keep a keen eye out for snakes. The pistol in its holster knocks against my hip with every step as I scamper up a low rise, struggling past spindly manzanita branches and clusters of thick sagebrush. With so few of us left in Kenworthy, there is no one else to come running as there once was. I do not know who or what I will find, but we must do what we can if we are to survive another winter alone.

The stone entrance comes into view as I rush over another rise with Bethany still on my hip. The mouth of the shaft is braced up with beams and thick side supports, all hewn from nearby pine, and the boards that barred entry have been taken down. Three mine carts are lodged at the entrance, one of which is turned over on its side. A man kneels on the ground there, hunched over. Whimpering beside him is the abandoned dog from a few days before. Head low, the dog skirts around the mine entrance.

"Mr. Conrad?" I set Bethany down and hasten nearer.

He looks at me, surprised. The skin above his right eye glistens with blood.

I crouch beside him, hoping the closeness isn't untoward. He brushes his hand against his brow as blood slides down his wrist. His hand. That's where it's coming from. More blood stains the dirt beneath the tipped-over cart.

"Just stay and wait," I call to Bethany, who lingers a few paces off, sage leaves still clinging to her dress hem. I do not have to glimpse Mr. Conrad's fingers a second time to see how badly two of them have been crushed. My stomach churns as I drop lower at his side. He's pale as ash. "Allow me to help you, Mr. Conrad?" I speak softly even as alarm draws me up tight.

The dog whimpers again. Mr. Conrad's chest heaves, and I don't blame him.

I'm far from a physician, but the town doctor pulled out three months ago. A plan scrambles together in my mind. "I'm going to fetch some water."

Rising, I hurry to the pipeline where water has been diverted in from what the miners dubbed Pipe Creek. After yanking loose an old sifting pan from a forgotten pile of rubbish, I crank the rusty valve handle. Dry as a bone. Returning the handle to its resting position, I scan our surroundings. Was there not a pump near the stamp mill? The operator's platform and station that rise above the nearest trees spur me into a run. After a few dozen yards, I pant to a halt near the side of the massive steel stamps where a pump once offered water to thirsty workers. I heave the pump handle up and down until a gurgle rattles the pipe. In a rush, the pan floods full. And I linger long enough to scrub the earth from my soiled hands. I've no soap, but this will have to do. Hurrying back, water sloshes over the side of the pan, darkening the front of my skirt and turning dust to mud there. It's a quick balance to reach Oliver Conrad's side again.

Kneeling, I take his hand and gently immerse it. He grimaces but stays silent. The clear water soils with dirt and blood, making it easier to comprehend the direness of his injury. These fingers will never be the same. They need to be splinted and bound. A nearby stick serves the purpose, and after beseeching him for a knife, he frees one from his hip with his uninjured hand. As a laundress, I know better than anyone that Mr. Conrad doesn't keep handkerchiefs in his pocket, so I pull one from my own, ignoring that it's what little I have left of John, and cut it in half.

Sweat beads on his brow as I secure his injured fingers to the stick. My fingernails are as filthy as his own, but there is no place for formality here. My hands have been laboring for survival in this place same as his own. Perhaps where etiquette was once a careful balance between the sexes, our understanding now springs from grit and grace.

He doesn't speak often, due to his stutter, so I offer enough words for both of us.

"You're going to fare just fine." It's meant to reassure him, though it's hard to say how his hand will heal.

I glimpse Bethany waiting where I asked her to, perched on the edge of a sun-rotted arrastra. The dog is lying at her feet as Bethany bends forward on the abandoned grinding mill to stroke the female's thick fur.

Despite everything, Mr. Conrad regards the dog as if concerned for its well-being instead.

Was the dog in the mine with him? I spare another glance, and she looks alright, but we'll check together.

I tie the cloth snug, and it's hard to imagine how the bones will grow back straight. A doctor would do much better, but to seek a physician means paying for the toll road that leads down to the valley town. Such a journey comes with a fee, and simply to reach that road alone is an hour by horseback through the woods—a luxury that neither Mr. Conrad nor I have access to. The choice will be his. At least this will help him get home.

When his hand is wrapped tight, he whispers through short breaths, but I can't understand. He rises, studying the patch job, and speaks again. "Y-you . . ." He tries again. "Thank. Thank you."

I stand as well. "Of course."

His full height is only a mite taller than me, and my attention lifts from his pained countenance to the blood smeared against his brow. His sandy-blond hair is matted with grease and dirt. Retrieving the last of the water from the gold pan, I use the wetness to wipe the streaks of blood away with what remains of my husband's handkerchief. Mr. Conrad's eyes fall to my wrist, then to my arm, then to the ground as I finish.

"There. That should do it. Be—"

The words fall short at a rustling in the brush just past the mine. Two wild dogs emerge, followed by a third. I call for Bethany to come to me. The dogs scamper down the hillside, likely drawn by the newest dog that has been left behind. Mr. Conrad calls for the skinny pup. With his stutter, it's hard to make out the name, but it sounds like Trixie. The dogs surround the female, sniffing and panting. She cowers away, and Mr. Conrad calls again, plowing past them to nudge her free of their crowding. He shouts, coaxing them farther off, and the dogs lose interest, pacing away. One slows and looks back. The new female whimpers but looks up at Mr. Conrad.

He holds up his hands, giving her freedom, and she surveys the wild pack again.

Finally, she sits and peers up at her new master. She's chosen to stay with him. Oliver Conrad's smile is of a man who knows how to find the blessings when few abound.

I smile too.

He scruffs her between the ears with his good hand while cradling his other to his waist. Seeing as he just gained his new companion, it surprises me when he risks that further by regarding the mud-splattered strays, their knotted fur and wagging tongues, then shifts his focus to Bethany and me. "W-walk you," he says, and his gentle gaze falls.

"Oh, you needn't do that." With the tattered cloth slipping from my hair, I tug it free and pocket it. The brown lengths blow free, which isn't proper, but this is neither the time nor place to tend to them.

"'Ss . . . ss . . .'" Grimacing, he repeats the sound a third time, but nothing else comes out. He swallows before trying again. "'S only right." He motions for us to start on.

I nod our thanks and coax Bethany to my side. We pass by the dogs as they watch from a distance. The dog next to Mr. Conrad cocks her head to him as though wondering what else the man might voice if he could string the words together. I, too, am curious what else this miner has to say. He's always been a kind man, albeit quiet. Why he has stuck it out here so long in a land with little rain and even less prospect, I don't know. I have no right to question his reasons, since I, too, have remained for a purpose that is hard to explain. I wait for a husband who may never return.

What is it that Mr. Conrad waits for?

I glance over to see that he has been watching me. He lowers his gaze.

As we walk, the other dogs lose interest and peel away. It's been so long since I've walked without feeling the need to search for signs

47

of danger. Bethany skips ahead, and I wonder if she feels more at ease as well. The bonnet she should be wearing twirls by its strings behind her. After a time, she slows for us and jabbers away to the reclusive miner. Her voice is so tiny and her skill with words still fledgling that it's hard for strangers to understand. As he casts me looks for assistance, I gladly translate. He angles his head toward her, appearing thoughtful enough to answer, but Bethany's constant chatter fills any need to do so. There's a pleased contentedness to him about it. They make good friends, her voicing every winsome thought, him with his easy silence.

Nearly back to the farm, I push a red-skinned manzanita branch out of the way and brace it as Mr. Conrad steps by its silvery-green leaves. Patches of blood have mottled the white of the handkerchief that keeps his fingers steady against the stick.

Why has he been in the mine? There is no gold.

When I pose the question, he takes his time in responding.

"Ga . . . gathering the carts. They're . . . they're sold now." From his pocket he retrieves a telegram with Edie's writing. The Fresno Mining Company has requested to hire a man for twelve dollars to unload all the supplies from the mine. They've purchased it all for a lump sum, even down to the very last brush and shovel. The toll road and doctor bill to fix his hand could cost that once he factored in lodging for a night, so like the rest of us here, he knows how to do without and get by. Such is life in the West. In these mountains.

Bethany listens as, by and by, Mr. Conrad explains that the company from Northern California has purchased the stamp mill as well as the remaining equipment and carts. It's all been sold for a fraction of its worth. Men will be on their way as soon as spring to disassemble the mill and . . . I wait as he struggles with the words of what will further redefine Kenworthy. No, not redefine. It will bring our very town, our home, to an end once and for all. It's hard to hear such a declaration and not give in to fear of what is to become of us.

Even the Hotel Corona is scheduled to be dismantled. There will be nothing left. If we must find a way to leave, I will have no choice but to abandon all hope of John.

Beads of sweat have gathered on Mr. Conrad's forehead again. It could be from the pain in his hand or the exertion of trying to say so much. This poor man needs to rest. I hope that whoever has hired him for this job is paying him well. If he's like me, though, he'll work for any wage, no matter how meager. Desperation has a way of doing that to a soul. He didn't put his life on the line just now for greed but for survival.

How had I not thought of his own stomach pangs? Of his own solitude?

"Please allow me to send you home with something for supper." I edge us closer to the house, but he slows to a stop. Bethany reaches up for his hand, and I catch her up, hoping the exchange will go unnoticed.

I kiss her cheek. "Run on inside and wash up."

She counters in her small voice. "But what about—"

"Yes, Mama," I offer.

"Yes, Mama." She trots off, waving to Mr. Conrad.

He returns the sentiment but hasn't accepted my offer.

I try another approach. "That hand'll be no use to you tonight. Might as well take something to eat so that you can rest it." Without waiting for him to respond, I head inside.

In the pantry, I fetch two pickled eggs and place them in a tin cup then wrap a square of last night's cornbread in brown paper.

"Grab me several of those potatoes," I call to Bethany.

She fetches a pair from the pail and holds them up.

"A little bigger?"

She returns to my side with two of the few that are larger than her hands.

"Good girl." Back outside, I'm relieved that Mr. Conrad has waited.

"Please. Take this." I extend the makings of a supper—two, actually—and he quietly accepts. A lock of his sandy hair falls onto his forehead, right where my fingers have been only minutes before. He balances everything in a cumbersome grasp.

"And please take care of those fingers. Perhaps soak them in warm water and salt. If you have any trouble, just holler." Since my cabin lies across the rise from his own, I'd likely hear him from the door of his shanty if he called loud enough. Something we both know he would never do.

He smiles, a small one, then turns away.

The garden still holds some of our harvest. It will all keep until tomorrow. For now, it's time to wash hands and faces, have our own supper, and say prayers. Then, once I tuck my sweet girl into bed tonight, I will sit down at the desk beneath the window and write to her father about our day. It's been nearly a week since I have penned a letter to John. Something about witnessing another man's raw determination reminds me not only of our own struggles but of my husband's. Of the possibility that he is somewhere out there facing dangers all his own, trying desperately to find his way back to us.

CHAPTER 6

JOHNNY

E leven heartbeats. That's how long it took for my truck to stop sliding across the asphalt.

I felt my wrist break—not even noticing my knee shatter against the underside of the dash. It wasn't until after I woke up in the hospital that I even knew there was something wrong. After a debriefing from the doctor, I was back in surgery for a knee replacement to pull out the broken bones and get me walking again. The wrist healed nearly as slowly. It doesn't bother me now, and while I sometimes forget about my artificial knee, there's times when it just feels weird to walk on. Like something inside me will never be the same and it's because I'd been reckless. I knew better than to take that corner so fast. I knew to be mindful of black ice. But my brain just shut down.

It was so dumb to let ambulance sirens be what woke it up again.

Kneeling in the barn, I feel the difference between my two knees as I unzip one of my climbing packs. This thing is a mess, but while

51

I won't be going on any trips this month, I did stash the keys to the side panel of my work truck in here after three days in Zion's slot canyons a few weeks back.

Digging to the bottom, I finally find the keys under my 60m static rope. Retrieving them, I brush away the sandstone grit that the canyon left behind. The rope goes back in along with my harness and an extra length of cord. I've hung most of my gear on pegs on the eastern wall of the barn, so I return the pack alongside the others, hoping to get out there again soon. Until then, there's lots of bouldering around here, which will be the perfect spot to teach the kids how to rappel. I've already ordered a child-size harness, and it should arrive any day. I'm heading up to town now so will check the post office.

At my truck, I unlock the side panel and find more rope as well as what I've been looking for all morning: the car charger for my cell. I have no idea why it's in here, but it's the one place I haven't looked.

Armed and ready to go to town, I make sure Rye is settled inside for the morning with food and water, then hit the highway. My sister is coming up for a few days, so it's a good time to stock up on supplies as well. I made sure she knew I hid a key under the mat for her so she can let herself in if she gets to the cabin first.

Town is quiet on this Wednesday, which makes it easy to grab the mail—still no harness—as well as some groceries that don't need refrigeration. After loading the two paper sacks into my truck, I walk over to the library to run a quick search on how best to restore the flooring in the cabin. It's so old that I don't want to lose the historic patina.

I could just access the web on my cell, but sometimes using a screen larger than a granola bar is too good to pass up.

Two clicks and one more password opens my email. It takes just a second to delete junk mail. One of the remaining messages is from a prospective client, describing the need for a kitchen remodel. I type a quick response, offering to create an estimate for what she and her husband are looking for. The job sounds pretty standard, so I'll give them a call early next week then crunch some numbers once I figure out how to balance their vision with reality. I hit Send on that, and just below sits a new email from the Realtor.

Nearby, a kid unloads a pile of books into the drop box then trips over a trash can when he races back toward his mom. I catch the can and hold it while he stuffs paper back in. He grins at me and hurries on his way. Straightening in my chair, I click Open on the email and wait for it to load.

> Johnny,
>
> I received word from the sellers, and they'll be in California this month. They'd like to come by in the next few weeks and pick up some items at the property.

I try to remember where the Cohens live. Wyoming, I think. From what I've heard, it's been years since they've come to the property. I read on.

> Basically, it's a handful of heirlooms that were on exhibit in the gift shop during the reenactment days on the property. The Cohens have indicated the heirlooms are in two lockboxes stored inside the barn. Any chance you've seen them?
>
> Either the sellers can come by and retrieve them, or you can drop off the lockboxes at the real-estate office. Any preference? If the boxes are too heavy, let me know, and I'll talk to the sellers about getting the code. The items were supposed to have been collected by the town's historical society, but after a series of phone calls, it sounds like they're

all still in the barn—so there's been a bit of confusion. Your help will be appreciated.

If you need to reach out to the historical society directly, I've copied them on this email so you have their contact information.

Also, one more request: I received an email from a student in Palm Springs who is requesting a photograph of the east side of the house. I think she found the property in the *Palms to Pines* magazine, and apparently the picture is for an important project she's doing. Would you mind sending one along? Sorry for the trouble with these requests, Johnny. Historic homes tend to hold value to a number of different people and sometimes garner extra attention or community needs than your everyday house. Appreciate your patience and help.

Best regards,
Daniel C. Hamilton
Mountain Realty

I shift on the hard plastic chair and start a reply.

Daniel,

I appreciate the updates. Yes, I'll take a look for those lockboxes and can drop them off on my way by your office this week. I'm picking up a stove and fridge tomorrow, so will plan to drop the boxes off before I hit Home Depot. As for the student, I can send the picture. That's no problem, either. I'll try and take one soon.

Johnny

I check my spelling then hit Send. After logging out of my email, I do a quick internet search on a few architectural details from the 1800s that I've been meaning to figure out for the house. The first is on how to properly finish antique floors and which type of sealant is best. I've gone over almost every square inch with an industrial-sized sander the last few days, and nearly fifty years of various varnishes have been worn to the natural wood. The only thing remaining is a bad water stain in the middle of the upstairs bedroom. About two foot in diameter, so I'm wondering if it wasn't the spot for an olden-day bathtub.

Through several articles, I scrawl notes then take off to get the sealant at the hardware store. When they show me the two canisters in stock, I buy both.

It's about fifteen minutes from town to the house. The drive home is relaxing, so I enjoy the cool autumn air that gusts in the open window and soak in the sight of the trees lining the highway, tall pines that soar skyward. The openness of it all—the vastness—has me thinking of the kids. The bite of loneliness, of missing them, stings the back of my throat, so I quickly clear it. The last time I came unglued, I wrecked both this truck and its knuckleheaded driver and risked losing them entirely. I swallow the ache and focus on what's ahead: the road, yes, but soon time with them. It's what I'll gain by signing the divorce papers.

I nearly signed them last night but paced away instead.

Why is this so hard?

At the property, my sister's minivan sits parked in front of the house. She's perched on the porch steps with a huge smile. A tray of brownies is balanced in her lap. She clearly found the hidden key because the door is propped open. Rye sits beside her, the yellow Lab nearly as big as she is. He's eyeing the brownies more than her. I ease to a stop and pull the brake as she stands. Kate jabbers a million miles a minute as I swing the truck door open.

Suddenly I'm engulfed in a sister hug, brownies and all. "Johnny. This place is amazing." She smells like chocolate and a sense of *home*.

Rye clobbers into my side, and I scruff his head. "Need me to grab anything?"

After strangling me a second longer, Kate pulls away. Swipes at her cheeks. "Nope. I moved my stuff to the porch already."

She's crying? It hits me that we haven't spent a lot of time together lately. As kids we were super close. As teens, we joined the same climbing gym where she met her husband and I met a love of heights. Things changed after that, both of us growing into adults and starting our own families. Now life has circled us back to a new and strange place. It will probably take me a few more years to call it good, but seeing her now, knowing that my sister has driven an hour with brownies to hang out for a few days, is something that triggers hope more than I can say.

Rye leads the way as we climb the steps to where Kate's suitcase and sleeping bag wait.

"So, what's first?" she asks. "I haven't actually gone inside yet. I just let the dog out since he started whimpering. I am so excited to see this place."

"If you're up to helping me finish the floors, we can arm you with a brush and tackle them together. I bought two jugs of sealant today, then you can put your feet up and give me tips while I rebuild the kitchen." I wink and grab up her stuff. The magazine peeking out of her sleeping bag has a newborn baby on the cover, along with "10 Answers to Fertility Questions for Women." She and her husband have been wanting kids for years and are now taking an all-new route. One that has her popping more vitamins than usual and visiting doctors on a regular basis. How I hope this works out for them. They deserve every happiness.

"Put me on the job, boss." She braces the door farther open as I work past with her gear. "Even better than popcorn and Netflix."

"That's good because unless you have a streaming device and microwave in your purse, we've got cold Pop-Tarts and tic-tac-toe."

She laughs, and I bump the outlet switch with my elbow. Her gasp floods the room even as light does. "Oh, my word. This is incredible!"

Kate moseys around the room for a minute, touching every nook and cranny and peeking into the alcove that might have been a pantry once. She's upstairs in two minutes flat, calling down to me from the top landing, "Johnny, have you seen this?"

"Yeah, I think I have," I chuckle. No clue as to what she's referring to, but the place isn't huge, so I've seen it all. In fact, I've scrubbed or sanded it all. Which reminds me of the tubs of sealant. Not to mention checking on the lockboxes for the Realtor.

I call up to her that I need to step out for a second. "I gotta check something in the barn real quick."

"I love that you just said 'the barn'!" she hollers back.

Chuckling again, I leave Rye to keep her company and jog across the yard. I fish keys from the pocket of my jeans and unlock the deadbolt on the barn door. The sun is lower in the sky, the afternoon air chilling. While there's no snow in the forecast, it's wanting to come. A week, maybe. Two, tops.

Inside the barn, I climb over the load of new lumber now piled there, aiming toward the far back corner where an old popcorn machine stands forgotten along with boxes of colorful pennants. Beside all that rest lidded storage tubs of employee costumes from when this place packed a crowd for historical reenactments.

It takes some effort to step over the tubs and not send anything sliding. In the far back rest the two metal boxes, each about the size of a large ice chest. They're stacked neatly, and while the boxes look as old as everything else around here, they're secured with modern code locks. These things are solid, so best to dolly them to the truck tomorrow while the floors dry. But at least now I can confirm with the Realtor that they've been found. Crossing the yard, I dart him a text along with a promise to drop them off at his office tomorrow.

When I lug the sealant inside, Kate has already stashed her stuff and is throwing her blond hair up into a ponytail. Her gray sweatpants have streaks of old blue paint on them, and her T-shirt says *Let's Do This.*

She watches while I get the brushes in order and open every window; then the cabin comes to life with the whir of a small shop vac while we suction up every last bit of dust. Kate takes over and carefully gets all the corners and even the windowsills. This takes some time, and I appreciate her attention to detail while I shake up the cans of varnish.

After a while, I call to her over the noise. "Hungry?" It's in my nature to worry about her.

"Not yet," she hollers back. "I want to do something construction-y first."

"You *are* doing something construction-y!"

She grins, and I'm never going to win this argument.

"Okay." I pull out the brushes and offer her one. "We can start on the sealant. And yes . . ." I toss her a cloth respirator mask. "You're going to have to wear one of these."

She eyes it. "But not you?"

I grin. "Joys of being big brother."

She rolls her eyes but puts the mask on while I work the lid off the top of the first tub of sealant. It's a natural oil wax, and the brand is biodegradable. It's safe enough for wooden toys, but I still want to be careful since Kate's trying to have kids. A journey that's been many years in the making, and so she doesn't argue. Instead, she plugs in the old CD player and hits the Power button. Country radio buzzes from the banged-up speaker, and she starts grooving to the beat even as I demonstrate how to apply the sealant. Then, noticing the way

Rye is watching us both from the couch, I call for him to go out. He whimpers, but I urge him outside to avoid a mess of paw prints on the floor and varnish on the dog.

Once the door's closed, I start in the far corner where the fridge will go in this week. The rest of the kitchen, including cabinetry, is on custom order, so for now two sawhorses make a temporary countertop. It's not glamorous, but it's as good a spot as any to whip up PB&Js and macaroni and cheese for the kids. They'll probably love it. Emily? Not so much.

I try not to think of what my wife is going to say. I try not to think about the meals we used to prepare together. How she would dance barefoot through the kitchen, fixing a salad—nibbling on veggies while she hummed a tune. The sight of her fades away and in its place dwells a hole in my chest.

Emily used to love helping me on renovation jobs. In fact, she's one of the best trim painters on the planet. The girl can cut in a straight line like nobody's business. She used to join me on jobs, crank up this very radio, and, with a handkerchief over her hair, paint anything that needed it. I'd finish cabinets, cut lumber, and install appliances, then together we'd celebrate with burgers and sweet tea from the local diner.

I glance at my sister, who's kneeling on a rolled-up towel again, this time applying sealant. The pair of them used to be the closest of friends. What would she say if she knew about Emily's final divorce ultimatum? These few days will be a good chance to talk it over with someone, especially someone who I can trust. Someone who knows and has loved us both, because I still don't know what I should make top priority: the time I desperately need with my children or making a stand for the woman I promised forever to.

"This wood is in such amazing shape," Kate says, having tipped the mask away from her mouth. "It's hard to believe it's so old. I mean, it looks old. But I imagined more of this place falling apart."

I grab a brush and start a few boards over from her. "They've taken great care of it over the years."

The mask is in place again, so her voice muffles. "What kind of wood is this?"

"Redwood. It's lasted well. Especially with this much foot traffic." I run my thumb along a smooth, dark knot, amazed at the wonder of wood and how it has the ability to live more lifetimes than any of us.

"And what are these marks here?" Despite my objection, Kate's peeled off the mask. Leaning back, she points to a rectangle border where the wood is still a lighter shade than the rest of the floor.

"There used to be display cases there. This downstairs area was a gift shop and museum for a few decades." I point toward the bolt holes. "Glass cabinets were bracketed to the floor."

"We used to come here as kids. Remember the hayrides?"

"Yep. And the potato-sack races." I tap my mouth to indicate she put the mask back on.

"Yes!" Her eyes sparkle with childhood memories as she slides the straps into place. Her voice is muffled again. "I always liked it when they did the gold-mining demonstration." She lifts the mask, ignoring me again, and I smile. "I actually found an old picture of both of us standing next to one of the historians who was teaching about how laundry was done in the olden days."

I turn the radio down when it hits a commercial break. "I'm trying to imagine you bent over a washboard."

"And I'm trying to imagine you in suspenders. Wait." She squeezes her eyes closed a second then laughs. "I can actually imagine it."

Her laughter brightens the time as it always does, and she hasn't complained once. In her true fashion, she's brought a joy to this project that's contagious. Granted, I've placed my trust in a whole lot of unknowns here, but it's been with a dose of trepidation at every turn. But right now? I'm seeing this house through all-new eyes. It somehow bolsters the dream—that this place could actually be a home.

When my cell buzzes from my pocket, I ignore it for a while. Then again, it could be the kids, so I tug it out. A new email has come in. I tap on the icon to see that it's a response from the Realtor.

Turns out the sellers have been delayed due to Mr. Cohen being ill. They won't be coming to California at this time after all. But there is an old nineteenth-century diary that they're looking for. It sounds like it belonged to one of the family members who used to live in the house—a Mr. John Cohen. He was a gold miner in the area long ago. The sellers have requested that we simply ship the journal to Wyoming directly. I have a hunch it will help save everyone time and energy if we just send it along. The code for both boxes is 22–15–6. If you can bring the diary to my office, we'll FedEx it same day. I'm sorry to have to ask this—but can you make sure the journal entries are signed from this John Cohen? It sounds like there might be a few diaries in the box. Thanks, Johnny.

JOHN COHEN

July 1894

This heaviness is too much to bear. I don't want to put it into words tonight, but if I don't, it will clamor out of me some other way, and I fear it will be worse.

My cousins and I have ridden out here to the far West, high into these hills where we learned of another abandoned gold mine. Already, we have salted three of them, and each sale proved profitable. It's almost too easy. Loading gold nuggets into a shotgun shell. Aiming the gun inside the mine. Firing it off. Even as the echo of the blast quiets, one can already see the glimmer of gold in the walls. Buyers are always impressed. Businessmen who run pristine hands along the walls, enamored with the wealth glinting before their eyes. Of the valuable ore they believe lies deeper still. Veins of gold that don't even exist.

Fools, all of them, and we are the bigger fools for deceiving them. We are the wolves in sheep's clothing, leading the lambs to the slaughter. For what? To line our pockets with dollars and to leave a city man behind with nothing more than a tomb.

This was to be the fourth mine we salted, the last man that we deceived. God, I wish we had stopped at three mines. I wish we had never begun at all, because now I lack the strength to sign my own name. No, I lack the backbone.

CHAPTER 7

JUNIPER

The sight of Edie spooning gruel into her father's slanted mouth is as tender as it is saddening. Such care, such domesticity, is a sharp contrast to the murmur of men's voices out in the storefront where they are gathered for our town meeting. Amid the din of their chatter, someone curses. A stool is tipped over and righted. A man guffaws. None of it startles me, though I do worry after Bethany and her knack for picking up words.

Standing there by barrels of flour and sugar, I silently count the men. Four ... five ... six ... seven. Sweat-stained shirts, many of which I will launder this week, are braced with faded and worn suspenders. Hats have all been removed, showing pale brows above suntanned faces. Hands are rough, some stained, and one hand in particular is bound in John's best handkerchief.

My focus lifts to Oliver Conrad's face as he stands near the polished counter, focus on a miner describing his recent sighting of a mountain lion. I listen, too, noting that the animal wasn't far from my farm. The stray dog that Mr. Conrad claimed lies slumbering beside his boots, and the bandage on his hand is in desperate need of changing. I will tie a fresh bandage into place before he leaves tonight.

From the porch of the mercantile comes the soft sound of a man plucking a banjo. The musician isn't very good, and the instrument sorely needs tuning, but it's pleasant all the same. We have so little here, it's hard to be picky.

The Cahuilla cowhand, Señor Tiago, stands in the corner smoking a pipe. The air is scented with its sweet, earthy aroma. He surveys the room but doesn't move or speak to anyone. Previously, when Reverend Manchester was a strong man, I remember seeing him and Señor Tiago speaking at times outside the mercantile. It seemed they shared a mutual respect, and I wonder if Señor Tiago feels the decline in the reverend's health as those closest to him have.

Señor Tiago's focus drifts to where Edie is feeding the last spoonfuls of gruel to her father, and then his dark eyes slide to me. I look away before I'm able to make sense of what I see there.

The banjo falls silent, and small footsteps sound across the porch before a woman enters, stepping into the light of the two lanterns Edie lit earlier. She is tall and lean. Her brown hair, threaded with gray, sweeps back from a severe part down the middle. The cut of her plain blouse is high, and her figure is as willowy as my own. But even so, all the voices fade to silence in the room. All eyes rest on her. Few of the men are her age or older, and it's those that let their gaze linger longer than a passing glance. Even the man who had been serenading us all has leaned across his bench to gawk. There are too few women in this town.

Like me, the woman has grown accustomed to such overt attention, so she pays them no heed as she pulls off a shawl. The knitted wool is as golden as the oak leaves that cling to the hem of her gray skirt. We've never met, but I sense she is Mrs. Parson, the school-teacher who has chosen to remain behind.

I meet her in the center of the mercantile, not caring that all the men are still silent. "Mrs. Parson, a pleasure." The formality hardly fits the fact that my hands are calloused and there's a pistol at my waist, but this is life as a woman of Kenworthy now.

She shakes my outstretched hand, and her own tells a silent tale of survival. Of the lives we lead here scraping by without men at our sides. More telling still is looking into the face of a stranger, and there's a shared understanding there in her smiling eyes. An outward dignity that doesn't reveal the span of hopes we as women feel within. It is one thing to have the determination to attend a meeting formed by men, then to do so with the sensibilities and compassion that define our gender. Making it as remarkable as it is difficult. Around here, the complexities of a woman's heart are best worn in secret, and I have no doubt that this woman has experienced her share of that raw hardship.

"I'm Mrs. Cohen. Juniper Cohen."

"A pleasure." Her smile is warm, and I introduce Bethany next, who is quickly as enamored with the schoolteacher as the woman is with her. It seems these two have a mutual love of learning, and I am grateful.

Bethany tugs at my striped skirt and whispers in her young voice that few can understand but me. Yet somehow Mrs. Parson navigates the words. "Is it the books she's hoping to look at?"

I nod. "The picture ones are her favorites."

The teacher holds a hand down to my daughter. "May we go and explore them?"

"I think they're waiting for that very thing." I give a little salute to my daughter, who grins up at her new friend. Bethany reaches for Mrs. Parson's outstretched hand, and together they move to the shelf of books near the back of the mercantile.

With only a few minutes to spare before the start of the meeting, I return to the far side of the counter to where a utility room and the two back bedrooms reside—one for Edie and one for her father. By lantern light, Edie is tucking a blanket up around his still, sleepy form. I gather the bowl from her abandoned chair and step out as she does.

Edie closes the door softly behind her. "He'll rest. He sleeps so often, June, I don't know that it will be long now."

She looks bone weary. A store to run, a father to care for, and a child growing inside her. Not to mention meals to prepare and dishes yet to scrub in the utility room that doubles as a place Edie hangs her coats and ammo and tends to dishes and meat. Even as I note the tired lines around her eyes, she tugs her coat snugly over her middle. The baby isn't showing much, but it's clear that Edie won't be too careful. I don't blame her.

It's difficult to return to the center of the mercantile. So hard not to survey these men again and contemplate who, if any of them, might be the father of this unborn babe. As the men gather around, some pulling close chairs or barrels to sit on, it's hard not to analyze if any pay Edie a special kind of attention. They all do, really, these lonely miners, so the effort on my part is futile.

These meetings have been held once a month in Kenworthy for as long as I can recall. Before, it was men who attended, but now I come in place of John. In truth, I wish I had always been bold enough to attend. Back then, the meetings were held outside in fine weather, or in the saloon during winter nights. Now, we have moved into the mercantile since the grand Hotel Corona is boarded up and empty. These men attend now to swap the latest news of safety and sanity. That Edie and I take turns providing a tray of sweets usually ushers in the most reluctant of attendees and keeps the naysayers at bay. As of now, all are gathered around the cream griddle scones I made today, and the plate is nearly empty.

As is customary since the relocating of the meeting, Edie speaks first, welcoming the men to all the hot coffee they want and reminding them not to spit tobacco on the floor. One of the miners swipes his boot across a board that's already soiled.

With that, Edie leaves it to those who have an order of business to share. Bethany and Mrs. Parson return from their perusal, and my daughter settles in beside me with a book on animal husbandry.

The man who had cautioned us all about the mountain lion addresses the issue for the room's benefit now. "Cougar's likely a male," he continues in a smoke-roughened voice. "Spotted just east of the shanties, heading back into the hills."

"When was he spotted?" I ask, and as the man answers that it was just yesterday, I feel Señor Tiago watching me from the corner of the room.

There have been mountain lions in the area before, and while they keep to themselves, it's hard not to be alarmed. I am just about to inquire further when I realize that Señor Tiago speaks English.

"Female. Not male. Four years old," he says in a cool, calm voice. "Walked north. Far from farm." His gaze finds me again, and after overcoming my shock at the sound of his voice, I nod my gratitude for the information. Though I know this man very little, strangely, I believe him. Still, I will keep a careful watch of our land and of Bethany's nearness.

Mr. Conrad speaks next, and while his speech is delayed, stumbling along like a twig in a brook, he manages to explain to the gathering that he is nearly finished unloading the mine of carts and equipment for the Fresno Mining Company, who will be sending out a crew to collect it in the spring.

When that discussion draws to an end, two more men speak, and then Mrs. Parson offers reading lessons in the mercantile on Monday and Friday evenings to anyone interested. Last to speak is Edie.

She swings her feet down from the shop counter where her boots were hitched up and crossed. "Fresh supplies are coming in from San Bernardino this Friday. We'll be restocked on most of the staples, and I put in for the saddle soap Mr. Hudson ordered as well as the gin ya heathens stripped the shelves of. With any luck, there will be a newspaper as well." She braces her coat closed as she speaks. "I'll keep it here on the counter for any who want to put those reading lessons to the test."

The men chuckle, and I smile as well. It feels good.

We are life. All of us together, and separate. But somehow, gathered this way, there is something in the blood that resembles a type of hope that's hard to conjure when alone.

"Any news of the mining gang that was arrested?" a man calls out.

This is the second time I've heard tale of these crimes, but I do not know the details.

"Perhaps we'll have some on Friday," Edie says with ease.

Señor Tiago shifts his weight, and the men disperse into soft murmurs.

I slide from beneath the weight of a dozing Bethany and rise to tend to Mr. Conrad's hand. When I close Bethany's book, Mrs. Parson offers to return it to the shelf. I thank her. Whatever it is about this mining gang and the arrests for their crimes, I'm curious, but as Edie said, we will have to wait until Friday to find out. Perhaps longer if no newspaper arrives. How refreshing it will be to have news from the world around us.

"Mrs. Parson," I begin to the woman seated on the other side of my daughter. "You've made a friend in my little girl."

"She's a gem. Smart as can be for one so young. How old is she?"

"Nearly three and a half." I smile proudly.

"She'll be ready for school soon."

"I hope so."

"Mrs. Cohen, may I speak boldly with you? This seems to be a time and place that calls for such." Her voice is kind.

"Of course."

"The school board has chosen to close Kenworthy school now that so few students attend. There are four children who come in from the nearby ranches, but no others. I may return home to Portland in the spring, or perhaps find a way to stay on longer. I would like to see them through this term at the very least."

Without pay? "That's more than generous."

"It's selfish, really. I don't much fancy the Oregon rain."

There is nothing easy about life here where rattlesnakes and ruffians are as common as drought. No one likes the weather here. It makes her choice all the more selfless—no matter how she is trying to color it.

"I no longer have lodging available, as I'm now on my own. I could take over one of the shanties, of course, but those all belong to the mining company still. Edie mentioned you might have a room for rent. I don't have much, but I can pay a little or would gladly help tutor your daughter. I know that's a poor offering for what I'm asking."

Here this woman is giving what little she has to others. Can I not do the same? We have a room we can spare, as Bethany and I can easily share together.

From my side vision, I glimpse the various men each tipping their hats to Edie before departing. Part of me longs to observe the exchanges, longs for some indication that might live there between her and the father she keeps a mystery, but I need to focus on what I have the power to change. For Mrs. Parson's existence—as well as Bethany's and mine—we all need the same things. Safety, and since the Lord is clearly granting it, some company to help push back the shadows of our quiet days here.

"Yes. We have a spare room," I say, lifting Bethany into my arms. "And we would be honored to welcome you to our farm."

CHAPTER 8

JOHNNY

S o get this." Kate turns back a page in the history book on her lap then sips from a sports drink.

She's seated in a camp chair with her feet balanced across my own chair that's empty. The mesh cupholder is her spot of choice for a pack of red licorice. From the top of the stairs where I've been staining, I shift the pail of varnish aside and dip the brush. The floors below have had twenty-four hours to dry, so now we'll have to keep off of the stairs for a while. Thanks to the type I grabbed, the varnish has put off little to no fumes, but just to be safe, we've kept the windows open.

Before smoothing the brush over the wood, I call down. "Are you going to send up this fun fact, or do I need to say something commemorative first?"

"Oh, shush! I was looking for the paragraph. This area used to

70

be that mining town. I forgot what it was called . . ." She flips back another page. "Kenworthy. There was a store, a big hotel, and even a schoolhouse. But that's not the most interesting part." She taps the open page with a piece of licorice. "It was a gold-mining town that this rich guy built, and he paid a ton of money to do so. Like fifty grand. Johnny. *Fifty thousand dollars.* And that's all the way back in the 1890s. And you know what it says?" She bites off the end of the red twist. "That the mine profited absolutely nothing. Wait." She double-checks a fact. "It made ten dollars. *Ten* dollars. Can you believe that?" She waggles the licorice even as her foot bounces with the same energy. "The owner built this entire town with his own money, then walked away from it after only a few years. Soon, everyone else left as well. There wasn't any gold. Imagine that. This whole place was built around the mine for nothing. It was all a ghost town before it hardly began."

"Wow." I hadn't known that. "I wonder if that mine is still around. I wonder if it's possible to find it."

"Gonna do some panning?" she calls up to me.

"It'd just be cool to see, I guess. It's probably caved in. At the very least boarded up. It has to be because there's nothing around. Not even a stick of wood left." This side of the story was probably explained during the historical reenactments, but we must have been too busy munching on cotton candy.

"Except this house is remaining," Kate adds.

True.

When I hold out a hand for a piece of licorice, she tosses one up to me. Next she sneaks a tiny piece to Rye, who is lying beside her, eyeing the snack. "And get this. They say that the fraud with the mine was that it was salted."

"What does that mean?"

Balancing the library book closer, she reads. "'The Kenworthy mine is said to have been salted. In this instance, salting occurred when a prospector loaded gold into a shotgun then fired it off inside the shaft.'"

The scene plays out in my mind, but it's hard to fathom. "Seriously?"

"Gosh, that would have been loud." She continues reading from the text. "'This was done so that a worthless mine would appear to be valuable.'"

So, it embedded gold dust into the walls. Crazy.

"'If the selling party found a gullible buyer, then that seller would walk away with a hearty profit. This is believed to have happened in Kenworthy due to its lack of gold and short life span in contrast to its high purchase price.'"

Setting the brush aside, I stand. Every muscle in my body hurts, but this shotgun story is more distracting. It's sad to imagine. "That's really something." I start down the stairs. "You've found some interesting stuff in there."

"It's been neat to read about this place. It makes it come alive, you know?" She uncaps her Gatorade again. "I can hardly believe that you own it all now."

"Well, I don't own the town." But now that she mentions it, the buildings that are no more would have been relatively close to the farm. It's tempting to head off on a hike right now, but I'll do that soon . . . maybe scope things out. I'm ready to do some climbing as well. It's amazing what you can see of an area after cresting a forty-foot boulder.

Thirsty, I grab a water bottle from the case in the makeshift kitchen. "I gotta head off in a bit to pick up those appliances. It'll take me a couple hours, so we can grab a bite to eat, or I can bring something back if you want to stay here."

"Hmm . . ." Kate's sweatpants are covered in streaks of varnish, but thanks to her help, these floors look amazing. "I might lie down and take a nap."

"Good idea. I'll bring back dinner." While I move my tools out of the way, she unrolls her sleeping bag and plops two pillows into place. Rye immediately assumes they're for his own comfort. While I call him off, Kate laughs that she doesn't mind.

I shake sawdust from my baseball cap, then slide it on backward before pocketing the truck keys. "I'll be back with the appliances before dark. You said you need to head back mid-morning tomorrow?" She's got to be missing her husband and home.

"Yep. We've got a doctor's appointment with a fertility specialist that I've been waiting two months for. Your kids are coming about the same time, right?"

"Yeah. Emily will bring them by in the afternoon." Eager, I resist the urge to check my watch and instead reach for my wallet. My sister and I have been snacking on carrot sticks and licorice this afternoon, so it's time I get her something heartier.

"I'm excited to see this new fridge!" she calls as I head out the door.

Me too. The thought makes this place feel even more real. Even more like home.

Outside, I aim for the barn, where the door is already open. Unlike the solidity of the house, the barn is sinuous. Standing here, it's different from the cabin. Here the boards are so old they're nearly black and bear cracks where light spills in. More pools in from original glass windows, and the whole building creaks even with just a hint of breeze.

The steeply angled roof is a good twenty feet overhead, and while the loft is still being used as storage, it looks fragile enough that it's time for it to be taken down. Now the barn is an open cavern. A storage house for the past. The earthy scent makes me wonder just how much hay and livestock it held over the decades.

Time somehow managed to stand still within the house, but it's moved twice as quickly out here. If the house has a story or two in the woodgrain, what of this place?

Picking a path around the lumber, I aim for the lockboxes again. The popcorn machine is kind of in the way, so I shimmy it aside. Taking a knee in front of the boxes, I twist through the code on one and the lock pops loose easily. There's nothing ceremonious about lifting the lid. I'm thinking only about making it to Home Depot before closing. But once the lid is raised, it's suddenly hard to move. The past has stepped forward in full force.

A brown cowboy hat rests on top of the pile, rustic, well worn, and safe inside a clear plastic bag. There's also a lacy shawl that would have belonged to a woman. That, too, is neatly packaged inside a bag. Bar codes declare the thick plastic as museum grade and offer ID numbers for the items inside. It's a little terrifying to touch all this, but I've got to find the journal. I lift out the wrapped hat that would have belonged to a man over a hundred years ago. The settler who lived here? John Cohen?

Wild.

I set the antiques aside, and next comes a stack of books. Three of them fill one bag. Maybe the journal is among them. I study the spines, but the titles and authors indicate the books are from a printing press, not a gold miner. I search deeper.

The following artifacts consist of silver spoons, a small glass pitcher with a chip in the base, and a pair of child's boots. The shoes are black and just above ankle height. Delicate buttons go up the sides. The boots look cut for a girl. They're much too small even to fit Micaela, so this girl would have been quite young. Old enough to walk, but not much beyond that.

Every heirloom is wrapped and labeled with great care, so I move them with equal respect.

Near the bottom of the lockbox rests a smaller box, this one of cardboard. I slide off the lid to find what I'm pretty sure is the object of the hour. The dark leather book has a blank spine. Am I supposed to open the bag? It seems that the only way to ensure the pages are signed by this John Cohen is to look. As carefully as possible, I slide the book out and lift the front cover.

Slanted writing pounds across the first page. Same with those beyond. Dates are scrawled at the top of many of the entries, all going back to what looks like 1894. The writing is the kind of cursive people used in the olden days, but it's rough enough that a man held the pen. The nearest entry is signed by *John*, so it has to be him. I can scarcely read any of the lines and am not trying to, but as I close the cover, I notice that a single word is repeated several times. Leaving the journal open, I angle it.

Juniper.

The word is capitalized, so it must be a name. Not wanting to probe, I close the book and carefully return it to its plastic bag. After sealing the bag tight, I set it aside to drop off at the Realtor's office this afternoon. Right where the journal had rested is a pile of antique letters, each one glinting from inside protective plastic. The top letter is signed *Juniper* and the heading above reads *Beloved John*. These aren't mine to probe into so I don't so much as reach the top letter. Needing to replace the lid on the cardboard box, I retrieve it but can't bring myself to press the lid down. Not with the black-and-white photograph resting in the open box—and the woman peering back at me.

My hands still.

She's young, maybe late twenties. Her hair is a few shades darker than her skin and must be brown since it's not as opaque as her black dress. Her eyes are quiet but confident. Almost questioning. There's a crease to her brow, as if she's wondering why the photographer is taking so long. Or wondering why I'm sitting here staring at her over a hundred years later.

These heirlooms aren't my business. I put the cardboard lid back, concealing the photograph once more. With care, I return the other keepsakes as well. The family will pick this all up eventually, but for now they'll have the journal as requested. It's hard to say what they need it for, but there's a satisfaction that something—even an old journal—is finally finding its way back home.

Or maybe this *is* its home. Maybe its heart would be breaking to leave the box with the photograph. That's if it had a heart to begin with.

I contemplate the name again. *Juniper.* Written in a heavy hand. Maybe even an urgent one. Over and over. Was it pain to spark such intensity? Or passion? Was this Juniper the woman in the photograph? Curiosity has me wanting to check. To flip that photograph over and read its label. But that would mean prying into business that's not mine. Besides, I have other things to focus on. Like the fact that Emily is bringing the kids up tomorrow and fridges and stoves don't deliver themselves.

The fact that I'm stunned into place right now is just because I've listened too much to my sister talk about the pioneers who first settled this county. All the dates and history must be getting to my head.

After everything is back in place, I reattach the lock to the metal box and double-check that it's secure. Time for a trip down the mountain. There's already tie-downs in the back of the truck to secure the new appliances for the windy drive home. The quick trip will do me good.

The thought of bringing back some burgers and fries for dinner has me carrying the diary to my truck. The thought of seeing the kids tomorrow has me sliding it into a FedEx envelope and cranking the engine to life.

CHAPTER 9

JUNIPER

OCTOBER 1902

Storm clouds roll in from the west, and I've just finished the milking when Mrs. Parson arrives at the farm. Mr. Conrad escorts her. The gentle miner pushes a handcart loaded with a well-worn trunk. His dog, Trixie, trots loyally beside him. The dog's eyes lift to him with every few steps as though to be certain that he and his kindness are real. Mrs. Parson carries a carpetbag as well as a narrow crate. Both would have easily fit in the cart along with the trunk, but she has made his burden less by bearing it herself.

They cross the yard as though blown in with the wind. Mrs. Parson's black skirt swirls against her ankles, and I haven't witnessed a lace hem in ages. The delicate trim is tattered now but would have once been quite fine. The carpetbag she clutches is woven in a pattern of thick stripes and is as coated in dust as the rest of the world outside is. She's some years past fifty. Kindness blossoms in the lines of her eyes and in the way she greets Bethany, who runs to open the door.

My efforts of greeting her as a proper lady get interrupted when Mr. Conrad carries the trunk inside and it slips from his injured grip. The thud startles us all—Oliver Conrad most of all when his face tints red. Bethany giggles, and Mrs. Parson thanks him for his aid, which softens his embarrassment as much as my own smile does. In taking his leave, he waves to Bethany as he starts off, and she bounds around the room, as smitten with all this company as I secretly am.

Mrs. Parson looks around the cabin, which was built for the town's founder, Harold Kenworthy. It's the finest house in town, which I sometimes forget since I think of it only as home. Checked curtains hang on the windows, and a string of pine cones decorates the stairwell banister. I remembered to close the pantry door so she doesn't witness the sparsely lined shelves. She'll find out in due time, and no doubt is accustomed to the same amount of provisions as we are. Not that Edie doesn't do her best to bring in what supplies are needed, but few of us have proper income to even up the tab.

Even so, Mrs. Parson's eyes soften as though feeling at home. "I heard tell that your husband was one of the builders of this house. As well as some of the other structures." She says it with ease, as though John has merely stepped out to till a field or cull a herd of cattle. As though he'll return in an hour's time and wash for supper.

"Yes. He did." I don't look around the room as I say it lest I recognize his craftsmanship everywhere. As it is, I am trying to stay strong.

But I can see that her compliment isn't to bring grief. Quite the opposite. There is a spark of optimism in her eyes, and I catch it in my heart, slip it into that hidden pocket. Where I have run low on hope, I will glean from what others are willing to sow. Like water to a thirsty meadow.

Mrs. Parson sets the crate on the table, and Bethany immediately rises onto her tiptoes to try and peer inside. My own curiosity has the best of me as I try to make sense of the foreign object that is a black leather box, braced closed by brass hinges and an ornate clasp.

"This," Mrs. Parson begins, "is a camera." She solves the riddle with a spark of amusement, and when Bethany climbs up onto the chair beside where I stand, Mrs. Parson lifts out the camera to make it easier to see. "Perhaps I can take your picture with it. If your mother says it's alright, that is."

Bethany crouches down into a little spring as though she'll shoot up the moment I say yes. I do . . . and she bounds back up to squeeze me tight.

I squeeze back. "Shall we help Mrs. Parson get settled?"

Bethany nods.

We show our new guest to the upstairs bedroom. The day before, Bethany and I moved her possessions to my own room. We washed and ironed all the linens, skidded a washstand into place, and set the finer of the pitchers alongside its matching bowl. The humbler tin one is now in my room along with the older of the hand towels. It feels good to offer the best we have to another, even better to help Bethany see the *why* of it. My daughter's brown eyes take in the scene of Mrs. Parson admiring every detail. This moment is a grander lesson than most I could have taught.

Our guest nudges aside the lace curtain. Golden light from the morning sun spills in, and it lifts her chin the way it does my own.

I think we're all going to get along just fine.

"Please take your time settling in. Breakfast will be warm on the stove if you're hungry."

Back downstairs, I stir milk and honey into the oats, and Bethany unloads the cabinet of not two bowls but three. A day's worth of laundry beckons—laundry that I always have dried, pressed, and at the mercantile steps each Friday, so I fill my largest pot with water from the pump and set it to heat. Not yet hungry, I settle Bethany to eat at the table then head onto the porch. There, I arrange the wooden tub and washboard in their usual places, sprinkle in soap, and sort out the laundry that men used to deposit on my doorstep at all hours of the week. Now I wash only for Mr. Conrad and a few other men.

Soon, I hear Mrs. Parson's voice joining with Bethany's downstairs. When I check on them, they're both seated, and Mrs. Parson is teaching Bethany how to shape new letters in their bowls of oats. My daughter giggles as she forms a backward *G*. The sight blesses me to no end, even more so at having help on hand with this girl who needs all the care she can get. How many times have I bundled my daughter onto a chair in the cabin while I went out to break ice from the water pump or pulled her along in a sled as we searched deep into the woods for limbs to tuck into the cookstove?

I milk the cow before my daughter rises most days, but on the mornings when I am slower to wake, Bethany sits in the hayloft, playing in the straw as I work.

The memories lift my gaze to our barn. There is so little hay laid in for the cow this winter that I try to imagine how we will garner enough, but such a need would keep a man busy from dawn until dusk for weeks on end, and it is strength and time that I lack. I consider seeking help from one of the lingering men, but I have no means to pay, and they have their own troubles in preparing for winter.

There has to be a way, but worry over that and other winter needs splinters the peace of this morning as I dip work shirts and scrub sweat from collars and sleeves.

The peace is fractured further at the sound of Edie's distant voice. Of the strain in my name as she hollers it up the hillside. I turn away from the grimy water to see her struggling along. She stumbles but catches herself. When she peels off her hat, a panicked face is lit by the sun. A matching fear jolts straight through me.

I push aside the wet folds of my skirt that tangle, making it nearly impossible to stand. "Is it the baby?" *Dear Lord, please, no.*

She shakes her head as I run that way. I'm nearly to her now.

Is it her father? When we reach one another, her face is flushed but her hands are ice. She grips my wrist and presses a folded newspaper page into my hand. Secret-like. As though not to let any other see. There are none to even witness the exchange, yet her hushed demeanor drops lead in my gut.

I open it with shaking hands. Edie's own are unsteady as she clutches my forearms.

"It's John." Her voice is grave. "Two copies arrived at the mercantile. I destroyed the other."

Desperate, I read the headline first.

Members of Confirmed Miner's Gang Arrested after Gold Fraud in CA and AZ Territory

There had been talk of arrests near Yuma, but these can't be the same men. Can they be?

Three Outlaws Hung at State Prison. Two Awaiting Trial.

The world spins as I try to comprehend what this has to do with John. My gaze plummets from the word *hung* to the rest of the declaration. Beneath the headline are the photographs of five men. Five outlaws. Five men who have been captured. Some who have been tried and executed. My eyes skim their faces, landing at last on the final man. My John. Bethany's father. With his steely eyes and calm demeanor, gazing back at me in striped prison garb . . . joining the other four men as ones I do not know.

CHAPTER 10

JOHNNY

Being late is standard op for Emily, so I stop watching the driveway for her silver sedan at 10:15 a.m. She'll be here when she's here, so I keep busy unloading a stack of old newspapers from the bed of my truck. Their new home is beside the woodstove for fire starting. I'll need to get firewood for winter, but for now lumber scraps from previous job sites have the stove roaring. The house is toasty for the kids' arrival.

After pulling off my beanie, I run a hand through my hair, using the window as a mirror. There's a number of things this place doesn't have yet, but . . . priorities. My hair probably still looks nuts, but Emily has seen it this way plenty of times. At least my T-shirt is clean. While my work boots and jeans are streaked with varnish, I managed to brush off most of the sawdust.

I cram the beanie into the back pocket of my jeans then haul the neon beanbags I bought for Micaela and Cameron upstairs. They look out of place in this nineteenth-century house, but the kid-sized blobs are part of what will make this place home. *Our home.*

At the top of the stairs, two doors open up from the narrow landing. A gabled window frames the east. I elbow my way into the smaller room and plop down the beanbags. Autumn sunlight makes the space soft and sleepy. A plastic tub of colorful blocks sits in the corner, the rocking horse that my dad made for the kids before he passed beside it. A soft nudge has me wishing he could be here. He'd love this place.

At the window, I check the driveway again for any sight of the woman my dad adored almost as much as I did. Still nothing. I crack the window to hear better. Thanks to my sister's help, the glass panes shine and the floor is satin smooth. The boards look amazing. It's tempting to snap a picture to show my guys. My three-man construction crew has been razzing me about this place since I put in the offer, nicknaming me Grandfather Mountain. The hard-wrought patina on those boards would quiet them down.

Desperate to keep busy, I check that the battery-operated lantern on the side table is at full power. The lantern is something that Micaela can easily access in the evenings, but just so they're not alone tonight, I'll crash in here with them. If the kids want me to stay longer, I'll sleep in here for as many nights as they need me. There's a floodlight up here as well, but I'll take it down soon. The window sash settles just above its thick extension cord, which plummets to the downstairs outlet. The cord could have been trailed up the stairs just as easily, but it wasn't worth risking my sister tripping and getting hurt. The setup isn't ideal from the outside, but proper electrical is at the top of my to-do list.

Dust churns in the distance as a car veers off the highway. They're here. Deep breaths. I aim for the stairs and instantly trip over the extension cord. The floodlight swings cockeyed, and I catch it before it slams into the wall. Well done, man.

Steadying the apparatus gives me a second to heave in a chestful of air before heading down, heart thumping. It beats harder as I nab the divorce papers and fold the thin packet. After pulling out the beanie, I slide the envelope into the back pocket of my jeans, taking care to tug the edge of my shirt to block it from sight. Rye's already at the door, staring at the knob. I'm scarcely outside when Micaela scrambles from the back seat of her mom's car. Bending down, I catch her running hug. Scooping her up feels like heaven. She smells like strawberry shampoo, and the ends of her short bob are so feathery soft they tickle the side of my cheek that's cemented into a grin.

"Hey, sweet girl." I stroke the back of her head and give it a kiss.

She burrows in for a tighter hug. "You forgot to call last night," she whispers.

"I called twice, sweet girl," I whisper back. It's hard to explain to a seven-year-old that sometimes the only thing I have a conversation with is her mother's voicemail.

Lowering Micaela back down, I watch as the very woman unbuckles Cameron from his car seat. Best not to crowd her, so I hang back. The dog? Not so much. He collides into her, and Emily scruffs the top of his head, knowing it's the only way he'll get a grip.

I call Rye back as Emily sets down our son, who waddles my way. I move to grab Cameron up next, taking care to make room for Micaela, who squeezes in against my side. I hold them both tight and, for a moment, forget all about the house. That is, until I open my eyes and see Emily gaping at it.

Well, she's gaping at the orange extension cord running along the edge of the porch and up into the second-floor window. It's probably still swaying.

"Please tell me you're joking." She lowers the kids' backpacks to the ground then brushes dust away from one of her sandals.

Micaela's jumping up and down now, begging to go inside. Needing to talk to her mother first, I take a knee. "I'm so glad you're excited." I squeeze her hand then point to the massive oak tree. "Why don't you and Cam go check out that spot while I help Mommy get the rest of your stuff from the car? Then we'll go in together." I smile to reassure her.

Micaela takes her brother's hand to help him amble over, and Rye trails them. I watch the kids for a few steps then turn back to my wife.

"Is that safe?" Her sculpted brows dip as she scrutinizes the setup.

The pair of swings I hung dangle from an oak branch that's thick as a Buick and older than my wife and me put together. "Pretty sure." Just to the side of the old tree is a picnic blanket that my sister spread out to hold a tin pail of plastic horses and soldiers. Cameron has parked himself there already. "Have a good trip?" I ask.

She nods then adjusts the zipper on one of the backpacks. "I forgot to pack pajamas for Cameron, but he has an extra T-shirt."

"No problem."

"Also, Micaela's shoulders got kind of sunburned at the beach. There's a bottle of aloe in with her stuff."

"I'll make sure we use it."

"She finished up her packet of schoolwork while we were there, and the teacher said she did great."

"That's wonderful."

We both go silent, and having contemplated for days—months, really—what I need to say, I try to think of where to begin. "I'd like to talk to you about the arrangement. The lawyer called." I pull out the packet of divorce papers, slowly shaking my head. "I appreciate the gesture to give me more time with the kids, but Emily, this isn't the answer . . ."

My voice trails off. Having tugged an elastic band from her wrist, Emily raises her blond hair into a ponytail and twists on the tie. Finished, she smooths her hand over the length of it a few times. I notice then that she's wearing a blouse that drapes loosely over her stomach. Is that a . . . maternity top? The way it hangs indicates that her midsection is not as narrow as it was a few weeks back. This is a woman who has never missed a morning at the gym.

I stare at the shirt for several moments, and while I hope to one day forget that it's yellow with white stripes, what I know will never be forgotten is the fact that there's a life growing underneath it. I've seen that mounded shape to her waist twice now. But unlike those times, it's not joy that floods me, it's despair. My wife and I haven't been within two feet of one another in nearly a year.

Pain clenches my chest. My eyes lock with hers, and for the first time since this nightmare set into motion, I know of the gravity of how I've lost her.

I try to say her name, but it doesn't come out.

She speaks mine instead. "I've been wanting to tell you."

Wanting to tell me?

"Please just sign the papers, Johnny." Spoken by the same lips that nine years ago kissed me beside a three-tiered white cake in a churchyard.

There's a different ring on her finger now, twice as big as the one I gave her.

When did this world become so backward? "You're . . . engaged?"

"J, you and I have been separated for nearly a year."

It takes me a second to comprehend what we're both saying. "That means *still married*."

"It's been over for a long time."

"Not for me." All these months I've been hacking through a wilderness, trying to coax her back from this trail she's stumbled upon. But she's determined to forge ahead without me. She's glancing over her shoulder at me. A goodbye so final I was probably a fool to try.

She draws in a slow breath and closes the car door. When her eyes lift to mine, they're resolute. Sharp. "Sign those papers, J, or it's going to get more difficult for you."

I turn the packet in my hands, trying to make sense of that.

"You're engaged. And you're pregnant?" Why do I have to say it out loud? Because it makes no sense.

"Johnny, it couldn't be more over. And if you don't sign those papers, I will turn this into hardball."

The whole world has slowed.

And it hits me: that's what life is. That's growing up and realizing that it's not like you imagined it would be. It's your life—your dreams—flipped upside down. Truck cab to asphalt as your wife stands there reiterating next that she'll take you to court to fight for the two kids you share if you don't finally sign the agreement that she and her lawyer drafted up.

She watches as my fingers, still holding the packet, grow unsteady. "Johnny, let this go."

I still can't speak.

The breeze catches the length of her ponytail, spraying the blond strands past her shoulder. I hate that it still hits me how lovely she is, but I've spent half my life noticing. The realization dies the same second because what isn't lovely is what she's doing. This choice she's made to destroy what we've worked so hard to build up. All because she thinks she's found a man who will fill her with more gratification than the one she started out with.

Or maybe I don't know anything at all. Maybe I'm the chump who has no grasp of reality. Everything I know fades to ash as I finally manage to speak. "Any chance I can ask . . ." Words failing me, I clear my throat. ". . . when the baby's due?" It takes so much determination not to envision her with Austin that I'm sick from the effort.

She hesitates, looks over at the kids, then back to me. "April."

Her drapey blouse flutters in the breeze, and there's a sting in the back of my throat that's about to close it. I hope she'll give that little one a good life. It's all I can do now. "Alright."

At first, I doubt she could hear me rasp the word, but she grabs her purse and retrieves a pen so fast it's a miracle her bag's still in one piece when she uncaps it. My heart rate is slowing, and my fingers tingle.

Everything is going numb.

It's the feeling of two EMTs pulling you from the truck window and onto the ice-slicked highway. Of fighting for breath past broken ribs. Of one paramedic pushing an IV needle into your unshattered arm while the other starts oxygen through a mask. One medic speaks into the radio, and it sounds like your heart rate. The number is so low you're sure it's the final time you'll drift off, but then you wake two days later in the hospital with eyes so swollen you can scarcely see. Your arm's in a splint, ribs bound in bandages, and a second chance at life with your kids lies on the horizon.

News reporters describe the near-fatal crash to the whole county—not a soul but you knowing that you drove too fast on an icy road, not by being reckless but because you had witnessed your wife checking out of a B&B with some guy. That you had just been wanting to get home so that you could collapse to your knees.

I glance once more to the girl who ran across the football field with me, wishing with all that's in me that I could have reached her in that wilderness. I unfold the papers, accept the pen, and this time it's not my arm that's broken in two places.

And there's no oxygen for this. No IV for this kind of pain.

Instead, there's two kids kicking up dust on the swings beneath the old oak. Even if it means that I'll be the only one watching them from the porch, I push the ink to the line and write my name. Not because of threats but because the girl from the football field is gone. She's long since hopped into the pickup of another guy and isn't so much as looking back.

JOHN COHEN

August 1896

It keeps me up at night—the memory of what happened that day.

Was it really over two years ago?

It was just to be a simple job. In, out, wait for them to fire off the shotgun, and we all get paid. As usual, I was going to keep to the edges. Keep to the background. My conscience lived easier that way.

But when that man stepped in to stop us, everything changed. None of us saw him coming. An Indian, right out of the hills, barely as old as myself and yet willing to defend the honor of that land with his life. An old gold mine that nobody cared about anymore, but to him it was a piece of the earth worth protecting. Who would have that type of conviction? Who would care about what we were there to do? Five against one . . . all over a craggy mine entrance. It was courage that made his back strong and his rifle steady as he aimed it at us. But his courage wasn't enough.

Everything happened so quickly, and by the time my cousins had their own guns drawn, I knew the Indian was a goner. I couldn't stand back in the shadows a moment longer. They already had murder on their hands. I grabbed up the gold-loaded shotgun and pulled the trigger myself. Not at any souls, but into the mine we had come to salt. The chaos gave enough time for the Indian to vanish, and when the dust settled, my cousins were plenty satisfied that the job had been done.

Now my conscience is as appeased as it is plagued. A man I don't know went free that day, but ruin came knocking my way instead.

I hear the mine has sold now to an Englishman named Harold Kenworthy.

I don't sleep anymore, and don't know how to get away from this darkness.

The sound of the trigger pull keeps me awake, watching shadows, listening to night. The new mine owner has succumbed to the trap we set for him. And I'm the one who pulled the noose tight.

John

CHAPTER 11

JUNIPER

October 1902

There's a heat to grief. It covers your very skin. There's a pressing that tightens your lungs. A piercing sharpness that rushes over you in waves. It sets a ringing in your ears that grounds you in reality even as mind and soul can't manage to agree.

I want anything but this pain. I can't think or move beyond sitting on the bed. Bethany slumbers beside me, oblivious to this plummeting ache that her father might be dead. Dawn is yet to crest the mountain peaks, so it's in a dark room where the crimes and sentences cover me in a shadow with even less light.

Five miners.

Three hung.

Two left.

It's all that circles my mind. I should be angry. I should be furious. If John has been part of illicit mining activity, likely it was much closer to home.

Did one of these men salt the Kenworthy mine? Did . . . John?

Five miners.

Three hung.

Coarse ropes would have been laid around their necks. Anguish flooding them even heavier than it does me now. Agonizing . . . those final moments before death. Tears burn my eyes at not knowing if John was among them. Or did he await within a darkened cell? Questions collide into broken understandings. All that I have known and everything I have conceived has been tipped upside down. There is a mess to clean up here and news to unearth, but I don't know where to begin. So I sit in the dark and try to keep breathing. Try to keep these wracking tears from making sound within me as Bethany sleeps. My body shakes with them. I don't have the strength yet to tell her anything of her father. Wiser would it be to wait until I know for certain.

Oh, God.

Tipping my face toward the ceiling, I try to suck in air through a closing throat. Then, curling back onto my side, I pull a pillow close and try to muffle the sound of more sobs.

It's a long while until merciful sleep claims me again. As I drift in and out of the fog between pain and numbness, Bethany's hand touches my shoulder. Some while later, I notice that her place is empty and cold again. Voices lift from downstairs. The alphabet is being sung in soft song form. The scent of warm oats and honey clenches my stomach.

It is impossible to move.

Time slides along—ever so slowly. Midday sun shimmers across the floorboards. I need to rise. Bethany needs her mother. We have a guest. But then soft footsteps enter. A shadow softens the light. A woman's hands place a cup of steaming tea on the bedside table, and comfort pierces the breaking, which hastens in more tears. Sleep stems in waves, dragging me, coaxing me toward unconsciousness.

Two words circle my mind as I dream. Words that have been penned over and over and over when the world was different and still holding a shred of faith.

Beloved John.

◆ ◆ ◆

I do not know how many hours have passed, but when I awake, sounds of life drift up from below. Bethany is humming, softening only to be replaced by a prayer from Mrs. Parson. Soft clatters on the cookstove whisper of a coming meal.

Rise, June, rise.

Finally managing, I slide a shawl around my shoulders. My whole body hurts, throat parched. Whatever will I say to Mrs. Parson to explain?

Crossing the floor takes great effort, and by the time I reach the door, the very woman is there, lending a knock. When I brave a new step forward, I find her grasping a tray that balances a steaming bowl of soup along with a biscuit. Carrots and potatoes scent the air, as does the richness of fresh game that must have come from Edie. I have no idea how to make sense of such an offering.

"Back to bed." Though softly given, Mrs. Parson's decree holds enough authority that I return to the mound of tangled bedding. "Feet up, please."

When I obey, she settles the quilt across my lap. Fluffs the pillow. I can't stem the tide of tears now. Why is this stranger being so kind to me? It is I who should be serving *her*. And yet it is her weathered hands that angle the spoon so that I can easily grasp the handle. Wedged beneath the plate is the folded newspaper clipping. It peeks out from beneath the blue-and-white porcelain. I must have dropped it between the yard and the house, and in truth, I recall little of the walk.

My eyes lift to hers. This woman knows.

The ones who salted the Kenworthy mine have long reigned a mystery. The citizens of this town would have surrendered the gold they didn't have to bring justice to those who fired such deception into the mine's walls. Now those suspects are stamped in black ink and folded on a tray.

Such should burn me with shame to be the wife of one of these men, yet it's only sorrow that floods me. I cover my face with my hands as sobs rise up. John's name presses to my tongue. How I ache to cry it out loud. To plead to God for mercy that he is still alive. And yet warring with that primal need is the agony that he has deceived me.

Mrs. Parson slides both arms around my shoulders, squeezing tight.

The article beside us is folded in such a way that John's picture stays concealed. I'm sure we would both agree that it's best Bethany not know of this now. Nearly a year ago, he was the one sitting beside me on this very bed, holding my hand as I described the cough Bethany had been battling then. He'd arisen twice in the night to check on her. I found him sleeping on the floor beside her bed come dawn.

Now that man could be lying in a shallow grave.

The date of the article is already ingrained in my mind. The sixth of September. Over one month ago. He would have died alone. His thoughts would have been on his daughter. On this little life he cherished so much. His thoughts might have been with me as well ...

What was I doing that day? Was I pinning laundry to a line when he received a sentence?

"He may still be alive." Mrs. Parson eases to sit beside me.

I nod numbly, but it's hard to find the hope. If he is alive, he is one of two convicts still awaiting trial.

Mrs. Parson whispers an answer though I have not voiced the question aloud. "The psalmist wrote, 'In God have I put my trust: I will not be afraid what man can do unto me. Thy vows are upon me, O God: I will render praises unto thee. For thou hast delivered my soul from death: wilt not thou deliver my feet from falling, that I may walk before God in the light of the living?'"

I hunger for this light she speaks of. This deliverance. This uprightness.

I hunger for it for me. For Bethany. And most of all, for the one who may already be lost to the cold earth. A man who may have stepped from this life not by the Lord's light but by the glow of gold mines. A shimmer that, while tempting, can hold neither the power to satisfy nor to save.

CHAPTER 12

JOHNNY

There's no glory to the brand-new stove as I dump a jar of spaghetti sauce into a pan. Pasta bubbles in the dented pot that's been dragged from my camping gear. Nearby, the kids play on their beanbags that they tossed down from the upstairs landing. Rye is curled up near them, oversized head on his paws. In any other circumstance their laughter would be contagious, but it sounds distant and far away, drowned out by the throbbing inside that feels an awful lot like being torn in two.

As much as I've craved these sounds—of them settling in—it's all shadowed. The divorce is on its way to being finalized. *Sutherland v. Sutherland*. Six months the state of California takes from filing to approval. Emily filed months ago, and I've actually done my part, so it won't be long now.

"This isn't happening," I mutter.

96

Sauce is starting to burn. Crud. It needs to be stirred, and my brain is disconnected from the rest of me.

The sound of Cameron's laughter from the middle of the living room shatters my heart further. The kids are so innocent. They have no idea that I just signed on the dotted line to make their home broken for good.

Do they know about the baby?

With a plastic fork, I try to revive the sauce and, with a bigger mountain of effort, attempt to corral thoughts of Emily aside. I need to focus on other things, but it's like wading through glue.

I angle to see the kids better. Needing grounding. A lifeline. Their presence here is my own kind of coming home. Like the house wasn't fully ours until their voices echoed within these walls. I only wish I could feel their joy. *Really* feel it. It's as though the information reaches my brain but not my soul.

"Is the spaghetti ready?" Micaela bounds over, jumping across the three holes that are now patched in the floorboard. They're from the old display cases, but she's already dubbed them bullet holes and is now playing Wild West hopscotch.

"Just about. Wanna fetch those paper plates?" I point to the "kitchen box," and she counts out three plastic forks and the same number of plates. It's a number I'm going to need to get used to.

I shut off the stove then carry the pasta onto the porch to drain the liquid over the railing. "So how does this sound for the weekend, you guys?" I ask, returning and desperate to rally. "I was thinking we'd just have fun tonight, then tomorrow maybe you two can help me with a few jobs."

The kids cheer.

"Sunday we'll head to church, and I've ordered a climbing harness that will fit you, Micaela, so maybe I can teach you how to rappel from some of the boulders back behind the house." There are bolts already in place, and I've tested each one with my own weight.

The cheering escalates, and while I wish I could match their excitement, I focus on forming words and plans to keep this night in motion. I'll have to do the same tomorrow and the next day and the next until someday, maybe, this will hurt less. I can't really imagine it, so my "Awesome," is strained.

Since there's no table yet, we all find spots in the living area. The kids sink into their beanbags, and I unfold a camping chair. I pop the top off of a Gatorade and fill plastic cups. We do a "Cheers" that doesn't reach its way inside me.

It must show when Micaela touches my knee and asks if she should pray for our food.

"Please," I say through a tight throat.

Her eyes squint closed. "Dear Jesus . . ." She peeks over to her brother. "Daddy, he's not closing his eyes."

Normally I'd chuckle at their antics, but tonight I just manage to speak. "How 'bout we close our eyes, Cameron."

My son squints his eyes tight, and Micaela folds her hands in her lap. "Dear Jesus. Thank You for this day and for this food. And thank You for Daddy's fun house and for the beanbags."

I smile, and the simple act nearly has me wanting to cry. Not for the sorrow but the way their sweetness cuts light into it.

"And thank You for the spaghetti."

I touch her hand, giving it a thankful squeeze. There's something about the way we say amen together. Like the word belongs here in this room. This house.

"So, what do you guys want to do tonight?" I twirl a fork into steaming pasta. There's no Parmesan cheese or even a salad, but we have something edible.

Cameron slurps a noodle, and while his tiny voice is hard to understand, I think he's asking for a movie.

"Sorry, bud. I don't have a TV yet."

"Can we still bake cookies?" Micaela asks.

That's right, I had mentioned to her I was going to get some dough last time she was with me. Thankfully, I grabbed two rolls and put them in the new fridge yesterday. "Good idea."

They both light up.

We take our time with the spaghetti, and as we do, I try to focus only on this moment right here. Me and these precious people. My people. The act softens the sorrow some, shoves it to a back cupboard of my mind where I know I'll be revisiting it once I manage to get them tucked into bed. For now, I lean into their happiness and let it ease the ache. I'm glad they've got an appetite because between all our second helpings, we empty both pans. Dishes are easy when we toss away the paper plates and I drench both pots in the yard with the hose. Cameron slurps the last of his Gatorade, then waddles over to the refrigerator. He can't quite reach the handle, so I hold it open and watch while his pudgy hands grasp for one roll of the dough. The tube of cookie mix is bigger than his arm, but he manages.

"Got it?" I ask.

He nods and tries to lift it up onto the makeshift counter—still just a slab of plywood laid across two sawhorses. Somewhere between trying to cut open the dough and preheating the oven is when I realize that I don't have cookie sheets.

Classic.

"Alright." I turn to Micaela since she's as bright as any bulb in the basket. "What should we do?"

She puts on her thinking face then hunts through the boxes of supplies on hand. After some digging and discussion, we decide to bake one giant cookie in the bottom of the pan the noodles cooked in. We spread the dough out with our fingers, and Micaela obliges us by poking eyes and dotting in a smile to make a happy face. Cameron eats enough dough that his mom would go ballistic, but I decide to just pour him a glass of milk and, after another "Cheers," eat my own piece of dough.

We slide the pan into the oven, set the timer, and then wipe sticky hands on a damp towel. It's getting close to bedtime now, so I lead the kids upstairs to dig pajamas out of their backpacks. If anyone is going to come unglued tonight, he's going to do it after the kids are in bed.

For Cameron, I tug on that extra T-shirt then get him set up with nighttime pull-ups. Micaela drags the hair ties out of her braids and unravels them. The timer buzzes then, and once we've downed nearly half of the ginormous cookie, we polish off our cups of milk.

"Toothbrushes?" I ask.

Micaela unzips her glittery backpack and holds up a plastic baggie housing bubblegum toothpaste and two toothbrushes.

"Perfect."

The Realtor had emphasized that the bathroom was rough, and while he wasn't lying, the kids get a kick out of the aged pine paneling, the two skinny stalls, and the fact that they get to stand on an old orange crate to reach the vintage sink and wall-mounted dispenser that serves up powdered soap. I refilled it the other day.

"I can't believe the bathroom has stalls!" Micaela cries. "It's just like at school!" Her voice filters from the stall on the left while Cameron is attempting to use the other.

"Awesome, right?" I lean against the wall and fold my arms.

"It is the *coolest*!" she squeals, dancing her slippered feet beneath the door. "None of my friends have stalls in their bathrooms!" She swings the door open. "Can I have a sleepover?"

Uh . . . "We'll see what we can do." I don't know if she's noticed that there's no shower yet. That's on my to-do list, stat. This house wasn't exactly plumbed to be domesticated. Instead, the bathroom was added against the downstairs exterior in the seventies to accommodate the crowds who visited during the reenactment days. In fact, I'm actually pretty sure that I used this restroom a couple of decades ago. There's even a retro hand dryer that packs as much punch as a leaf blower. Micaela hits the metal button. Cameron covers his ears in terror, but his sister dries her hands like she's died and gone to summer camp.

Tomorrow we'll drive to my buddy's house and take showers—something I've been doing throughout the week while simultaneously clearing my stuff out of his garage. I've got a corner shower stall on order at the hardware store and will have it in place by month's end. For now, we'll stick with glorified camping. The kids don't seem to mind.

Micaela finally notices the lack of tub. "How did people take a bath in the olden days?"

"Um, I think they heated water on the stove and used washtubs." I shape the size of one with my hands. "It was a tight squeeze, but I think you'd do alright."

"Can we do that?"

"We might have to." I wink.

With teeth brushed, the kids hurry back upstairs, climbing the steps without a care in the world. As though this place is becoming home already. Their bare feet pad on the newly refinished steps, and their small hands glide along the one-hundred-year-old handrail that's now up to modern height codes. In the spare bedroom, we roll out sleeping bags, toss pillows into place, and I set the battery lantern to low. Rye stretches out beside Cameron's sleeping bag and sighs.

"Do you guys want me to sleep in here with you?" I ask.

"Yes!" Micaela calls out.

Cameron nods, still looking traumatized by the encounter with the air dryer. He's already holding on to a portion of Rye's golden fur for continued protection.

"You got it." I grab my own gear and spread it out between them. I've spent nearly half my life bunking down in a sleeping bag, so it feels natural. Already in sweats and a T-shirt, I lay back, fold my hands behind my head, and peer up at the ceiling. "I'm really glad you two are here."

"I like being here with you, Daddy. I like it no matter where we are."

I angle my head to see Micaela. "Thank you, sweet girl." She and I talk softly, going over our plans for the following day as a way for us to all settle in and for them to get sleepy. Within a few minutes, Cameron is out like a light. His round cheeks are soft and slack.

I lean that way to kiss his forehead. "Good night, bud."

When I turn back to Micaela, she's drifting off. I tuck her little arm better into her sleeping bag, rise, and dim the lantern. Settling back quietly is easy, but now that it's silent, thoughts of Emily come tromping in, and the ache in the pit of my stomach returns. Part of me wants to shove it aside, but instead, I face it for a while. There's really nothing else to do but stand boot to boot with grief.

In most slot canyons, there are spots that are so tight they only get a few minutes of sunlight each day. We call these *narrows*.

Is this what I'm facing now? The narrows?

It's hard to see the sun here. Nearly impossible to feel the light. But one thing I've learned in all my years of canyoneering is that you have to keep moving . . . and the scenery will change. It's the narrows that make you braver. Stronger. It's the narrows that change you.

By the time I'm swiping at my eyes and am just about ready to drift off, I say one more prayer, adding it to the one that Micaela said over dinner.

"Help us get through this, Lord." After brushing aside my daughter's crazy hair, I kiss her cheek as well, then angle onto my side, close my eyes, and take hold of Cameron's tiny, sleeping hand. Hoping that somehow, someway, He will.

CHAPTER 13

JUNIPER

OCTOBER 1902

They've suggested I do what?" Bent over the woodpile, I adjust two gnarled chunks of oak.

Wrapped in an embroidered shawl of red and brown, Mrs. Parson speaks beside me. "Cook for the crewmen when they arrive. It should be by spring. The Fresno Mining Company wired into the general store this morning, offering to pay a cook to keep the crew fed."

I straighten to make sure I've heard her right when she declares the amount. It's not something to balk over when I need income so badly right now. I shouldn't have missed the town meeting this afternoon but haven't left the farm in over a week. I've managed to rise again, not because I am strong, but because I must be strong for Bethany. In truth, I feel like a paper doll, somehow able to keep shape and yet about to crumple. I've hardly left the cabin walls. Mrs. Parson has been more than understanding, which is why I'm so surprised by this piece of news she's brought back. "I don't know how equipped I would be—"

"You would be perfect for the job." She bends to help me move more firewood beneath the eaves of the wood crib where it will stay dry. A cobweb catches on her tight bun, and she swipes it clear. "It seems weighty right now, but the job is still a few months off. If you step out in faith? Who knows? Maybe it will even give you something to look forward to."

It's hard to imagine such. It's hard to imagine anything these days.

"I'll think about it." Inside, all I can think of is that those men will not be John. So what would I want to do with them? God hasn't heeded my prayers all that much this past year. They rose, turning to vapor upon reaching His ears. I'm not in the mood for doing much for anyone else either.

"They'll need to know soon. Edie will be laying in supplies, and we both know she'll need help with that." Mrs. Parson smiles, and despite the storm inside me, I know she is trying to draw me forward through it. Forward from these shadows where she's trying to lend me courage.

"Then I'll walk over in just a bit." The words are stiff, but she's right. I have to keep going even if I don't feel it inside. I move another wedge of wood onto the pile. "And I'll tell Edie . . ." I glance at my mud-splattered boots and soiled hem then to the schoolteacher. "I'll tell her that I'll do it." Somehow I need to keep hands and heart busy. As for the income? It's sorely needed.

We return to the house together and enter quietly since Bethany is napping. She has begun going to school three times a week, and on the days she remains home with me, she often falls asleep in the late afternoon. Dear girl. Growing so fast and yet such a wee thing still. It's hard to believe that she will be four this spring. Too young to attend school in most districts, but the Kenworthy structure is now being run by Mrs. Parson's rules, and so Bethany has been more than welcomed to join the other four students.

After washing up, I start on biscuit dough—the fresh mound of flour in the barrel is from Mrs. Parson. One of her contributions for lodging, and it is a gesture we are thankful for. Mrs. Parson preps the kettle for our usual round of thin tea. We don't have any sugar for it, but sugar's a luxury I hardly recall.

Bethany joins us for tea, and I have yet to speak about her father. Not of the crime or the trial. Least of all that he could be dead. Not yet, and Lord willing, more will be made clear soon.

For now, when sorrow overwhelms me, I retreat to the barn, returning with stinging eyes and a fresh smile just for her. It is not that I mean to deceive my daughter, but there is no sense in terrifying such a young heart until answers become certain. To unearth them is as unsettling as the lingering silence. While all I can think to do at this time is pen a letter to Yuma prison directly, inquiring about John, it's a step that I pray will bring those answers.

Bethany helps me with the biscuits, slicing out rounds that I move to the greased cast-iron skillet. Standing beside me on a chair, she sprinkles down more flour and wiggles the cutter into the pressed dough that's as white and clean as her pinafore. With two small hands she guides a cut round into the skillet, and I kiss the top of her head. Her sweetness brings me life. Even though my heart is broken, God is showing me how to bind it up tight in grace and press onward. Hope remains fractured. That which I held on to for John is like ash, and I do not know how to revive it. I do not believe I should try. But for Bethany and me? Hope must bloom and blossom.

It must.

We finish our task, and I carry the pan to the oven. "Will you two be alright pulling these out? I'll pay Edie a quick visit."

Mrs. Parson swipes flour from the board with a wet cloth. "Most certainly."

Bethany asks to come along, but I should do this alone. I need to check on Edie and the growing baby, and it will be easier if Bethany stays behind.

"Won't you help me grade papers, Bethany? You can help me hunt for all the right answers." Mrs. Parson dries the table with a clean towel. In the corner rests a small stack of exams in a basket. Bethany settles on a chair, distracted by the challenge.

I whisper a thank-you for the teacher and drape a shawl around my shoulders. The day is frosty, so I button up John's thick coat on top of it. After pulling my braid free of its stiff leather collar, I head out. A cold chill seeps against my neck, biting at my cheeks. The air smells of coming snow, and the collar still holds the scent of the man I have loved. Walking has been my salvation of late. A way to move forward in body even if all else lingers at a standstill. A gentle nudge within reminds me that God is always moving, always working, but I'm sorry to tell Him that I cannot see it.

The cow is in her pasture but soon will need to be boarded in the barn. In all of my spare time, I've been cutting hay in the far fields but do not have the time or strength to put in the day of a man, so what has been gleaned will not last long. By taking the cooking job, I will be able to pay off the grain Edie helped me purchase for the heifer. An extra food supply for the cow when her pastureland is between thaws. As the burdens of all to come weigh my shoulders, I square them back and lift my chin toward the horizon.

I have always enjoyed the walk from the cabin to town but, with a darkening sky overhead, keep my pace quick. Thoughts of John plague me, as does the wondering of what others in town know. Dare I ask Oliver Conrad if he has any news or information? It doesn't seem as though others in Kenworthy have heard yet of the trial and its convicts, and too much of me wants to keep it that way. Edie has carefully checked all other papers as they arrive for any word before she splays them on the counter for others. No other news has appeared.

I know well enough to hurry so as to beat the storm, and I'm breathless by the time I cross the borders of my farm. It's strange, the way autumn leaves linger, blending with dew. The way the dark, gray sky hails in promise of a frost-laden land while oaks still bend beneath the weight of leaves of red and gold. The leaves are soft now, spent. They make no sound underfoot as I peer up at the sky to gauge its darkening mood.

I've heard of the blizzards that strike other parts of the country, but here, winter snow will fall gentle. The Pacific Ocean is only eighty miles to the west, so the climate is milder, even in these mountains. Snowfall here begins softly and often remains that way. I take comfort in this when the first flakes begin. They dust the path in front of me, and by the time I reach town, a soft haze of white tumbles from the California sky.

Yet despite such a gentle dusting, on the wind spins a woman's angry voice. At first, I imagine the storm is taking a turn, but that voice is . . . familiar. It does not swing in from the woods or sky. It's Edie. I hasten onward until the store appears in the distance. Light glows through the windows. The door rests wide open despite the cold.

Edie is on the porch, and to my surprise, Señor Tiago stands just below, facing her from the road. This is the cause of her row? A brown horse lingers just paces away from the man, loaded with saddle and supplies. Though dusted in snow now, the creature is neither tethered nor anxious. Not even when Edie throws a box of salt at the man standing across from her. It slams him square in the chest. The native doesn't move. Edie swears and grabs another box of salt. This time it sails past him, and while he still doesn't budge, his hat flies off. Señor Tiago seems reluctant to retrieve it. As though the woman before him would win if he were to lift it from the ground. He finally does, his eyes on her all the while as he brushes it clean of snow. Señor Tiago places it over his long black hair that lays past the collar of a leather coat.

Having halted, I take several steps back. Why do I feel as though this is a private moment? Somehow . . . personal to these two. This is not the row of a shopkeeper with a customer. This is different. Edie would not be so heated if it was business. She tromps down the stairs and rams both of her fists into the man's chest. She is a tall woman, nearly as tall as the native who stands solid and proud as the son of a shaman. But her frame is much narrower than his strength. He angles away, picks up a pack made of rabbit fur, and throws it over one shoulder. She screams at him again, slewing curses I wouldn't say to my darkest enemy.

And that's when it hits me. These two aren't *enemies*. They're lovers.

Nothing else would draw such passion from Edie. It is not fear in Edie's face. It's anguish. A grief that I have been walking in every moment of every day.

"You don't know his name." It's what Edie told me when I asked of the baby's father. I never envisioned it could be Señor Tiago since he is no stranger. Perhaps she meant his given name, for no one in this place knows it. It would be just like Edie to have meandered the truth so.

Her coat has fallen open now, revealing her belly. The small curve of it is arresting and stark beneath a thin, white blouse. Señor Tiago must see it, too, because he returns to her, clutches the tiny mound between his bare hands, and brushes his forehead to the unborn child. Straightening, he slides a hand behind Edie's head. Her long braid drapes the length of his forearm, and the brown of his hand, his wrist, is like a different season entirely. So strange against the pale neck cradled by his palm. Caring neither for the contrast, nor the public avenue, he kisses her.

Though they are shrouded in snowfall, shock has me looking away. His passion must have thawed her own because it's a stately stretch of time before loud thumps ring through the clearing. I lift my gaze only to ensure that my friend is safe, and once again it is not Edie under fire, it is the man whose nearness prevailed over her wits. Edie smacks another fist against Señor Tiago's chest.

The horse, impatient now, paws at the ground. With a shake of her majestic head, the mare rids her mane of snow.

Edie picks up a tuft of ice that fell from the store eaves. She flings it at the Cahuilla man then, when he turns away, lands another into his back. He makes no sign of pain. Does nothing to indicate he even felt the blow. Never once has he raised a hand to her, and it has nothing to do with chivalry due to passersby. He has yet to see me here. The snow is thickening, blurring between us, but I am not hard to see. This man only has eyes for Edith Manchester.

Then, just like that, he takes up the lead rope and trudges away. His horse follows. Edie plops herself down on the porch steps, folds her arms across her chest, and pouts. Her emotions are not so unlike what this storm may yet yield. Soft once, angry the next, and then melancholy . . . finally reaching a welcome thaw. But this? I cannot yet grasp the gravity of what is happening.

Not only is Edie carrying a man's child, but that child will be half Cahuilla. There are other mixed-race people in the region. Those who are as native as they are white from the way some settler men have, at times, sought Cahuilla women. Never have I met one, as they are rare to see. I cannot fathom what this will mean for Edie. This is why she's so urgently kept her pregnancy a secret.

Señor Tiago trudges onward, boots making tracks in the snow away from the mercantile. Edie retreats into the shop and slams the door behind her. Though I am frozen into place, he glimpses me. He stills for a measure of time that seems to offer some sort of message. I cannot fathom what it is, but I now understand that he hasn't been visiting the mercantile every day due to a tobacco habit. Finally, he surveys the log walls of the building that brace up a slanted roof and stout chimney, which billows smoke. The very building housing the woman who carries his growing child. Judging by the brew of tears that swelled in Edie's voice, and the way she let him hold them both, he in turn carries her heart.

In moments, this man disappears into the haze of falling snow. With winter blowing in and his tracks north fading away grain by icy grain, I can only pray that he loves her as desperately.

JOHN COHEN

February 1897

Construction began at what is now called Kenworthy. After some time in a logging camp up north, I returned here—God knows why—to help form the first foundations. To lift the first beams into place. Word is that there's going to be a whole town eventually. Mill, general store, even a cyanide plant that's slated to process 100 pounds of ore a day. I don't know why this man, Kenworthy, dreams so big. Why he lays down so many dollars on optimism. I hate it when I see him in the streets. Hate it when he shakes my hand, congratulating me on my work, on my skill with wood.

He's even requested I be one of the men who helps to construct his very own home.

I will do so—the pay is good—and yet every splinter and every nail will be ones that I feel into my very soul.

I can build and dig and toil, and still I cannot run from the truth:

This town is going to fail.

Nearly as terrifying? One day they will discover that it was because of me.

John

P.S. We crossed paths again today. Myself and the Indian from that day, years back now. Did he recognize me as I did him? He's older now, as am I. I wait now, for something to happen, but there was a quietness in his eyes—a solidarity—that makes me sense my secret is safe with him. The problem is that I don't want it to be safe. I dread and long for its liberation.

Yet just as strong is the urge to tear this page, and several others, from my journal. That way, no one will ever know the truth of my shame.

PART 2

CHAPTER 14

JOHNNY

FEBRUARY

The morning is cold and hard. A lot like my mood. It's going to be another Everest of a day—near-impossible odds and hard to breathe. In fact, all the days have blurred together to where I can't even remember what this climb called life is really for.

My boots crunch on the frozen driveway as I transfer a tarp and chainsaw into the bed of my truck. No snow yet this week, but we've had our share following the turn of the new year. Only a week's worth of firewood huddles on the left side of the wood crib, so once the kids wake up, we'll drive to one of my job sites in town. The homeowners offered us wood they don't need now that I converted their living-room stove to gas. The felled pine in their yard is thick, so my buddy José is coming along. He's on my payroll but is as much a friend as he is an employee. A true kind of friend that let me bunk in his garage all those months back. Together, we'll get the wood split before the storm.

115

I tug open a side compartment in the truck bed, checking that there's two pairs of work gloves. I dig to the back, past snow chains and a broken flashlight, and what I find instead is a pink sweater. It's lightweight, with the flower logo of Emily's favorite beach brand on the front. Even as it lands in my hand, her perfume still scents it. I crammed this in here months ago after finding it under the seat in the cab. How did I forget to get rid of it?

Trying to ignore the soft feel of it, I drape it over the side of the truck bed and wipe my hands on the sides of my pants. As I do, the memory is as fresh as the day I stashed it here. She and I had gone to a drive-in movie last year. We sat in the back of my truck, sharing a bucket of popcorn but not so close that we touched. Having barely spoken on the way there, we watched the film in silence. I remember finally grazing the side of her hand with my own—hoping to connect even in a small way, but she pushed her hand into her lap, eyes not leaving the screen.

It was our last date. The last time she and I were ever out together.

"Dad." Micaela's gentle voice calls me from the house.

How did it come to this?

"Dad?" She's nearer now.

"*What?*" My tone is sharp. I turn and see Micaela standing in the yard in her nightgown. Her bobbed hair is wild, and she's holding a blanket around her shoulders. Her bare feet have to be freezing. Her toes curl under, and the start of tears dwells in her eyes.

"Micaela, I'm sorry." I cross to her, trying desperately to feel something more than pain. But the sight of her sorrow only intensifies the hurting.

"It's okay, Daddy." But her chin is quivering, and a tear drips down her cheek.

I take a knee and grip both of her hands. "Daddy didn't mean to be grumpy. I'm very sorry."

She nods quickly.

Come on, man. Everything inside me is trying to rally as I touch her cheek. It's warm to my cold, rough hand. Instead of turning away, she leans into it, and another tear goes sliding. My own eyes fill. I seem to cry all the time these days.

"Sweetie, Daddy's just having a hard time." The words barely squeeze out. I cough into my shoulder to try to fight it. "I'm sorry for the ways that I haven't been as much fun. I'm going to keep trying, okay?"

She nods again. "It's okay."

Numbness battles with sorrow inside me. Two constant companions. If only one would just snuff the other out. But it's terrifying to think of which one would remain. There's got to be another way. Some way for goodness or courage or even hope to join the battle, but I don't know how to let those into the ring, and God help me, they're not showing up on their own.

"How about I get some breakfast ready for the road." The voice is half dead, which means it's mine. "And you can get dressed?"

"Okay."

Back inside, she runs to get dressed, and I fill two travel cups with milk, a mug with coffee, and grab three muffins from a package on top of the fridge. The kitchen is complete now, including a farmhouse sink and butcher-block countertops.

"Can you help your brother too?" I call up the stairs to Micaela. "We're gonna head up to town for firewood and hot chocolate."

Floorboards shake overhead as she scurries into action. With mini mama on the job, I top off the dog's food and water then finish loading the truck and toss a blanket into the back seat for the kids. A crank of the engine gets the heater going. The interior is almost warm by the time the kids run outside a few minutes later.

"Good job, sweetie." I squeeze Micaela's shoulder then lift Cameron into the cab. He's dressed—not matching, mind you—but she put a sweater, hat, mittens, and rainboots on him, and that works in my book. I buckle him in while she climbs over to her booster seat. I wish I didn't glimpse my reflection in the window. The gray shadows under my eyes are getting worse. Harder to see is the deadness in my eyes. Do the kids notice? Or can I keep faking my way through until I reach the other side of this? Whatever *this* is.

Last night, I found the bottle of painkillers they gave me in the hospital. Powerful stuff and enough to knock a guy my size out for hours. A single one would have allowed me to sleep like a stone— exhausting grief tackled by compacted chemicals. But I couldn't. Not with the kids here. Better to hurt and be alert for whatever Micaela and Cameron need. Part of me wishes I'd just upped and flushed the pills down the toilet, but I slid the bottle back into the bedside drawer. I'll take care of them later. When I got out of the hospital, dealing with a just-about-broken everything, I had to admit they had a good effect, making it easier to sleep and keeping the pain further away. I eventually set them aside but didn't discard them entirely. I felt bad about it then, and do today, but one hurdle at a time . . .

After settling in, I slide the truck into gear and head for the highway. "We're going to make a stop for some firewood. We'll pick up José first, and he's gonna help Daddy. You guys can help, too, and be good listeners?"

They promise to, and we wind higher up the mountain. On the sharpest curve, a quadruple yellow line warns motorists to go easy. After my incident last winter, I take it extra slow.

When we reach town, most of the shop fronts are still asleep. José, best friend and lead man, lives just behind the hardware store in a small apartment, and by the time I pull up out front, he's heading out the door with chainsaw and gloves. The hood of his gray sweatshirt is pulled up over a baseball cap. Having moved here from Mexico six years ago, José really doesn't like to be cold.

I smirk as he climbs in the truck. "A little frosty this morning?"

"Ay, *vato*." He grins. "Is too cold here."

He angles to give the kids a fist bump each, and they light up. Cameron holds out his half-eaten muffin, and José obliges the kid by pinching off a piece with a wink.

It's just another half mile to the house with the firewood. The homeowners dropped twenty grand on the living room remodel, which included new overhead beams and custom tile from Italy on their overhauled fireplace. We still need to seal the tile, and after that, we'll throw all our focus onto some refurbishments for a local restaurant. The job will keep me and my guys busy until summer.

I park close to the pine tree. The homeowners gave us permission to pick up the wood anytime, and with it just past ten, it should be fine to cue up the chainsaws.

I settle the kids on the truck tailgate with the blanket then explain a few rules for staying clear while the chainsaws are running. After sliding on leather gloves, José and I crank the motors into action. With a double glance to ensure the kids are good, we make the first cuts. José and I work a few yards apart, blades carving steadily into the fragrant wood. Sawdust sprays, and we take turns glancing back toward the kids every minute or two. By the time both saws are nearly out of gas, there's enough thick rounds of pine to fill the bed of the truck.

Now for the heavy lifting. I let the kids hop down to play with sawdust while José and I lift each round into the truck bed. Pine is a middle-of-the road kind of wood. Not as hard or slow burning as oak or eucalyptus, but it doesn't go up as fast as cedar. Working side by side with José reminds me of the day my sister came up to help seal the floors. Maybe I'm a sap, but it's just good not to be alone. I've never really spoken about Emily or the divorce with my guys; while they know the basics, I haven't been able to explain more. It's hard for me to clarify what life is like on this side, or the bleakness that has somehow clouded up my world.

But as José cracks a joke with the kids, I have a feeling he grasps what we're going through. I don't need to explain. Your best friends don't rally around you at odd hours and for little compensation because they don't get it. The realization has me squeezing José's shoulder and making a mental note to make sure he has all the wood he and his family of six could possibly use.

By the time we get the final round loaded, it's nearly past lunch-time. I call for the kids to climb back into the truck. José checks that the tailgate is secure while I buckle them in.

"Thanks, man," I say as he climbs into the passenger seat.

"Anytime. Let's go get some grub."

"Done." I'm starving.

We decide to grab sandwiches at the deli, and the nice thing about a town this small is that it only takes a minute to get anywhere. We're standing in the short line outside the deli door when Micaela tugs on my sleeve.

"Daddy, look!" Her breath fogs in front of her face as she points next door to an old cabin where an elderly woman is hanging up a flag with the town's name and logo on it. On the windowsill is a bowl of peppermint suckers and a sign that says *Free Coloring Pages*.

"Can we go over there?" Wind whips Micaela's shoulder-length hair, and Cameron's cheeks are pink.

They've been in the freezing cold all day, and that pocket-size cabin has smoke billowing from the chimney. It will be warm inside. But if we go now, we'll lose our spot in line. I squint at the folding sign that describes the building as the town's historical society. The sign lists their hours of operation. "We can always come back another time." There's a storm to beat, and this wood needs to be unloaded before it rolls in.

José tips his head that way. "I'll grab the food and meet you guys at those tables." He points to picnic benches in front of the historical society.

It's not a good time, but the kids are so hopeful, and his offer is more than generous. "Thanks, man." I thumb through my wallet and find a twenty to cover lunch, but he declines it.

"I got this one." He pulls his hood off to twist his baseball cap around backward.

"I promised you lunch. It was part of the deal."

He grins, flashing white teeth against his brown skin. "Next time." He waves us off like a mother hen, and the chuckle that rises inside me feels so different than numb. This will give the kids a few minutes to warm up and to just be kids without needing to worry about chainsaw rules.

"Thanks, man." I lead the kids toward the cabin. "But we've just got a few minutes, okay?" I add for them.

"Deal!" Micaela dashes up the gravel path and inside while I lift Cameron to my hip to enter. The elderly woman greets my daughter, then she offers us the same warmth. "Good morning."

"Morning, ma'am."

The air inside is toasty. Twinkle lights are strung across the ceiling, and it smells like dust and cinnamon sticks. I hadn't realized how cold we were until the warmth has us tugging off gloves and hats.

"You new 'round here?" the woman asks.

"No, we've lived here for a while but don't often get to play tourist."

"Well, have a look around, and take your time. We're open until four."

"Thank you." I set Cameron down.

The kids run to a pint-sized table that holds coloring pages and a basket of crayons. Micaela settles on a knotty-pine chair that's just the right fit, and they both dig in for a crayon.

With them settled, I survey the perimeter of the tiny museum. Artifacts cover shelves, and on the walls hang giant black-and-white photographs of the pioneers who settled this area. The oversized images show men leading teams of oxen up a steep grade, hauling cut logs not so different from the ones now stacked in the bed of my truck. A pioneer woman stands in front of a one-room schoolhouse with a dozen children around her long skirts. The photograph on the opposite wall portrays a Native American woman weaving a basket. Several baskets fill a display case beneath, showing their age and intricacy.

Another picture is of a slender woman in pants. She grips the barrel of a rifle, and the long handle rests on the ground at her boots. Behind her is a building labeled *Manchester Mercantile*. A cowboy hat perches on her head at an angle that might as well say, "I dare you to try." The bottom of the picture has a handwritten date: *1905*.

Above that looms a stuffed mountain lion. A brass plaque beneath the cat declares that it died of natural causes while dozens of others were hunted by sportsmen and ranchers over the century to such lengths that sightings are now extremely rare. The cougar is hunched down, one large paw holding the side of the branch as if for balance, while its face is downturned. The angled eyes are outlined in a haunting black.

Imagine facing such a creature in the wild.

"Are there still mountain lions in the area?" I ask.

"Very few." The historian settles behind a polished counter where a rack of postcards leans near an antique window. "They were over-hunted in the 1800s, so their numbers diminished drastically."

I contemplate that while the kids continue to color. The woman smiles over at them, looking glad to have guests. The building is so tucked away that I really hadn't noticed it before. Since the historian is perched patiently on her stool, I toss out another question.

"What do you know of the Kenworthy mine? It seems there used to be a town there."

She nods, jade earrings wavering beneath her cropped silver hair. "There's not much on record about Kenworthy. It came and went so fast. But some of the history books have a few pages on it." She returns to the shelf and pulls out a book. "This has some good information on Kenworthy."

I flip it open. "Do you know anything of the Cohen family?" It's a shot in the dark, but this lady seems to know her stuff.

"Oh, yes. There's a copy of a letter written by one of the Cohen family members in here."

As I balance the open book, she finds the page. It's a photocopy of one of the same letters that still resides in the box in my barn. My gaze skims to the bottom.

Dearest John.

I've never read the letters. They're not mine to paw through. But with this one published, maybe it's plenty worth the fifteen bucks.

Out the window, I spot José returning with two paper sacks and a cardboard drink holder. Cameron waddles over to me and holds up his picture. Brown crayon covers a pinecone in dark scribbles.

"Good job, buddy."

Micaela colors faster, tongue sticking out the side of her mouth. I show Cameron where José is just outside and tell him he can go start lunch. The little guy scurries out, and José catches him up, settling the toddler on his knee as they dig into a paper bag together.

After tucking Cam's picture into the back pocket of my jeans, I examine the cover of the book again. *A Local History of Our Mountain.* I pull out my wallet and thank the woman as she drops a handful of peppermint suckers into the bag with the book.

"We'll have new coloring pages next month, so be sure and come back." She adds Micaela's picture to a corkboard behind the cash register, and my daughter beams.

"We sure will. Thanks."

Outside, I give Micaela time to eat. I try to focus on my burger, but it's hard not to wonder about the book in the bag.

After cleaning up our trash, we return to José's house and unload half the wood. The kids wave him off, and I do too. As I pull away, both Micaela and Cameron look sleepy around the edges. On the drive home, Cameron sinks his blond head against his car seat and yawns. Town fades from view behind us as the road winds down the mountain. Thick forest hedges both sides of the highway, evergreen branches hazed by the fog still rolling in. Mist begins to dampen the windshield. Both wipers pump slowly back and forth. The rest of the storm holds off until we reach home.

The kids are conked out, and since they're warm and safe, I keep the truck heater running and nestle the blanket better around them. The cold air bites through my coat when I climb down. Wanting to hurry, I drop the tailgate and heave out the first round. This wood still needs to be split into wedges, and for now I roll them into the barn to keep dry. A gas-powered wood splitter sits ready and waiting for action.

The light mist has vanished as though the air is drawing in a breath so as to blow down something icier. The air stings my fingers when I tug off the work gloves. It's almost four, so it will be best for the kids to sleep a few more minutes. A nap will do them good and give them enough energy tonight for the board games they brought over from their mom's.

After fetching the gift-shop bag from the passenger seat, I settle on the porch that's over a hundred years old. Maybe it's the creak of the antique wood, or the underlying grief in me, or a growing need for purpose, but I need to know. I need to know who the people were who once made a life here. And why.

What kind of person . . . besides me . . . is determined enough—*desperate enough*—to call this farm home?

I slide the book from its paper sack and thumb to the spot the historian bookmarked. The photocopied letter catches my eye again with its yellowed paper and slanted writing, but on a whim, I turn to the page just before it. And in a single moment, I'm once again struck dumb by the sight of the pioneer woman. Juniper Cohen. Of the sight of this very cabin behind her.

It's the same photograph from the barn, and it's hard to describe the satisfaction for the original to exist only yards away. This very person from history once lived here. More important, she seems to have a story to tell. While I didn't pay full attention at the historical reenactments as a kid, it's clear that the depth of this legacy—whatever is in that journal and those letters—was not fully on display.

Why is that?

The photocopy is grainy. Her chin is slanted up, eyes straight at what would have been an antique camera on its tripod. Is the directness in her gaze due to the inconvenience of having to stand painstakingly still for the flash? Or is it a depth she's conveying in that single glance? It's a look that unveils one soul to another, as though she's trying to state something that can't be declared in words. For a moment, I wonder who was on the other side of the camera. Crazy because now I sit in the *exact* spot it was taken yet on the other side of that look. She doesn't know me. She never would have.

But for some strange reason, I want to tell her that I'm sorry.

I'm sorry for whatever her life was like here. As the first snowflakes begin to fall, I'm sorry for whatever she endured to be alone in a photograph surrounded by a spread of land that perhaps puzzled and astounded her as it does me. Perhaps she knew something much deeper than even I do. Some remarkable loss or even desperation. If that's the case, then maybe her joy was also more intense. Perhaps she knew a type of assurance that I can't begin to imagine as she glimpsed the sunsets here, or the way an eagle sometimes soars over the far-reaching sky while the horizon burns golden.

I touch the page, and either I'm losing my mind, or she once lost hers, but whatever grit dwelled within her, some must still linger because I want to rise.

I want to stand and tell this life that it will not defeat me.

I want to tell the lawyer and my wife and anyone else who will listen that I may be busted up into a thousand pieces inside, but those pieces are worth gluing back together one sliver at a time. I was made for some purpose, and even if it is only to be a father to my children, it is as noble a purpose as a man could have.

And it's worth accepting.

Rising, I push the book back into its bag. There will be time to consider it all more, but for right now, I want to be the man who turns on the lights and starts a crackling fire for the kids. I want to have a smile on my face when they wake up and for it to be genuine.

Just like the prayer from the night I signed the divorce papers, I could really use some courage. If God could send some more my way, this is as good a time as any. It might not be as simple as asking for it, but it's also impossible to ignore the fact that this breathtaking land had a Creator. One wilder than this territory was and is.

The mighty pines towering above the barn declare that the One who crafted the mountains that brace up these woodlands drew it all up from earth. That's a God who wields a strength like none other. Can I draw on that strength? Can I trust that even a speck of it lives inside me? Even as my heart hollers out for the answer, I return to the truck and pull two sleeping children into my arms. Trusting that moving forward is the only way to find out, I shield them from the falling snow and carry them home—hoping and praying that God is doing the same for me.

CHAPTER 15

JUNIPER

Kneeling on the cookhouse floor, I dip a scrub brush into a bucket of hot water and lye then scrape the bristles over the nearest floorboards. The friction is as steady as the racing of my mind. The letter I mailed to Yuma prison some weeks back? Has it arrived? Will someone there pen word to me of John's fate? I do not know, and so it's with a quaking spirit that I inquire each week with Edie if a response has arrived. Each week, there has been nothing for me in the limp mailbag. Shadows rim my eyes each day from crying and lack of sleep, and so I am grateful there are no looking glasses here in the cookhouse. I do not need to be reminded.

Though we press on with duties, longing for those who are far away is a constant companion. It is a silence between Edie and me as we both watch an empty road. Determination keeps us moving forward, as does our friendship. This knowing that we are not alone in this place. More so now that Reverend Manchester has passed away.

He went to heaven in his sleep not long after the night Edie pitched salt boxes at Señor Tiago's chest.

Edie's grief was gentle—her having waited for her father's passing for over a year now—but I sometimes sense her missing of him. There are moments, while she's in the mercantile, when she wears a look about her as though he is unaccounted for. My heart has ached for her since his passing. Yet it was a peaceful homegoing, and there is comfort in knowing that Reverend Manchester is now safe at home with the Lord he cherished.

Why must this grief feel so endless? Is it better to never have loved than to have loved and lost?

Despair does no good, so I search for hope moment by moment, throwing ropes to it with weakening hands as though it is a ship and I am afloat in a vast and stormy sea. Sometimes I am holding on by mere threads, but God is teaching me how to keep my head above water. It is a daily struggle. An hourly struggle.

As I push bristles over wood, and John's memory lingers with me, it is minute by minute.

With Bethany at school today alongside Mrs. Parson, I take this rare moment to let tears flow freely. I feel foolish, at times, when they do, but I know of no other way forward. I have tried to stuff down the missing of John, the unknowing over his life or death, and yet it flows as steadily through me as the blood in my veins. God's Word reminds me to lift my eyes to the hills. That there is where my help comes from. I do, letting my gaze lift to the snowcapped peaks through the cookhouse window. A cold breeze lifts through the open doorway, reminding that for all of my worries and sorrows, the Lord is greater. I must hold on to that.

Wiping my eyes, I force myself to rise. At the door, I pitch the filthy water over the side and move to the pump for a fresh fill.

In the distance, someone is walking this way. I shield my eyes with a hand. It is a woman. I squint harder. A Cahuilla woman. As she ventures nearer to town, her native heritage gleams with an elegant mystery. Her golden-brown face and black hair are striking beneath a blue sky. Her clothing indicates that she works at one of the nearby ranches. She wears a simple cotton blouse atop a calico skirt. Her feet are bare and her hands seasoned. As she nears the mercantile, she is close enough that I can see the smile lines that have spent perhaps half a century catching the California sun.

Soon, she is gone inside the mercantile. As curious as I am about her visit, Edie can't keep much to herself, so I'll be hearing of it soon.

Already, I've learned much about Edie's romance with Señor Tiago. I have learned that his given name is Santiago Del Sol but that most in the region call him Señor Tiago out of respect for his position in the tribe and community. He is only thirty-five, but as the shaman's son, he is as close to nobility as the Cahuilla have. More significant, Edie has explained that she and he are in fact married. Husband and wife . . . joined together by Reverend Manchester upon Edie turning eighteen. That was well over a year ago.

I guess Edie knew how to keep *some* secrets.

That she did not tell me prior is not something I will hold against her.

Edie, in all her spirit, has claimed one of the tribe's finest men. He would have strong standing among his people. By taking a Cahuilla bride, it would have furthered his pureblood heritage. And yet Edie is the woman he has chosen. The one to claim his heart. I have known Edie long enough to understand why she captivated him. She is feisty and impulsive and glorious, all at the same time. Her spirit is wild, perhaps not so different from his own. Each of them have been shaped by this land they were raised on, her with a preacher father, him as a shaman's son. Two drastically different worlds.

And yet, Edie has also described him as a Christian, a religion he chose through his schooling at one of the local missions operated by the Spanish—one reason so many Cahuilla have Spanish names.

From what I have known of the Cahuilla, being made to learn the ways of the Bible has not been a welcome change. While I hope that all can come to hear of the love of Christ, it is only right to respect the many centuries they have worshiped in their native beliefs. Because of that, I do not blame them for disliking the way they were swept up into missions and forced to learn another way.

Santiago, however, seems to have truly formed a faith in Christ that now directs his every step. Perhaps that had something to do with the mutual respect he shared with Reverend Manchester? I am curious about this and hope for the chance to better understand the husband of my dearest friend.

It's clear why this union has been kept secret. Here in California, the tension between settlers and the Cahuilla is as charged as it is across the nation with other tribes and those who have moved onto their lands. Aside from those who take work at the ranches, rarely do the two cultures mingle. This pregnancy, this marriage, is a rare testament that sometimes they do through love.

I glimpse the mercantile again through the cookhouse window, more than curious to learn about Edie's visitor, and by the time I have finished the floor and scrubbed all the tables and benches, the woman exits. Hands raw and weary, I move to the window and glimpse Edie giving her several items—a tin of tobacco and sack of what might be coffee. Before parting, the Cahuilla woman touches Edie's belly. Her fingers move like water, dark eyes steady as small stones. There is wisdom and care in her quiet, gentle movements. I am thankful that there is someone else who can look after Edie and the coming child. Someone who holds much more wisdom than myself.

When the woman departs, Edie strides my way. She waves overhead, and I wave back. It is good to see the smile on her face. Her belly has grown over the months, and yet she manages to keep it concealed beneath all of her layers. If I didn't know she was with child, I would be curious, but I doubt the few remaining townsfolk give it much thought. Perhaps Mrs. Parson has taken note, but the woman has never spoken of it. If there's one thing I've learned about Mrs. Parson, she's discreet, and I'm as thankful with my own secrets as Edie surely is.

"Oh, June. I feel so much less afraid now."

"I'm so glad to hear it. Come and tell me." Pouring focus into other things, be it tasks or this dear woman beside me, is blessed relief. I dry a bench for her to sit, and she settles near the cookstove where it's warmest.

There, Edie explains that the woman is Santiago's aunt from the same ranch where he works. "She's a housekeeper and has delivered babies—both Cahuilla and whites—for decades. Before his leaving, Santiago asked her to check on me when the time drew nearer." Her eyes glisten with tears. "He's looking out for me, June."

I pull her close to my side. "He is. Did she give any indication of Señor Tiago's whereabouts?"

"Nothing beyond what he already told me. That he promised to return by spring."

"There is comfort in that promise, Edie."

She hangs her head some. "Yes, there is. I wish I hadn't been so angry with him. I wish—"

"I know." Still near, I circle a hand across her back. "He knows how much you care, and I believe he will do as he has promised. Take heart in that."

She wipes her eyes, and when she looks at me, she seems ashamed. For crying for her husband? There is no shame in that. Or because she has a promise where I have none?

That is not her fault.

"I hope you'll come to know him as Santiago," Edie says, inviting me to address him less formally just as she does with John. "He doesn't really know how people came to call him as Señor Tiago, but it must be because the two sound so similar. He eventually stopped correcting people." She winks. "I suppose the pronunciation is difficult for most people. It was for me at first as well."

"Of course. It would be my privilege." I will try to think of him as Señor no longer. The Spanish equivalent of *mister* always seemed more befitting, but Edie's invitation is a warm one. I will honor their marriage and my friendship with Edie, thinking of him as Santiago. I have never spoken his name so informally, but here with Edie, his wife and my dearest friend, it seems only natural to begin.

Desperate to keep Edie and my thoughts busy, I ask more. "So tell me how it went. What did she have to say about the baby?"

"She said the baby was growing well. A good, healthy size. And that I looked well too." Edie leans her head close to my own in a sisterly way. "It was good of you to hide my flask of gin from me. I looked behind the counter last week and noticed it gone."

I smile. "I'm glad you're not angry."

"No. I need to do all I can to help this baby be safe and strong. Oh!" Edie perches her boots up on a nearby bench. "She said that this little bit is going to be a girl."

"A girl? However would she know that?"

"Well, she used this length of string. Almost as though she were gonna play cat's cradle. She held it right over my middle and, after watching it a spell, declared the baby a girl. I dunno, June, but it was awful nice to hear. I like the idea of a girl."

It is a lovely thought. "Boy or girl, I am praying for a safe, smooth delivery."

"Thank you. You'll be with me, won't you? And Santiago's aunt has promised to be with me as well."

"I'll be by your side."

She sighs, looking satisfied and even spent. It's been a long day for her. A long winter for us both. So I'm surprised when she looks around and asks if there is anything she can do to help.

"You just sit there and keep your feet up." Her chatter brightens the room as much as the sun does.

"Alright, then. Have we finalized our list for supplies?" She slides a fold of paper from the pocket of her britches and reads off the ingredients we've already listed.

Plenty of flour for biscuits. Salt pork for gravy and lots of coffee. Cornmeal for grits and cornbread. She's ordering dried apples and sweet currants, as well, which I can stew and turn into pies or jellies. The men will be well fed.

This task is a good feeling for both of us, I sense. It is life coming to our town again. Even if it's only for a few weeks. We will each face the aftermath as we must, but for now, we've thrown ourselves into this job as though it were oxygen. We will not be alone, and it's that notion that spurs me on to ready this place to welcome guests.

The pots and pans beside the giant cookstove all still need to be scalded and scrubbed. It's been over a year since the cookhouse was used, and every inch of its abandonment shows. Cobwebs cloud the room's corners at the ceilings, but after today's work, the floors are polished once more.

At a sound coming from the pantry, I fear something living might be scampering inside an empty barrel. When Edie volunteers to investigate, I assure her that I'll see the tenant relocated.

Was this place truly integral to the town of Kenworthy? It's hard to imagine, but it was. If the mine was this town's hope, the cookhouse was its heart. Dozens of men ate here—mostly bachelors in need of refreshment amid summer's heat. Nourishment during the bite of winter. Two full-time cooks handled it all. Now it's just Edie and me leading the charge.

For today, it takes a bit of that courage to drag the nearly empty barrel out onto the porch and tip it over so that a squirrel can dash off. I swipe the back of my hand over my forehead, tip the barrel upright, and am thankful for this day and the God who grants the strength to keep going. That strength is always around us—I see it now—but how often do I forget to reach and grab hold? To lay down troubles of the heart and breathe in peace in their stead? It is a trying thing to do, but one that must be pursued with abandon or else . . . what do we hope in?

What do the abandoned hold on to?

For Bethany and me, God is seeing us through. For Edie, I pray she will feel the same.

Nights still fall when I think of how I could take Bethany away from this place. We have just enough to make it to San Francisco, and she and I would have family to lean on. She would meet her grandparents for the first time. Lord knows we could use the refuge. But I haven't yet had the grit to write to them of John's disappearance, nor do I have the ability to leave this place.

I lack the strength to go where he won't know to follow. I could leave word, yes, but at risk of it turning to an empty echo we remain here. I will remain here until it is impossible to do so, or until it puts my daughter at too great a risk. For now, John is still alive in a corner of my heart. I will continue to drink thin tea and sprouted potatoes for sake of the impossible.

And for now, and these coming days and weeks, preparing the cookhouse will be our purpose, the exhaustion of cleaning it from top to bottom and stocking it with fresh supplies more than a task or a chore. It has already become a sanctuary. A place where we will do so much more than prepare meals and scrub dishes. The men we will serve will not be our husbands, but we can serve with the same fire of purpose and prayer, even as I pray that if John is still alive, someone— even a stranger—is able to show him a kindness. This will be a place warm and safe and dry. A place for our broken hearts to find a mending and for the weary to be welcomed home.

CHAPTER 16

JOHNNY

Y ou're doing great, Micaela!" I call from below her. "Be sure to keep your feet in front of you. Thatta girl."

She's maybe twelve feet up the boulder, leaning into the harness buckled securely around her hips and thighs. Her pink beanie covers her shoulder-length hair, which sways with each inch she lowers. I've turned my ball cap around backward so as to see her clearly overhead.

Being able to rappel properly is one of the biggest keys to canyoneering. I won't take the kids out on beginning trips until they're older, so now is the perfect time to teach Micaela how to rappel down a rock face. That way she can get comfortable with trusting the ropes, bolts, and harness. Since this boulder is just a hundred yards or so from the cabin and already set up with bolts, it's the perfect spot to practice.

Micaela's tennis shoes slip against the rough granite. Grit flakes

135

and falls. I give the rope some slack, helping her lower farther. She takes small steps down, feet out in front of her, and she's trusting the gear like a seasoned pro. Finally, her feet hit ground again and I ease up the slack on the rope so she can get her balance.

I step around a low cactus to give her a high five. "You did amazing!"

"That was so fun," she cries. "Can I do it again!"

"Absolutely. We just gotta get you back up to the top."

From the flat surface of rock beside me, Cameron is busy with a PB&J and juice box. Rye slumbers at his side.

Keeping tension in the rope, I show Micaela how to get back up the easy route we discovered. When she's higher than my head again, we practice her rappel once more. She's loving every minute, so we do it several more times before we've got to get back to meet up with the Realtor. He's coming out today to grab a few more items from the lockboxes. Turns out the family is wanting more than the journal. They want the letters as well. The letters I have yet to explore.

Micaela helps pack up both of our harnesses while I get the rope coiled up and put away. She carefully zips my hiking pack closed and makes sure that the side pouch is secure.

"Thatta girl," I say proudly. The tasks we do together aren't all that complicated, but I know each one matters. Whether it's gathering kindling or emptying out the ashes in the stove, each chore is teaching them valuable skills that develop purpose and confidence. I hope the lessons we're learning out here together will stretch a lifetime.

The hike back home is only about five minutes, but between the heavy pack of gear and Cam on my shoulders, it's a solid workout. Rye paces beside Micaela, who tows along our jug of water. We get back to the farm just in time to see a silver SUV in front of the barn. The Realtor has already climbed out and is peering through the barn window. Beside him stands an elderly woman who looks strangely familiar. I call a hello, and they both turn. The woman waves, and suddenly I recognize her from the historical society up in town when the kids did the coloring pages and I bought the book that is now dog-eared on the nightstand.

The historian's smile reaches us. "Hi, Mr. Sutherland. Hi, kids!"

The Realtor opens the back door of his SUV, retrieving a file folder. "I hear you've met Mrs. Hollister," he begins. "The Cohens suggested we get some help with moving the other artifacts. Never hurts to have a professional around."

"I agree." My response, while warm, lacks energy. Why?

Because I haven't yet had the gall to rifle through the letters in the barn. I've not yet broken the seal on the privacy of the past, since it's never been my right. Now the stories stemming from this place are about to slip from my grasp.

"Lemme grab my keys and we'll get inside." I take the kids to the cabin and settle them in front of a TV show with two containers of vanilla pudding. I leave the dog with them then grab my keys and head back out.

The historian pulls a box of latex gloves from the back seat. This is getting real. "Thank you both for allowing me to help with this," she says as we cross to the barn. "It's a real honor. When you came in the museum, I had no idea you were the new owner of this farm."

It makes the way she treated us with such kind consideration even more meaningful. We were just strangers, and that was enough. Somehow her involvement is making it a little easier to let go of these letters. A little . . .

"And, oh . . ." She slides off a glove to dig inside her vest pocket. Retrieving a folded flyer, she offers it over. "We're passing these out at the museum. The historical society is hosting an event with the Cahuilla tribe down in Palm Springs in late April. If you're able to make it, you might find it interesting."

"Thanks."

We slow just beside the lockboxes. The window overhead is

cracked open, letting in fresh air and light. I wonder who might have been the one to open it a thousand times and as many seasons before.

"Have you seen them?" the historian asks. "The letters?"

"I've glimpsed them, but that's it. I'm pretty sure they were the ones written by Juniper Cohen."

"Yes. Wife to John who wrote the journal."

"Exactly." In the dim light, I kneel in front of the lockbox that I've nearly opened again twice now. But both times I decided not to for the simple fact that the boxes aren't mine. These letters—these memories—belong to others. I'm just a caretaker, and I've done my job in keeping them safe. These pieces of the past have stayed safe. Now they'll venture on to wherever it is they're meant to be.

That just won't be in my hands, even though I've longed to discover more.

There's nothing I can do or say that would justify any different outcome than unlocking the box for her and stepping aside as she pulls out the plastic-packaged letters. She reaches in next for the photograph of Juniper Cohen. I glimpse the young woman's face as the historian places each item inside a thick, padded envelope that is already postmarked to the family in Wyoming. Beneath that photograph is another. Mrs. Hollister studies this one, and I lean nearer to better glimpse it.

This shot is of a small girl—perhaps three or four. She's seated indoors on a stone hearth, and it's definitely the cabin interior. Her composure is still, ladylike, but her face is blurred. It's just possible to glimpse the smooth curve of her cheek and her pert little nose, but the rest of her face is hazed. A split second captured in time.

"It's as though the child turned her head the moment the shutter went off," Mrs. Hollister muses. "It took some time to sit still for one's photograph in these days. Images like this aren't uncommon among children. This is likely the Cohens' daughter." When she turns it over, we glimpse *Miss Bethany Cohen* written in slanted cursive across the aged paper.

I squint at the image again, intrigued by what look like feathers tied in the end of the girl's braid. It still astounds me that this was taken in my own home. That this child sat in the very place where I still build a fire each and every morning.

"I'm curious as to who was the photographer," Mrs. Hollister muses. She moves a few items aside with care as she checks to make sure there is nothing else the family has requested. One of these items is a thick binder that she sets on the lid of the box. She opens it, flipping through plastic pages protecting a dozen or so brochures from the museum in its heyday. Following that section are several pages' worth of old newspaper clippings as well as more black-and-white photographs that I've yet to see.

Leaning against a broken refrigerator, the Realtor talks as the historian continues her careful search. "Say, I got an email from that kid again who is doing a history project on this property. The one who needed a few pictures of the cabin exterior. Okay for me to let her know she'll be hearing from you? I'll forward the info along again if you want."

"Yes, I'm sorry about that." I completely spaced. Has that poor kid been waiting for the pictures of the house all this while?

The historian sifts farther into the thick binder, past more memorabilia. That's when she reaches a section near the back that resembles the original letters. These ones are photocopied, three-hole punched, and protected in more plastic. There are dozens of them. All written in the handwriting I've only glimpsed. I just watch, having grown a little numb, but something sparks inside me.

Closing the binder, she examines the back.

Property of Kenworthy Heritage Museum. 52647 Ridgecrest Rd. Mountain Center, CA.

"Hmm." She offers it to the Realtor.

"This thing'll be a ton to ship," he says as he gives it a quick perusal.

"Additionally, it doesn't belong to the family. Not technically." Mrs. Hollister rises and peels off a latex glove. "This was part of the museum organization itself."

"What does that mean?" I ask.

"Well, it was part of their property—the museum, which was run by a third party, not the family. Some of these items are technically a part of that, like the soap dispensers or old banners, et cetera. Probably even this popcorn machine. The family only owns the original artifacts themselves, and of course the property, prior to selling it to you. This"—she nods toward the binder again—"probably ended up in the box when the museum organization was dissolved, workers and volunteers going their separate ways, and everything packed up." She motions for the Realtor to hand me the book.

It's solid and heavy in my hands. It feels as though a copy of every letter Juniper Cohen left behind resides within it. I open it up to the very first letter. The exact same one that has been printed in the history book.

July 7, 1902

Dearest John,

Crickets are chirping this evening, stirring up a ruckus. Do you remember the sounds of this land, or have . . .

"So, wait. What happens with this binder?" I lift my gaze.

Mrs. Hollister indicates the address printed on the back of it as dust motes swirl around us. "The museum is no longer a corporation, so ownership may as well be *52647 Ridgecrest*."

The Realtor thumbs toward the address sign staked into the ground at the front of the driveway. Then nods to the book I now hold. "I guess that means *you*."

JOHN COHEN

January 1898

She's due on the stage tomorrow. Her name is Juniper. It's an awful pretty name, and I've said it to myself each day that I've been awaiting her arrival. I don't know what she looks like, but I like the way she writes to me. What is she going to think when she sees me? What am I even going to do? I've never been close to a woman before, so I've observed the couples around me of late. The way men make sure and open doors or offer their arm. These things I can learn to do, but could I ever really make her happy? Can I truly give her a good life?

The shanty's clean. I've swept and cleared every inch of it to be ready for her. Even washed and folded a quilt that I purchased at the mercantile. The colors are like fall. She said, in her last letter, that it's her favorite time of year.

Still no gold in the mine, but there never will be. Sometimes I wonder that if I dig harder and farther than any man here, I will find some. When I do, my soul will be free. But until then, it burns with shame. I don't want to think about shame tonight. Not with Juniper coming tomorrow. I will return to the mine soon and keep digging and scraping for the sign of promise the town desperately needs, and will do so with each day that follows. I don't know if it gives me assurance or fear that Juniper will be by my side in this life, when that means that she, too, will know the outcome. She, too, will eventually know my crime.

John

CHAPTER 17

JUNIPER

MARCH 1903

D o you remember the next step now that we've unfastened the
clip?" Mrs. Parson asks Bethany.

Standing on a kitchen chair, Bethany unlatches the shiny brass
brackets on Mrs. Parson's fancy camera and slides it open. The
wooden face rises to horizontal, and the black bellows accordion up
like a swan's neck.

Scrubbing the dinner dishes, I watch, imagining during this
stage that the camera is being awakened.

"Well done." Mrs. Parson tightens a knob. "And then . . . ?"

"Then this?" Bethany points to the lower portion of the device
that Mrs. Parson taught her how to adjust.

A pair of feathers, one blue and one amber-gold, is tied into the
ends of Bethany's braid, something she urged me to help her do after
we found them in the barn loft the other day.

A storm rages outside, pelting snow against the windowpanes, but in here with the glow of the fire and lantern, and Mrs. Parson's added cheer—all is cozy.

"Correct." With skill, Mrs. Parson slides the back plane toward her. "That keeps the folds from being worn out, or risking holes."

Bethany touches the bellows, and her face is soft in the light.

The teacher smiles at Bethany's joy with the camera. "We're almost ready to take our picture. Who should be our subject?"

"Mama!" Bethany cries, momentarily drowning out the howl of the storm outside.

"Oh, no." I fold the wet dishcloth over itself and reach into the tub for another pot to scrub. Thanks to an offering from Mr. Conrad, we had fresh game for supper. I insisted on sending him home with the last of our bread, and while he tried to decline, he finally tucked the muslin-wrapped loaf under his arm for the trek home. "I'm not so good at sitting still. How about a picture of you?"

Beaming, she turns to her instructor, who nods agreement.

"I think that's a fine idea," Mrs. Parson says. "Why don't you settle over by the hearth, and I'll get the shot set up?"

These lessons have been a welcome distraction during a frosty week. Over the last days, and with school closed for the storm, we have kept busy tidying, but the house is so neat with three females in it that there is nothing left to sweep or straighten. That's when Mrs. Parson offered to tutor Bethany in photography, and the two have been engaged with these lessons each evening. While I have kept to the outskirts, I've listened to it all, soaking up the knowledge. The idea that a photograph can link two worlds and even two different times is beyond my imagining. To think that decades from now a picture could remain is a phenomenon I can hardly reckon with.

Perching on the edge of the hearth, Bethany straightens her calico skirt of brown and white, then crosses her ankles in their dark, woolen stockings. She pulls her small braid to the edge of her shoulder, letting the feathers tied there catch the light. Behind her, a fire crackles in the woodstove. Mrs. Parson angles the camera and adjusts another knob. She lowers her head to the viewing pane and moves the knob another half turn.

With the kettle nearly hot, I pull teacups from the cupboard and sprinkle a tablespoon of black tea into the bottom of the pot. The addition of boiling water sends up a comforting aroma. Outside, evening is settling in, casting a blue tint to the soft snowdrifts gathered over the land like a blanket. Though we keep the fire stoked around the clock, a chill still seeps in from around the windowsills. We've stuffed rags beneath the door where gusts howl past cold and lonely.

Mrs. Parson instructs Bethany to tip her chin up and to balance her hands just so on her knees. My daughter's spine is straight, neck turned elegantly toward the camera. She looks so grown up. Mrs. Parson drapes a black velvet cloth over the back of the camera and slips it over her head, blocking out the light. Gears squeak as she adjusts the focus and tightens the planes. From how she's explained it, the view she's peering upon is upside down within the camera. I looked in it just the other day and was astounded by the phenomenon.

Mrs. Parson closes the lens and slips out from beneath the dark cloth. Next, she inserts the film holder. "Now hold good and still."

I hear Bethany inhale. Mrs. Parson is just releasing the shutter when something slams onto the porch outside. Bethany's head whips that way. I, too, startle.

A loud *thunk* hits the porch again. A horse whinnies.

I unholster my pistol. "You two get upstairs," I whisper, and Mrs. Parson hoists Bethany up from the hearth.

I'm just to the door when something pounds against it. Bethany shrieks.

The gun, cocked now, feels too light in my hand for whoever might be on the other side. "Who's there?" I demand.

The voice that presses through the thick slab is strangely

familiar, emboldened by the wind and cold. "Mrs. Juniper. Open the door."

Someone has moved to the window, and I can just glimpse a shape through the curtains. A hand presses to the glass, the muscular wrist wrapped in a beaded chord. Santiago. Why doesn't he go to Edie? Or perhaps he has and it's why he's come. Panic rises as I reach for the knob.

"Dying here," he adds. Then his words turn to Cahuilla, even more foreign than the Spanish sometimes spoken in this land.

I don't understand them, but am too panicked not to open the door.

I push the slab outward and Santiago lumbers in, nearly shoving the door off its hinges. I stumble back. He moves in a rush of power that is far from the edge of death. He's clad in a thick overcloak that's as coarse as a horse blanket. A slit has been cut in the middle, allowing it to be pulled over his head like a *vaquero*'s poncho. A belt cinches his waist, bracing the horse blanket to his body. His fringed, leather jacket is not so much missing . . . but placed elsewhere.

It drapes the form of a man that is limp beneath his arm. Another Cahuilla man? Is this who is dying? Dark, muddy flannel has been cut into rough squares so as to wrap around the man's hands, binding closed at the wrists by dried grasses. Pauper's gloves, and in desperation at that. The same type of covering binds the stranger's feet that drag across the floor as Santiago tugs him inside. The man's neck dangles forward, limp and unstirring. A canvas sack covers his head.

I bite back bile even as I fight to keep my wits. "Lay him here!" I push two chairs clear of the table.

Bethany, who's now halfway up the stairwell, starts to cry.

Turning back, I see that Santiago has removed the sack from the dying man's head.

And that man—so covered in filth that I can hardly recognize him—is not one of the native's kinsmen.

It is John Cohen.

Bethany's father.

My husband. Unconscious and near frozen. Returned somehow from the clutches of death, only to be lowered to the floor at my feet.

CHAPTER 18

JOHNNY

MARCH

5th of September, 1902

Dearest John,

Three wagons pulled out today. Loaded into their weather-beaten frames were several families but mostly miners. One of those miners asked me to marry him only the day before. As he stood there, lit by the sunrise, I thought of you. And as he turned his hat in his hands, beseeching me with his request, I thought of you.

I'm shamed that I was tempted to say yes. To shake the dust of this place from our shoes and to give Bethany a life that is filled with more hope than the one we have here. Do you know why I said no? Do you want to know what thought crossed my mind when I refused him?

It was the dawn that we stayed abed. It was nearly time for us to rise for chores. The milking, breakfast, bringing in wood. But on that morning, there you were, your head pressed to the side of my stomach that was big as a washtub. Your hand held the other side, and it was so warm and right against my nightgown. You looked at me then with a sheen in eyes that were green as the pines, and you told me that you could feel her. Our sweet girl.

How you knew it was a girl inside me, I'll never know. But she was made in love and was growing in love. You kissed me then, and rose, bidding me to keep both me and the baby warm. You went downstairs then, moved the kettle to the stove with a soft clang, and headed out to do the chores in the frosty dawn.

You are missed not only for your goodness, but because your soul somehow knew how to speak to my own. This silence terrifies me not because you have been silenced. Quite the contrary. I feel you and hear you in nearly everything still. I am afraid because I do not know if you can hear me in return.

You are missed more than I could ever describe.

Juniper

CHAPTER 19

JUNIPER

Edie's husband shoves back the kitchen table, and chairs tumble, slamming into the wall. I help him make space as he drags John closer to the fire.

"Make him warm," Santiago demands.

Rushing to the stove, I yank open the iron door and cram two more wedges of oak inside. Tears blur my vision, and I fight them back. The whole world spins as I try to make sense of this moment. Of this relief that bends with pain inside me. Shaking hands reach for the kettle. I fill a cup, not even bothering to steep tea leaves. I carry the warm water to where John is lying, and with Santiago's help we lift his head. John is unconscious, and the hot water only sears against his lips, dripping down his bearded jaw where the overgrown whiskers tangle with mud and neglect.

Santiago moves the cup aside. "Make warm," he demands again.

Yes. But I don't know how.

Santiago works on the nearest sleeve of the fringed coat. I start on the other. As we peel off the stiff jacket, the intensity of how foul John smells increases. I cover my face with the back of my hand. Gulping back the urge to recoil, I move into position to help Santiago get John nearer to the fire. But the native man presses on my shoulder, bringing me lower to John. It's a grip that I haven't strength to resist. It's not rough, only adamant.

"Make him warm," he says a third time.

That's when I realize what he's bidding me to do. I cannot.

I *cannot.*

John has deceived me. He has betrayed others. He has broken every vow he has ever made. But in this moment, his lips are tinted blue, and his skin is so stiff with cold death hovers over him. It chills the room itself. I lower myself to stretch out against his side, and the scent of him pulls bile to my throat. It is the sourness of a man who has not bathed in weeks.

Santiago rolls John onto his side, making it easy for me to fit my chest to his own. I do, and sight of my husband's face blurs as my vision does. He is home. And somehow still alive. With help, I manage to get an arm around John, and as I move in closer, something hard and square pegs me in the chest. I try to ignore it, but it digs into my ribs so sharply I feel it against the front of his shirt.

A book?

"There's something here." I begin on the buttons of John's shirt. The fabric is so crusted the buttons won't be coaxed loose. Brandishing a knife, Santiago slits the shirt up the front to reveal even more cloth binding a canvas-wrapped book to the center of John's chest. He cuts this cloth next, and the book within a dingy sack falls away. For John to carry it so far, so close to himself, it must hold great value, yet there is no time to ponder the book's contents as I settle against him again. This time there is nothing between us but my flannel blouse and the layer of dirt on his bare skin.

Mrs. Parson returns with blankets, neither shocked nor repulsed as she places one over us, followed by a second. I cannot breathe. So foul is this man that I cough against the stench. His overgrown beard brushes the side of my face, and I fight the urge to recoil.

"Bethany's asking to come down," Mrs. Parson says. "She's calmer now. Knows it's her papa and that he's alive."

"Yes. Have her come." I will shield her from the truth no longer. She is a brave girl, carved out of this West like the water carves its canyons.

Mrs. Parson's footsteps rush up the stairs and she returns with Bethany.

I know by the sound of my daughter's voice. "Mama?"

"It's alright, sweet girl. Your papa needs some help being warm." Sitting up, I pat the blankets where John's feet are tangled just beneath, still bound in cloths that are thick and dark like an old saddle pad. "Can you sit right here and help?"

She perches against John's feet, still wrapped in her blanket. She looks like a bird, wide-eyed and fragile, nesting there against her father. Her warmth will help.

Mrs. Parson slips into place with a bowl of warm water and a rag. She starts first along the side of John's neck where bruises and grime are etched into his skin. Santiago stuffs more wood into the stove. The kitchen is so hot now that sweat gathers at my temples and against the bones of my corset. Despite the heat, John is as cold as a side of meat that has been hanging out to cure in midwinter.

His hand, limp on the ground, is wedged beneath my stomach. His firm knuckles press without meaning to the place where I once carried our child. Crouched beside the fire, Santiago rubs his own hands back and forth, chafing heat back into them. He blows into his cupped palms once and then again. This man needs something hot to drink as well, and gratefully, Mrs. Parson is already on the task.

Though every breath is stifling, I must ask. "Where did you find him?"

Santiago's eyes slide to my own, telling a story more vast than the single word he utters. "Yuma."

The prison referenced in the article where I sent a letter only weeks ago. A place known in Arizona territory as the Hell Hole. Tales of that prison have been whispered across the West. Such bleak accounts that I have turned an ear away, not wanting to know the horrors, yet John has been immersed in them. Has it been all this while?

Santiago rises, and my gaze falls to John's still face. I don't dare touch him there, yet the longing intensifies in knowing where he has been.

I brave another question. "Why was he covered so?" The sack that had draped his head lays crushed beneath us now.

"For travel. No one stop us."

I don't understand.

"We walked many days. Not be stopped. White men don't bother with worry over dead Indian. I say take home for burial." Bitterness tints the words, and their truth is grievously true.

When the men first entered, I had thought John a Cahuilla man. Santiago had camouflaged him in plain sight of passersby who would have regarded him little in territories where hostility and censure are still prevalent. It is a bleak truth. The journey would have taken hundreds of miles and many, many days past territories thick with white settlers and lawmen.

I must ask . . . "Has he escaped?"

"*Netéteyamaqa pé'iy*. I found him on the roadside by his prison."

His prison. I know nothing of the Cahuilla language but understand enough. A thousand more questions burn within me of how this man knows all this—knows John enough to risk so much and journey all the way to Arizona territory.

THE GOLD IN THESE HILLS

The man steps to the door. "I'll help the horse now." He pauses, contemplating before speaking again in Cahuilla. "*Héspen peqéyl-laqmu'qa'.*" His brow plunges as though trying to find the English. "Much pain. She's very injured." His words dance between two languages as he rifles through the kitchen wares until he unearths a clean cloth. He beseeches Mrs. Parson to fill a pan with hot water. She does so, placing the pan carefully in Santiago's blood-encrusted hands. He's still wearing the saddle blanket, belted around his waist as a crude poncho.

The horse. That is where the wound is.

With the saddle pad and blanket having been cut up for coverings to keep the men alive, the horse had nothing to protect its hide beneath a saddle. It's no wonder the creature has become bloodied. "It will be warmer in the barn. And dry," I say. "There's a little hay. Take all that you need."

Santiago nods and steps out into the falling snow. Mrs. Parson swipes the rag down the side of John's face. She helps me adjust so that my head is farther from John's chest and I can take a breath of cleaner air. Warmth has grown between us. Is it seeping into him?

Mrs. Parson dumps the soiled water into a pail and partly fills the pan with what remains in the kettle.

As she returns to her ministrations to clean John's face, I watch her calm, concerned expression. "Do you think this will help?" I ask.

Water trickles in the lantern light as she wrings the rag. "We will pray so."

I have lost the ability to pray for this man. "Will you pray for the both of us?"

Mrs. Parson squeezes my shoulder. "I'll pray enough for many."

Tears sting my eyes. The heat is beginning to crush me, as is this nearness to John. I release my grip around his back long enough to swipe a tear. While it's impossible to mine for a prayer within the cavern of my heart, I can at least remain here, warm against him. The wool coverings that shroud us are stifling, but he needs the reviving. It's unclear if it will be enough. Beneath these blankets, beside this fire, I look at John and imagine for a single, brief moment that he did not shatter my heart into a thousand pieces. I imagine that this unconscious man pressed against me is good and honorable and kind. If I think of him for what he truly is—a convict—my stomach knots in ways that have nothing to do with his need for a bath.

Pinching my eyes tight, I try to imagine that all I once dreamed of is real. I must. For tonight, so long as it is needed, I will be by him to help his heart beat closer toward life. As to what is to come after that, God will tend to it and prepare me to face it, just as He will also be preparing John.

"Mama?"

At Bethany's fragile voice, I shift to try to see her better. Before I need move far, she steps behind John and sinks to a crouch. Her nightgown is a puff of white. So different from the grime of his clothing that holds most of Arizona and half of California in its creases.

"Is he warm?" she asks in her small voice. "Can I say hello to him now?"

"He's very cold still." Even with the rising heat, he feels like death. Fear needles me that he will be a corpse by morning. That I will have lost the chance to see him alive once more. "But you're being such a good helper."

Bethany's green eyes trace the length of her father. If she is repulsed, it shows not in the gentle slant of her brow. The way she silently considers him. Her soft face is so full of compassion that it breaks my heart. The two feathers still twined in the end of her hair flutter as Bethany sinks lower until she vanishes from sight behind the span of John's shoulders. Only a moment passes, and then her small hand rises to his upper arm. She holds on, gripping the fabric of his tattered shirt.

"It's alright, Papa," she whispers, and her voice on this earth is small but it stretches wide inside this room.

My tears that fall are silent ones. Near the stairs, Mrs. Parson conceals her own behind damp hands.

"We've got you now," Bethany whispers again, the assurance strong and sure as she holds John as close as I do. "We've got you now, Papa."

CHAPTER 20

JOHNNY

I'm deep asleep the next morning until Rye starts barking and the UPS guy tromps up the porch steps, drops a heavy box against the door, and cranks his truck back down the driveway. Blinking awake, I go to sit up when the binder across my chest slips. I catch it before it slides to the floor. Closing the binder, I place it on the bed beside me and rise. My sweatpants are thick, but the cold of the morning still causes me to shiver. I reach for a long-sleeved thermal shirt and slide it on.

How many letters did I read last night? And did I fall asleep in the middle of one? Judging by the binder that had been tented across my chest, I must have.

Crossing the floor, my bare feet move once more over the circular stain embedded into the floorboards. No amount of scrubbing or refining would remove it. Apart from peeling up those boards and

156

laying new ones, the dark water stain is here to stay. I don't want to compromise the integrity of this place for something so superficial anyway, but it's times like these that I wonder again at what caused these markings. What rested here over a hundred years ago?

But maybe I'm probing too deep this morning. These thoughts are too heavy on an empty stomach.

Juniper's voice is still in my head as I lumber downstairs to switch on the coffeepot. It's still in my head as I fill a cup of steaming brew, and as I stand in front of the window, watching fresh snow fall, I can hear her. It's as though she's here, peering out at this same view. Chills cover my skin, and I search the living room for a sweatshirt. It's easier to chalk up the sensation to the cold as opposed to the fact that I have somehow peeled back a layer of time, looked into the past, and hurt for a woman—for a family—that I don't know. But for some wild reason, we've shared this farm, and after reading over a dozen of her letters last night, I realize that we have shared something else.

Pain. Hope.

It seems to spring up from this place. It settles around the land like dew. It's in every creak of the stairs and every knot in the pine walls. It's a cry for home and, in some ways, for renewal.

She and I . . . We've wanted the same things.

It's why I had to know last night if she got them. If the cries of her heart were ever satisfied. Did her husband return? This John fellow who seems to have just vanished into thin air. What would make a man do such a thing? Why would a husband and a father simply leave with no trace of his whereabouts? I'm tempted to return upstairs and keep reading, but the next letters will have to wait. Right now, I've got to head down to the nearest city in the valley where the Home Depot is. I've placed an order for supplies for a new set of clients and their bathroom remodel.

I don't feel like cooking so grab half of an egg-and-cheese burrito from yesterday and pop it in the microwave. It spins slowly as it warms, and I take the moment to top off my coffee and Rye's dish of food. With breakfast finally in hand, I settle on the couch and watch sunlight part the clouds. It's only a dusting of snow on the ground and will be gone in a few hours tops.

I manage just two bites of the burrito when my phone rings from the kitchen.

It's an achy kind of rise, but I reach my cell in time. "Hello?"

"Hello, this is Mrs. Hollister from the historical society. I hope I'm not bothering you too early."

"Not at all."

"Well, I'm calling because I've got a young lady here who came in to ask about your property. She's from Palm Springs and is doing a project on the local history and some of the connections between the Cahuilla natives and the white settlers."

Oh, this must be the high school kid I finally sent that photograph to. What was her name? Sonoma, I think.

Mrs. Hollister continues. "She and I have been talking about your property as it's pertinent to some of the research she's doing. Would you have a chance to talk with her? I don't know if you have time to swing by the museum today, or maybe we could set up a time that suits you both. She's happy to come back." Her voice lowers to a whisper. "I don't think she wants to inconvenience you, but the information she has is pretty amazing. I think you two might be able to solve a few riddles if you put it all together."

"Right. Oh." My brain isn't working fast enough. "I think I'll swing by there." I can spare an hour before Home Depot. "Maybe twenty minutes? She mind waiting?"

"Not at all! Gives me time to put on a pot of coffee. We'll see you soon."

◆ ◆ ◆

There's one vehicle parked out front of the history museum, which makes two cars in the snow-dusted lot by the time I pull my truck in beside it. The morning is all sunlight now as I step toward the front entrance, making it hard to see that there's a person seated at the picnic table where the kids ate lunch with José.

A moment later, I glimpse that it's a woman. With the day warming, a snow jacket rests on the table beside her.

Rising, she swipes her hands on the sides of her jeans before walking over. There's something graceful in all of it. Something elegant and earthy. Her skin is a soft brown, and her long, sleek ponytail nearly black. She looks as though she could have Native American heritage in her, but not full blooded. She's way too young to be the mom of a teenager.

I extend a hand. "Thanks for waiting. I wasn't sure about having a kid at the farm all on her own, but if I knew she had company, it would have been totally fine. I should have asked. I'm sorry about that."

Her thin brows lift. "I'm sorry?"

"Sonoma," I clarify. That was the girl's name, right? "I just wasn't sure if she should come to the farm without a chaperone, so thought this would be a better way to go about it."

Her face melts into a smile. "That was very responsible of you."

I'm not sure what she means by that. I wasn't trying to make a big point of it, but also wanted to be respectful, and why is she still smiling at me like that? "Is she . . . inside?" I ask.

She shoves back the sleeves of her gray sweater. "Mrs. Hollister?"

"Sorry, I mean Sonoma. Is she inside?"

This woman is nearly laughing now. "Not exactly." A set of beaded bracelets jangles on her wrist as she extends a hand. "I'm not in high school anymore, but I hope it's okay if I introduce myself. Sonoma Del Sol. I wrote you the email."

I wish my brain had an extra circuit board, because when the main one cuts out in that moment, all I can do is stand there dumbly.

She finally gives in to a laugh. "I can see that we had some crossed wires. Anything I can do to troubleshoot that?"

It's as though she can somehow see that crashed circuit board and its flashing lights that are desperately attempting to compute. "Uh. I'm sorry." I stumble over the words. "I thought it was a high schooler doing a class project."

"Oh, yes, a class project." It's a mercy the way she motions us to sit at the table, because I really need to sit down. "But it's for a few final credits through an online academy. I'm attempting to get a bachelor's in cultural studies, then go on to start my master's program. A little late in the game, but I had to work two jobs to cover tuition and ended up taking off several years to care for my grandma who had dementia. So, I'm finishing up my degree program a few years later than planned." There's a leather bag on the seat beside her, and she pulls out a manila folder. "I believe there's some hot coffee inside. Would you like some?"

"I, uh . . ."

Her eyes don't quite meet mine as she rises again. "I think I'll grab a cup."

She heads in, and the few minutes gives me a chance to regain my wits. Partway through, I glimpse both women watching me through the window, probably discussing how I'm a total nut.

When Sonoma returns, there's an air of hesitancy about her, but the face that settles across from me again is a friendly one. She places a steaming cup for herself and offers a second to me. "I brought it just in case."

"Thanks." I take a sip. It's prepared differently than I usually drink it but tastes good. Maybe it's the graciousness with which it was offered.

She sips from her own mug, and the quiet seems to be offering room for me to respond with more than a single word.

I swallow the scalding drink too quickly. "That's great. About your degree programs, I mean. You're already doing better than I've done."

She braves a look my way again.

"The only classes I passed with decent grades were math and woodshop."

She smiles at that.

"So, I do construction." I shrug.

"Well, that stands for something," she says warmly then suddenly looks a little mortified. "No pun intended."

I chuckle, and it feels good. Like the tension somehow floated off with the breeze. "So, tell me more about what you're looking for." I'm curious about her file.

"Absolutely." She opens it and, after brushing a few stray flecks of last night's snow aside, shifts the papers closer for me to see. "First off, thank you so much for sending that photograph. It gave some answers, but . . ." A dimple appears in her left cheek as she smirks. "It's also brought up a few new questions. That always seems to be the way with this kind of thing." She straightens the papers, and I lift the nearest one. "The bulk of this is genealogy research. I've made a lot of progress over the last couple of years but hit a firewall that I can't seem to get around."

"What's that?"

"Well, here . . ." She touches a series of empty squares in what looks like a family tree. "There is a portion of Cahuilla bloodline here, but nothing is set in stone yet."

From here, I can read one of the boxes that is filled in. *Santiago Del Sol.* That's the same last name as her own, if I'm not mistaken. And if I'm counting up the boxes right, he'd be farther back in time than a grandfather. The square beside him, what would have been a wife, is empty. As is the one below it, their offspring.

She slides a picture forward. It's the one I emailed her the other day. It's been blown up and printed on photo paper. She's put a lot of effort into this. "At first, I had been thinking that my ancestor was with the desert Cahuilla because there were some ties there. But other indicators suggested the mountain Cahuilla. There were half a dozen groups of them in the area, some spanning all the way toward the Salton Sea."

I lean forward on my arms to study the image better.

"I haven't been able to know for certain, until you sent me the photograph."

"Really?" Her enthusiasm is not only contagious, but for the house to be such a critical piece to her puzzle has me wishing I'd gotten the picture to her much sooner.

"Yeah." She shifts through to the back of the file where more black-and-white photographs are compiled and pulls one out.

I take it, angling the glossy image to the light. And there, in black and white, is my house. It's been stripped of a century of wear and looks nearly new. Standing in front of it are two men, similar in height. Similar even in build. But what is strikingly different between them is that despite the fact that one has an arm of comradery draped over the shoulder of the other, one man is Cahuilla and the other is white.

"This man," she says, touching beside the white settler, "is the man who is alleged to have built the house. A John Cohen. You are familiar with him?"

"Yes." Even as I answer, I study his face more closely. He looks about my own age. His beard is neat and his cropped hair combed off to the side. Though he's not smiling, there's something youthful about his face, perhaps in the way it is shaded by a hat from the southwest sun.

"And this other man"—she touches the photo where the native man stands, dressed in cowboy garb—"is who might be my great-great-grandfather. But . . . it's hard to say exactly. That's where I've hit that firewall. Many Cahuilla in this era had several names. People often had two Cahuilla ones—given to them as a child and then again as an adult. For those who attended school at one of the missions, they were given a Christian name—which was typically Spanish since the missions were Catholic." Reaching up, she tucks a piece of hair behind her ear. "Ultimately, this man had *four* different names."

"Wow."

"And that's what has made it so difficult to match up the genealogy. Even then, I might be wrong, so it's still a theory right now. You've already been a huge help." She shifts papers around. "I don't know his Cahuilla names, and sadly, I doubt those will surface." She nudges her coffee cup aside so that there is nothing between us but the file and its mysteries. These two men—one with a shadowed past and another with several identities. "What I do know is that his Spanish name—or his Christian name, if you will—was Santiago Del Sol. That's how I discovered him in a genealogy search, but I'm still not certain that this man is a match."

"Why is that?"

"Well, look here." She touches the bottom of the page. "He's been listed as a Señor Tiago. That's what the photographer wrote on the bottom corner of the photograph where two names were written by hand long ago. *John Cohen, Señor Tiago, 1905.*" Sonoma continues. "So was that what he was known by among the settlers in the area? If so, it makes sense, but . . ." She angles the photograph and studies his face for several seconds.

"It's still sort of a riddle."

"It is." Her smile is sad. "But I think it's enough of a match to be confident."

"It sounds like you're on the right track. What about his wife?"

"That's what I still need to figure out."

It's fascinating. "So how can I help you?"

"I'm wondering if there is anything else that might have some answers. Anything else on the property or that you've learned. I hadn't originally thought to link my heritage with this house you now own, but there's something about this photograph that indicates a link of some kind."

"It certainly does."

"If you've heard stories, or have any names or resources that I could research further, well . . ." Gingerly, she places the photograph back in its file. "Often these riddles are answered in the unlikeliest of ways."

My coffee is growing cold now, but my focus lingers on this person across from me.

"That's not to say that it will be. But it seems worth it to try. So much was lost when my grandmother got dementia, and now, trying to piece it all together has been like building a bridge, stone by stone." She smiles, and it's a bittersweet contrast to the sheen in her eyes. It's a look that has me wanting to know more. More important, wanting to help. "And maybe the answers are gone, and maybe they'll never really be found. But for my family, to have a clear understanding of where we came from . . . It would mean a lot."

I think of the letters. Of what I've slowly been learning. But there hasn't been a single reference to any of the Cahuilla tribe in the area. "I don't know if I have anything that can help, but I'll be on the lookout. There are some old letters that I'm reading through, and I'll let you know if I spot anything that could be connected." Now that they're in my possession it's hard to think of passing them along, but maybe they weren't meant for me in the long run. Maybe there's a greater purpose here. "If so, I could get them to you. I've got your email address and can be in touch."

"Thank you, Mr. Sutherland. That would be amazing."

"It's no problem. And please, call me Johnny."

"Just the one name?" she jests, and it's fitting, all things considered. I smile. "So far as I know."

CHAPTER 21

JUNIPER

MARCH 1903

I wake to John's fingers pressed against my hip. It's in this half-conscious stage that I can't comprehend why they're still bound. For a few hazy moments, I think, *Why has my husband come to bed in mittens?* Then it hits me: we're not in bed, and this man against me is less of a husband and more of a criminal. The notion jolts me further awake. Eyes open, I inch away from his heat. He's warmer now, not fully conscious, and his forehead glistens with sweat. John's hands shift again, bound fingertips grazing the front of my blouse, as though he, too, is dreaming, perhaps wondering what this prison of coverings is about.

Any person who has been imprisoned would want freedom—even in sleep.

I push myself farther away and remove one of the two blankets covering us, stopping in my movements at the sight of Bethany curled up against him still. Her forehead is pressed to his back, and her face is at peace. I settle the second blanket around her for warmth. I am afraid to remove the wrappings on John's hands for fear that they will show signs of frostbite. But lack of knowledge won't help him. There is not a doctor here, should he need medical attention, and it calms me to think that Santiago may have some skill here. He clearly knows how to keep a person alive.

The dried grasses that bind John's wrists are so snug they're difficult to unravel. I finally manage, and the grasses fall away, brittle. The portions of spliced saddle pad are coarse and nearly as stiff, but the first one peels away from his hand. Where I feared blackened fingertips, I see only the filth of his skin. Dirt and grease have filled the creases, embedded under his nails. These hands—that I now see are well—are ones I have known, and they have known me in return.

Do not cry, Juniper.

Rising, I swipe at my eyes. It's early yet, the sun just turning the sky to gray. How strange it is to leave John sleeping on the floor, but sleep is healing, and he will need all that can be summoned. Santiago is nowhere to be seen. He must have gone to the barn again. It's unsettling to be here alone with John.

There's only one piece of firewood left, so I grab a shawl, slide on my boots, and step out into the gray haze of dawn. The storm from the last few days has passed. The sky is clear and the fresh snow looks deep. I halt in the doorway at sight of Santiago seated on the steps, pipe in hand. Smoke wafts from the end, and with his head low, he blows the rest toward the ground.

I gently step around him. "I'm just . . . I'm just going to fetch some wood. John is still asleep. Have you seen Edie?"

He nods. "In the night." He rises, and when I step from the porch, he follows. My feet sink with every step that's a struggle.

At the wood crib, I pick up several chunks of pine. Beside me, Santiago begins to take the wood from my grasp. The lightening is a relief. I don't expect him to take it all, and yet piece by piece, he claims the whole of it.

"I get wood. You make John clean," he says.

Hesitating, I reach for more wood. The motion serves to pretend that I don't understand.

Snow clings to the legs of his pants as Santiago strides to the porch, where he deposits the wood. I follow with my own addition. He waits until I lower it beside his own. "I do this. You make John clean," he repeats.

"No." I square my shoulders, careful to keep my voice low so that it will not drift into the house. I will not make him clean. "I listened to you when you said, 'Make warm,' and he's warm." My voice falters. "But he . . . he can clean himself when he wakes."

"If he does not wake?"

"Then what does it matter?" The bitterness in my voice sickens me.

It shows no effect on this man. "The vows we make." Santiago angles so that he stands in front of the sunrise now. I see more of the amber glow than his face. It's only the shape of him that I make out as he speaks on. "Love. Respect. Provide."

"He has not upheld his vows." Where have I found this boldness? It must have been a long time coming—this chance to say what I must.

"You know this? You have sat in prison in Yuma and see these things?" He slants an arm toward the east as though the fortress were on the other side of the crest and not hundreds of miles away.

I don't answer him.

He touches his chest. "*I* will not make clean. Not disgrace John." He holds his hand out toward me. "Bone of my bone. Flesh of my flesh."

These are Bible words.

This man is quoting Scripture to me?

Sun rises past his shoulders now, and the light is enough that I can make out the grief in his face. "Flesh of John's flesh must make him clean."

Who is this man? Who is this man who thinks that marriage is so simple? He does not know the beast of betrayal. He wouldn't, or he would not preach to me so. "He will clean himself when he wakes." This man does not dictate my actions. And neither does John. I swing away, intending to stomp back inside, but Santiago's hand is faster, cradling my wrist with his fingers.

The touch is not unkind, only intent. "Come." He releases his hold and starts for the barn. When I don't follow, he adjusts the saddle blanket still draping his shoulders. It must itch terribly because he shifts it again. "Come, please, wife of John."

Sighing, I follow across the snow, vaguely recalling that I wear no pistol at my hip this morning. What does it matter? This world no longer makes sense, and there is nothing that I fear more than the man lying on my floor opening his eyes. Seeing me. Me truly seeing him.

At the barn, Santiago pulls open the door, entering first. I follow in silence. His horse, tall and shadowed, stands quietly in a stall. The lantern is still warm when I touch it to light. This man was here only minutes ago, judging by the heat still in the tin. Now the new spark glows into a flame that flickers. Shadows and light dance around us, and Santiago's steps are soundless as he comes around me.

The horse is still, watching us with unblinking eyes as we approach. Her keeper slides a hand to the side of her face, then down the length of her brown neck. He enters the stall, and the mare doesn't so much as shift. A white diamond stretches the length of her long nose. A regal mark for a lovely creature. Her eyes are wide and innocent, watching me.

She's a tame soul, and her gentleness bleeds an ache into me.

Strips of thin cloth are speckled with some kind of leaves where they drape her back. With a slow hand, Santiago lifts one of the cloths.

The horse shifts for the first time. One hoof, and then another. He whispers in what can only be Cahuilla, for it sounds a thousand years older and a world apart from all that I have ever heard. *"Pé' ish pé' chém pé' áchakwe' pichemtéewwe."* Then he beseeches me in English, "Lantern."

I lift it from its hook and step nearer. There I see that the mare's flesh is torn across her back. Where there should be soft brown hide, there is only raw meat where horsehair has been worked away beneath weeks of John's weight. Over two hundred miles it is from here to Yuma. A saddle blanket and pad would have protected her, but her blanket went to keep John's fingers from turning black. Her saddle pad kept Santiago warm so that John could have a coat for the journey. This creature stands here, worn raw and uncomplaining for it. By her sacrifice two men have come home.

"Say no more to me. Tell her." Santiago takes my free hand, presses it gently to her warm neck. Her heartbeat pulses soft as a hymn beneath my palm. "Tell *her* that you will not make John clean."

The horse blinks long, straight lashes. Her innocent face blurs as my vision does. I blink quickly, seeing now that her dark eyes are like jewels. They do not quite meet mine, as though she feels unworthy. My hand slides away. It is I who am unworthy. My throat has swelled, and it hurts to swallow, let alone speak.

Turning, I start for the house, aiming not for the kitchen but for the water pump. The ache lingers as I fill a bucket, and then another. It stands beside me as I heat water, fetch soap. It lingers, hovering, as I kneel beside John and peel back his blankets. With Bethany near yet, I won't sponge him properly until she and Mrs. Parson are at school in a few hours' time, but by the soft glow of the cookstove, I dip a rag and begin on his hands. The creases and lines that I have always known. The coarse planes of his knuckles and palms that once dug for gold and spent countless hours loading ore and rock into wooden carts.

These hands hold scars and the remnants of splinters that have calloused over. They held me with tenderness throughout summer nights and on snowy mornings. They brought Bethany into this world. They have been to the fortress of Yuma and back, and as I clean them in the dim light, I realize that all the months of writing to John on pen and paper did very little to prepare my heart for the reality that he very well could return. And that in the return the greatest testing of our courage would begin.

CHAPTER 22

JOHNNY

MARCH

A windchime rattles softly from the porch eaves. Micaela made it from treasures she found around the farm. On a thick paper plate, she drew the silhouette of a black horse, then tied on strings of sticks, creek stones, and feathers. The feathers—blue, charcoal, and sunset orange—are from the birds that inhabit the pines above our farm. When the breeze hits it, the rustic chime is as much a part of this place as the wind itself.

Bottle of water in hand, I cross the porch and claim one of two chairs I put there. Rye settles at my feet, watching, as I do, the two hawks soaring overhead. One cool thing about California is that spring comes quickly. Not that snow doesn't still appear in the early months, but today the air is a mellow sixty-eight degrees. The sky is blue, white clouds shift by, and sun dapples the land. It's perfect weather.

171

It's my birthday today, and so far I watched a game and read a few texts from my sister and some close friends. The kids are coming early this evening, so I've got some fun plans for us. It's still a surprise, but we'll hike into the hills, a little farther than the day Micaela learned to rappel. It's sandier back there, nearer to the creek. More tall boulders and open skies. I already lugged up some wood and a few camping chairs and now have a backpack loaded with s'mores supplies and matches. It's hard to think of a better way to celebrate another turn around the sun than to see their faces lit by the glow of a campfire beneath a star-studded sky.

The kids are due within the hour, but a cloud of dust is rising from the top of the drive. I strain to see better. Emily wouldn't be early . . . The thought dies as soon as I see a FedEx truck rounding the bend. I didn't order any packages.

I stand when the driver parks and climbs out with a large envelope. He offers it over then asks me to scribble my name on a screen. I don't open the envelope until I'm seated again on the porch. It's addressed from the lawyer's office. My heart is racing.

My fingers move of their own accord. Not because they want to, but because whatever fate this envelope holds, it's already signed, sealed, and delivered. Stalling won't win my wife back. I slit the top and slide out the official document. My heart knocks harder as the printed text sinks a rock in my gut. The divorce is finalized. Emily and I are no longer married. The news comes with a hollow feeling. Nine years of life—of marriage—unraveled. Just like that.

Breaths come slow now. *Don't cry, man.* The gnawing in my chest is a peeling back of all that was whole or somehow still steady. Clearing my throat, I head inside and stuff the papers into my briefcase. I'll file them away better another time. Right now, I rub my thumb against my wedding ring. It needs to come off now, but I can't seem to tug it from my finger. The warm golden band is coated with scratches. Scuffs and dents from lumber and brick. This band also brushed against Emily's fingers from a decade of holding her hand. It cradled the downy heads of two precious newborns.

I read in the Kenworthy history book that it takes nearly two thousand degrees to melt gold. Strange to think that the heart can withstand even more heat. It has to or we would never make it through this life. Right now, that searing heat is trying to knock me flat, so I pull the ring from my finger, press it into the pouch of my briefcase, and slide the zipper. The kids are going to be here soon. Time to keep it together.

Normalcy takes over in picking up my work boots to settle them by the fireplace. I crack a window, letting in fresh breeze, and finish the last of the dishes in the sink. My empty finger feels weird in the soapy water.

Hands dried off, I fill three aluminum bottles from the tap with cold mountain water then stash trail mix, beef jerky, and dried fruit into my hiking pack. I also grab a box of packaged cupcakes, which are the closest thing to a birthday cake that can be carted out there. There's no candles on hand, but the campfire will more than make up for it.

If the kids insist, I'll try to make a wish. But it's hard to think of what it would be for.

When they arrive just shy of dusk, I hang back from the porch, letting Emily send them up the steps, backpacks and smiles on. I just don't have the courage to face her today, and it might be a while before that courage comes knocking. The kids have known the divorce was coming, but they're so little, and have been adjusting well, that it's best not to bring it up afresh. If they have questions, I'll answer them. If I sense they're confused, or hurting, I'll speak into their hearts as best as I can. But for right now, they're jumping back and forth on the beanbags, and despite the fact that I am a fractured man inside—and probably will be for some time to come—it looks like it's time to party.

If there's one thing this process has taught me, it's to keep moving forward.

Looking down at their smiles makes it easier to find my own. "So, what do you guys think about an adventure?"

◆ ◆ ◆

The kids run ahead with Rye as soon as we hit the trail. After months of snow and rain, the gritty earth beneath my boots is soft. Perfect time to be out here without worry of rattlesnakes, but with cactus scattered around, I urge the kids to be careful all the same. Cameron finds a stick and swings it as he toddles forward.

Micaela runs up to a boulder, pressing her hands flat to it. "Look how big this rock is, Daddy! Can I rappel down this one too?"

Her enthusiasm for the sport I love means more than I can say. "This one doesn't have bolts, but maybe we'll find another one that does." I wink, and she immediately begins scrutinizing all the boulders we pass, searching their craggy surfaces for those subtle glints that mean someone has already created a climbing route—fastening bolts into the rock with a drill.

"None of them have bolts," she assesses at last. "Can we put some in by ourselves?"

"It's doable." While I'm neither equipped nor trained, I like the idea of speaking into the possibility. "We just need a drill and some courage."

Now it's her turn to grin.

Up ahead, we spot the pile of firewood and the three lawn chairs already in place. Rye chases a lizard then halts to lap up water from the narrow creek. Cameron gathers up two craggy rocks that shimmer under the setting sun. Micaela is instantly convinced they're gold.

These two are good medicine for my soul. Warmed by the short hike, I unzip my jacket and lay it over the back of a chair.

Cameron tugs it onto his lap as a blanket. "Mash-mawwos!" he hollers.

"S'mores *and* cupcakes." I tousle his hair. "But first we'll need a fire."

At this news, the kids freak out, which is nothing compared to what they'll be doing once the sugar rush kicks in. Three points to Dad for packing beef jerky to balance things out. Not wanting to alarm the locals with smoke or the worry of a brush fire, I wait until it's nearly dark to strike the match. Within moments, paper and kindling catch, the earthy scent of smoke rises, and the warmth hits us instantly.

Overhead, the first stars wink down.

We pierce marshmallows with sticks, and Cameron climbs into my lap as I help him balance everything over low flames. Micaela's marshmallow catches, blackening, and we blow it out together. I was one of those kids who intentionally burned marshmallows, so when she wrinkles her nose in disgust, I gobble it down and reload her stick with a fresh one. This one she toasts gently, perfectly, because she's so much more like her mother than me.

But maybe that's not true. Maybe the kids will be a perfect mixture of us both—all the while bringing their own unique traits to the table. Micaela has her mother's blond hair and small ears, but she has my brown eyes and long fuse. Cameron is passionate like his mother, but his baby pictures look just like mine. It's a blend that eases the ache this night.

As the three of us settle in watching the stars come out, there's no hurry to get back. We've got flashlights, and the trail home is a cinch. Leaning back into the folding chair, I peer up at the sky. Cameron is keeping me warm, and I'm probably doing the same for him. Micaela hums the birthday song as she licks white goo from her fingers.

When Cameron shifts, something crinkles in my jacket pocket.

Checking what it is, I find a folded paper and tilt it to the light. Oh, right. It's the event flyer that Mrs. Hollister gave me. I'd forgotten all about it. It's a struggle with just one hand, but I manage to get it unfolded and, in the glow of the campfire, can just make out the large text.

GRAND OPENING OF THE NEW
CAHUILLA HERITAGE MUSEUM
32344 YUCCA DRIVE, PALM SPRINGS, CALIFORNIA

The flyer advertises food, festivities, and cultural demonstrations. It also emphasizes the opening of the exhibits that will showcase historical Cahuilla artifacts that have never been on display before. Reading further, the museum is proud to become the most extensive representation of our local tribal history ever compiled for the public. I think of Sonoma and her connections to the past. Her desire to unearth more of her family's heritage.

Last of all, the flyer lists the speakers who will present on the tribe's history and how it pertains to society today. Everyone is invited, which makes sense of why Mrs. Hollister gave me this. Struggling to read the bottom, I pull out my phone and tap on the flashlight for a better look at the list of speakers and their pictures.

11:00 a.m.—Glimpses of the Past
  Presenter: Alana Alvarez, Director of the Southern
  California Tribal Institute
1:45 p.m.—An Ancient Purpose in a Modern Era
  Presenter: Diego Cortez, PhD, Regional Anthropologist

The first two sessions pique my interest, but it's the final name and photo that's newly familiar. One that doesn't have a doctorate or fancy title, which makes her presence all the more noteworthy.

3:15 p.m.—Blended Origins: A Guide to Genealogy Research
for Partial Cahuilla
Presenter: Sonoma Del Sol

Though we only met once, I feel pleased for her. This is a big deal.
A testimony of hard work, especially since her own questions are still
out there to be answered. I wonder, then, if I could have helped her
more . . .

Micaela screeches, and I nearly drop the flyer, certain she's been
burned. But she's rummaging through her coat pocket, complaining
that she forgot my birthday present.

Hand to my heart, I try to calm my breathing. "We put it in my
backpack, remember?"

She hops down and unzips the pouch. Wrapping paper crinkles.
I open my arm to draw her closer, and she leans into my shoulder,
handing it over.

I give the small package a shake and kiss the top of her hair. "Can
I guess what it is?"

She leans back and nods.

"Is it a shower?" Turns out the one I picked months ago is still
on back order.

"No!" she giggles.

"But I really want a shower."

"A shower's too expensive, Daddy!"

"Naw. You just need to open a line of credit." I shake the package
again.

She giggles and clambers into my lap next to her brother. Rye lies
at our feet, leaning his massive head against my boot. This is a good
birthday.

"Okay," I whisper between the kids. "If it's not a shower, what
is it?"

"Auntie Kate took us to the store and helped us pick it out."

Now I'm really curious.

"Open it!"

I do, and the first thing that falls out is a chocolate bar. My favorite. I sniff the plastic wrapper and make a show of how awesome it is. Micaela urges me to dig farther, and I feel a book. The paper falls away to a leather-bound journal. Opening it up, I tilt it toward the fire and see that the pages are blank and new. Nestled in the paper is also a pen that's nicer than any I've ever owned. My sister is a good shopper.

"You guys. This is really neat. Thank you."

"The candy bar was my idea," Micaela says.

"Uh-uh." Cameron jabs her with his elbow. "Me!"

I squeeze them tight so they stop arguing. "You guys are the best. It's all perfect."

We settle back in the camp chair, the kids leaning against each side of my chest, the opened package still in hand. The kids grow limp and sleepy, which means I just might be carrying them home. As the fire crackles and the night deepens, Rye sighs and I do too. Finally, I shift to the beginning of the book, and there inside the cover are words that have to be written by my sister.

For your own Kenworthy story. It's going to be a good one.

JOHN COHEN

December 1899

June's in the rocking chair with Bethany. Over half a year, and she's like a brush of heaven. I swear I see glory every time I peer into her face.

I want to hold on to them for every moment that I can.

I don't know how long that will be, and it scares me more now than it ever has. They know where I am, my cousins. They know I've returned to this mountain to try to work off a debt of guilt and regret. I don't know where on this earth they are, but I've heard whispers that the law is after them. Which means it will ultimately be after me as well.

God, if I could stay hidden just a while longer, I'd thank You. I know I don't have the right to ask, but I'm asking all the same. You've seen them, both of my girls, and so You know why I have to try.

John

CHAPTER 23

JUNIPER

MARCH 1903

No school, Mama." Bethany, who has adored visiting the school-house ever since Mrs. Parson first took her there, clings to my skirt.

I kneel so as to take those two small hands in my own. "Oh, sweet girl."

"I wanna stay with Papa!" Her eyes lift toward the stairs where John is now resting thanks to the help and strength of Santiago. Edie's husband has returned to the mercantile to be with her, which is for the best since John still hasn't woken. John's color is fuller now, pulse stronger, so it could be any moment.

I smooth Bethany's braid. "And your company is helping him to mend." Her cheek is too close to not give a soft kiss. "But Papa needs to rest a little longer. I promise you. He is going to be here when you return."

Her lip quivers.

"How about this? You go to school with Mrs. Parson so that I can give lots of good care to Papa, and I'll fetch you on the break. You can help me fix supper. I'm sure it will be fine for you to attend only half the day."

Thankfulness sparks in her eyes. "Promise?"

"With all my heart."

Mrs. Parson waits in the doorway with a smile, then, hand in hand, they start off. I wonder in that moment—as the both of them are lit by the morning sun—if my child's father will ever look upon a sight such as this. If he will see and *know* how brave and good and lovely his daughter is becoming.

From where I had already set a pot of water to boil, bubbles spill over the side, hissing on the hot iron. Filling the enamel pitcher, it waits steaming on the table as I fetch more rags and a new bar of soap. All in hand now, it's time. I softly tread up the stairs, and what I see at the top is a world away and a lifetime ago.

John sits on the edge of the bed, facing the window. His posture is neither squared nor slumped—he simply is. With his back to me, it is almost as though nothing has ever changed. As though he will turn to me, smile, and rise. When I step back, the boards beneath me creak. He shifts, glancing back. There is confusion in his face. He blinks, and the dip between his brows is as much shock as it is puzzlement.

Neither of us move until I brave more steps. Even with a window propped ajar, the air smells of his lingering odor, and I pity him for it.

He won't have the strength to stand, but his eyes are clear and fixed on my face.

"You're awake." It's all I can think to say.

"Juniper." The word holds hundreds of miles and as many days.

"John." A thousand questions.

When he tries to rise, I move nearer. "Please don't." Whether it's the plea or the way I reach out to insist, he sits again.

His body is thinner than it once was. Frame masculine, but in a modest way—one that speaks louder than a striking appearance. It's resilience. He's made up of the same angles and lines as most men, but while his presence fills this room somehow, there's a leanness to him that speaks of hunger and hardship. It speaks of the will to survive. His scraggly beard brushes his open shirt collar, mustache fringing his mouth in wiry strands.

"I have hot broth on the stove if you're ready to eat." I settle the pitcher on its stand and notice that his journal rests on my desk where I placed it the night before. I have not opened the cover and do not plan to. "And here is hot water. Perhaps . . . perhaps you would like a bath now that you're awake?" The question is such a simple one, but it's all that comes in this moment.

His eyes follow me. "Both would be . . ." His voice is weary as it trails off. All he can do is nod, and for a moment I fear he is going to topple.

"I'll fetch you something to eat then fill the washtub."

Hand to the side of his head, he nods slowly. "Would you like me to move?" He lowers a glance to my feet. To the place I stand here in this bedroom. *Our* bedroom. "I don't have to be here." His hand curves around to his neck. "I'm not even sure how—"

How he got here? "I don't mind staying downstairs tonight."

I don't see his reaction, but his response lifts my gaze. "Bethany?"

"She's at school for the morning, but she's eager to see you awake. I'll get her very soon. The schoolteacher, Mrs. Parson, boards here now, so she will be returning this evening."

He nods. "How is she? Bethany?"

"She is well. She's strong."

"And you?"

I lay the rag beside the pitcher, having no answer to that. "I'll get the broth." Retreating, I make my way down the stairs and take plenty of time filling a bowl with rich stock. I dip a spoon into place and fold a small napkin beneath the rim of the bowl. It would have been easier if the meal were harder to prepare, more taxing to finish, but I need only carry it back up the stairs and deposit it into his hands. When I return, John has moved to the chair beside the window. I lower the bowl for him to grasp, making sure he has a good grip on it before letting go. It's all too easy to keep our skin from touching.

"Take your time. And there's plenty more. I'll prep the bath."

"Much obliged." His gentle tone says more still.

Downstairs, I heft my two largest pots to the pump and fill them to the brims. There's just enough room on the stove for them both to heat. The washtub hangs on a wooden peg on the side of the house, and it's a relief to have an excuse to escape outdoors. Thoughts pummel me regardless.

John is alive.

Awake.

Eating broth from a bowl.

There is so much to say. So many questions to ask. But I can only focus on basic comforts—on nursing. I will give him this care but no more. There will be time for thinking beyond, and even then, I do not want it.

My strength fails me today because it takes many trips to lug all the hot water up the stairs, and that's with shaking hands still unsteady from the shock of it all. The tub is half full and steaming at the end. John watches it with a base need, the soul-deep hunger he displayed when accepting the broth. He braces the empty bowl now as I sprinkle dry soap into the round washtub. The water fogs. This soap is meant for laundering, so I use it sparingly. It is sharp and what he will need to become fully clean. With a sturdy rag and a bar of lye soap at the ready, he has all he'll need.

"I'll leave you now."

Nearing the door, my skirt snags on a sliver in the knotty-pine bed frame. This he built by hand before I first arrived here. I shake the tattered hem loose, harder than necessary. Angry. Angry at God for answering my prayers—for bringing my husband home to me—but in a way that is outside how I imagined it could be. God has answered my prayers, yes, but it feels as though He is mocking me. It's a childish thought. Worse, heretical. Who am I to dictate how God wills our lives? Did He not ask His servant Job upon being questioned, *"Where were you when I laid the foundations of the earth?"* Still, I'm angry . . . and I can only hope that one day God can forgive me for it. I will need to make peace with it first—and do not know that I will ever be able to.

John watches the way I right my tattered hem before that same considering of his reaches to my face. He has yet to rise still. Whether it is shame or longing or something in between that tints his voice, it has not changed from its soft tone. As though his words are reaching for me in a way that only they would be allowed to. "Thank you."

CHAPTER 24

JOHNNY

Emily picked up the kids early this morning, and they aren't gone but half an hour—the house sighing with their absence—when my guys show up. José's driving the work truck, and a couple more of them are on hand to help tear down the old barn loft, salvage what wood we can, and rebuild an all-new loft from fresh, new lumber.

José is barely out of the truck when he's got a radio cued up, Spanish music blasting from the speakers. Antonio, who is a genius with tile and grout, has brought a case of bottled water, and Raúl, my strongest guy who can heave just about anything into place, tosses two bags of lime-flavored tortilla chips onto the folded-down tailgate. These guys are good for the soul.

Emily told me while she was here that she and Austin are getting married in a week.

That with the divorce final, and their baby due soon, it was time. I just stood there and listened. Nodded. Then watched her drive away.

Raúl claps me on the shoulder with, "We doin' this, man, or not?" and it jars me back to the moment.

I squeeze his shoulder back. "Let's get started. Thanks for coming." I've already arranged to pay for their time, but it still feels like a sacrifice on their part. They don't have to help me on a weekend when they have other things to do with their families. But they enter the barn with me, and all three of them peer up at the soaring space.

"*Dude.*" Antonio drags out the word. "This place is old. Like *super* old."

We all chuckle.

With the volume cranked on the radio, we grab gloves, sledgehammers, and skill saws and set to work on the remaining loft fragments. It takes the rest of the morning to get the rotted wood down and stacked in the yard. The air is filled with sawdust and a smell that whispers of time. The dust lingers in José and Antonio's black hair as they drag a massive beam out into the yard. It's rough around the edges, but it holds unspeakable value as an accent beam for a farmhouse.

Near noon, José's wife, Marta, arrives with a crockpot of homemade refried beans and a tray of hot enchiladas covered in foil. Two plastic tubs hold homemade salsa while extra tortillas steam from inside a striped towel. She takes the spread inside, and we feast on the porch, washing it all down with ice-cold Coke from glass bottles. Rye lies on the porch, watching Marta the most as though knowing she is the bringer of the food. When she pinches off a piece of meat and lowers it to the floor beside him, he laps it up and watches her with even more adoration.

"So, hey, man," José begins after a swig of soda. He swipes a loving hand across his wife's back, who is seated beside him. "We all talked and just want to let you know that we don't want this to be on the clock."

I shake my head. "It's on the clock. I asked you all to come, and you've been working your tails off. There's no way I'm not paying you."

"No, man," Raúl counters in his thick accent. His English is patchy, so the two words are enough.

Seated beside me on the steps, Antonio balances his meal on his lap. "It's already done, boss. We won't take it."

I hang my head, overwhelmed and trying to think of a way to counter them, when Marta rises, gives me a tight hug, and places another enchilada onto my plate. "Eat up." There's a warm smile in her brown eyes. She winks at me and then kisses the top of her husband's head. These people . . . They're the salt of the earth.

After we eat, Marta asks for a tour, so we head inside, and I show them all around. The guys admire the historic details and wood finishings while Marta gives me tips on how to better organize my kitchen.

Having wandered upstairs with the guys, Antonio calls down. "Hey, boss, what about finishing off this floor? I thought you said you did it already? Looks kind of awful still."

After climbing the stairs, I reach the bedroom doorway and see the circular water stain that he's eyeing. "Yeah. I could have probably gotten it out, but didn't want to sand down too far."

Kneeling, Antonio touches the wood that is slightly warped and uneven from the damage. The circle, about two and a half feet in diameter, is a perfect round.

"I think it might have been from an old bathtub," I add. "It might have sat here too often. Or too long, perhaps."

"These are some steep stairs to haul water up," Antonio says. He's a genius with flooring, can cut trim on a dime, and so it doesn't surprise me that the roughness of these floorboards stumps him.

Especially since I could have renovated it all to a more pristine shine.

I crouch beside him and touch a portion of the warped flooring. "I guess I liked the idea of leaving some of the history intact."

Antonio nods slowly. "Yeah, I can see that. Is all good, man. This place is really something."

"Thank you. And hey," I add as we rise. "Let me know when you want to help install a shower downstairs."

"No way." He grins. "I've seen that bathroom. Too scary to touch."

"It's not scary. It's . . . vintage."

"It's scary!" Marta calls from the kitchen. "But I like this place all the same, Johnny. It's a good home." Her cheery voice continues up the stairs. "A really good home."

CHAPTER 25

JUNIPER

MARCH 1903

S now blankets the land, cocooning my every step as I tromp toward the mercantile. The bag of laundry I had draped over my shoulder has lost any sense of balance as I now drag it behind me, trailing a rut through the white drifts from my cabin to the town. Up ahead, smoke curls from the chimney of Manchester Mercantile where Edie will be holed up and cozy.

With nary a sound to be heard, business will be slow today. I doubt even the ranchers or their families will have cause to venture out in this deep of snow. Yet when I arrive, stomping my boots outside of the open doorway, a plethora of activity buzzes within. Two men stand at the long wooden counter in threadbare coats. Supplies drape the counter before them. Their faces are chapped—the skin worn raw with cold as though they blew in with it. They've a rough look, but I feel no uneasiness at the sight of Santiago lingering in the corner of the shop. He's feigning interest with the display of tobacco but will likely choose the kind he always purchases from the wife he comes here every day to see.

Glimpsing him again, it is impossible not to recall encounters of late. Of the way he dragged John's body into the cabin only nights ago. Of him standing with me in the barn, forcing me to see the pain and anguish of an innocent mare. Of the way he helped get John upstairs and into bed. There's much I need to say to this man—so many ways I need to thank him—but this won't be the time.

The oversized coat that Edie wears is buttoned up the front, and a thick, knitted scarf is tucked beneath the collar. The padding is sufficient to distract from the fact that she's eight months along. Her height works to her advantage, allowing her stomach to nestle more closely within her slim torso. The scarf wound around her neck was once a favorite of the reverend's and now serves as warmth for his daughter . . . a shield for her unborn child.

One of the men is eyeing her manner of dress so seriously Edie's cheeks are flushed. Does he sense her secret? His eyes skim down the length of her, and Edie's jaw clenches.

"Say, miss, that jacket's too big for you." He shrugs broad shoulders beneath his own coat that has seen one too many winters.

Edie yanks the lever that opens the cash register. "That's 'cause I took it off a man I shot."

The man's eyes widen. At the display of tobacco and cigars, Santiago observes the conversation with a spark of amusement.

"I have something that may suit," I say, announcing my presence for the first time. I haul the laundry bag nearer. Inside linger several garments from miners who are no longer here. After digging to the bottom, I pull out an offering. The outerwear is tailored differently than this man's bush coat, but the wool is thick and warm and the seams still plenty sound. I shake it out and hold it up. Since the man I laundered it for never paid me, I decide to try my luck with tossing out a price. A way to pay off a few more dollars of my tab here at the mercantile.

The stranger pulls several bills from his pocket and places them in my hand. He takes the coat with a nod of gratitude and then a glance of apprehension Edie's way. "Much obliged, ma'am. Ladies." He touches the brim of his hat then introduces himself and his comrade to me as scouts for the Fresno Mining Company. The same company leading the charge for the stamp mill and hotel to be disassembled. "We'll be seein' ya next month. About six wagons and twenty men altogether. Laborers, drivers, and two foremen."

"We'll be ready." Edie swipes her own payment into the register, and a bell dings as she closes the drawer.

How I hope she's right. There is much to do in the cookhouse still. Work that ground to a standstill with John's return. Somehow I must divide my time.

Slipping behind the counter, I deposit the rest of the laundry. "These are Mr. Conrad's things. He'll collect them soon as usual." I have no idea what to do with the other items, but maybe Edie can look through to see if anything will fit Santiago.

Through the shop widow, we watch the travelers mount their horses. Santiago comes to the register, pays for his tobacco, and considers Edie and then me before politely giving us a moment to speak.

"Oh!" She turns and pulls two paper bundles from the shelves behind her. "Your order came."

"My order?"

"The sugar and flour. You were gonna put together a cake for Bethany. I've been fixin' her up a little gift."

How did I forget? Her birthday is only days away. With all that's happened, it slipped my mind entirely. "Thank you, Edie."

She pencils the total onto my running tab, and I slide her the fresh bills to put a dent in the sum.

"She'll be so pleased." Edie comes around the counter, giving me a comforting squeeze. Does she know what thoughts circle my mind? That this return of the men is so much harder on me than it is on her? Tears well in my eyes, and when her own grow misty, I sense she understands.

So much has passed in the last months and now days. Both of our husbands gone. Both of them returned. The mystery surrounding them both yet unsolved. I long to whisper to Edie further . . . to glean what she knows, but if I am honest with myself, I want it from John's lips first. I've waited so long, it is only right. The chance to speak plainly and unearth answers has come. I need to begin with the man resting beneath my roof.

"I'll be off." I squeeze her hand.

Santiago stands on the porch now, watching the snow, giving us time.

"I'm so glad he's home," Edie whispers.

"I knew he would come back to you. It's apparent how much he loves you."

Edie shakes her head. "Thank you, but I was speaking of John."

I offer a weak smile that won't fool this woman.

"June. Talk to him."

A nod is all I can muster.

"Please." She hesitates then says more. "If I could speak to my pa just once more, I would." Her eyes glisten. "We never know how much time we have with someone."

Her sentiment humbles me. "I will." Where I ventured off into the unknown to marry John, leaving behind the only home and family I had, Edie has been planted like a tree here in this place. Rooted in the very mountains, she grew from under the care of a loving father. What different paths we have walked as daughters and women. Her counsel is one I would be a fool to ignore. "And you are well? The baby?"

"Wiggling like a ground squirrel in the brush. Darting this way and that." She presses a hand to her middle that's still buried beneath layers of leather and wool. Nestling past the folds, I press my hand to the same place atop her blouse, feeling the blessing there. This child who was knit from two different heritages. While no man could ever tame Edie Manchester, it is clear that a man has learned how to love her and to garner her love in return. That is no small thing, nor is the blessing of this coming child. This unborn baby is a testimony to the wonders that the Lord can weave in the unlikeliest of places. It is the same God who chose that the glory of gold should be harvested from the grit of the earth and that I should face what I am avoiding.

"Speak to John," Edie whispers again as I take my leave.

I give her a small wave of assurance before returning to the winter's day. Shawl wrapped snug, I head for home quicker than I left, not because I am eager to cross the threshold, but because I have nothing to carry except a small sack of flour and another of sugar. It's another working of the Lord. To strip us of what we mean to cling to. Of what weighs us down—or, in my case, keeps us from facing what we fear most.

At the cabin, I'm scarcely inside its warmth when Bethany's laughter rings out. She's kneeling beside the washtub, as is her father, and they are both scrubbing laundry. I halt. John looks up, and his face does not hold the carefreeness of his daughter's. His hands are red with what can only be the heat and too much lye. Bethany uses my wooden paddle to push a billow of white beneath the foamy surface. They look like bedsheets. Why would John bother?

And then it dawns on me. The scent of him. The filth. He is tending to it so that no one else does. This is shame he's pushing beneath the surface, and it makes my heart ache worse for him.

"What a good helper you're being, Bethany." I say it for her benefit. I cannot address John, and silence would leave our daughter unsettled. I fetch a turnip from the bottom of the barrel in the pantry. "Would you mind pausing a moment to bring this to Mr. Santiago's mare? She'll be needing some company for a spell." I wink and hope it's cheery.

"Are we finished, Papa?" It's clear she doesn't want to go, but John must sense what I'm about.

"You've done well. Do your mama's bidding now, and we'll look through your books when you get back." He speaks clear and kind. His beard is neatly trimmed again, and he's growing more robust with each passing day. "Take good care of that horse. Your company will do her good."

Bethany nods, accepts the round turnip, and dashes off without a coat. I nearly call out to her to come back, but she will be warm in the barn, and her dress is spun of thick wool.

John silently watches her depart, as though her presence here is as much a lifeline for him as for me. She is made from pieces of our souls, so it is no wonder we both watch her go. I feel her absence instantly. The room seems colder. Smaller. Despite the chill, our aloneness sweeps in. I step closer to my husband and kneel across from him. The washtub steams between us. His brow, damp with sweat, has taken on a healthier color in these few days.

It has been the same stretch of days that he has waited on me. He is being a gentleman, not pushing words. Not pushing anything. So it is *I* who must begin. "We only have a moment." As we both know. "So I'll speak plainly."

He wipes damp hands on the sides of his pants.

"You have come from Yuma prison?"

He lifts his chin, answering with the readiness of a man who recently stood trial. "Yes."

"How long were you there?"

"Four months."

I try to let that make sense. The last dozen letters I wrote—letters of doubt and fear and longing—he was in a prison. If only I could have known. I speak slowly to this man who has been a convict. That he may still be makes the next question difficult to voice. "You were set free?"

Something shifts through his eyes—regret and despair. That I asked such a question? Or that I have cause to? "I was released. My sentence has been served in full."

My mouth is too parched to swallow. "And what was your crime?"

Now it is his turn to swallow hard. "I was tried alongside four other men. There were several accounts of mining fraud, punishable as a felony in Arizona, which was why we were taken to Yuma. In addition, there were three accounts of murder."

He says it so matter-of-factly.

The cold of the room seeps into my bones. My fingers feel numb, this man too close. Traces of truth, of knowing him, rise in my spirit even as he presses on.

"I was not a part of the killings, June. I wasn't even in the same territory when they happened. I need you to know that. I was young and foolish when I met up with them. My cousins, that is." His wrists rest on the edge of the washtub, and it's impossible not to imagine those same wrists clapped in irons. "Among the five of us, the mines were salted, but please know that it was long before you." Years of pain dwell in his eyes. Eyes that linger on my own even as the crease in his forehead bows beneath the weight of it all. "Please believe that I had no part in those killings. It's why they didn't hang me. It took a fair deal of trial for the jury to concur."

The cold is replaced with heat, and a lightness sweeps over me. "Are you the one who salted the Kenworthy mine?" I don't realize until now that my hands have slipped into the water, where his own have returned to the sharp heat. It's as though he cannot be rid of his filth. And as though my hands long to help him. That longing is ingrained within me, serving as master over even my sensibilities. It is a master I will serve no longer.

"Juniper."

"It's a simple yes-or-no answer." I pull away, drying my fingers on the hem of my apron. The man either fired that gold-loaded shotgun inside the Kenworthy mineshaft or he didn't.

His eyes—and all that lies behind them—consider mine. Moments that bleed into the spaces between our words, a telling that there is more to this than a yes or a no. Yet he does as I wish, speaking only a single word. "Yes."

CHAPTER 26

JOHNNY

I was never much of a runner until I moved here. I much prefer the slow trek down through a desert canyon. But here there's a hundred miles of open land from one end of this mountain range to the other. A few houses speckle the landscape, and white fencing lattices the fields where horses roam. Beyond that in this high-mountain valley is just me and air and sky.

Keeping a steady pace, Rye lopes along just in front of me. There are endless places to run here, but today we chose a nearly abandoned mountain-biking trail that heads into the woods. It means being creative with my footwork over fallen limbs and gopher mounds, but for the most part, the narrow path is smooth. There isn't a pine-scented product on the market that can even touch the clearness I'm heaving into my lungs. By the time we finish the mile and a half to the end of the bike loop, it's time to turn and start back down.

There's more of a rise this time. Breaths come hard. This is tough.

197

It's a kind of tough I like because even if it beats me, I can try again tomorrow. But maybe a lot of toughs are like that. Maybe we just don't have the courage to say we failed—for now, but with the willingness to strap up the next morning.

Despite the crisp spring weather, sweat draws my T-shirt against my shoulders. It clings to my torso. I tug at the fabric, aching for water by the time I reach the farmhouse. Perspiration drips down my forehead, hitting the dirt when I bend forward to stretch. Rye ambles up to his water bowl and wolfs down huge gulps. Finished, he flops across the porch and nuzzles his face into one of my slippers. I reach him, move the slippers, and push inside. I'd give anything for a shower right now, and the new one is slated to arrive any day now. Finally.

A moderate stand-in has been a camping shower, which takes just three gallons of warm tap water to fill the rubber bladder. With soap and a towel, I head outside to where I rigged up a temporary partition, and it's another handy reason neighbors are sparse. And since three gallons flies by, I'm upstairs dressing in no time. I'm just pulling a sweatshirt down to the waistband of my jeans when my phone beeps with a new email. I've learned to keep a close eye on emails since the logistics of homeowner renovations can change by the hour, so even though it's a Saturday, I tap the icon.

But the message is not from one of my clients. It's from Sonoma Del Sol.

Our past encounter was relatively formal. This message also holds the warmth of character I have come to see in her. She's inquiring about the letters I mentioned. I type a quick response, letting her know that I'm still on the lookout for details but the offer still stands for me to get them to her at any point. I don't have to finish them first. Technically, I could have copies made of every page, but I don't know when I'll be going down to the city next, and I don't mind bookmarking my spot and sending them to Sonoma. Her use with them is more pressing, and since the history around here is so pertinent to her research, I send an invitation for her to stop by at any point if that would help.

Her response comes an hour later.

That's a really nice offer, thank you. But I would just want to make sure your wife would be okay with it. I haven't met her, though I'd like to. I just don't want to show up unannounced.

I stare at the message. My wife?

My thumb hovers over the keyboard. How to respond to that? Then it hits me. The one time Sonoma and I met in person—I wore a wedding ring. I was still a husband. A few weeks of massive change isn't something she'd have been aware of.

Oh, man. She must think I'm such a jerk.

Mortified, I'm practically sweating again as I type back. It takes about ninety-two attempts before I've pieced together a response that feels right.

That's really good of you to check. Actually, I'm recently divorced. It was finalized just a few weeks ago. Forgive me for not thinking that through and for putting you in a weird position. It's just me here, and if you're okay with that, please feel free to stop by anytime and I can show you some of the historical sites, especially the one you're looking for. If you'd like, Mrs. Hollister could come along. I'm sure she'd be thrilled. Whatever works best for you. And either way, I'm happy to get those letters your way! I could even drop them off at the historical society with Mrs. Hollister for you to pick up sometime.

After hitting Send, I tap Play on the radio. Country music fills the house as I start a pot of water for spaghetti tonight. It's really one of the few dinners I've gotten good at cooking, and while I am totally over spaghetti, it's what's on hand. I find a package of pepperoni in the back of the fridge as well as some garlic and zucchini and, after some slicing and dicing, manage to jazz up the jarred sauce. Back on the porch, plate in hand, I take a bite as the sun goes down. Rye hasn't moved from his napping spot since our run a few hours earlier.

The sky starts to burn a brilliant pink. Phone still handy, I snap a picture of it and am just saving it to a special folder for my sister when I realize the email icon is lit up again.

It's Sonoma, and for a split second I feel like I'm still married and this is wrong. Like I shouldn't just be emailing a lady. But I'm not married. It's not wrong. And somehow, stuff like this will become a new normal. Won't it? I both dread and welcome it.

For now, I barely know this gal, but I like that she's nice, easy to get along with, and cares about the history of this place. These mountains. The people whom she calls ancestors. It has me eager to read her message, and as warm a feeling is the response that's come through. That yes, she's glad to come by and check out those spots. And that if tomorrow works for me, it would be great for her.

◆　◆　◆

It's by the glow of another campfire—this one in the yard and with just one canvas chair pulled close—that I open the binder of photocopied letters again. I've read nearly every one, but half a dozen at the back lay waiting.

Maybe *they're* not waiting. Maybe it's me who has been waiting.

I kind of don't want them to end. There's something about not knowing the end of the story yet that gives me hope that perhaps, in some crazy, wild way, things worked out okay for this woman and the man who vanished from her life. I want to know if he returned. If he came back to her. And if he did . . . what did he say?

Even though the letters are duplicates, it's a habit to turn them carefully. They're the only copies I have. More could be made, of course, but I'd rather take care of these. These are the ones with my address on them, given to me by those who have the authority to do so. This album is more than just a duality of what once was. This one is different somehow. It's mine, and now I have the honor of sharing it with someone it might help even more than me.

I turn to the first of the last letters.

Dearest John,

You have been gone one hundred and fourteen days. Each and every one of those days has been wrapped in silence. How I long to begin each letter with "This is the last one I will write," but my heart still moves in my chest, my hand still knows how to hold a pen, and the dwindling pile of stationery is not yet exhausted.

So, I pen your name. The name that lives in my heart—a beating that is pain. A pulsing that is longing. And a hope that will not die.

There is so much to say. To ask you, to share. But tonight, as Bethany sleeps burrowed beneath the blankets on our bed, I cannot recall the happenings of the day or even the week. I can only recall your face, and it is such a rare remembrance that I will do all I can to hold the sight clearly until sleep forces me to forget. This is what you have done to me. This is how much I miss you, and for this night, even if only for a handful more hours, I will not be ashamed to do so.

You were worth this heartache. I need to believe tonight that you were worth it.

Yours . . . still,
Juniper

CHAPTER 27

JUNIPER

MARCH 1903

John slides his knife down the center of the hatbox lid that once hailed from San Francisco. The floral box busted out on the bottom some time ago, and now Bethany watches, spellbound. Over and over he does this, adjusting the size and curve of each shape of the cardboard cuttings until each floral piece is resting in a pile between the pair. It's a puzzle he's made for her. When he begins to reassemble it, Bethany moves in to help. Their hands work in unison as though they were never apart.

What would it be like to forgive so easily? To forgive like a child? One who keeps no record of wrongs?

I've stopped mixing cake batter to watch them. John's focused solely on his daughter. Bethany has longed for him—has prayed for him—through months of silence. This reunion is a gift to the girl like no other. I can only pray it will last. But will I, too, make peace

202

with him? Otherwise this marriage will continue on as a strained existence. One where we speak little and touch even less.

Will this be our lives from here on? John would never force anything else upon me. And for there to be change? Hurt has left its mark, and I do not know how to smooth over the gullies in my soul that his actions have left.

How is there a way out? A way forward?

I pour in butter and the golden swirls fade as I whip it in. Edie gave me a tin of candied ginger, and so I slice that into fine pieces and sprinkle them in to flavor the cakes. I'll dust them with sugar come morning so that they're good and ready for Bethany's birthday dinner. A thick stew bubbles on the stove, and there seems little else to do but to get through another night. Ever since John washed and dried the sheets, he has claimed a spot by the fire. Without a word between us, I have returned to the upstairs bedroom with Bethany. Mrs. Parson still boards with us but spends most of her time at the schoolhouse, in her room, or out in the barn where she's continued Bethany's photography lessons. When she is downstairs, it is in times when her presence is a welcome distraction for us all. She is a wise and gracious woman, and based on recent ideas she's voiced to me, she will be looking for somewhere else to board soon so that our family home can go back to its natural balance. I see the wisdom in her choice but can't help but worry what it will be like without her presence here.

A printed rose takes shape as Bethany turns a piece to nestle into another. John braces it to the floor with his thumb as she slides another into place. She searches for the next, and though it sits right before her father, he waits, watching not the piece but his daughter. He is waiting to see if she will solve the riddle. Waiting so that her determination will grow.

Is that how God is with us, His children? There to guide and direct us, but in a way that gives us the space to grow in patience? I believe so, and as I watch John challenge and even delight his daughter, it makes me long to be wrapped in the same kind of care. One that comes from the Lord on high. But these thoughts? Why do they betray me so? I should not be watching John and thinking of God. The two do not go hand in hand.

The stew is bubbling more than it should. A glance in the pot says it's about to burn. Reaching across the stove for the wooden spoon, my nervous hand grazes the side of the pot on accident. The spoon clatters back to the stove louder than my cry. I turn for a way to cool my skin, and John is already at the door, rushing down into the yard and back. He's at my side before I can think to use the water pitcher. His hand folds a mound of snow against my skin. He braces it there. The sting, his hold on my wrist, is enough that fidgeting flees from mind. Instead, I stand still as granite while pain pulses through my skin and up my arm.

The burn is numbed by the snow as my fingers become warmed by his touch. His hold is gentle but steady.

I pull away. "It's fine. Thank you." Snow melts down my wrist, tracing in a coil across his forearm.

At the washbasin, John brushes his hands clean and dries them. He says nothing as he returns to the half-finished puzzle, but the magic of their game has ended. Bethany kneels upon the seat of a chair now, watching me.

"Mama's just fine, sweet girl," I say, drying my reddened skin on my apron.

John gathers up the pieces of cardboard. Worse than the sting of the burn is seeing that they didn't finish their puzzle. The pieces remain unsolved. For another day, I hope.

With supper ready, I serve up steaming bowls. In another life, John would have blessed the food, but I do so before he can. The meal would be silent if it weren't for Bethany, who chatters away to her papa. Her sweetness softens the night, and by the time dishes are stacked and I've filled both cake tins and slid them in the oven, she's dressed for bed. Bethany sits upon John's lap, and he reads her a story from the Bible, this one of Adam naming all the animals in the Garden.

Bethany is nearly asleep by the time they finish, and he carries her up to the bed she and I now share. When he returns, his steps are slow.

"I'll check on the horse now. No need to wait up." The words, as always, are grace.

I nod, and he's gone for nearly half an hour. When he returns, the smell of baking cake belies the late hour. I didn't plan this timing very well. He doesn't seem to know what to do with himself. This is where he sleeps, on the floor near the fire. But he won't do so with me here. Neither of us will have peace until I go upstairs, but I slide the kettle from the stove, fill two tin cups, and set them on the table. This isn't a night for peace. We slide our chairs out at the same time. Sit with equal determination.

"The mine," I simply say.

His hands that have been resting in his lap grip the edge of the table. He yanks his chair farther forward. He's ready for this. Am I? "Do you want me to start at the beginning, or do you have specific questions?" he asks.

Questions have pummeled me for ages now.

Why did you bring me here? Place an ad for a wife in the newspaper all those years ago?

Why did you choose me?

And the hardest of all. *Why did you deceive me?*

But I slay them all, asking instead what is most relevant. "Why did you salt the mine?"

It's a slow bleed—the way wetness fills his eyes. He looks around the room, and I give him time to assemble his words. He speaks, and it's haunted and steady in equal measure. Like the midnight sky, pierced by countless stars and still refusing to fall. "Because it needed to be me."

Wind stirs outside, rattling the tin cans hanging from the porch eaves.

"Explain that."

The air grows sweet with rising cakes as he seems to gather his words with care. "I was young and foolish when I joined my cousins in these acts. We salted three mines together, all long before Kenworthy, and always, I was simply on watch. I've already said it, but it bears repeating: this was long before you. Long even before the dream of you." Reaching up, he unfastens his flannel collar. "Why I joined up with them is something I will always regret. I was alone in the world. My parents were gone. I was young and impetuous and seeking purpose. But it was the wrong kind of purpose." He shakes his head, frustration palpable.

I cross my ankles, too weary to sit upright and too desperate to move.

"As time went on, things quieted down. We had enough silver in our pockets from mine sales, and things settled some. I moved on. Started working at a logging company in Oregon. It was a few peaceful years. When the murders happened, I didn't know of them at first, but my name was still linked to theirs."

Rising, I step into the pantry, lift down an empty tea tin, and return to the table. The lid slides off with the clatter that is louder than the soft crinkle of newsprint as I unfold the article. "These are your cousins?" I slide it across the table to him, and John squints, seeming to glimpse this for the first time. His face is sheer agony as his eyes meet mine.

"Yes." He touches the picture of one of the men. I do not know if this man was hanged or not. "They caught up with me soon after with the law on their tails. I didn't want to join them, but June, there was a hold on me that I can't describe. One that had me looking over my shoulder at the logging camp every moment. Waiting for someone to know. For someone to see my guilt. I felt like being with them was the only way I would truly be free. I can't tell you how wrong that was."

It's so much to take in that more questions surface, but I silence them to let him speak.

"I was back in it then. Deeper than before. I didn't want to die, but inside I was already a dead man walking because I was doing the bidding of those who held power over me. I was just a shadow of a man." His hands rest on the table, only inches from my own. "When it came to the mine here in Kenworthy, yes, June. I pulled the trigger. It was me and me alone. I pulled the trigger of my own free will, and the whole town of Kenworthy came of it, and the whole town has been dying of it. Because of me. I don't have an excuse."

"And the hangings?"

"Three of them were hung for the killings that had taken place years before. At first, it looked like I might be, too, but I was spared."

My eyes are transfixed on his own.

"Because of my work at the logging camp, I had an alibi against the crimes. It's complicated, but I'll explain everything you want to know."

I don't realize I'm worrying my wedding ring around my finger until his focus steadies there. "It took some time for the law to unravel the evidence, but my old foreman from Oregon testified in court that I was on payroll and working there at the time. Had documents to prove it as well as bank deposit slips that I had signed, confirming that I couldn't have been anywhere else. My trial took four days, and for every one of those hours, I didn't know if I would see you again or not." His voice grows thick, eyes solely on me, his wife. "There's more to say, June . . ." he adds, his voice weak now. "But may I continue tomorrow?"

Tenderness presses into the edges of my soul. A softness for his beseeching. "Of course. Thank you, John, for saying what you have."

My rising is slow, and he simply watches. Watches from his chair as I pull two pans from the oven, center them on the stovetop for morning, and silently retreat upstairs. There, I curl up beside our sleeping daughter, listening to his sounds below. Of him stoking the fire. Of him sliding the bolt in the doorlatch. Of the way the boards softly creak with his quiet bootfalls until he finally stops just below. Everything goes silent, and I know he's spread out his blanket and taken to his meager bed. One he neither complains about nor lingers in after the sun. He will be up before I am, and so will begin a new day. One of me wondering how to make a soul-deep sense of him. Him likely wondering the same about me.

CHAPTER 28

JOHNNY

C hurch ends with a hymn I've never sung before: "Lead, Kindly Light." It's one of those old songs that you don't even realize exists until a worship leader places it up on the projector, finds the first notes, and the congregation lifts the words up high.

Standing in the back, I sing with the others—not loudly, granted, as my voice isn't very good. Afterward, it's handshakes and small talk with people I don't know all that well, but should. The interaction is nice. The pastor calls it fellowship. I forget how often I'm alone these days until surrounded by a church full of people. Even a small country one like this. It's good to be here.

Later, in my truck, I drive home thinking of the kids and what this week has in store. But first, Sonoma is coming by today at two o'clock. I've got just over an hour to change out of my collared shirt and grab a bite for lunch. I do both with plenty of time to spare, and she arrives shortly after, pulling in with a small, blue truck. She angles to park behind mine.

The driver's-side door opens, and her long, dark ponytail nearly touches the ground as she bends out to look at something under the truck.

I step closer. "Everything okay?"

"It's making a weird rattling noise. It didn't start until I got gas back at that station around the corner. I have no idea what's wrong. Just started out of the blue. I almost pulled over twice but figured I might as well just get here."

Kneeling, I grip the bottom edge of the driver's side and peer beneath the truck. There's a small pine branch wedged up in the axel. It must have gotten lodged there from the highway. It takes a second to wiggle it loose, but it finally snaps free. I pick up the two ends of the stick and show her.

She laughs. "How much do I owe you?"

"Repairs are on the house." I step back so she has room.

She climbs out wearing hiking boots and fitted jeans. Her T-shirt is faded and stamped with an LA Lakers logo near one shoulder. It's too tempting not to ask what she thought of the last game. Sonoma snorts as she drags a petite backpack from her truck. "I don't even want to talk about it."

"There's always next season."

She smiles, and her teeth are white against honeyed skin.

It's been so long since I've stood alone with a woman who wasn't my wife that it's hard to know just what to say. "Uh, need anything before we head out? Bottle of water?"

She pats her backpack before sliding it on. "I'm all set, thanks."

"Okay, great. I'm gonna fetch Rye, my Lab. Okay if he tags along?"

"Definitely."

She waits by her truck while I call for Rye, who comes barreling out of the house to greet Sonoma. I shut the door, and the two are already fast friends by the time I reach them. Really, my presence is superfluous at this point. Sonoma ruffles his floppy, yellow ears, and he tries to lick her face.

"He's a sweetie!" she says in dog voice, which only excites Rye further.

"He's a pain in the butt, actually. Also, he likes you more than me at this point."

She laughs as we start off toward the clearings near the farm. The bare spaces spread like patchwork, laced through with trees that might have been saplings a hundred years ago. Gravelly sand crunches beneath boot treads as we trek through this curious maze of bare earth where the buildings of Kenworthy once stood. In the hills beyond would have been miners' shanties, but I still haven't explored that way, nor have I searched out the location of the mine itself. One of these days, I'll go on that adventure, but this one is more important. It's good to know that there's time. That this land is in no rush to tell its story.

We're standing in the middle of a long, narrow clearing when Sonoma halts. "You know what puzzles me?"

"What?"

"That the town stood for nearly five years, and at one point there were *several hundred* people. Yet there is no mention anywhere of a graveyard."

"Morbid, kind of," I quip.

She smirks. "I'm saying that people would have passed away during those five years. But as far as I understand, there wasn't a town cemetery. You'd think a place with a schoolhouse, hotel, and dozens of homes would have had a cemetery."

It makes sense to see it the way she does. If genealogy is her gig, then headstones and death records would be a huge deal in figuring out family trees.

"Well, maybe . . ." I slow to a halt. "We could be standing on it right now."

We each survey the clearing around us. If crosses were made of wood, they wouldn't have lasted through the heat of California summers nor the winds of high-desert winters. After digging through her backpack, Sonoma consults a map that looks copied from one of the history books. She scans the earth around us.

I do the same. "Want a shovel?"

Her laugh sounds like it belongs here. "I think I'll pass on that one."

"Yeah, me too."

Rye sniffs at a rabbit hole and immediately starts digging downward. We holler a panicked "No!" in unison, then she melts into giggles. I'm grinning so hard my face hurts.

"How about we move on from talk of a graveyard." Her honey-hued cheeks are rosier.

"Agreed."

We walk on, but slowly. She's thinking still . . .

"Just say it," I offer.

Her eyes lift to mine amusedly. They're a dark brown with a soft slant that whispers of native blood. "It's not so much that I need to find the exact graveyard, but I'm just . . ." She turns, looking across the valley. Her eyes lift to trees, scan boulders. Finally, they land on my face, and her expression is warm. "Just thinking, I guess. Seeing if something will click into place."

I nod, though I don't fully understand. I'm more of a lines-and-numbers kind of guy. This is all harder for me to wrap my brain around, which makes it intriguing. I can practically hear the cogs moving in her mind. It's kind of cool.

We explore on, and with her gentle pace, I don't lead us far into the hills. Instead, we take our time, and it's focus she has, not hurry. I like that.

It's late in the afternoon when we finally walk back to her truck. Rye, dusty and covered in twigs and bits of dirt, canters over to the porch, where he flops beside his water bowl. Sonoma sips the last drops from a plastic bottle.

I thumb toward the house. "Lemme go grab you another one for the road."

"I appreciate it."

In the cabin, I snatch two cold bottles from the fridge and return to her truck. She's just tossing her backpack inside.

"Hopefully this has been a help somehow." Droplets slide down the plastic as I hand over the bottle.

"It's been amazing. Actually, can I show you one last thing?"

"Totally." I am in no hurry.

"Do you remember the spot just down there?" She points to where we came from, the last clearing we explored, which is just out of sight but not far from here. "I think that's where the mercantile might have once stood. And get this . . ." She tugs more historical documents from her backpack and unfolds another photograph. "This is the same one that's hanging up at the historical society. Her name was Edith Manchester. There's only a few accounts of her in the books, and they don't indicate who she married, but that she did have two children who were recorded as stillborn."

I glimpse the sorrow in Sonoma's face.

"Much of what I'm researching is that it's possible she married a Cahuilla man in secret. He's linked to my family tree, which you might recall—Santiago Del Sol. Apparently, he had a wife in Kenworthy as opposed to within the tribe. So, it's possible it was her. She was one of the last to live here, as was he, and so it makes sense."

I nod, curious.

"It's taken me nearly a year of searching, but I've unearthed two different accounts of her death. One source, an old county census, has no record of her in 1910, so she either passed away or left a few years after they were wed. Another source indicates that she didn't pass away until 1946. So, I'm not sure. My great-great-grandfather, Santiago, was married until late in his life, but was it this woman?" Sonoma scans the splayed-out documents on the hood of her truck. "Did he remarry? I've found records of two additional deaths, which might have been his children. If there are no records of a living child and a second marriage, where did my family come from? That's what has been the biggest riddle to solve." Her water bottle sits forgotten, and there's a crease to her brow that only this purpose can smooth away. "I need to do some more investigating. That seems to always be the way of it."

I debate for less than a second. "Would you still like those letters? They're from the original homesteader of the property here. It's possible she might have even interacted with this woman who worked at the mercantile. I haven't noticed any references, but you would see details I'm missing. Why don't I go grab them, and you can take them home and see what you find?"

She gapes at me.

"If you want to, that is."

"I found one letter in a book not too long ago, but there was no mention that there were more. I didn't realize these were the letters you have."

I set my water bottle beside her tire. I could invite her in to show her, but something about us being outside feels more casual. Sonoma seems most comfortable in the yard, and I mean to keep it that way for her. "The folder's back in the house. Let me go grab it." I haven't finished the final letters, but it's time they help someone else.

Hurrying inside one more time, I hustle upstairs to where the binder sits on the nightstand. I'm breathless when I reach Sonoma again, and surprisingly, it feels right to let go of the folder, placing it in her grasp instead.

"This is incredible." She shakes her head, still looking in awe. "I promise I will take such good care of it and return everything as soon as possible."

"Take your time and let me know what you find. I just hope there might be something in there that could help."

She beams at me as if hoping the same. "I promise to."

CHAPTER 29

JUNIPER

APRIL 1903

A string of cloth pennants is stretched between the young oak tree and the eaves of the front porch. Their edges are ragged, but the colorful triangles have been cut from scraps of old garments, so they're a playful display of taffy-yellow, indigo-blue, and a wash-worn violet that was once my favorite apron. Just right for a day of festivities. They catch the breeze just as much as the fringe on Edie's leather breeches. Facing out toward the open yard, Edie aims her pistol, steadying it with both hands, and pulls the trigger. A hole blasts through the center of the paper target that John nailed to a fence post. Her bullet struck just shy of dead center.

Edie swears.

I remind her that one person in our midst just turned four.

Winking over at Bethany, Edie moves out of the way so that John can help Bethany take aim next. He kneels behind her, his hand holding the gun and trigger. Bethany braces her hands around his. Her tight braids are tied with one of the same patterns of cloth as blows in the breeze behind us.

Just beyond, we've set up a makeshift table that holds a pitcher of sweet tea and the two-layered ginger cake. A stack of plates and polished forks glint in the sunlight.

Even Oliver Conrad has joined us for the festivities. His dog, Trixie, lies in the shade of the cabin's porch, far from the noise. Bethany wanted to invite the entire town so that everyone could have cake, but after explaining to her that most everyone else was gone, she agreed to the present guest list. It's the first time Mr. Conrad and John have been side by side, and while they worked together in the mine over the years, it's only fair to acknowledge that something has changed. In John's absence, Oliver kept an eye on Bethany and me from afar.

"Let me know when you think we've found the target," John says to our daughter.

Squinting one eye closed, Bethany helps him align the destination, and then she steps back and covers her ears. John glances to her, ensuring she's good and clear, then pulls the trigger one moment after he tilts it even more in line with the target.

A hole blasts into the bullseye, and Bethany cheers in her little voice. "We're winning!"

"We are indeed. But now it's Mr. Santiago's turn to go." The earrings I've worn today swing as I turn my head that way. Though made only of brass, the short dangles were for my wedding to John. There have been few instances to wear them since, and a day such as this was a welcome reason to don our finest.

Bethany clambers up onto a wooden chair, as wild as the beautiful day around her, and puts two hands on her hips to watch Edie's husband. Santiago steps from behind his wife, grazing fingertips against her lower back as he does. He accepts the revolver from Edie and, with it aimed to the ground, loads it fresh. After clicking the chamber closed, he steps ahead, sets his aim at the dying target, and fires.

A hair shy of the bullseye as well. Edie and Santiago are as good a shot as John, so their misses are for the benefit of a little girl whose birthday we're celebrating today.

Bethany clasps her hands over her mouth and erupts into giggles. She and her papa are the victors. With an air of ceremony, Mrs. Parson pins the ruffled first-place ribbon we cut from cloth to the front of Bethany's dress, announcing her the winner of the competition.

With the shoot-out now over, the men each take a few more shots just for fun. Edie does the same. There is a camaraderie about John and Santiago. I had never witnessed it before, and perhaps it's because they treated one another as near strangers. But after Santiago found John outside the prison in Yuma, their bond has not only become clearer but stronger.

"Let's see what Juniper can do," Edie calls.

I touch my hip, and it dawns on me that I stopped wearing a pistol sometime since John's return. He turns his own around, offering me the wooden handle. It's warm when I take it, and there's amusement in his eyes as he steps aside for me to stand before the target. I check and see that there are two bullets left.

Everyone is silent as I take aim, and I can feel John watching me. I pull the trigger. Two inches high of the bullseye. A poor shot considering the expertise around me, but seeing as I grew up in the city, I'm rather proud of the hit. Aiming once more, my second shot is nearly center. I smile. John's eyes are alight with pride.

"I believe Mr. Conrad should have taken a turn," I say.

The quiet miner unholsters his gun, steps clear of everyone, and raises it to eye level. The fingers I once cleaned and bound are not on his shooting hand, and from where I stand, it looks as though they have healed well. He and John have made small talk this afternoon. My prayer is that nothing inside Mr. Conrad is hurting. I don't think he would show it if it did, and so while I hope he bears no regret over John's sudden return, I cannot assume that Mr. Conrad didn't think more of me than simply a neighbor. If I have learned anything about this quiet, gentle man, it is that he is more complex than that.

Wind stirs across the short April grasses. When Mr. Conrad pulls the trigger, the center of the bullseye blasts away. Everyone cheers. Hopping down from her chair, Bethany starts to unpin her blue ribbon, but Oliver Conrad insists she keep it.

John shakes the miner's hand, and despite my worries, Mr. Conrad smiles. Mrs. Parson begins to pour glasses of dark, sweet tea while I press a knife into the cake. It's a rich amber color, and the fragrance of ginger and sugar is heavenly. As I spread out a quilt on the grass, Edie starts to sing out, "For she's a jolly good fellow . . . ," and the rest of us join in.

Bethany is pink cheeked and grinning by the time we finish, and I am thankful that my daughter has this special day. It's good to see her laugh. To watch her play. For so many to be gathered around, and most especially for her father's presence. John scoops Bethany up to his shoulders, and she eats her cake from the high-up perch. Sugar dusts the tip of her nose.

I offer him his own slice, and while he cuts into it with his fork, he doesn't lift any to his mouth. We already had a filling noon meal, and though his appetite has been steady, I've noticed him pacing himself. As though he can only stomach so much at a time, even though his body may be needing more. He'll graze on it, as I've seen him do with most of the meals he's taken. A slow regaining of strength.

He finally lifts the bite to his mouth but doesn't go in for a second.

"I've a feeling they about starved you in Yuma," Edie says. She states it matter-of-factly, as though commenting on the field a man just plowed or if he means to sell his new colt at auction.

Everyone goes still. Including Mr. Conrad.

Santiago, whose expression is always collected, slides her an apprehensive look. My breath catches. Not because she tapped into something we've spoken so little of, but because we'd been working to keep this news quiet between only ourselves. It's why we took such pains to collect any newspapers that arrived, and why I am thankful that even then, the few lingering miners don't read much.

John glances to Mr. Conrad as though to gauge whether or not he just heard what Edie said. That John had served time in Yuma. Served sentence for a crime.

Though he's off free and clear now, most folks would still imagine such a man in striped prison garb—freed or not.

Santiago clears his throat, and Edie's brown eyes widen. She's realized her blunder.

Oliver Conrad has kept his focus on his cake, neither acknowledging nor inquiring into what was just said.

John has always had a kind spot for Edie. Like an older brother who has never minded the unpredictable antics of a kid sister. He picks up his fork again and cuts another bite. "It was enough food. But the heat made it hard to stomach at times."

I can't help but glimpse Mr. Conrad again, who has observed John's absence from afar all these months. For John to have spoken of it freely, instead of tucking it under the rug, means that he either trusts this man or is willing to take the fall for his actions. I don't know why. It would be so much easier to keep it hidden away, keep it in darkness so that no other souls in Kenworthy know that a convict lives in their midst. Let alone one that is responsible for the demise of this very town.

"They . . . they say . . . ," Mr. Conrad says as he balances his dessert in dirt-creased hands, "the h-heat hits over one hundred and . . . one hundred and . . ."

John steps in to help. "Over a hundred and twenty degrees in summer."

Oliver Conrad nods. "I would l-lose my appetite too." He gives John a nod of assurance. One as filled with grace as everything else this man has done.

John claps him on the shoulder. "Then it's a good time to eat up, so I'm thankful to my wife." He nods in my direction. "And to you all for gathering today to celebrate our little girl."

Mr. Conrad holds up his glass of tea in Bethany's direction. "T-to the best shot in the W-West."

We all do the same, and Bethany takes a bow.

◆　◆　◆

Upstairs, I pull the chair away from my writing desk and sit. It's been a glorious day, and with evening harkening in, I came up for only a moment to see the sun set through my favorite window. Edie and Santiago are gone home now, and their company today was a welcome addition. After supper, Santiago and John pulled out pipes and shared a light while Edie and Mrs. Parson shared stories. The house is still warm with the memory of their laughter and fragrant with the smell of tobacco. From downstairs lift the voices of Bethany and Mrs. Parson poring over the book of paper dolls the schoolteacher gave her for her birthday.

I'm ready to be rid of this corset, but it's too early to turn in, so I ignore the sight of my nightgown draped over the desk chair. I've gotten so used to sitting at this desk, writing to John, it's strange now not to pull out a fresh sheet of paper. To dip the pen into the inkwell.

There's a soft knock, and with the door ajar, I turn to see John standing there—a hesitant look on his face. "May we speak a moment?" At my nod, he enters but doesn't come much closer. With the sun going down behind me, there's a rosy tint to the room. It lights his skin with the same tone, softening everything around us.

I'm not sure what to say, but something in particular has been on my mind all afternoon. A furrow of worry. "About what Edie said . . . ," I begin.

"Edie?" He steps closer.

"In front of Mr. Conrad."

His brow pinches then smooths as dawning comes. "I'm not worried about that."

He's not?

"I was afraid before, but I'm not now. I spent too many years being afraid. Regretting. It was too much time fearing the truth. Now the truth is out."

And paid for, though he doesn't have to say that.

He gestures to the edge of the bed. "May I?"

I motion for him to sit. Reaching across the desk, I turn the knob on the kerosene lantern, and with a lit match, it brightens the room softly. The scent of sulfur lingers as I shake out the match. This desk is the place I have penned his name with longing dozens upon dozens of times. How many nights did I peer at this dark window, hoping and praying that he would somehow be safe? That he would somehow return to us? Now he is here, in this very place.

"May I tell you something about Yuma?" His eyes search my own as though to be certain I'm comfortable in learning what he's about to say. "Perhaps it's not so different from most prisons, but it's the only one that I know." He pulls his hat off, and I notice once more the way his forehead is soft and pale. Not as weathered as the rest of him. The weathering—inside and out—has only made him more handsome. "I'd heard rumors before arriving, as all of us have, but I was not prepared. There's a reason they call it the Hell Hole. There, in the middle of the desert, the summer heat was excruciating. A gritty, red sand blows in all the time. It coats your skin endlessly. Beyond that, the rest was hopelessness."

His gaze shifts to the collar of my dress. Lace. My Sunday best.

"We were several men to a cell at times, and one chap in particular was tough to get along with. Maybe it was the heat that messes with your mind, but we came to blows at one point and were taken out for punishment." His eyes gauge my own before continuing. "I never found out where they put him, but for me, I knew they were taking me down to the basement—which I'd heard of. Below the prison there's no light. Not even a spark. It's through this room that the guards lead you to a central cage. I do not know how high it is, but when I was inside, I couldn't go more than a few paces before feeling iron again."

A cage with no light?

"They don't hang men at Yuma, June. There is no death there, only suffering. Unless someone dies from fever or is shot for trying to escape, everyone just *exists*. A slow, agonizing existence. Two of my cousins had already been transferred and executed, and I feared my time was coming next. That I'd never see you or Bethany again."

Closing his eyes, he wets his lips. A slow shake of his head.

"It felt like an eternity, and it's a darkness I will not describe to you. It's darker than even a mine. It's alone and empty. Void of hope. When I was brought back up, an old man in the cell they placed me in said it had been three days. The minutes, they had crawled on like torture. I was used to darkness because of the mine—but that was something else entirely. It crushes your spirit."

When a breeze stirs the curtain beside us, I move to close it, but he asks me not to.

"Please," he adds.

Fresh air, no matter how chilled, must be heaven-sent to him.

I return to the chair and watch the way his face now leans in the direction of the night. My gaze traces the profile I have grown to know and love. And now? Now, there is an ache in my spirit that I can hardly put name to. It lands there somewhere between loss and longing.

"I wasn't underground anymore," he continues, "but I couldn't shake the memory of that cage. I could scarcely eat and in some ways was hovering against death. I think I had begun to give up, to give in to despair, but that time in the cage also taught me something." He squares his boots, which are as roughened and dusty as my own shoes. The pair of us somehow belong here together. "It reminded me what it was like to stand there in a courtroom, awaiting my sentence with wrists handcuffed. Shamed and not able to say much about it except to answer the questions given to me." John's voice falls to a whisper now. "And I remembered the moment that the judge read my sentence and brought the gavel down . . ."

There is a look in John's eyes that says he will never forget.

"And I began to realize—to question—what I would have done if instead of bringing the hammer down on my guilt, the judge brought it down for himself. That the judge chose to take my shame—to enter the darkness and the confinement and the hopelessness of that lightless cell. On *my* behalf . . . so that I could be set free."

I've forgotten there is a whole world around us still. In this moment, I see only him.

"I slowly began to realize that it was what Christ had done for me. The Bible says 'while we were yet sinners,' and for the first time I truly understood the gravity of that and the abundance of the gift. That He took our place. Served our sentence and faced the darkness so that we wouldn't have to." John angles his face toward the window, then his eyes return to my face. Staying there. "That's when I knew that if He deemed it right for me to find my way back to you, I would do everything I could to not lose you again."

Rising, he leans forward and kisses the top of my head. The movement is so gentle—so familiar—that I don't move.

"I'm horribly sorry for the ways I snuffed out the light for you. That I wasn't open with you from the start."

Lifting my face, I see the sheen of tears that is in his eyes.

"I promised Bethany I'd read her to sleep, so I'll go fetch her and get her tucked in."

In other days, I would have joined him, but I want Bethany and her father to have the time together.

"I'll finish the dishes." I rise, and as I do, his hand squeezes mine.

Stepping from the room, it's an effort not to look back at this man who has always been a dream I don't want to wake from. A dream that I was shaken awake from with such force, I am afraid to close my eyes again. Yet he is also the same miner I once knew. The one who brought me here . . . won my heart . . . and is still battling to keep it.

CHAPTER 30

JOHNNY

Halfway out the door for a morning climb, I halt. As much at the sight of the red sports car sitting in my driveway as of the four women who are walking around the barn, some of them pausing to peer into the windows. They all have rain boots on and skinny jeans. Flatlanders—city folk. A few are huddled inside designer jackets, and I haven't seen that much artificial hair color outside of a cosmetic aisle in my life. One bright red, one bluish-black, and two bleach blonds.

"Lost?" I call, setting aside my day pack that's already loaded with gear. Eventually, I'll get better at addressing the occasional strangers that pull in here looking for the museum, but there hasn't been much cause for practice yet.

"Is this the spot for the Kenworthy Heritage Museum? We might have missed the parking lot."

I've *got* to put up a *Private Property* sign. "No, you didn't miss anything." I leave the steps to meet them in the yard. "This is the spot, but the museum's been closed for a number of years."

"Oh, no!" The redhead who spoke peers up at the cabin and pouts like Christmas just got canceled. "We used to come here as kids and thought we'd get out and see it again."

"Yeah. Sorry. It's all closed."

"Even the souvenir shop?"

Unless they want to poke around some dude's messy living room, yes. "Like I said, sorry." It takes just a minute to give directions to the smaller museum up in town where I've been a couple of times now, but while they thank me, they seem more interested in this place and the history this farm wears on every surface. Can't say I blame them.

"Is there a bathroom around here?" the blond in a plaid scarf asks. Her rain boots are doing a little dance in the dirt that says they've been on the road for quite some time.

"Uh . . . gas station is about ten minutes up the road. By the lake."

The lady blanches.

It's hard not to feel bad for them. I unclip the ring of keys from my belt. "Okay, hang on just a second."

In the cabin, I cross through to the bathroom and to the exterior door that still exists from when it was a public restroom and visitors entered from the outside. I've only opened this outer door once since moving in, so it takes a few tries to find the right key. Finally, I manage to creak the stiff door open and step out into the sunshine. I thumb into the bathroom. "There's two stalls."

All four women rush in at once. A few minutes later one of them calls out. "Are there any paper towels?"

I am not getting paid enough for this.

"Just a sec." After grabbing a roll from the kitchen, I head back out and toss it in through the open door. I don't know why they can't just use the—

"Thanks!" calls whoever caught the roll.

Their voices muffle together as they all wash hands, and while I'm trying really hard not to overhear, someone whispers, "Totally hot," and the others giggle. I sure hope they're talking about the hand dryer. Finally, they're back to their car and heading out of the driveway. I let Rye out of the house, and we head off toward the boulders behind the property.

By the time we're there and my hands are chalked, I've forgotten all about the visitors, and it's just me and the rock. Rye lies down near the manzanita bush where I anchored a leash for him. I don't make a habit of tying him up around here, but on the off chance he spots a rabbit while I'm eighteen feet up this boulder, I'd rather he not vanish.

After dipping both hands into the chalk bag at my hip again, I survey the granite slab in front of me, decide on two handholds, and grip them. I settle my left climbing shoe onto a narrow flake of rock and lift my right foot up against a slope that's bulging from the boulder just enough that I can get my balance. The ground is gone now, and I work my way higher, taking the time to decide on the best route since this is a boulder I've never climbed before. It's slow going. Climbing without a rope isn't a good time to make mistakes. If I fall, it's only a couple of meters, but it's gonna hurt, and breaking something is plenty possible.

I chalk my right hand again, then reach up as high as possible, pinching a narrow rise in the granite between two fingers. The hold is sketchy, so I don't hang out there too long. A few more moves and I'm at the top, pulling myself over the edge. Dust and rock scuff against my T-shirt and waist, but I get up relatively unscathed. Sitting, I brush at my white, chalky hands that now have a few fresh cuts on the fingertips. The skin is calloused enough that they don't sting.

Once up, there's no reason to hurry, so I soak in the view. The craggy landscape stretches out for miles, dry and arid. Closer to the farm grow dry grasses from old cattle-grazing lands, but farther back

THE GOLD IN THESE HILLS

into these hills it's dusty earth and boulders of the same pale color. Different-sized cacti jut from the hard ground here and there, but trees dot the landscape, bringing a richness that says this portion of land is more mountain than desert.

About a mile away, I can just barely make sight of the highway.

I wonder if those ladies found the other museum. Thinking back on it now, I imagine one or two of them might have been single—judging by the way they were talking in the bathroom—but it hadn't crossed my mind to even glance for rings. My mind hasn't been wired to work that way in so long, it's hard to kick-start it. I'm free to date now if I wanted, but the desire is more convoluted than it is straightforward.

Do I want to be alone for the rest of my life? Definitely not. I long for a life partner. Someone to share everything with. But my heart is still raw and far from healed. Even more than that, it's intimidating to think that the chance for marriage could ever come along again. Do people love more than once? Truly love and be loved in return? I don't know. Part of me doesn't want to find out that the answer could be no . . . but it could also be yes.

While I don't imagine one has to be fully healed to begin dating again, well, I guess I will know when the time is right to think about trying. It's a weird thought—getting back out there. I'm kind of cringing at the idea, but a strange sense of comfort eases that away when I think on someone I know.

Sonoma.

Not that I'm suddenly trying to date her or that she would be remotely interested in dating me. It's because she's been kind and is so comfortable to be around and talk to. I hope the search for a potential wife could look something like that.

A lizard darts from behind a bush, but while Rye lifts his head to watch, the dog stays where he's parked and doesn't fight the leash. It's a reminder for me to do the same. So many times, I want to chase after what might be coming. Or what I fear I'll lose. There's something about a guy being single that reminds him of the chase. Yet there are also times to be still. To wait and watch and even grow. I'll be the first to admit that patience straight up scares me. For most of my life, I haven't wanted to lean into God's timing. Instead, I've just worked hard to make things happen. Dating Emily was like that. Starting my own construction company. Even buying this property. I plowed forward and trusted that I'd figure out how to land on my feet.

But something about this piece of my future feels different. It feels like if I rush ahead and try to force something, I'm going to end up doing more damage than good. And when I think of Sonoma—whether it's being friends or the possibility of something more—it's not a price I want to risk. I like knowing her, and if it means moving forward with great patience, then that's what I'm going to do.

I'll need some help from God for that. Truth be told, I'll need a heck of a lot of help. Because life is very possible to turn out differently than I imagined. It's one of the lessons I've come to learn lately. I can try to envision how I think things could unfold, but unexpected twists and turns weave a different kind of outcome. But the twists aren't unexpected to God, and there's assurance in that.

Seeing as He hasn't failed me yet, can I believe that He won't start now?

It's shocking, sitting here on the edge of this boulder, far from the home I once shared with Emily, to think of our divorce as yet one more piece of life where God hasn't failed me. While I don't know yet the purpose behind it, I want to trust that time will eventually tell. It's kind of scary to look around, to see so many unknowns, and not to know the plan. Kind of like scaling this boulder. Each hold took time and patience. I didn't yet know where the next hold would land, but with some time and diligence, I get to testify that the top has a pretty incredible view.

CHAPTER 31

JUNIPER

APRIL 1903

The cold of night seeps through the cabin walls as though the dense log walls are mere twigs. Tugging the patched quilt tighter, I nestle deeper into the mattress, nearer to Bethany. The warmth of the stove isn't enough to stem the night's bite, and I don't want to traipse downstairs and risk waking John to stoke it. He's tended it of late but must be deep asleep. I'm grateful he's at peace this night. I snuggle deeper beneath the blanket, longing for the same. In this sleepy state—the place where my guard is down and my heart is unfiltered by practicality—there's a renewed sense of comfort that John is near. With that, I finally drift into a sweet, sleepy haze.

I awake to darkness and a banging at the door. The fog of drowsiness is blown to bits when the knocking pounds again. After reaching for my robe, I stumble down the stairs.

John's already at the door. "Who is it?" he calls as I push aside the curtain.

"Beg pardon, sir," comes a young man's trembling voice through the door. The soul on the other side sounds nigh unto frozen. "The shopkeeper missus sent me over to fetch ya. The men are making camp. Just pulled in, we did, and they's all right famished."

His muffled voice grows clearer as John opens the door. I move in beside him.

The lad shivers as he speaks. John reaches out to beckon him inside, but he shakes his head. "I best be off again, but came to tell ya that we ain't had a proper meal since dawn, and even that was cold."

The cabin is too dim for me to glimpse the clock on the mantel. It must be near midnight if not later. With the cookhouse locked, they would have no way to pilfer for supper even if they wanted to. "Of course." Simply speaking helps shake the last traces of sleep. "I'll be right over. Please tell your men that supper is on the way."

"We thank you, ma'am."

After closing the door, I hurry upstairs. Mrs. Parson is on the landing, holding a candle.

"All is well," I say at the top. "We'll go over now. Would you mind looking after Bethany? It's possible we won't be back by sunrise."

"Not at all."

In the bedroom, I pull my woolen skirt over my nightgown. As I button up a flannel blouse, the silence in the house is softly broken by John tending the fire. It's a cold night. No snowfall tonight, but the chill is sharp. I wrap a shawl around my shoulders, tucking it in the waistband of my skirt on the stairs. Below, I reach for John's old coat when I realize that he needs it more.

He catches my hesitation. "Take it, please." He sinks into a chair to pull on his boots.

"No. It's yours."

"It's a cold night, June. Please put it on." Rising, he pulls the coat down. Holds it open. Hungry men are waiting, so I slide my arms into the sleeves. The comforting weight of it settles around my shoulders as he offers it in full.

He doesn't speak until I've fastened every button. "May I accompany you?"

"Into the night?" He has no coat . . .

"If you'll allow me. I can carry the lantern. Help get that fire lit. Whatever else you might need."

A second effort at protesting churns within, but it is silenced as the first. The night is dark as tar, and the cookhouse stove will take coaxing to produce warmth. Have I even laid in enough kindling yet?

"Should I bring some wood?" he asks before I've even agreed.

"Please." It's easier to speak than *thank you*.

John disappears into the night. Despite all the pain of the last year, I pray his two layers of plaid shirts will be enough.

An empty tin can serves as a way to lift ash from the stove and layer it inside. Several hot coals come next, and I nestle them carefully before banking them with more ash. The tin warms in my hand as I join John in the yard. He's bracing a mammoth amount of wood against his chest. His strength is weak yet, but I say nothing.

"I'll need you to hold the lantern," he says, steadiness in the words belying his condition.

"Of course." I take it from the porch railing, and we start off together, him with his heavy burden, me with the clutch of warmth in my hand. The contrast seems unfair.

We walk quickly, and if his breathing grows labored, I hear only my own. The snow—this deep in the night—is frozen stiff, making the descent toward town easier.

I see nothing beyond our reach of light, until all around the night quakes with the rattle of wagons ambling on the rutted roads. Lanterns bob and horses whinny. Men call orders to one another— all under a moon that glows cold and white. Kenworthy is a loud, jostling ruckus. A memory of what it once was. I step aside for a horse and wagon, bringing me closer to John, who has matched his pace to my own.

Here in this land we are the few who have kept asylum in Kenworthy, and now these men seek the same. Men uprooted from their lives to further unroot our own.

I unlock the cookhouse door as John deposits wood beside it. Inside is black as pitch, and the lantern chases away shadows. John joins me at the stove, using a hatchet to split a soft piece of spruce into splinters that will catch quickly on the coals I sprinkle inside the iron grate. Kneeling there, he tends the flame, and I try not to think of how cold he must be, his breath fogging by lantern light in this icy building. My body, tucked within his coat, is warming further with each task.

Before I've even set water to boil, the men are pushing their way inside. At their lead is a tall, wiry miner who pulls off his Stetson so that he can stretch to his full height beneath the low ceiling.

His sober eyes are fixed on me in confidence, but his words are respectful. "Our apologies, ma'am. We've put you out with the odd hour." He addresses John next with a nod of comradery.

"Do not think of it." An earthenware bowl clangs as I set it into place. "You've all arrived safely, and that's what matters. I'll have hot coffee real quick. Biscuits on the way as well." Fixings that can be prepared on the spot, which is what these men need.

"We thank you, ma'am." He shoos out those who have followed him inside and barks orders to several who are leading a team of wagons to the wrong side of the town center. Men pass by the door, some casting me curious glances. In the dark, they are little less than shapes of men, of glistening eyes in the moonlight and weary footsteps.

After grinding the coffee and filling the percolator, I place the enamel pot to boil. The stove is roaring now. Flames crackle and pop, lending the spread of heat. John moves benches around so that they edge the tables at easy angles. My heart warms with gratitude, but there is no time to thank him as we hurry about.

At the flour barrel, I scoop out no less than six cups. After surveying more men unloading supplies into the nearby bunkhouses, I add two more scoops for good measure. I'll mix up a gravy as well. I've bacon grease that can give it enough flavor to pass as supper. It will be more pallid than I would have planned for, but it will be hot and filling.

There is no room for apologies or excuses in a mining camp. Men are here to work, and they're promised a meal, which is my task and mine alone. Though . . . John's quiet presence somehow alters the ownership. The burden.

After mixing dough and rolling it in a rush, I cut quick rounds with a clean tin can. Turning for a second baking sheet, I bump into John. He steadies me with a grip to each arm. His expression, which has been unflinching since his return, is suddenly as vulnerable as the day we first met. He releases me, stepping away, and I take care not to turn so fast, lest that happen again. I'm glad I couldn't see what my own expression was like. Probably not all that different than when I first saw him as well.

The ruckus of men continues from the dark of night. While the first biscuits bake, I scoop the rendered bacon grease into a second skillet and stir in flour as the makings of a gravy. The percolator bubbles and steams, filling the air with the smells of home. Men pass by the door more slowly now. Some have gathered just beyond. They linger in the traces of light spilling forth, and in the curious looks they cast, I see that their eyes are hungry.

"Please come in if you wish," I call to them. "It's warmer inside."

No one moves. Men stay close to their belongings, their horses. Not sure how to set them at ease, I grab a dented tray and splay out as many tin cups as can be filled. I can only take out trays of coffee and hope that it begins to warm them. I'll need to make another pot right away, but at least they'll have something to heat and nourish them while the biscuits finish and the gravy thickens.

Tray in hand, I step out the door, harnessing more courage than

I feel within. John lights a second lantern, hanging it just outside, beneath the rooftop eaves, and while our daughter slumbers back home, we serve coffee to road-weary men by its light. They accept the offering with gratitude. Humble nods and "Much obliged, ma'am" are what I gain in return, and it is strangely fortifying. More nourishing to my soul than the peace of sleep could be this night.

Maybe there is cause for this that goes beyond what I see. Is this how God tends to us? To me? A soul seeking refuge in the bleak hours before dawn. For so long I have doubted God's purpose here. That God brought my husband home to me, but in a way I did not ask for. With a past that I did not ask for. Do I stand outside the door of warmth and provision, unsure how to move forward? Unsure how to accept?

I glance at John—considering what we have lost—but his humble presence continues to patch some of the pain, filling emptiness with something warmer. I do not deserve it. Not with the pain I have harbored in my chest, letting it block out the light.

For the first time since John arrived, I wish it was only him and me standing here so that I could speak these words. I wish that I could speak them up to the heavens, more so.

But we must keep moving. Men begin to come indoors. One or two strike up a conversation. A few hold their hands out closer to the stove's warmth. I dish up plates of food as quickly as possible while John works tirelessly at my side. As I hurry from man to man, stepping in and out of the cookhouse with plates and the steaming coffeepot, I can see in these miners' faces that they are receiving a patching-up all their own. I see in John's face a care and intentionality that speaks how much he knows of what they have endured to journey here to this mountaintop. He knows as much and more.

The sun is nearly risen by the time each of them are fed and the dishes have been washed. I don't know how many hours we've been on our feet, but if we don't get some sleep now, there will be no one to feed the workers come their first workday. In the now-empty cook-house, John is just reaching for his coat, handing it to me, when I finally brave what needs to be said.

I speak his name, and it is enough for him to still. He grips the leather coat, and it is I who needs to bridge the gap now for him. It is I who needs to forgive, who needs to humble my own pride—my own anger—and to acknowledge this man's sacrifice. But forgiveness is not what I offer. I offer something we both need so much more.

"Will you forgive *me*, John?" I say, and the breeze doesn't steal it away this time. I speak the words as much to my husband as I do to God. "For so many months I prayed for your return—for your safety. But when it came to truly facing what that entailed, of my purpose as your wife, I grew faint of heart. I have always loved you. I just haven't known how to tell it to you."

John nears me in long strides, and his answer is not one that he speaks.

Instead, he kisses me.

He kisses me, and it's memory. It is the way I have known him a thousand moments in my heart. In the hours I once shared with him. Knit to his side as two souls, two lives, learning how to make a new one. It's a gift being reborn inside me, and I realize I had forgotten such tenderness. Because now it is not memory—faded and grayed. Now it is real.

I open my eyes to the blue of his shirt where it draws tight against his shoulder. The glisten of his cheeks as the sun rises through the eastern window. The brush of his beard and the strength and deter-mination in his hands. All those months of heartache grate a rawness across my spirit, and yet this moment . . . one that is not memory . . . smooths the valleys over, binds them up, and brings the rest of my heart back to life. And what rises, even more than longing and the sacredness of his touch, is in knowing, in *feeling*, that he's kissing me from the same summit of hurt and healing.

CHAPTER 32

JOHNNY

H ave the doctors scheduled it yet?" I ask Emily through the phone.

"For four o'clock." Her voice is calm on the other end.

I set my cell on the windowsill, tap the speaker icon so it's not as though she's so close. There's something very memorable about the sound of her voice against my ear. With the phone now wedged against a wilted cactus in a cheap dollar-store pot, it's not so personal.

She called moments ago to explain that the doctors have arranged for her to deliver by C-section the following evening due to low amniotic fluid around the baby. She'll go in tonight for monitoring until then. Everything about this conversation is at once numbing and newly familiar. There's no other way but to have it and to keep pressing forward.

"When do you want me to get the kids?" I ask. "I can come and pick them up."

238

"Is noon too early? That will give me time to rest, and I still need to finish packing."

"Yeah." I check my watch—10:13 a.m. "I'll be there in a bit." I will watch our children. And she will have Austin's baby. "How are the kids doing?"

"They're excited to meet the new baby."

I swallow hard and decide to ignore the onslaught of emotions on that one. "I'm sure they are. Okay." I clear my throat, needing this call to come to an end. "I'll head off here within the hour to be there when you need. And I can keep the kids for however long until you're ready for them again."

"Thanks, Johnny."

I can't say "You're welcome"—or anything, actually—so I just nod even though she won't see. When she hangs up, the rest of the morning still feels like a fog.

On schedule, I pick the kids up.

On schedule, Emily goes to the hospital.

And all else happens as smoothly as the sun changes places with the moon. It's later that evening and the kids are in the back seat, asleep with empty milkshake cups in their car-seat holders, when the first update is texted through. It's a number I don't recognize, so it's gotta be Austin. I don't have the courage to look until my truck is parked in front of the cabin. Crickets chirp outside, and Rye is at the cabin window, nose fogging against the glass. It's then, and finally then, that I open the message from Austin.

Em wanted the kids to have a picture tonight.

The image loads next, and on the screen is Emily in her hospital gown, holding a cup of some kind of juice. Her hair is French braided, and she's traded her contacts for a pair of thin-framed glasses. Though she looks tired, she's flashing a thumbs-up and a cheery smile that I know is for the kids. A monitor is strapped around her belly, and in the background, a nurse is doing something to an IV bag.

I stare at the image. How to text back? How to get these fingers to work? I blink quickly and in my mind hear her voice from a century ago. A voice that met with heartache and spoke grace into the empty unknown.

Dearest John.

You find the words because you have to.

I manage to type to the father of this coming baby.

I'll show them. They'll be glad to know their mom is doing well.

I mean it too. The kids stir awake as I unfasten them each from their car seats. Micaela manages to walk sleepily toward the house while Cameron rests his head against my shoulder. Inside, we do jammies and teeth.

Once they're each settled in their new beds, I perch on the end of Micaela's mattress. "So, Baby is on the way tomorrow, and your mom is doing really good."

Her eyes grow wider. It's the excitement of a girl who loves dolls and life and her mother. This baby will encapsulate all three joys for her. It's with eager fingers that Micaela accepts my phone and peers down at the picture of her mom.

Cameron hops out of bed to peek at the screen. "Hi, Mommy!" He kisses the picture then leans into me for a sleepy hug. I squeeze him tight and ruffle his hair before he clambers back into his toddler bed.

Micaela settles in against her pink pillowcase, staring at the image fondly. I give her some time with it, answering her questions about how babies handle their first few nights. "She'll probably spend a lot of time sleeping, and your mom will too. When they're home from the hospital, you can be an extra-big girl and help out."

She nods and offers my phone back.

"Thatta girl." I kiss the top of her head, rise, and dim the light.

After cracking their door, I step into my room and, with enough of a glow from the moon, cross over the old floorboards, over the history of this place, and take a knee in front of the nightstand. There, I slide open the drawer and dig toward the back where a forgotten bottle of painkillers sits. It rattles gently on the way back down to the kitchen. The childproof lid isn't hard to wrangle off, and I sprinkle two pills onto the counter then grab a bottle of water.

Somewhere out there Emily and Austin are bringing a new life into this world.

And I'm still trying to reckon with why it hurts. And for how long . . .

Maybe it's always going to hurt. Maybe it just slowly begins to hurt less. Is that how grief eventually takes its shape into finding wholeness again?

I place both pills into my palm. I told myself I wouldn't do this if the kids were around, and conveniently, it slipped my mind until now. If the kids need me, I need to be alert. Blowing out a sigh, I slide the two pills back into the bottle with the others.

The bathroom is freezing when I enter and flip on the light. It takes just a second to shake everything into a toilet bowl and flush it all down. The Rx bottle empty now, I pitch it into the can and hit the light off. No sense in postponing a possibility that's really not going to get me anywhere good. Life is marching on in new ways, no matter how much I wish it wasn't.

I sink onto the couch and rub a hand down my face. Rye hops onto the cushions beside me, using my leg as a pillow. The night is young still, only seven o'clock. I'm not in the mood to go to bed yet and don't feel like TV. I could call my sister or a buddy—but on a crazy whim think about shooting off a text to Sonoma. I don't want to be reactionary, though. Or desperate. But just like with the kids, this has been a bright spot, so I roll with it.

How's the research?

I check the spelling and hit Send. She sends a message back right away.

Interesting! Would now be an okay time to talk?

The words are just the warmth I needed, but I force myself to play it cool for five entire minutes before calling her up. She answers on the second ring and, to my relief, jumps right in before I need to explain about why I texted her out of the blue.

"These letters have been amazing," she says.

I smile. "What have you discovered?"

"Well, I've noticed a few things. First, as you know, there are no references to whether Edith Manchester was actually Edith Del Sol. But there are other clues that indicate this woman *is* part of my family tree."

"Yeah? Tell me." I want her to keep talking for as long as she wants. Settling more comfortably into the sofa, I close my eyes and just listen. Not because I have the hots for her—I mean, she is pretty and super cool—but because of her energy and life. There's something really nice about it. Something comforting. Especially lately.

"Okay." There's a smile in her voice, and I wonder if it's the same for her. If it's nice to just have someone to talk to tonight. Regardless of where we've been or where we're going, we have this in common. This place and this time and the history that came before it all.

"In the letters there is an early reference to Señor Tiago, who, if you remember, is Santiago Del Sol. Juniper Cohen was telling John about the final few who remained at Kenworthy in the winter of 1902. It was only a few people at that point." Her voice goes quiet, and I wait. "This would have been a more formal way to address him, if that makes sense."

It does.

"Then, in a later letter, there is one more reference of him, but this time she calls him Santiago."

"Oh, yeah, I remember that one. She wrote to John to tell him that Santiago had disappeared just as he had." That letter was a sad one.

"Well, did you notice the change in names?"

"Yeah," I say even though I didn't.

She laughs because it's obvious that I hadn't picked up on the switch. "Well, that might be a clue. See, it changed over the course of what looks like . . ." She goes quiet again, and I hear the shifting of the plastic-protected letters. "About a month's time."

"Okay . . ." I'm not fully getting it.

"That means something changed."

"What is it?"

"Well, I'm not certain yet. So I need to keep thinking on it. Maybe Juniper began to know him more. It almost seems like a familiarity. Or kindredness. If Edie and Santiago were already wed, it could have to do with the fact that Juniper was more at ease. It's hard to say, though."

I smile because that means she's filling me in on her process even though it's incomplete. It's a nice place to be—here, as her friend and confidant with this mystery.

I don't realize I'm quiet until she speaks up. "I'm sorry, I probably just totally wasted your time. Calling to tell you a half-baked idea."

"It's more than half baked. And besides, I called you."

Her laugh is soft.

"Anything else? I'm curious, so don't feel like you have to worry. I'm genuinely interested to know more."

Giving her the space to do so opens up an all-new door of intrigue. The hour stretches on as she explains about the marriage practices of the Cahuilla back then. Not only was Sonoma's great-great-grandfather Cahuilla, but he was a part of the Coyote moiety, which she explains is sort of like a clan. As she speaks, I glean that there were two separate clans within the tribe. The Coyotes and the Wildcats, and that in order to marry, a man's father would arrange it with the woman's father, so long as they were not from the same group.

"That's really something," I say when she finishes.

"It is. And it means that if Santiago did indeed make Edith Manchester his wife, he would have not only defied his father's way of doing things but that of his entire tribe."

I think I get what she's hinting at. It's something he would have had to do for love. To defy one's heritage and family? That's no small thing. "If it turns out that he did marry this woman, and that they did have a child, then you are from that line."

"Exactly."

I don't know much about Native American culture, but I've always assumed it's kind of more prestigious to have a higher amount of native blood. Sort of a status. It even counts on things like college grants and such. When I voice this, I can practically sense her nodding on the other side of the line.

"It's true. We're proud of our heritage and in being Cahuilla. For me, this would answer whether I have some Northern Europe blood in me, likely English since Edith's maiden name was Manchester. I don't yet know."

"And what are you leaning toward?"

"It's hard to say, but I can't help but be intrigued by this woman. If Santiago married a Cahuilla woman instead, there are no records of it. Native American names were altered and changed so often in those days that it's incredibly difficult to track down a lineage. So, there's a gap there as well. One that keeps the questions going."

"And with Edith?"

"There's something about her that I can't quite put my finger on. The way she is somehow connected and yet so impossible to trace. I feel crazy even just saying it because the data on her is so sparse. But the timing of her presence in Kenworthy during the late 1890s and even after suggests that she was one of the few available white women in the area. And my family has always sensed we weren't full-blooded Cahuilla but haven't quite been able to pin down the why."

I think of Sonoma's picture on the flyer and how her coloring is just a shade fairer than that of the other speakers. "So, you're hoping she might finish off your family tree?" That would mean Sonoma has less Cahuilla blood in her and not more. I want to understand this.

"I think so." Her sigh is wistful. "I'll try to explain that more, but I just realized it's getting late. I've been keeping you so long already."

No sense in making her feel pressured. "No worries. It's been nice talking to you. Thanks for telling me all about this, and I definitely want to know more as it comes to you. I'll try to see if there's anything I can add to the riddle. Maybe I'll hike back out there again and see if any inspiration strikes."

She laughs, and I'm glad she didn't take it too seriously. "That's a deal."

"And also, good luck with the event that's coming up. I saw you're going to be one of the speakers at the big museum opening down in Palm Springs."

"Oh, yeah. I'm kind of nervous about that. Public speaking is not my thing."

"You'll do great. It's clear that this history is your thing. And that kind of passion is hard to contain. You'll do wonderfully."

"That's nice of you."

I've been thinking about going, but it feels weird to just blurt that out. Maybe I'll bring it up if we talk again. I hope we do.

Not wanting to hold her on the line too long, or make her feel shy, I end with, "Have a good night, Sonoma."

"You too, Johnny."

JOHN COHEN

September 1903

I dreamt last night that it was not Santiago who tried to stop us from salting the mine. I dreamt that it was myself. That it was others who were bent on the destructive, selfish deed. That it was I who stood in the way, willing to risk my life for justice. When I awoke, I remembered it only for what it was. That was the reality. Not the dream.

This morning I hiked up to the ridge, needing to see as much sky as possible. There, the world was blue above and green below. We cannot see the ranches from home, but I know Santiago is there each and every day, raising horses, training them. He is a noble soul for the task. This man who walked all the way to Yuma in the deep of winter, scooped me up off the side of the road where I had collapsed only days after being released, and brought me home.

I wish the dream had been true. That I had the courage he had.

But maybe God is growing it in me. Maybe it is growing day by day.

I don't even know why I'm writing these words. They have to go. Another page that will need to be torn out. Not for me. I've already faced my shame, already served the sentence. But for my family. For this place. I do not want my sins to be their legacy. God, set them free of it. Set me free as well.

John

CHAPTER 33

JUNIPER

APRIL 1903

The hotel roof is half bare, wilting like the side of a cliff on the coast. It stands pathetically now beneath a robin's-egg sky where men dismantle it piece by piece. Boards are loosened as workers straddle rafter beams. The wood that splinters is tossed aside to be used elsewhere, but what comes down whole is loaded onto wagon beds to be carted away. She is weeping, the Hotel Corona. Her once pristine form bowed beneath the loss of her dignity. It is a sweeping loss as I watch it through the cookhouse window. Edie works quietly beside me, adding roughly chopped onions to a pot of beans. Her belly is at its fullest now—and she pauses to press a hand to her lower back. The baby will come any time now. I stir the mixture so as to remember my purpose here. It is not to watch this grinding machine of men and crowbars as our town nearly ceases to exist.

John is among those on the roofline where he straddles the ridge. He and another man lower down a board to waiting hands below.

They work well as a team. Over the course of the morning, I've witnessed John receive instruction twice as often as he issues it. He has always been a quiet leader that way. Willing to do the hard work—able to communicate his way of seeing things only when needed. He is a miner by trade, but at his heart he is a builder. Having helped construct this hotel with his own two hands, I wonder if he, too, is weeping inside.

It's hard to see him perched so dangerously, laboring beside men who are getting paid, unlike himself. Yet he's worked since they arrived, and I doubt he will stop. Having been behind bars for months, perhaps the busyness of hands eases mind as much as it does soul. Or is it a burden that he bears? Of knowing that by his own trigger pull, this town was dead in the water before it even came alive. It is a secret he bears inside as he lowers another board. It's a secret he carries as the men around him do not know what fated this town to wreckage.

He worked in the mine every single day, laboring from sunup until sundown, all the while knowing there was no gold. I now know why his quest was so extreme. It wasn't greed that had fueled him but something as hard to wrangle. Is it still shame that keeps him going from dawn until dusk? A man doesn't come home to his wife and child with a face so covered in grime he's barely recognizable, nor dip bleeding, split hands into a basin of water each nightfall, for lack of caring. If anyone wanted to find gold in that mine, it was John Cohen. I cannot imagine the agony to plague him in knowing more than anyone else in the earth's depths that there would be none. What a hellish existence, fragmented only by the light of possibility that would have dimmed with time.

We did not speak of faith often, he and I. We attended church during the short time there was service, but neither of us pulled the Bible down from its shelf unless it was a Sunday. How I wish it had been different. That it could even be different now . . . now that I sense something new about him. The same newness I long for within. A fervor for the hope and freedom we've been granted.

"Biscuits are about to burn, June."

I startle at the sound of Edie's voice, which is silly since she's been up since dawn, helping me. Dear girl. She bustles to the stove, grabs a rag, and opens the iron door to slide out the pan. Culinary arts are not her specialty, and yet she has patiently observed how to prepare a meal. This woman has blossomed in the wake of so much. As I watch her hum quietly while sprinkling sugar on top of the next biscuits—her idea, not mine—I smile and know that it is not she who is learning from me. It is I who am learning from her.

Today she wears a wool skirt of dark evergreen. I didn't even know Edie owned a skirt, but now that her belly has grown full and low, she's declared it one of the most comfortable garments she's ever worn. The leather belt slashed low around her hips leaves a place for her pistol to reside in its holster. With no men inside, she's tucked the skirt hem up into the waistband. Her slender legs, clad in gray long johns, peek out each time she crosses the cookhouse floor.

With it an hour shy of noon, the dinner bell is poised to be rung as soon as the beans finish softening. Beef-and-barley stew simmers on the back of the stove in the largest pot the cookhouse has to offer. Edie slides the last of the biscuits into the oven, and I turn my attention to opening a dozen jars of stewed apples, tucking the sweet contents into a pan so as to layer on a sweet, crumble topping. A treat for the men.

The song Edie has been humming is a hymn.

Wind stirs across the land, stealing two hats along the way, as well as an oilcloth tarp. Men scramble to gather up the chaos even as the others climb down from the roofline, beckoned by hunger. In short time, I ring the bell, and it chimes like a church song, twining in melody with Edie's voice. There is peace here as I lay plates and watch as some of the men say grace to themselves. Dirt-creased brows bow over hot meals. Eyes close in silent reverence.

THE GOLD IN THESE HILLS

John is among their numbers, his own head bowed, scuffed hands loose in his lap.

Edie arches her back in the corner of the room, looking uncomfortable. She should rest, and it's a relief when she tucks into a corner bench while I serve up more stew into tin bowls. It's a dance here in the cookhouse, my skirts swaying from table to table as I make sure no bowl goes empty until its owner leans back, insisting. For some of the men, it takes three ladlesful. Others, four. The cookpot is about to echo empty. Seeing it, John stops me after his second serving. I offer him another hot biscuit and then heft the empty pot outside to the pump for rinsing.

The cookhouse is vacant again when I return. Edie still rests in the corner with her eyes closed, and I take care to work with quiet. Wind drifts in through the window, lifting the strands of whiskey-red hair that have come loose from her braid. A pale hand rests atop her belly.

Tables sit askew—laden with crumbs and drippings of broth. It will take some time to clean, but I enjoy this purpose.

From her spot, Edie speaks softly. "June." Her voice is weighted.

"I can finish. You sit and rest."

She shakes her head. "I don't want to rest." A tear has slid down the side of her face.

At the hush in her voice, I come around to where she is slouching now. Her grip on the windowsill is tight.

I have never seen Edie Manchester so still in these five years, and now two more tears streak down. She wipes them away and dries them on the side of her skirt. "I haven't felt the baby in a while, June."

"How long has it been?" I force calm into my voice.

"Days. Maybe three or four." She breathes out slowly through her nose that is freckled now that skies have been brighter. Her slender hand circles her belly protectively. My hand follows her. Eyes closed, I try to feel, to sense.

"Wiggled like an octopus on Saturday. Or was it Friday?" Her eyes are still closed as she slowly shakes her head. "Then just went still."

"Does Santiago know?"

Another shake of her head. "I haven't had the courage to speak of it."

"Edie." I say it with as much steadiness as I can. This young bird. This sweet girl. "I am going to go fetch your husband because we need some help. Do you understand?"

She nods, eyes still pinched tight.

"Will you lie down and rest?"

Edie shakes her head.

"I'm gonna have to insist that you lie down."

Another shake. This one more urgent. "I can't. When I do . . . When I lie there at night. I can feel that she's gone."

She.

The splintering is shattering into me.

"She's gone, June. The baby's gone. There's no other explanation."

"Edie." I grip her hand tight, turning her so that she faces me some. "Let's get you home, and we're going to summon help." I can send John for the Cahuilla housekeeper who helped Edie these months past. We will need her wisdom.

Finally, Edie nods, and with my arm around her, I slowly usher mama and baby toward the mercantile, where I settle Edie down on her bed, pull a quilt up snug around them, and pray like I have never prayed before.

CHAPTER 34

JOHNNY

Willy Wonka and the Chocolate Factory flashes across my laptop screen that's balanced between the kids on the couch, snuggled under a shared blanket. I pass over bowls of sliced strawberries and whipped cream. The kids are entranced as they accept them. I don't usually park them in front of a movie like this, not when my time with them is so precious, but we've all been restless as we await word that Emily is safe through surgery and that the baby is born and healthy.

I'm just not in the mood for puzzles and laughter tonight, so I cued up a movie and loaded up a third bowl of strawberries for myself. I hate heartbreak. I don't mean to sound like a wimp, but there's a reason that most of the songs on the radio talk about love and loss. It's what we as humans must endure in this life. To love . . . and, at times, to lose. The last time I felt the weight of it, I was about five minutes shy of that icy curve on the highway. The one where I rolled my truck and found myself strapped to a gurney. I want tonight to be different.

So a movie and treat are a better trade. God's teaching me, I guess. Hopefully even growing me to endure the pain and to step into it with courage, instead of running from it. The thing is that the hurting doesn't change. It's just as present one way or another. But to no longer be thrashing against it?

There's something freeing about it.

My watch beeps half past six. Is Emily done? Is everyone safe and well?

The text comes in three minutes later from Austin's number again. It's a picture of a small infant wearing a pink cap, all round cheeked and sleepy.

8 pounds 13 ounces. 21 inches long. Mom and baby are
     doing great.

I reach for the remote. Tap Pause. "Hey, guys. The baby's here."

You say it because you have to.

I lower the phone so that they can see their new sister.

You do it because you must.

Like walking through a desert. One foot in front of the other even though the challenge seems endless. You just do it.

The kids gasp and ogle their new sibling, and I give them all the time they need with the image. I do my best to answer their questions about when their mom and the baby will be able to come home.

Dang it, this desert's dry. *Keep walking, Johnny.*

It's healthier to think of what we do have instead of what we don't. I have two beautiful, incredible children. I've had a good life. I have friends and family that mean the world to me. I live in a place where the scent of pine and the sun on mountains greets me in the mornings. I have air in my lungs and hope in my soul, and so I swipe at the tears forming in my eyes before the kids can notice.

Micaela is clutching my phone still, admiring the little girl.

"She's beautiful," I whisper and kiss her cheek.

Grinning, Micaela curls up on the couch, still holding the lit-up screen. I don't slip it from her hands until the credits are rolling and she's fast asleep. Cameron's out too. I turn off the movie, gather up bowls, and dim the kitchen light. Not wanting the kids to sleep down here alone, I grab a blanket from upstairs then stretch out on the floor.

It seems like forever until I'm asleep, and the few hours of unconsciousness are hardly enough when I feel a little hand shaking my arm again. Cameron's wide awake and asking if we can have cereal. After swiping at my eyes, I sit up. "Yeah, bud. Just give me a second, and we'll eat." I tousle his blond hair. Last week I taught Micaela how to switch on the coffeepot, so she runs to do it for me. Next, she grabs cream from the fridge and sets it on the counter.

I touch the side of her head as I reach for a mug. "Thank you, sweetie."

The machine trickles to life, and soon the scent of coffee is as inviting as the glow of morning through the window. It's a good day to keep busy. It's a good day to enjoy. The kids and I do just that as I wait for further word. It comes in spurts. An update from Emily. One more picture for the kids from Austin. Just like the climb up one of the boulders around here, I take each message in stride, each grip and reach with patience that I'm learning can only come from experience and grace.

◆　◆　◆

The kids spend several more nights with me, giving Emily more time to rest and acclimate with the baby after her surgery. I get them to and from school, and life goes on like clockwork, even though it's changed now. By Monday afternoon she and Austin are home and asking for the kids.

It's time.

So goes the routine of refolding clothes, packing up two back-packs, and watching the kids say goodbye to the few stuffed animals that have accumulated on their beds. I guide them down the stairs, glancing back just to notice that the colorful beanbags still have Micaela- and Cameron-sized dents. This heart desert feels dry beneath my boots, but we descend the stairs. The sun on my soul is parching, but there is a quenching that rises up from an even deeper place, one of hope, as I buckle the kids into the back seat of my truck.

It's twenty minutes from here to where Emily and I used to live together. The porch light is on, and Austin opens the door the moment we pull up. The kids hesitate when they see him, their eager-ness perhaps more for the baby than him, and I'm secretly relieved. But that will probably change as they get more accustomed to him.

Not wanting the guy to come closer, I climb out and unfasten both car seats. I lift my daughter down, and then my son. They start for the house timidly now.

Austin kneels and asks if they are ready to meet their new sister. There's not a reason in the world that has me wanting to follow them up the lighted stone path, but the kids both need their backpacks still, so I slide them from the floorboard and carry the bags toward the house. Emily's voice filters softly from the doorway. It's impossible not to imagine the new life lying in her arms. A life that is now being introduced to the very lives that I value more than my own.

I don't look Austin in the face as I hand over the backpacks. Barely nod to his appreciation for me watching the kids the last three days. I want to tell him that they're mine . . . and that I don't need his thanks, and I try to ignore the way blood is hot in my veins again. So I just turn away. The warmth of the porch light is soft on the path as I reach my truck, climb inside, and pull away slowly.

As I do, I glimpse the second-story window where Emily has gone upstairs to rest with the baby and the kids. I've learned since the delivery that the baby was in grave danger and that the C-section had been performed just in time. Despite everything, I have to acknowledge that Emily and Austin have a lot to be thankful for. It's a bitter reality that had she tried to deliver this baby a century ago, either baby, mother, or both might have been lost.

With the house now behind me, I don't have to look back to remember the glow from the upstairs window, or to know that Emily would probably have been humming. She always sang to her babies.

This time, I just won't be there to hear it.

Despite everything, she's always been a loving mother.

It's funny the way the scar in my arm seems to burn as I aim for the highway. A reminder of all that has been lost, of all that has been done, and of all that remains. I still have my life. And because of that, I take deep breaths, drive more slowly, and use the quiet drive home to focus on all that I have to be thankful for.

CHAPTER 35

JUNIPER

It takes three more days for Edie's labor to begin. The tightening on her still, firm belly brought her to in the middle of the night, sending Santiago to wake me from where I was sleeping on a pallet on the mercantile floor. Now the brightness of Edie's smile—a memory in the dark—is all I can think of as I set water to boil on the shop stove. The memory of that smile is a vision that I have seen thousands of times. One ingrained in my mind with every breath this dark night. An unassuming beauty that God granted to this earth to brighten the world around her. I must keep her alive.

She is in the back bedroom now, huddled on the bed, moaning. Her pain is my pain as I cram more wood into the fire. It is just her and me. Mrs. Parson is back home with Bethany, and John rode to fetch the Cahuilla housekeeper from the nearby cattle ranch. Santiago has hurried into the haze of what will soon be coming

258

dawn to fill two more buckets with fresh water. His absence stretches out, and though Edie cries for him, I can only assure her he will return quickly.

When Edie rests between pains, I move clean towels into place and check that the water is at a steady roll. The mercantile door opens, and Santiago braces it with a strong arm. John hangs back as three women enter like starlight—silent, able, and so very welcome. They slip inside, one woman after the other, until I see the one who has cared for Edie these months past. Each of them bears a small basket, and they each pass behind the counter to where Edie's moans draw them nearer. I follow, unsurprised as Santiago hangs back, as it is the custom of this land regardless of what tribe or town a man hails from.

In the bedroom, one woman lowers a shallow basket that holds bound herbs while another one holds a filled carrying net woven from agave. Their dark hair glimmers in the lantern light, and their brown, plump faces shine with wisdom. These are women who will know so much more about birthing than I. Their wisdom is rooted into the earth around us for more than a hundred miles, and as many decades. I breathe lighter, but it's short-lived when Edie cries out in pain. Will they know if the child is alive?

"What can I do?" I ask.

I realize that Santiago has moved to the doorway when he repeats what I've said in the Cahuilla language.

One of the women I have not yet met replies in the same dialect. Their exchange is sure and swift.

"She asks that you bring the water," he says to me.

I hasten to the stove and fill a pitcher, nearly sloshing the scalding water over the side as I balance it into the bedroom. There, two of the women are trying to coax Edie from the tangle of sheets she's perched atop. They wait patiently until this round of seizing has passed, then together they ease her to a stand. Edie moans but doesn't resist. The third woman motions for me to help her with the bed. She nudges against the frame. They mean to move it? Brooking no argument, I step that way and offer my strength. It is not until the bed collides into the wall that she nods her satisfaction.

Next, the woman pulls a blanket from the bed, fanning it out onto the floor. I move to help her settle it into place even as the other two lead Edie to the center of it.

Edie's slender legs bow as she is swept up in another birth pain. The cries that follow are as raw as the earth and old as time. The ache claws through me that I can do nothing to aid her pain. This is her path to becoming a mother, and yet hers is not lit with the lamplight of joy. She walks now in darkness, hoping to hold Santiago's child in her arms, alive and well. A child that is as much of Edie as it will be of the man waiting in the shop front. Their child does not hide beneath coats and scarves this night. Instead, it bows out from beneath Edie's sweat-drenched nightshirt, protruding and proud. A brave little soul who must be as stunning and wild as its mother. Gentle and proud like its father.

Will its first breaths bring a blessing to this family that has hungered for it? Or is it a child who in this moment is already dancing with the angels?

The Cahuilla women guide Edie to kneel on the center of the blanket. One of them sings softly in her native tongue. A gentle, rhythmic melody that Edie pants to, adding her own melancholy that is a primal, desperate need for release and a knowing-of that ushers in life.

Hours crawl by as Edie labors, her pain and her agony as vivid as her need for this child. With a rush of waters onto the floor, her baby is born after the moon makes its arc in the sky, bending low to kiss the sun. And when it slides into this world, it is a Cahuilla woman who cradles it. The babe glimmers in the glow of dawn, and the room goes quiet. I am on my knees, bracing Edie's trembling waist with both of my hands, and the other women are gathered around—Edie and the babe their full focus of skill and strength.

The baby doesn't cry.

She is plump and still, her skin ashen gray. It is not the warm, golden brown from the dreams of those who have awaited her.

No ... no ... no ...

My soul cries it.

Edie is moaning it.

Death has come to this room. It has been here as long as Edie first sensed it. Her cries that follow are not the pain of birth but of a mother who has lost her very heart.

CHAPTER 36

JOHNNY

Three days after the kids go home, I meet Sonoma at a coffee shop. We sit across from one another at a table painted with a checkerboard, her holding a steaming frappe, me balancing a tall iced tea on my knee. It's just a jeans-and-T-shirt kind of thing, but I can't help noticing that the sleeves of her black top are trimmed in white lace and the earrings dangling against her cheeks are a soft green. She's smiling, but not the big, bright one from a week ago when we were laughing in the sunlight of Kenworthy. Today it's a nervous kind of smile.

I'm nervous too. There's a herd of butterflies in my gut, and my palms are sweating. I'd be lying if I didn't recognize the *why* and the *what for* of these long-forgotten sensations. The truth is there's someone quite lovely—inside and out—sitting across from me, and a man notices that kind of thing. Even a guy with a bruised and battered heart.

Tracy Chapman is singing "Change" alongside drums and a guitar through overhead speakers. Sonoma unloads a cloth bag with books and a series of plastic folders, including the binder of letters I lent her. Yesterday I reached out by text to see how things were going with the research, and she announced that a few discoveries had been made. I stood in the kitchen, holding my cell, debating for about ten whole minutes on what I *should* say, while wrestling with what I *wanted* to say. The *want* and the *what* became an offer to meet up for coffee to talk through it all. She said yes.

Now here we are.

She arrived first and ordered, so I didn't pay for anything, which means it's most definitely not a date. This is a classy gal, so I'm guessing she did that on purpose. Maybe a grace to me? To her? Likely both of us. Just a way to make this less complicated.

"I'm eager to hear about what you've figured out," I say as she opens the nearest folder.

It's clear she's just as eager. "I can't tell you how helpful those letters have been." She's flushed now. Something good has happened.

"Well, come on, let's see it!" I toss it out in a teasing tone to try to set her further at ease.

A little laugh. "I'm trying to find it!" A few of the letters are marked with sticky notes, and these she thumbs through, scanning the pages, a treasure hunt.

I wait, sipping the sweet tea—in *no rush at all*.

"So, I read through the letters this week—"

"All of them?"

"Yes, and I found a few indicators that I wanted to run by you. Since you've read Juniper Cohen's writings as well, and know some of the history surrounding them, I'm hoping you might be able to confirm what I'm thinking."

She's offering me a position I'm not qualified for. Faith from a woman I barely know. "I'll do my best."

"So, this here"—she places her drink off to the side—"is from the winter of 1902, and it says . . . Well, I'll let you read it for yourself."

She touches a bottom paragraph, and I read the slanted cursive.

We buried Reverend Manchester yesterday. My friend is alone in Kenworthy now. We watch the horizon now, the pair of us. Two women both hoping for the same thing. For a returning. For answers.

I read the line again. I don't get it. Sonoma's ten times sharper at this, so my gaze lifts to her face.

"Do you see?" She touches the page. "Most people might not notice what she just said, but they're waiting on the same thing. A returning. Answers."

I squint at the paper. "Answers . . . answers . . . ?"

Sonoma smacks a palm to her forehead. Did she just roll her eyes at me? Her soft laugh confirms it. "Johnny. Edith Manchester was also left behind."

The clue clicks into place, and I read it once more, this time seeing what Sonoma spotted. Two women waiting for someone to return. They wouldn't be waiting on the same man, so it would have to be two different ones. "I think you're right. Whoever it is that Edith was watching for, it certainly wasn't her father. He was already gone. So, who was it? This Señor Tiago—er, Santiago?"

"Possibly." Her eyes spark with the likelihood. "That's where the photograph comes into play." She pulls out a 5x7 of the shot I sent her of my house. She's printed it in sepia tone, but the high res is clearly modern. Next, she opens up an old history book and turns to a marked page near the back. "Look at this photograph."

The image is grainy and in the same golden tones. A group of men stand in front of a cabin, but the structure itself isn't the focus of the picture. Only a portion of it is captured, and that is blocked by several men in front of it. I note the caption: *Miners stand in front of the newly built cabin for town founder Harold Kenworthy, circa 1897.*

There are no names listed. All of the men—four total—are white. I lean closer, searching for more significance. Searching for what Sonoma must see. Before I have to admit to being lost again, she slides forward yet another history book. It's open to another old photograph. Same cabin. Only two men this time. One is white and one is native. The white man is staring at the camera, and the native man is standing tall and somber, except his eyes have drifted to something that's behind the photographer. I've seen this photograph.

"Maybe I'm jumping to conclusions, but I'm thinking that if these two men were friends, then the woman that Juniper is referring to could be . . ." The wonder of it lights in her brown eyes. "Edith Manchester. Or perhaps Edith Del Sol."

Wow, she's good. When I say this, she beams. From the speakers, Tracy Chapman is slowly singing "The Promise" now, which means it's got to be a CD playing.

"It's in the details. It just takes time to find them. Nothing is certain, of course, but the clues might be lining up."

I shake my head, amazed.

"Okay, are you ready for more?" she asks.

"Hit me with it." I gotta admit, this is pretty fun.

She moves to another marker in the book. This photograph, while smaller, is the same one hanging in the historical society of the woman with the rifle. She's tall and slender and peering back at us. Through the power of photography, this fiery gaze has somehow spanned more than a century.

Sonoma reads the caption aloud. "*Edith Manchester, daughter of Reverend Carl Manchester, mercantile proprietors.*"

Beside the image is a close-up of the woman's face. As though the author of this history book decided to zoom in, clip out the landscape around her, her rustic manner of dress, even most of the shotgun.

This focal point is simply of her face. The close-up is grainier, but it's obvious that her skin is smooth and young. There are shadows under her eyes. That double-dog-dare-you look I noticed from a few months back is more complex than I first realized. Instead, the stoniness of this face might stem from a profound strength. "You said she lost two children by this point?"

Sonoma nods slowly. "If everything lines up as I think it does, she would have lost them both already before this photograph was taken."

I lean closer to see the pinch between the woman's eyes. It's one of courage. One that's hard wrought. Perhaps this woman had been fighting for it.

It's a feeling I've known in ways. Our stories are different—our losses different—and I am saddened for her. It's impossible not to respect this woman that I don't even know. In fact, I've been so caught up in all this, my iced-tea glass has soaked condensation onto the knee of my jeans. I set the cup aside, swipe at the damp circle, and glance to the woman across from me. "This is really something."

I examine Edith's face again, grieved that she would have endured such an amount of pain. I think of Emily's C-section—a modern procedure designed to keep mother and baby alive in dangerous circumstances. This woman wouldn't have had such an option. Not even if she would have hoped for it. What would that have been like?

"I like to think that Edith could be my great-great-grandmother," Sonoma says softly.

I lift my focus to her bittersweet expression. If that were the case, Sonoma would have *less* Cahuilla blood in her, not more, something that clearly holds value. "Why is that?"

She smiles softly and touches Edith's picture with great care as she angles the book back toward herself. "Because if I am somehow a part of their family tree, it would have to mean only one thing." Hope floods her face. Not for herself but for another. "It would mean that she eventually had a child that lived."

CHAPTER 37

JUNIPER

APRIL 1903

The ache of the heart can pulse as sharp as death itself. It's a fighting toward life—and at times a losing battle that skirts the unlit paths of despair. Twining within it. The sun but a memory that can no longer be conjured. Victory—*hope*—dwells at its edges, and even in the in-between places, but it is a long wasteland to cross. That battle is pulsing inside Edie as she sits abed, staring out the window. Heated river stones have been placed against her hips, just atop a light blanket. The stones were brought by the Cahuilla women, warmed on the stove, and now curve round Edie's body for healing and comfort as is their custom. Edie's pale face and auburn hair are clean, as stark as fire and ice. Her pale hands rest limp at her sides. Her eyes rest unblinking on the snowy horizon. Her tears have quieted. She held her daughter for hours in the night, until Santiago finally coaxed the small body to his own.

Edie peered up at her husband with an ocean in her gaze and

finally let go. And in his strong embrace, a tiny girl was ushered from her mother's sight as must eventually be done. The sweet child looked to be slumbering in Santiago's strong grip. Bundled in a knitted blanket, she lay nestled against his slit-top shirt, her face close to the span of his sinewy chest. Her lips were plump and perfect, and her feet so small and wrinkled.

I turn away from my friend now, so that she will not see my tears spilling again. Shame floods me that I ever declared my life unfair. Who am I to have ever complained? This moment, as Edie mourns the death of a child, it nearly brings me to my knees that I allowed bitterness to take root in my soul over my lot in life. God has been generous with me, and regret spreads that I did not acknowledge it sooner.

At the washstand, I swipe at my vision so that it clears enough to mix her up a tincture from the herbs the Cahuilla women brought. Two of them have returned home. They traveled speedily that night. A whole four miles on foot to be with the woman their nephew and cousin chose as his wife. To be with Santiago and the unborn babe. One, Santiago's aunt, has stayed behind today. She is aged and wise and gentle.

As we work quietly, tending to comforts that can scarcely pierce the darkness for Edie, the old woman looks at me. I stir a teaspoon slowly around the cup, and when she pats my hand in loving assurance, we speak the same language. We long for the same things.

CHAPTER 38

JOHNNY

Kneeling in the barn, I slide open the bottom drawer of the file cabinet and pull out the real-estate file on the cabin. José's due at noon to help me with some finish work on the barn loft, but nearly as pressing—and, surprisingly, as important to me—is that the Cahuilla heritage event is in just one week, including Sonoma's genealogy presentation. I'm no expert, so there's probably little I can do to help her, but I want to try. I dig past escrow docs and find a series of emails that were pertinent enough to the sale to be saved. I thumb through to a document from the sellers themselves. At the bottom of the email is the Cohens' address and phone number in Wyoming. Hopefully it's a current number. Only way to find out is typing the digits into my phone.

It rings twice, then there's a raspy, elderly voice. "Hello?"

"Hello. I'm sorry to contact you out of the blue. This is Johnny Sutherland who purchased your house."

"Oh. Hello, Mr. Sutherland."

I glimpse the paper to confirm the correct first names for the Cohens—Lynn and Herb. "Thanks for taking my call so unexpectedly. Is this Lynn Cohen?"

"Yes, it is."

"A pleasure, Mrs. Cohen. I don't want to keep you long, but I have a question about the journal that was recently shipped to you. Did it arrive okay?"

"Safe and sound, and we appreciate you getting it home to us." There's a tenderness in the way she speaks of the old journal. One I understand now.

"It was my pleasure. It's also the reason I'm calling." I hook a thumb into the front pocket of my jeans. "I'm wondering if there's any possible way of getting the answer to a research question." I explain the details and, from where Mrs. Cohen is, hear a teaspoon rattle in a glass cup. It's easy to envision her there in Wyoming, enjoying warm weather with iced tea. She listens as I explain about the history I've been learning—that she's already versed in—and as I divulge Sonoma's discoveries that pertain to Santiago Del Sol and *possibly* Edith Manchester, there is genuine interest in Mrs. Cohen's voice as she offers her two cents.

That yes, she sees potential in the connection.

"So, you think it would be possible?" I ask.

"Certainly. But I know you don't need my hunch. I'll ask Herb and see if he has any ideas as well. He's read John Cohen's journal twice through now over the years, and I'll have him reach out to you with any further insights on this man. He's heading into the hospital this week for a routine procedure, but soon as he's home and in recovery, I'm sure he'll be on the job." She goes quiet a moment. "We'll do what we can to help. This is the number to reach you at?"

"Yes, please. I can't tell you how much I appreciate it."

"It's our pleasure, Mr. Sutherland. Thank you for taking such care of the cabin. We know it's in good hands. Oh, and one thing about the journal."

"Yeah?"

"There are some pages missing. About five—" She pauses a moment, and I hear her husband in the background. Mrs. Cohen chuckles. "Okay, Herb is telling me it's six. They've been torn clean out. There was never any record or indication where they went, and according to the stories Herb heard from his parents as a child, the entries have been torn out so long as anyone has had the journal."

I let that sink in a moment.

"It's possible they were removed by John himself or someone in his family. We don't know what the content would have been, so there is a missing piece to the story that will never be understood."

I nod slowly. "Thanks for letting me know." Interesting. And in all honesty, I guess I wouldn't blame the guy. I don't know that I would want the world to know everything I'd write down about my life. Whatever reason he—or one of his family members—had for tearing out those pages, it would have been significant.

"We'll be in touch, Mr. Sutherland."

"It's been an honor, Mrs. Cohen." Speaking the name, I realize I could have been expressing the sentiment to Juniper Cohen herself. "It's been an absolute honor."

When we end the call, I slide the real-estate file back into the cabinet and secure the drawer. I try to imagine John Cohen tearing pages from his journal. What secrets . . . what stories would those pages have held? Would he have crumpled them up and discarded them? Hidden them somewhere else? If they were worth removing, he likely destroyed them.

There's a thought building, and it's not even fully formed yet. Probably because I don't want to give it full attention in my mind. To zoom in on the pieces—of what's here and of what's missing—would mean to consider a bleak moment in time.

Was it John Cohen who salted the Kenworthy mine?

The timing of it all combined with his disappearing adds up in ways, but there's no evidence to point to it. Six pages torn from a journal and destroyed. What story did those pages tell? It's a story that died with them . . . that died with time and the way a present eventually turns into a past. That's the way life works, and it's the mystery of it all.

No matter what, I don't think harshly of John Cohen; this rabbit trail isn't because I think little of him. Quite the contrary. I'm learning from him, from his family. I'm awed by them and the struggles they faced. The hardships they endured, and yes, even the choices they made. The thing about a bad decision is that there can be, with grace and wisdom, more to come. The other half is to remedy what was wronged. Was that ever done? Judging by the glimpses I've had into the past, it sounds like restoration came, which means that John Cohen reached the end of his life far from a coward, but a man who stood upon courage. He had a wife who did the same.

Slowly I shake my head, realizing how far my thoughts have wandered. It's all just speculation, and I won't pursue it any further. If John wished for those matters to lay buried, I respect the man enough to do the same. There's no way of knowing, and the past certainly can't be changed. But I'm reminded suddenly of what I can do . . .

At the house, I climb the stairs to my room and grab the new journal Micaela and Cameron gave me. I've yet to write the first entry, and it's more than time. While my life doesn't have the kind of intrigue that other journals from this cabin hold, I can at least begin documenting these days here at home. *For your own Kenworthy story*, my sister wrote.

After jotting down the date, I begin the first page, taking my time so that my writing is legible. I'm not used to writing in a journal, so the first few lines feel unnatural, but then a momentum hits. And as nearly an hour goes by, I've begun the start of a story that's not only in full motion, but I have the honor of living it—hurts, hopes, and all.

CHAPTER 39

JUNIPER

The baby is buried at the point in the land where the sun is last to touch each dusk. Well east of where Pipe Creek springs from the mountains. Here the ground is soft, the land protected from wind by the rocky hills that steeple above the valley. Pine trees rise on either side, plummeting down blankets of noontime shadows that will be cool in summer. It is a gentle place for so small a creature to rest. A place near enough for her mother to visit, to lay wildflowers down in the spring, and to peer out upon from the mercantile during winter months.

Wrapping the land—this hour—are dozens of people who have come to pay their respect. There are those of us who remain in Kenworthy, including Mrs. Parson and Oliver Conrad. Most of all are our Cahuilla neighbors who stand in honor of a grandchild to their deceased shaman. That shaman's son is neither Señor Tiago to these people nor even Santiago Del Sol. He bears a name that I do not know.

Today it is the name of his people. Of him having become a man amid this tribe in a language that roots right into this earth.

His fellow tribal men stand and sway as their deep voices cry out into the evening air. In their hands, rattles shake. Slender handles catch the glow of dusk, the round gourds filled with seeds, clattering out a rhythm to their melancholy songs. Bird singers, they are called. Singing the "bird songs" of the Cahuilla tribe. This is told to us by the Cahuilla cowboy beside us, soft and slow in patchy English.

So empty this town has become . . . so sparse its people . . . that we have not had a funeral since burying the reverend.

Now, all who call this land home stand in reverence of the child being lowered into the earth. Santiago is on his knees at the graveside, lowering the wooden casket himself. Edie huddles beside me, her body trembling with exhaustion, but most of all with grief. Beside me, John observes it all in silence. The bird singers grow quiet. Wooden rattles still.

Now only Santiago is singing.

The Cahuilla cowboy speaks again beside us. A gift for Edie so that she can know the manner in which her child is being surrendered to the earth by her husband's steady, sad hands. "He sings the moon song now," the cowhand says. "Because the child is a girl."

Tears slide down Edie's cheeks. I can scarcely see myself. I didn't know a heart could hurt this badly. However is Edie able to stand?

She does it for her child. She does it because this moment will never come again. There will be weeks and months and years to crumble, but right now she stands for her daughter who is being honored by a tribe of people and even distant cowhands who did not have the joy of seeing her beautiful face.

Soft and sad grows Santiago's voice. His cries are clear, rising toward the sky as dusk hearkens in. The language of this moon song is as foreign as it is sweet. The Cahuilla men and women gathered around sway in a rhythmic shifting of skirts and dusty pants, as though they, too, are speaking this language with him. I'm bracing Edie now, so severely she's trembling. She's not yet healed, and no mother should have to labor forth a babe only to labor harder still at a graveside. And yet Edie Del Sol has not once lowered her chin or closed her eyes. She watches the two whom she calls family.

Tanned throat bent skyward, Santiago's guttural song fades into silence. The dancers cease their swaying. Not even a rattle is moved. In the quiet, blue jays call to us from the trees, offering up their own harmony of loss and life.

A new song begins. This one not in Cahuilla but English.

It's a hymn the church congregation sang often when there were enough residents to gather for Sunday service at the schoolhouse. "Lead, Kindly Light."

Santiago's voice is no longer strong and clear; the melody dims as faint as starlight. In his voice linger tears, pronouncing his broken heart, but on his tongue dwell words of peace and of longing for a home that cannot be found on this earth.

The night is dark; and I am far from home.

Edie's shoulders shake with grief. Broken for this dear soul, I pull her close, holding tight as her husband sings to a God who is different than his people worship, and yet they stand reverent for the man who was raised in their midst, and who walks as much in their ways as he does in our own.

Keep thou my feet; I do not ask to see.

Lead, kindly light. That is the promise springing from a father's broken heart—one of trust in a dark, dark hour.

The man with four names sings to his God as he lowers his daughter with only one into the earth. *Little Bit Del Sol*, her cross reads. The humble name was chosen by Edie and carved into the wood by John the night before. It took nearly until dawn, so often John swiped at his eyes. That cross now pierces the spring ground that is soft and fertile. The piercing spreads to my chest, and it is so hard to breathe,

I hardly know how to hold Bethany close to my skirt. But I squeeze her tight, thanking God that she is safe and well.

Beside me, Edie swipes an edge of the blanket across her eyes. This spirited lass is a child no longer. She is a woman who has known a loss greater than I have ever known, and in this moment, I do not feel worthy to stand beside her. I am not worthy to stand beside a woman I helped bind with linen strips around her chest to stem a flow of milk that has nowhere to be needed. But God has gifted us one another in friendship, and I vow to walk with her every step at her side that she allows me to. I cannot hold her pain, nor can I sift it away. But I can be a hand to hold, and a voice in the darkness as nights come in. And as I glimpse my friend's agonized face, I am thankful beyond measure that her husband sings of the light. How deeply she needs it this hour.

Beyond us, the mine is silent—the work of disassembling the stamp mill ceased for this day. Some of the newcomers have even gathered at the edge of the work yard, watching what is happening below. They've pulled off their hats, standing as sentinels, a respect that people say doesn't exist in the West between the white and those who lived here a thousand years before. Yet it exists this day, and I am only sorry it has taken the loss of an infant's life to spark such unity. I pray it is a legacy that will linger on.

They say there is no gold in these hills.

But as a father lays dirt over a wooden box, there suddenly is. She's the most precious thing that this stretch of mountain has ever had the honor to hold.

CHAPTER 40

JOHNNY

Saturday afternoon traffic is light in Palm Springs as I merge my truck north on Highway 111. To my right, stucco buildings hold shops and offices, while to the opposite side snowcapped mountains rise high from the desert landscape. I love this view because somewhere up there is home. But down here, soaring pines have been traded for towering palm trees. Always an astounding switch on a drive that drops four thousand feet in elevation along a one-hour stretch of mountain road.

GPS says I'll be to the Cahuilla Heritage Museum in less than fifteen minutes. I'll hopefully make it in time to find Sonoma and give her a vote of confidence before everything begins. It sounded like she was nervous about speaking in public, and maybe it can help to have a familiar face in the crowd. I roll my eyes at myself. What a dumb thought. Of course she'll have familiar faces in the crowd. She'll have friends there, maybe even family.

Maybe I should just settle into the back and not bother her.

My palms are sweating now, and it has nothing to do with the desert heat outside.

By the time I reach the brand-new museum and park, I decide to just go on in, and if I see her beforehand, great. If not, then I'll wave or say hello when it's all over.

The parking lot is packed. A great sign. Tables span the front courtyard with refreshments, and most of the attendees look to be of Cahuilla descent. I'm one of the minorities today, and it's kind of cool that way. There's a buzz of energy in the air. It's almost an other-worldly feel. It's as though the past is calling out again, but this time it's not of the settlers. It's of the natives who cherished this land long before it was taken from them.

I approach the courtyard, where several women wear traditional beaded costumes as they sip sodas and balance paper plates. They'll probably be performing at some point during the event, and I'm look-ing forward to all of it. I pay admission to an elderly woman whose friendly smile is set deep within golden-brown wrinkles. Her long silver hair is parted down the middle, and silver bracelets jangle on one arm as she hands me a ticket and the change.

"Welcome," she says with another smile.

"Thanks." I check the top button of my collared shirt and slide the ticket into the pocket of my khaki pants.

After ducking beneath an archway of brightly colored balloons, I pass around the courtyard fountain and into the entrance to the museum. Inside, a refreshing blast of AC drowns out the desert heat. The hallway smells like brand-new tile work and fresh paint. One of my favorite smells. The museum is filled with visitors, but there's still enough walking space to navigate down the corridor, where alcoves showcase various exhibits. The first one holds baskets and pottery. Another, weapons—bows, arrows, and even several historical rifles. I'm tempted to check this room out better, but I spot Sonoma instead, speaking with a middle-aged couple near the entrance to the conference room.

She's wearing a calf-length black skirt and a bright yellow top. The colors match the energy of the event, and the wide, beaded bracelet around her wrist is nearly the same pattern as one of the baskets I just passed by. Seeing her this way, surrounded by so many of Cahuilla descent, I can see the strong ties of her heritage to their own. I don't realize I'm staring until she waves.

Great. Nice job, Johnny.

I start that way, wishing I'd thought out more of what to say, but winging it works too.

"I'm so glad you made it." Her eyes are bright.

When she smiles my way, the couple she was speaking with excuse themselves.

Sonoma waves to her friends, then angles back to me. "I'd shake your hand, but I'm so nervous that I'm trembling."

I cram both hands into my pockets so she doesn't feel any pressure. "You'll do great. You're the last speaker, right?"

"Yeah, and I think that makes it worse." The words are light, but when she adjusts her bracelet, her hands really are shaking. "My parents are running late from freeway traffic but are going to be here before it starts. I hope."

I glance around, wishing the act could get them to appear. Instead, I give her a friendly smile. "They'll make it. Anything I can do to help? Can I grab you some water?"

"That'd be great. I'll walk with you, though. That might help settle my nerves."

We turn together and start on side by side. We're turning down the main corridor when the sound of drums begins in the courtyard. Sonoma angles toward the large glass doors that showcase the outside happenings. "Oh, the bird singers are beginning. Come on. I want to show you this."

Though my mind and heart are still crossed wires of hope and pain and wondering what God will have for the coming days in my life, I'm honored that she wants to show me anything. I can't help but be. Not with this woman—one who says that joining me on the search for water would be just the ticket to settle her nerves. She's unassuming, and gracious. Qualities that, among many others, are hard not to value. I hold the door open so she can pass through and her smile is shy enough that I wonder if she's having the same internal thoughts that I am.

Probably not. I can really overthink things sometimes.

I pass through the invisible curtain of heat—AC now a memory behind us. But amid the outside swelter lives a world like no other. A world that would have existed a hundred years ago and beyond. Unlike the women who are dressed up as the days of old in their brightly colored skirts and jewelry, the male singers wear jeans and black T-shirts with a printed logo of the tribe's emblem. Some of them have black bandanas tied around their foreheads, while a few of the older men are wearing cowboy hats. They all shake rattles carved from gourds. The men are bent at the waist, focused. Most of them move their feet with the rhythm of the song. A swaying that pulses out the sound as much as their instruments. It's as though the courtyard is no longer around them and they sing and dance with memories of old.

Sonoma is at my side, but she has to lean the tiniest bit nearer to speak over the rise of voices. "This is called the moon song. It served an important role in ceremonies. It was also played at funerals if it was a female who passed." Her eyes lift to mine, and though I'm struck at first by her nearness, my thoughts center instead on the sorrow I see there.

Of the child that was lost long ago in Kenworthy. The Cahuilla infant. Sadly, the first of two for the Del Sols.

I draw in a sigh, nod so that she knows I understand, and lift my focus back to the dancers. What would it have been like to listen to such a lonesome sound, such a pulsing beat as steady as time itself—all because a little girl was lost to the earth?

We listen and watch, and halfway through I remember that bottle of water I'd meant to get Sonoma. I edge closer to the nearest table and fish a bottle from a huge bucket of ice. Returning to her side, she thanks me and uncaps it. The music fades, a softer, second song now building beneath its echo.

I nearly say it then and there—that I wasn't able to get Sonoma the answers I had hoped from the Cohen family. They're trying, but time just wasn't on our side with this one. I could say that to her now, but I don't. Another time, because it's not a disappointment that's going to derail her. Whatever facts she's spent her life discovering are going to be more than enough today. This woman didn't need my help, but I'm thankful to have at least gotten the chance to try.

She proves it, too, when a few hours later, in a room of a hundred museum guests, Sonoma walks up to the podium at the front of the conference room, lays down her notes, and describes the purpose and passion behind her genealogy search. And not because of her own lineage but because the process is empowering for any person to hear the stories of those who went before them. To learn their names, their lifetimes. To see their humanity.

I think of all that she and I have discovered in our own ways through the land surrounding Kenworthy. I think of the Cohens and of the Del Sols and of dozens of other families, both settler and native Cahuilla. There is so much story there. More important, there was so much life. And now here we stand, all of us in this room, living our own lives. Our own stories. As Sonoma speaks, I notice, as I've come to with her, the loveliness of her mind and spirit. Of all of her. This woman has been a joy to encounter, and I'm growing increasingly thankful that God granted me the chance to know her. I hope it won't be for only a short while.

Her lecture is brief. Just a half hour, but when she finishes, the crowd offers up a thunderous applause. Her parents, who made it in time, are on their feet, clapping proudly. Their faces shine with love for their daughter. Even though the echo of all those hands—all that energy—drowns out any other sound, I can still hear Sonoma's closing words echo all the deeper. I think on it again during the drive back up the mountain later that evening after Sonoma and I shared a plate of appetizers in a quiet corner of the courtyard with her parents, and I walked her to her car, where we sent one another off with a wave.

"We search and we ask because it matters. Because history, without understanding the hearts of the people who made it, is just a bunch of dates. Let us change the course of that wind. Let us teach the next generations what it is that truly matters."

Stars are overhead when I reach home that evening. I climb the steps slowly, tired but contented. On the other side of the door, Rye is scraping to come out. I unlock it, and he bounds onto the porch, more interested in sniffing at my hands than running out into the dark. He scampers around me, tripping over his water bowl before dashing off into the yard. I leave the door open since he'll be back before bedtime.

Just before entering the cabin, I spot a white envelope leaning against the porch chair. It's from FedEx. I hit the lights in the living room, which gives enough glow to see that it's addressed from the Cohen family. With a tear of the envelope, a packet of papers slides out.

Photocopies that I instantly recognize as John Cohen's original journal.

Suddenly I'm wide awake, and within moments, there's a century of a fissure running across the sands of time. No, this didn't come in time for Sonoma's talk, but there's a deeper purpose here that has me reading late into the night. Not with the same raw need as I did the letters. This time it's different. This time, I don't feel like a man clawing for air. Instead, I read of a man who is in a place much like I am. One of desire and resolution. And for some miraculous reason, we've met across a century, in the very same place.

The answer that Sonoma has been seeking is still pieced in riddles, but with the attached promise from Herb Cohen—that he'll be poring over these pages again himself once recovered from surgery in the coming weeks—I think we may be onto something. With a little more digging, and a little more time, we may find a way to help her.

PART 3

CHAPTER 41

JUNIPER

Five months have passed. Long enough that Edie rises from bed for hours on end. I know because I have gone to be with her nearly every day since the birth. At first, I laundered her linens while she healed, brought her cups of tea that often sat untouched, and made sure something hot and nourishing was placed into a bowl and into her hands. That, too, often sat abandoned, often while Edie bit back tears from the pain—mind, body, and soul—of having no baby to nurse while the front of her nightgown dampened to her skin. She has been suffering, but while she is far from the edge of peace, she is up again. A *Closed* sign hung in the window of the mercantile those first few weeks, until Edie craved busyness more than rest.

In her face now lives a determination that is as much Edie as it is a woman who is going to fight the shadows of despair. The heart never heals to wholeness after such a loss, and the shadows beneath

Edie's eyes are testament to the depth of pain she still walks in and will walk in the days to come. The truth about then and now is that it will take time. It's what we all know. It's what our parents knew and our grandparents knew. It's what loss needs from us. It takes time. It drives its fists against the very soul, tempting it to give up, forcing the soul to cling to a courage unlike any other.

In the wake of Little Bit's death, Edie slipped away to a place that no one could reach. She was a shadow of the Edie we all knew. The love and comfort we surrounded her with was scarcely a silhouette of the love she longed for—that of and for her child. There were many days when she did not want anyone near. Days when she did not even speak.

Now, her eyes often brim with tears, yet she has placed one foot in front of the other—slowly, cautiously, achingly. It's what has made her steps more profound than any of mine have ever been. It's what has made these months and weeks so very raw for the woman who has wept and shown courage in ways I cannot fathom.

Is there hope in this place? In the world that Edie now finds herself within?

There has to be, but there is no easy way to harness that hope. To even see it at times. Even so, it is there, and God does not come at a woman like her as though He is a tyrant. Instead, it is a gentle coaxing of sunrises and sunsets. Of His promise that He has not forgotten her. I pray for Edie each and every day that the slow spread of healing will continue to grow within her.

Today, I take down clothes from the line behind the mercantile. I come for an hour every day, just before school is let out. At first, Edie pleaded for me not to, but there are so many tasks for her to undertake, and she is the last person who would complain. This young woman who once lacked the patience to unravel a box of rope but who now can watch the sky for hours. The quiet of the outdoors has been what has helped her venture from her bed more and more often.

She's needed moments of sunshine, and the glow of morning. She's needed cups of strong, healing teas and hours sitting on the lowest boulders where Cahuilla women once ground their acorns and the day shines the brightest.

Santiago has scarcely left her side, and it is good that way, but this day he and John hiked over the ridge to hunt. They will return by dark, and with Bethany at the schoolhouse and the workers gone with all the lumber and equipment they could haul away, I keep a close eye on Edie, who is a striking contrast to the men in this town who have moved on from the death of Little Bit easier than the rest of us ever will. We hear news of tragedy in newspapers or on the wind, and rarely does it affect us until it reaches inside our homes. I learned this the moment I held the newspaper clipping of John's arrest, and Edie knows it in her own way as she sits upon a grassy knoll now, a handwoven blanket wrapped around her shoulders.

Edie doesn't move. Only the breeze that blows stirs her hair. It is a craving she has now for the quiet. What we can do in these weeks and even months to come is be a strength around her in any ways that will help. Much like the way the Cahuilla tribe stood around the day of the burial in song, we can summon up a type of music that she desperately needs.

In the distance, the school bell rings. Bethany will be along any moment.

Finished at the laundry line, I carry a basket of fresh sheets inside and set it on the bed in the back bedroom. Edie has insisted that while I do the laundering for her these days, she wants to iron and fold, so I leave the basket on the floor beside the nightstand where a clay jar sits. One shaped from the mud, dried by the sun, and charred by fire so that it can sit here, glazed in red ochre from the mountains. It holds a salve that the Cahuilla midwife made for Edie especially, which she used in the weeks after the difficult birth. I fold her night-gown and drape it over the metal bedstead, then tidy the blankets. It is evidence now of the way she and Santiago have lived in secret these past two years. It is a secret that I will continue to keep for them so long as they desire. But something is in the air—that secret drawing to an end by way of the funeral. A bittersweet end in that it has been loss that sparked their steps toward freedom.

Finished tidying, I fill a fresh glass with water and mean to carry it up to the hillside where Edie sits, but she has returned, and now she and Bethany sit in the center of the porch. Though she's only been here moments, Bethany has already unraveled her blue ribbon from her birthday shoot-out and has it pinned to the front of her dress. She has hardly been parted from the prize in the months since, and while I make her take it off for school, she often returns it to the front of her dress the moment she's home.

Legs folded in, Edie's back is straight and still. Eyes closed. Kneeling behind her, Bethany braids her hair. She's weaving the long amber locks in rough fashion, but it is beautiful all the same, as is this afternoon. On the wind, autumn storm clouds blow over the land. The gray of them dance over the fields. It charges the air around us that smells heavy like coming rain.

My daughter's hands move gently, and in Edie's still, quiet face I cannot begin to fathom what she is thinking or feeling as a little girl twines her hair round small fingers. Edie draws in a shuddering breath, and it's heartbreak here, in every twist of Bethany's girlish hands, and yet an aliveness of soul that Edie is welcoming regardless. To feel is as much a blessing as it is a curse, and Edie is caught in its incomprehensible dance.

"Tell me more about the colt." Sitting, I lift a bowl of milk onto my lap. In it is soaking one of Edie's blouses so as to work loose an ink stain.

There is a soft smile at the edges of Edie's mouth. The gentle, subtle curve is a beautiful sight.

With a rag, I scrub at the stain that has begun to soften.

Edie's eyes remain closed. "She's somethin' else, June. Black as night and ever so soft. Santiago said she's nearly a year. She pranced around like a dream as he led her over yesterday."

Thank God for Santiago's ability to nurture this woman's spirit. Over the last months he's searched for ways to coax her toward another dawn.

John has begun joining Santiago in his work with the horses. He's on payroll now at the ranch, and the work is welcome for him with the mine closed. Welcome for us all. I see the way the gentle mares and majestic stallions have given John a renewed sense of purpose here. A way to press forward now that the mine is boarded up and sealed.

"Have you thought of a name yet?" I gently swish the front of the blouse around in the milk.

"You know I'm no good at naming things." As Edie says this, the softness in her voice clips to silence. Moments later, there's a quiver to her chin.

My rocking chair squeaks as I reach over to touch her knee, clad as always in rawhide britches. "You are wonderful at naming things."

When her brown eyes angle my way, they're wet now. Her mouth, though, while still holding the bittersweet, is more softly set than it was months back. "Thank you."

Bethany ties a yellow ribbon roughly around the end of the braid. "So pretty!"

Edie reaches back to stroke my daughter's handiwork. "Bethany, you spoil me." She smiles over her shoulder at the girl, who's beaming.

"Can I do your hair next, Mama?"

"How about you do mine tomorrow?"

She nods, then Edie bids her to pick a taffy from the jar on the counter. Bethany rises and darts inside.

The sound of the glass lid being lifted is eclipsed when Edie softly speaks. "You've a beautiful family, June."

How to respond to that? I set the bowl aside to settle on the steps beside her. The ribbon that Bethany tied at the end of Edie's braid falls loose. I reach over to tighten it.

"Edie . . ."

"I mean it." The fringe edging Edie's britches sways as she shifts her boots out, crossing her ankles. "We all . . . we all have something different, don't we? We all lose and gain in different ways. There's really no telling the how or the why. It just comes, doesn't it?"

Slowly, I nod.

"For the better part of a year you didn't know of John's whereabouts, and for all that while, I watched you be nothing but strong."

"I wasn't strong," I admit. If she really knew how I felt inside, or the ways I wept on my bedroom floor when another night fell with silence . . . And now? Now it is the same bedroom where John and I settle in at night, knit together once more. How I savor the warmth of his hand as he presses it to my back, to my shoulder. Or the way he always finds a hidden curl at the nape of my neck, coils it around his finger. The way he often lowers a kiss to that spot before saying good night, or tips my face toward his own as we remember, together, what we once had, and the newness we have gained.

Some nights I wake to a lone candle beside him as he reads through the letters I wrote to him in his absence. Words I penned at the desk of our cabin while he sat in a cell in Yuma. There are times, there in the glow of the lone flame, that I sense him swipe at his eyes. And whenever he snuffs out the light, he lowers a kiss to my head. Weaves his arms back around me and holds on a little tighter.

Why is it that I have been given the gift of my heart when Edie has lost her own?

"You were strong. Because you bore an unforeseen pain with grace," Edie says. "That's strength, Juniper."

Reaching over, I squeeze her hand. "If I had half your strength."

Her eyes grow moist again. "We gain it when we have to, don't we?"

I nod again. "I believe so."

"But it's possible." Her long lashes are wet with unshed tears. "It's possible to put one foot in front of the other. Sometimes I want to give up. To just lie down and not rise again, and do you know what I think of? I think of you. Of all the days and nights that I had Santiago by my side, looking after me, and you were alone. And yet it didn't break you."

"It broke me inside."

"But you pressed on all the same. That's what makes it all the more meaningful. Thank you."

I can hardly understand the grace of this. It is I who am amazed by Edie. That she has the ability to press on in the most broken of valleys.

"'Lead, kindly light,'" Edie whispers, and it's the hymn that Santiago sang skyward the day of Little Bit's funeral.

And I remember what comes next—"*Keep my feet, Lord. I do not ask to see*"—even as I recall John's account of the lightless room. Of the minutes being agony.

Edie walks in an agony all her own, and yet words of hope are rising from her heart. It is a heart that has been forged in gold. It is the gold that dwells here in Kenworthy. Perhaps the mine has always been empty, but we have a fortune that cannot be dug from the soil. Instead, it is in the lessons we have learned, the people we've come to love, and the way our faith grows in the desert and deep in the mountains. That is the gold that dwells in these hills, and it is an honor to have witnessed its glory.

CHAPTER 42

JOHNNY

The canyon rises on both sides, curving skyward in walls of rippling stone. My pack is loaded with climbing gear. Ropes, carabiners, and ascent shoes that I'll change out of once I get to the waterfall. It's a spot I've rappelled from a half dozen times, which is why I chose this place to bring my sister to on her first expedition to this canyon that's hewn in shades of orange and gold, set deep within the San Bernardino Mountains. Just one range away from home. I had to leave Rye behind since it's not the kind of terrain a dog can navigate.

Kate and I have climbed together in the past, but this is different. It's more exciting, but there's also more at stake. Because of that, I triple-checked weather reports for any kind of flash flood warning. Since we're about to rappel down a waterfall, then descend farther into the wet depths, we can't be too careful about the risk of rainfall. Not in a place as dry and arid as this canyon that would collect rainwater like a bathtub. Skies are clear overhead and scheduled to stay that way, so we're proceeding as planned.

Kate talks as we walk, and it's a sound I don't tire of. She slides her hand along the canyon wall of rough stone that has been shaped and curved by time and water. "This is incredible."

"Pretty cool, huh?"

She adjusts her backpack. "It's amazing. I'm so glad we came here today. I've been wanting to see this place ever since you first showed me those pictures last year."

"It's a good spot."

Her head tilts skyward. "Look at how blue the sky is. The colors here are *unreal*."

She's right. Being in a canyon somehow makes the world more vivid. Sound is different down here, and so is texture. But most of all, it's the light. The sun only hits you at high noon, and beyond that, you're wrapped in a strange dance of shadows and the fragments of sunglow that fight their way in. A dappled existence where the rest of the world fades away, voices echo softly, and the narrow passages force you to angle just right at times. Like half the risk is in just not getting stuck.

Gosh, that's like life.

A slot canyon is not the best for people who are claustrophobic, which is why I never brought Emily down here. She hated it the one time we ventured out, and so I stuck to this part of the adventure alone. It makes having Kate here with me all the more meaningful.

When I pull out my phone to check the time, I notice an unexpected text from Sonoma. There hadn't been a *ding*, so the text must have come through a while ago when Kate and I were busy unloading our gear from my truck. That's the only place I can think of that would have had service around here.

The surprise and pleasure of it all is spliced by Kate, who leans around my shoulder with a "Who's So-no-ma?"

She says it like we're twelve.

I smile and slide the screen away. "It's someone I know." The message was to let me know she's finished with the letters now. I'll text her back as soon as I'm out of the canyon to respond. I've also got something for her now that I've unraveled one more piece of the mystery within John Cohen's journal.

"Johnny—oof!" Judging by the squeak in Kate's voice, she just got stuck. I glance back as she pushes past a narrow spot. "Be more specific!"

Now I chuckle. How to explain? "She's someone who was interested in the history near the cabin, so we got to talking about it. That's all." I've already pulled my phone out to glimpse the sight of her text again.

Kate rolls her eyes. "Yeah." She lowers her voice an octave to impersonate me. "It's totally nothing."

"Oh, shut up." As the canyon path angles left, I decide to just fess up. "No, she's really interesting. Nice to spend time with. I heard her speak a while back at an event in Palm Springs, and it was really cool. I think she's the youngest member on the council with the tribe down at the Cahuilla reservation. Has some family ties, too, which we've been trying to unearth the last few months."

Kate's gaping at me.

"What?!"

"Johnny, that's super cool. And you went to an event where she was at, huh?" Her eyebrows wag. "Is she pretty?"

I'm not going to answer that.

"Ooh, she *is* pretty! And you drove like an hour just to hear her speak!"

"Will you stop?"

"I want to see a picture."

"I don't have a picture. We just hang out now and again. Why would I have a picture?"

"Why are you getting so defensive about it?" she teases.

"We're dropping this subject." I take a right around a sharp curve with a twinge of satisfaction when Kate trips a little.

"Fine." She laughs, shoving my shoulder from behind. "But just until the ride home, and then I'm going to hound you again."

"Fine." I slam to a halt so she crashes into me, then start walking again.

She throws a pebble at my pack, which dings off one of the helmets hanging there.

As we walk, the canyon opens up enough for us to hike side by side. Kate pulls out two granola bars from her stash and offers one over. Judging by the change in sound, the waterfall isn't far away. There's a faint hum in the air now, and as we get closer, it turns into an unmistakable pulsing.

Kate's face lights up. "I can hear it!"

"Almost there."

"Mind if I get a couple of pictures of this spot first?"

"Take your time." This is a good place for a break anyway. The hard work is ahead of us, and we've been hiking for over an hour. I unstrap my pack and lean it on the ground against the canyon wall. Sinking down into the sandy dirt, I polish off the granola bar and wash it down with a swig of water.

Yeah, Kate stopped teasing me about Sonoma, but in truth, her name has entered the new journal my sister gave me for my birthday. The kids are in there, penned on dozens of pages now. Their laughter and energy. From swinging beneath the oak tree to finding another creek out behind some of my favorite bouldering spots. Cameron and Micaela splashed and played while Rye dove in right after them. All of this in the wake of a divorce. No, the sun isn't exactly right overhead, but if I search for the dark, that's what I'm going to find. If we search for the light? We'll realize it's glowing more than we first noticed. But that's what it takes—the noticing.

Noticing.

Such a simple concept, but I think, as I'm sitting here, that it's just faith in form.

Camera out, Kate angles the lens down the stony corridor we've been traversing. The shutter clicks, she shifts the camera, and clicks it again. "This light is incredible."

It really is. Tipping my head back, I gauge the sky again. It's nearly noon, so the sun will be overhead in less than an hour. Right now the air is simply warm and bright. There's something about sitting here in the shadows that reminds me of life. The sun is up there—but just out of sight. Why is it that the things we desire are often as near . . . and yet as out of reach? We wait in the shadows, seeing the possibility and the promise of what could come, and when it arrives are so stunned by its glory that we forget it could pass on again.

Maybe life has made me pessimistic these days, but maybe it's the opposite. Maybe it's making me into an optimist. Knowing that while, yes, hard times come, there's good too. We just have to wait and watch for it and, as important, even in the shadows realize there's still light all around. I can see my hands, my hiking boots. See the navy-and-orange weave of my neoprene pack. The way my sister turns my way and scrunches her nose in delight before snapping a picture of me sitting here. All of this without the sun overhead. It's all still good, and it's all still in view. I guess the secret to life just might boil down to counting our blessings one moment at a time. And that maybe as we do, we realize that even though the sun isn't right overhead, it's been light all along.

CHAPTER 43

JUNIPER

S itting on the porch steps with Bethany at my side, we go over the alphabet on the slate. She's been doing marvelously in school and can now shape all of the uppercase and some of the lowercase. With her finger, she erases a crooked *r* and tries again. Since it's a Saturday, there was no school, but the cabin is empty of Mrs. Parson's company now that she rents the spare bedroom in the mercantile. A blessing to all now that John is home, and Edie can use the helping hand and motherly presence.

In the yard, John and Santiago seem to be discussing their guns. They've each unholstered their firearms and are examining them. I have no idea why, but the pair of them have been working so hard at the ranch, the diversion must be a welcome break.

In the distance, I spot Edie striding this way in her rawhide pants and neat blouse. Her loveliness beneath the evening sun is only made more so by the dried flowers she carries at her side. The flowers were likely laid on Little Bit's grave only days ago. Edie visits the grave every day, and rarely does she travel out to the site without a fresh bouquet of goldenrod. I used to wonder what she did with the dried flowers she brought back home, but I've since noticed jars of them appearing all over the mercantile. Dried blooms that she saves and cherishes not only for their raw, golden beauty but for the hours they spent keeping watch over her daughter.

"What are those scalawags up to?" Edie nods toward the men before sitting beside us.

John has retrieved a crate of old tin cans from the barn, and together he and Santiago are walking out to the farthest fence.

Edie's words are warm, but her eyes are rimmed in red. She's been crying. With her near, I swipe a hand across her back, and she brushes the side of her head to my shoulder. *Dearest friend.*

"A competition is my guess," I say in answer. "They started discussing revolvers, and now it looks as though we're in for some entertainment."

In the distance, John and Santiago begin lining up several tin cans atop the fence. Beyond stretches the meadow and acres upon acres of open land. The heat of a September day is softening. Edie watches quietly, as do Bethany and I. Inside the cabin, a venison pie is bubbling away in the oven. It's enough that I hope Edie and Santiago will stay for supper.

With five rusted cans lined up, John backs away dozens upon dozens of steps. Finally, he turns and takes aim. After five shots, three of them have fallen. The men return to the fence to restore the numbers, and now it's Santiago's turn. He manages to take out four cans. John claps Santiago on the back, and together they seem to be discussing the final can and where the shot went. Santiago reloads but misses again.

The blue ribbon ever pinned to the front of Bethany's dress flounces as she tugs at Edie's hand. "Come on, Edie. Show them!"

Edie shakes her head, though a wry smile is forming. "Aw, no. Maybe some other time." Her eyes still glisten as though tears began moments ago without a sound.

I cannot begin to fathom the grief her heart is swimming in. It makes me admire her courage and strength all the more. If I have learned anything from this woman, it is how to be brave in the face of impossible loss.

Bethany tugs again. "Show them!"

Edie smirks and swipes at her eyes in such a fashion that Bethany doesn't even notice. This little girl who will one day know a woman's heartache. I pray the Lord will be merciful, and yet I am thankful she has such a woman as bold and beautiful as Edie to observe and learn from.

Bethany tugs again, giggling now. The laughter rings out through the bright, crisp evening.

Lowering her head in defeat, Edie inches to the edge of the porch. "Fine, little miss. But you tell them to set up more than five cans. If I'm gonna show them, it might as well be properly."

She rises, and as my daughter runs toward the men, hollering out for them to "Line 'em up good!" I rise as well. This I have to see. Edie unholsters her six-shooter and inspects that the cylinder is fully loaded.

In the distance, John lines up six cans along the top rail of the fence. Bethany points toward three more waiting in the dry grass. "You forgot those ones!"

Chuckling, he glances over his shoulder to his daughter, probably as intrigued by the spunk growing in her as I am. "How about you come and help me?"

At his permission, she scurries over, gathers the rusty cans into her arms, and John hoists her up so that she can balance them beside the others. Finished, he settles her onto his shoulders. John returns to my side, where he cups the back of my head to kiss my forehead. I savor the feel of it.

Since this is a competition about distance, we all stride back to the shooting point, Edie behind us all. Santiago slows so as to take her hand as they walk. Their fingers twine together.

When we're far enough away, Edie waits for everyone to step clear before cocking the revolver. From atop John's shoulders, Bethany covers both ears. The fringe lining her pants rustles as Edie takes her stance, aims the pistol, and, after a breath, fires the first shot. The can flips backward. Then the second and the third. Breeze stirs her hair that's as warm and brassy as a glass of whiskey. A shift in the air that she no doubt calculates into every aim. The rustiest of the cans shatters away, and the fifth follows a moment later. The sixth flies clean off the fence, and Edie reloads. She does this with the speed of the wind, and soon there's not a single target left on the fence rail. Nine perfect shots.

John's eyebrows are raised in admiration.

Santiago is grinning.

Bethany cheers, and after bending to whisper something in her papa's ear, he nods and lowers his daughter to the ground. At my daughter's bidding, Edie takes a knee. As Bethany pins the ribbon to the front of Edie's blouse, my friend's eyes fill with tears again. She smiles at the young girl who is giving away her most prized possession. Arms open, Edie invites Bethany in for a hug. When my daughter leans into Edie's embrace, she is once again the child who draped her arm around her father as he lay unconscious and freezing. I've come to understand that Bethany has a heart that sees people. Eyes that know others are in need of comfort. She is once again the child lending life. Even as the blue ribbon flutters on the breeze of a grown-up blouse, Edie's eyes slide closed, holding tight to a little girl's embrace as though the greatest gift of all.

CHAPTER 44

JOHNNY

Sonoma arrives right at ten as planned. I'm on the porch, down into the yard, before she's even parked. The choir of birds in the pines dims as she climbs out of her truck. Rye gets to her first, nearly knocking her over with eighty pounds of Labrador.

Sonoma laughs, ruffles his ears, and tries to keep from falling.

I'm to them in two seconds, giving a tug to Rye's collar so that all four paws hit the ground again.

Sonoma brushes yellow fur from her black leggings, not in the least bit fazed.

"Thank you for meeting me." I brush the same fur from the front of my T-shirt then flip my backward ball cap around.

"I wouldn't miss this for anything."

I like her faith in me. In this outing. I still haven't told her what we're on the hunt for. "Got everything you need?" I hardly notice what she's wearing—but the colors are earthy, and she's ready to hike.

302

The distraction comes not from a lack of interest, but because it's hard to look away from her bright smile and brown eyes. There's an energy there that's impossible to ignore, that's hard to not want to be around.

"Should I bring more than water?" Her voice muffles when she retrieves a water bottle from the center console of her truck.

"I think we'll be fine. It shouldn't take too long to get there."

I've spent the last few weekends scouting out where we're headed, and after cross-checking the spot once more with John Cohen's journal, I'm 99.9 percent certain it's the place. Sonoma explained to me once that tracing her exact family line has been nearly impossible due to the drastic changes Native Americans experienced in the previous century. As part of that, it sounds like very little of her family tree has been traceable beyond the forming of the nearby Cahuilla reservation. Now, I hope change unfolds around that. Even if only a little.

Nerves now make it hard to stand still while I zip up my CamelBak. The weight of what Sonoma is about to find is a sobering anticipation. There's no use stalling when someone's past and future are about to collide.

We head off across the farmyard to where the town of Kenworthy used to reside. The actual townsite isn't on my property, but it's a cinch to access. We only have to step around an old stretch of fencing that crumbled some decades ago. There the land opens up into the series of grassy patches where long-ago buildings stood. Since I don't mean to lead us toward those old sites exactly, we walk out beyond them, across the dusty land. Sonoma is quiet as we stride through tall autumn grasses and past fragrant sagebrush. I've got too much nervous energy for small talk. Maybe it has to do with this place.

I couldn't begin to count the things I've learned here in Kenworthy. I've grown more patient watching the sun set between towering trees. I've grown wiser in knowing that my footsteps are not the first to dent this soil.

I want to know them one day. The Cohens and the Del Sols. These couples who overcame more than I ever have. If there's not a seat beside them in heaven, I'll just have to summon up the courage and walk over and say hello. Something tells me it would be like meeting old friends.

And now, the woman beside me has come to have her own experiences through them. She doesn't know this terrain to the degree that I've explored it, but she knows its heart. Maybe we teamed up well for that. I scarcely know where my ancestors came from because I never put enough thought to it. So today, it's incredible to fathom that her very ancestors once walked this exact stretch of land. And right now we have the honor of walking side by side, me trying to figure out how on earth to make small talk and her quietly soaking in the sights. How is it that caring for someone works that way? We're only friends, she and I, but to know that something is about to touch her heart in a way that can't be measured has me anticipating these next steps so much more than if they were for me.

"I think . . ." I begin, slowing so that she does as well. "I think this is the spot."

"I'm so curious as to what it is." With a hand, she swipes at her ponytail, then glances around at the outcropping of boulders we've arrived at.

"Well. I want to show you something." I pull out the copy of one of the journal entries from John Cohen. "Take a look at this."

She accepts the page, and it's impossible not to watch her lowered face as she reads. A loose tendril of brown hair stirs against her cheek, and her lashes move with the words.

September 1903

Juniper should be walking down from the cabin any minute to
fetch Bethany and me. The smells of her supper has me craving to

be there at her side, but I'd be wanting it, meal or no. Beth's here
in the hayloft, playing paper dolls in the straw. I ought to fashion
her something for them. Maybe a box to hold them proper. I'm
sitting beside her now for no other reason than the soft sound of her
humming, and the way the evening light catches her blond hair.

Santiago and I spent most of the day stalking deer—two does and
a forked horn. We came home empty-handed, but the conversation
was as good as the company. We seem to be made for that—he and
I—this cause to keep one another on the higher path. The path that
leads home. He's gone off now to sit with Edie at the place where
she kneels most every evening. I can just make them out from here.
With sunset coming, their shadows stretch as long as the boulders
bookending them. At dusk, like this, the hues of this landscape are
deep as the sorrow they have faced together. A sorrow I can only
imagine, but one that lives on their faces, and in their every step.
I pray that God continues to cover them with His grace. Most
especially in the hard. In the waiting and the yearning.

Listen to me now, talking like I'm some kind of poet. I think June's gone
and rubbed off on me. I don't mind so much. If anyone were to draw
the world in a way that I can somehow see it more clearly, it'd be her.

John

Sonoma inhales softly. "Everything is beautiful here." Her eyes
move over dirt and stone. Cactus and manzanita, then to the sky
overhead. This woman also has a way of seeing things that others
might miss.

Her focus lowers to my face, and her question is soft. "I feel like
you are telling me something, but I don't know what it is."

I grin. Here's a first—me piecing something together for once.
"Well, *I'm* not telling you something. They are." I touch the paper
again.

As she reads it a second time, her fingertip traces the names. Is the answer unfolding for her? Her brow is pinched now. She's close to putting it all together. I could just tell her, but this woman has a way of unearthing things, and this is too big to spoil for her.

Her demeanor shifts, and she absorbs the sight of the two boulders bookending where we stand now, glances back toward the farm, squinting in the direction of the barn. Of the eastern window.

She's almost got it . . .

She looks at me, her eyes wide. I nod.

"Oh, my goodness . . ." Stepping back from the outcropping, she lowers the paper at her side. It's as though the wind has left her sails. Now it is a tide that brims not beneath her but in her every glance as she looks around with wet eyes. "Are you serious?" The words are whispered.

Struck by her emotions, I can only nod.

This is the place. The place where a tiny infant was once buried. If there was a marking—a cross—it's gone now. A hundred California years will do that to an exposed piece of wood. Her eyes scan the ground as though trying to find a remnant. I did the same thing this morning, but it's only earth now.

Sonoma sinks to her knees. Dust taints her leggings as she sits back on her hiking boots. Her shoulders slump, and she draws in a shaky breath. "I can't believe it," she says with matched softness. "They stood here." Edie and Santiago Del Sol. "They . . ."

"Knelt here."

Hands that are a few shades lighter than those of the man with four names touch the earth. Sonoma's fingertips graze the pale grit as she arcs her hand slowly in a half circle. "Hello, little one," she whispers, and I realize that we've yet to come across a reference to the child's name.

I'm not much of a crying man, but I have to blink quickly to keep dry eyes.

Far behind us twines the highway where travel trailers meander toward local camping spots and tourists have come up for a day in the mountains. Not a soul who crosses this land today will know that the woman kneeling here is glimpsing not only a piece of her past but a new window into the heritage that has been slowly fading over the centuries.

A heritage that is in the process of being preserved as Sonoma pulls out her notebook and flips to the page she's sketched up about the Del Sols. There she has already penciled in information about Santiago and Edith, and now she draws several fresh lines with her pen. As she writes quietly, she pauses every few words to examine the surroundings as though making as much a note about the location as the tiny infant who is a valued part of this family's tree. The Del Sols' legacy.

Finished, Sonoma caps her pen and slowly closes the notebook. She touches the ground again, and her voice is soft. "Your mama was very brave." She sits quiet for a while. "I have spent so many years trying to make sense of this. To piece together what I can of my heritage. Not just of my own, but for others as well." Judging by the notes she has in hand, including what look like links, dates, and more, she would have spent countless hours at it. "So much of it has been misunderstood or forgotten entirely." Her eyes rise to mine, and it takes no effort to recall the way Sonoma stood at the Cahuilla museum and addressed a roomful of people.

When she rises, it's to step closer to the dried brush and autumn flowers lingering in the craggy ground where the boulders give shade. She gathers several and lays them on the spot where she just knelt. When the wind stirs them, unsettling the stems, I shift a rock into place so as to brace the flowers securely. It's now a marking—an offering—that won't again be lost. At least not by us, and if I know anything about Sonoma, she'll make sure that the world knows the story of a precious Cahuilla baby, the parents who loved her, and the legacy that such a family left behind.

"I know this doesn't solve the mystery for you. The connection," I say at her side. "But I believe along with you that this was where you came from. Until you know for certain—and even if you never do—I think . . ." I search her teary expression, seeing the depth of bond and care she has for these people. These lives, including her own, somehow rooted in Kenworthy. The place I have the honor to call home. A place I hope she will return to many more times. "I think it's obvious where you belong."

She smiles, swiping at her cheeks, and I cave, braving a reach around her shoulder. The first time I've hugged her. I pull her in to my side, and she carefully brushes her head to my shoulder. Though I want to hold on a little longer, I let her go.

Her smile is shyer now, but there's a look in her face that says she didn't mind the hug at all.

"I'm glad we're friends," I say and wish I could explain all the ways she has blessed me, but slow is good. No matter what happens or doesn't happen here, the heart beside me matters. It matters to me and this place more than I can say.

EPILOGUE

JUNIPER

Facing the camera, I try to smile at the apparatus, but it feels unnatural. "I don't think I can hold a smile," I say to Mrs. Parson.

"No need to." Her voice is muffled from where it's draped beneath the dark cloth just behind the camera. "Just stand still and steady. Don't move."

Ten minutes ago, I was hanging laundry on the line, and now I'm standing here, posing for the first photograph I've ever taken. Mrs. Parson is leaving Kenworthy today and asked if we would allow her to photograph us. She's taken a position at a school in San Bernardino, and we are all going to miss her. Bethany, who has blossomed these last several years under her tutelage, most of all.

I remind myself of Mrs. Parson's instruction to be still.

Be still.

Is that not the very thing God asked of me in John's absence and even beyond? *Be still. Wait.* Such a decree is hard for me. When it came to the adventure of leaving my home to join John here on this mountain, I was ready and willing for the risk. To step into the unknown. But when the unknown requires stillness? When the unknown calls for submission and surrender? A much harder calling for me. When we cannot act or take or do enough to gain what our heart desires—I believe that *being still* is the greatest challenge of this life.

As Mrs. Parson adjusts levers on her camera that Bethany knows so much more about than I do, I straighten my spine, peer straight at the black lens face, and tip my chin up. A few seconds pass. From the side of my vision, John is watching me. Bethany is at his side. So grown now, at six. Ribbons dangle from her long braids, and her nose is dusted in freckles from a childhood beneath the California sun.

"Alright, Juniper. Steady and still." Mrs. Parson clicks the shutter, and I flinch. John grins, his eyes shining as he watches me.

"Was that it?" I ask.

"Lovely. I won't be able to develop the images until I arrive in San Bernardino, so I will mail them back here."

It's a nice thought. I've never seen my photograph before, so I will be curious when the package arrives. Maybe we'll get a boughten frame to hang it in. More likely, John will fashion one, and it will be even more lovely.

Some time back, Mrs. Parson brought over one of the photographs she developed here in Kenworthy. It was a shot of Bethany sitting on the hearth. It's a perfect capture, except that Bethany's head turned toward the door the moment the shutter clicked, which blurred her face. At first, I wondered why Mrs. Parson would have taken such care to bring me a photograph that most would view as flawed, then I realized what she had captured. It was the moment of her father's arrival. When Bethany first witnessed his return, and all her focus went to the door where he was being carried through. Though blurred, it is a picture, a moment, that I treasure.

"How about the men now?" Mrs. Parson slides a plate from her camera, then replaces it with a fresh one. There's a notepad in her hand, and on it, she writes the numbers that coincide with the plates, adding the names of those who are in the photograph as well as the date.

Santiago shakes his head. He's been eyeing the camera warily all morning. At his side, Edie smiles at her husband.

John squeezes Santiago's shoulder and grins. "Come on."

Head down, the Cahuilla man follows. He casts the camera one more look of distrust. When they take their places, Santiago's stony expression softens. John has turned them both to face the lens, arm draped across his friend's shoulder. They are handsome men. So different and yet so alike.

"Would you like to take this one, Bethany?" Mrs. Parson waves her over.

Bethany dashes to the camera on its stand, and together they work through the steps needed to capture the image standing there. The hem of Bethany's calico dress hits just below her knees where her stockings have been worn through from too much time spent playing in the fields with her papa, Santiago, and the spring colts.

With their heads bent together, Mrs. Parson reminds Bethany how to press the shutter switch, so it is my daughter who bids the camera to remember this moment so that we will as well.

"Oh, that will be fine," Edie calls from where she stands in her shade. The baby in her arms stirs gently. She bounces the child. A boy. Her third born to this earth and the first to live. I prayed on my knees every day that he was inside her.

When we all suggest she pose next, Edie shakes her head, so Bethany offers to show Edie how to do it.

"It's real easy." Bethany perches on the steps of the porch. She sits straight and tall like a lady. Her eyes are a glorious type of happiness as she peers at the camera. *Click.* Her image is etched forever. In my heart, I want to remember it always as well.

The last two photographs are of Edie.

The first is of her posing with her son, Elias. The babe cries the entire time, his little arms flailing inside the woven blanket while Edie grins from ear to ear. It takes no effort for her to hold the smile. I don't think it will be leaving her face until the day she dies. Her eyes have been aglow since Elias's birth three months ago, and it's a light that was hard wrought. A reminder of God's faithfulness even through the darkest of valleys.

For the last photograph that Mrs. Parson captures, Edie makes a special request, and it's a good one. Santiago carries the camera while John hoists the stand, and by the time we've all walked down to the mercantile, I see afresh the sign overhead that is so much a part of Edie's life and heritage. *Manchester Mercantile.* I sense why this picture will mean so much to her. It's the place where she grew into a young woman and spent years by her father's side. It's where she and Santiago have made their first home, and the place where all her babies were born.

Edie stands on her own in front of the mercantile and hoists her husband's rifle over her shoulder. She stares at the camera, and when the shutter is pressed, I wonder if we will ever see these images. If the package will arrive safe and sound in Kenworthy once more. Mrs. Parson has promised them to us, a parting gift that we will remember always, just as we will never forget her kindness.

With all the plates packed away in her leather bag, Mrs. Parson and Bethany latch the camera back up like a turtle hiding inside its shell once more. John is taking Mrs. Parson by wagon to the train station in the valley tomorrow, so for this evening there are a few hours left to enjoy one another's company.

We return to our cabin where the oak tree, while small still, stretches out an inviting shade beneath its late-summer leaves. At our bidding, the men set up makeshift tables, and Mrs. Parson and I drape cloths. Edie settles wildflowers into glass jars. Bethany bounces Elias on her knee beneath the oak, and the baby babbles to her all about it. This tree was meant to hold children in its shade, and I hope it always does.

Perhaps someday this land will be inhabited with more souls, but on this quieting evening it is wild and free, and it is us who are the voices that rise toward the first traces of starlight. There is laughter, and there have been many tears.

As sunset hearkens in, we serve up hot rolls with Edie's sweet cactus jelly. Two roasted chickens grace the table, and Mrs. Parson's chocolate pie is the crowning glory. We feast in stages, talking and sharing stories as the night stretches on. There is no hurry, and as John lights lanterns, we all seem to be in silent agreement to make the most of this night. Bethany stays up way too late for a girl her age, her shadow cast against the cabin wall as she listens to the tales that are swapped, chiming in with a few of her own. My brave, sweet girl.

I hold Elias by moonlight, and Edie sits beside me, touching his tiny hand as though not wanting to let him out of her sight. There is life here, and it is lovely. So much to thank the Lord for.

As laughter fills the air that still holds the kiss of warmth, I thank God for His goodness, His faithfulness, and for the mercy He has been showing to all of those in this yard. Mercies that are new each and every morning and that settle like dew each and every dawn. Life is a journey, and while our lives here in Kenworthy are unlike what we set out to accomplish, they are right and good all the same. This is the story that God has woven for us, and I am learning to trust that He knows the way.

A NOTE FROM
THE AUTHOR

I n the spring of 2020, just one day after the state of California
closed many businesses for COVID-19, I slipped out into what
I think of as my *greater backyard* . . . heading to a remote place I had
dreamt of for nearly two years: Kenworthy.

Tiptoeing around curfew this way felt a little bit like being an
Old West outlaw, but fortunately, I wasn't alone on the adventure.
Meeting me at the trailhead was a local rock climber and friend who,
armed with some hiking gear and his husky dog, was ready to explore
with me into the dry San Jacinto Mountains in search of the noto-
rious gold mine. He had digital maps and climbing apps and I had old
history books and loads of notes, and combined, we pieced together
a direction of where we thought Kenworthy *might* be, and set off on
foot down the dusty trail.

We didn't find a gold mine that day, and the Kenworthy site was
all faded to dust and picked clean—nothing but meadows and rocks
where buildings once stood. But what we did find was a mutual fond-
ness for a place that we would return to time and time again. Ground
that somehow became just a little bit sacred with each visit back. A

place where conversation passed the miles and snacks and laughter kept morale high as we continued to explore.

Sometimes on our visits to Kenworthy, we got stuck in brambles, or had to find shade because of the heat. Other times, we put a new spin on *social distancing* while I sat against granite boulders, scribbling down story notes with a sleeping husky at my side, while her owner climbed some of Kenworthy's countless rock faces. We even named several, which I'm pretty sure makes us pioneers!

Once, I was halfway through jotting down a new idea for the story when my cell phone rang from my hiking pack, and it was my friend, some sixty feet higher, showing me the incredible view at the top over live video. A sight I would have otherwise missed. But more on that in the acknowledgments!

Those were good days. Good adventures. The sunshine and comradery and even the rattle of ropes and carabiners wove their way into nearly every page of this novel. From the routes that Johnny climbed, to the trails that he and Sonoma explored, to the views that Juniper and John had the honor to look out upon, to the place where dozens of miners called home . . . Kenworthy wasn't just a place in history books anymore. It was—and is—real and dusty and beautiful. And I am ever so thankful that I got to be a part of it.

ACKNOWLEDGMENTS

O h, the gratitude that stems from all who were involved with this novel. It was an incredibly challenging story to write—the most difficult to date—which makes the support behind it all the more meaningful.

My thanks to agent Sandra Bishop for once again guiding me along this writing journey that feels less like a career at times and more like an adventure. Thank you for your wisdom and guidance along the road.

To my editors, Jocelyn Bailey, Leslie Peterson, and Laura Wheeler, for making this novel shine in ways I could have never done on my own. Your expertise and eagle eyes made this manuscript far and above what it was before it landed in your hands. It has once again been a joy and privilege to work with you.

To fellow writers and kindred spirits who surrounded me with encouragement during the writing of this novel: Amanda Dykes, Jody Evans, Savanna Kaiser, and Kara Swanson. Thank you for your steadfast friendship and your own beautiful words. And to non-writer friends that are just as deserving of praise: Robyn Mucelli, Jennifer Cervantez, and Katie Gehring for never letting a week go by without sending me your cheer and prayers.

Here's to local librarians—Susan Righetti and Shannon NJ for always being so supportive of my stories, for gathering stacks of research books for me, and for going the extra mile during the writing of this story. (Shannon, our head librarian, even let me borrow research books from her own personal shelves!) Thanks also to neighbor and friend Susan Gray for immense help with all topics relating to genealogy research. Sonoma's character took on even greater depth thanks to your wisdom. Lastly, loads of local thanks to the Idyllwild Historical Society who confirmed my understanding that historians have never known who in fact salted the Kenworthy mine with a shotgun. Because of this, I felt peace in crafting the fictitious tale that *could* have answered the question.

My appreciation to a number of books that aided in my research, including *A Dried Coyote's Tail*, volume 1, by Katherine Siva Sauvel, from where I drew the Cahuilla language and phrases that Santiago voiced. Such history and preservation not only made those moments possible but are keeping a priceless piece of California heritage alive for decades to come.

To rock climber and friend Jeremiah Carlsen—there's no one else I would have rather explored Kenworthy with. Thank you for making the adventures so much fun and for teaching me that life is kind of like climbing, and that by trusting in Christ, we can have peace and confidence that He's the one who belays us.

To my parents for your endless support in everything I do. You are the best kid-watchers, late-night brainstormers, and all-around encouragers that I could ever have. I am so thankful to you. To my kids, Mabry, Caleb, and Levi, who have been endlessly patient while I slip away to write *just a few more words*, and who joined me on local research adventures like champs (including the historical society that appears in the book!). And to Aunt Laura, who this book is dedicated to, for your perseverance and courage through cancer that shine a light for so many of us to see. I signed this book contract the same day of your surgery, and as Mom and I both realized, this one was meant to be yours.

Through and for everything: all of my heart's thanks to God for being the greatest leader, friend, and hope-giver this girl could ever have.

DISCUSSION QUESTIONS

1. Juniper found the land around her as captivating as it was challenging. Has there been a time in your life when you have lived in such a place? What was your experience? How did you find strength and endurance?

2. What contrasts did you find between Juniper and Edie? In what ways were they different? How were they similar? What ways did you find each woman growing over the course of the novel?

3. If you could share a Bible verse with one of the characters in the story, what verse would it be and who would you share it with? What scene or experience has you choosing that verse for them?

4. Little Bethany's personality stems not only from who she is but from the place she was growing up. In what ways did Kenworthy mold her into the girl she is? In what ways did your childhood adventures shape who you are today?

5. Johnny made the big decision to buy the Cohens' cabin on the spot, which brought some angst as he toiled with the idea. What is a big decision that you have made in your life that was worth the challenges surrounding it?

6. Sonoma's heritage is rich with the different cultures that have shaped her. In what ways have your own cultures and heritages shaped you and your life? Are there any stories or traditions that you are especially proud of?

7. The Cahuilla are the native tribe of my homeland of Southern California. What native tribe is part of your local heritage and history? What intricacies have you learned about their culture? Is there more you would like to explore and discover?

8. The title *The Gold in These Hills* is meant to represent what *truly* matters: the people we come to care about, the lessons God teaches us, and the way a place shapes us. How do you think this title was reflected in the lives of the different characters?

9. If you arrived in Kenworthy during the late 1800s and early 1900s, where would you imagine yourself settling? What might have been your role or your family's role in the community?

BIBLIOGRAPHY

The following books were essential in researching the Cahuilla tribe, the history of the San Jacinto Mountains, the ghost town of Kenworthy, and gold mining in Southern California:

Hatheway, Roger G. *Rim of the World Drive: Images of America*. Charleston: Arcadia Publishing, 2007.

James, Harry C. *The Cahuilla Indians*. Banning, CA: Malki-Museum Press, 1969.

Robinson, John W. *Mines of the San Bernardinos*. Glendale, CA: La Siesta Press, 1977.

Robinson, John W., and Bruce D. Risher. *The San Jacintos*. Monrovia, CA: Big Santa Anita Historical Society, 1993.

Ryan, Marla Felkins, and Linda Schmittroth, eds. *Tribes of Native America: Cahuilla*. San Diego: Blackbirch Press, 2002.

Sauvel, Katherine Siva. *Isill Heqwas Waxish: A Dried Coyote's Tail*. Vol. 1. Banning, CA: Malki-Museum Press, 2004.

Trafzer, Clifford E., and Jeffrey Smith. *Native Americans of Riverside County: Images of America*. Charleston: Arcadia Publishing, 2006.

ABOUT THE AUTHOR

Mike Thezier Photography

Joanne Bischof is an ACFW Carol Award and ECPA Christy Award–winning author. She writes deeply layered fiction that tugs at the heartstrings. She was honored to receive the San Diego Christian Writers Guild Novel of the Year Award in 2014, and in 2015 was named Author of the Year by the Mount Hermon conference. Joanne's 2016 novel, *The Lady and the Lionheart*, received an extraordinary 5 Star TOP PICK! from *RT Book Reviews*, among other critical acclaim. She lives in the mountains of Southern California with her three children.

◆ ◆ ◆

Visit her online at JoanneBischof.com
Facebook: @JoanneBischof
Instagram: @JoanneBischof